To Justin and Theo,
the bringers of pain and delight

First Montag Press E-Book and Paperback Original Edition July 2015

Montag Press
ISBN: 978-1-940233-23-9
Jacket and book design © 2015 Rick Febré
Interior illustrations © 2015 Richie Israel

Montag Press Team:
Project Editor – Mara Hodges
Managing Director – Charlie Franco

A Montag Press Book
www.montagpress.com
Montag Press
1066 47th Ave. Unit #9
Oakland CA 94601 USA

Printed & Digitally Originated in the United States of America
10 9 8 7 6 5 4 3 2 1

{ Dysmorphic Kingdom }

a fairy tale

Colleen Chen

None of the usual rules apply in this tale of heart and humor—
Dysmorphic Kingdom is a rollicking, unpredictable, fantasy-filled ride.

Karen Park, Hot Pink Books

A fairy tale for adults...delightful, fast moving,
with complexity and depth.

Art Riggs, author of *Deep Tissue Massage*

{ Dysmorphic Kingdom }

a fairy tale

Colleen Chen

CHAPTER 1

SHE WOULD NEVER BE ABLE TO LOOK AT Nim the same way again. Vesper watched her neighbor standing in front of her house, staring up at her bedroom window, masturbating.

From her vantage point at the side of the house where she'd been hiding the last twenty minutes, she could see Nim in profile, holding a bunch of wildflowers. His other hand beat a furtive staccato on the ruddy, slightly curved member that poked out of faded trousers.

He must have arrived right after she'd left the house from the back door, heading for the ramshackle structure near the front of the property where the mule was stabled. Despite the dawn hour, she should have guessed that he'd come today—he'd always been an early riser, and his visits had increased in frequency since he'd heard of Aren's engagement and realized that Vesper, being the elder sister by two years, must also be of marriageable age. Had he made the masturbation a sort of pre-courtship ritual all those other weeks, too? The thought made her shudder and then grimace as she noticed Nim also shuddering—and mouthing "Vesper" with a terrible scrunch of his entire face—before he tucked his penis away and straightened his clothes.

Now she had better make a run for it, because soon Nim would start calling her name, and the house would wake up. Sharrua, Vesper's mother, had managed to scrape up enough coins to commission the services of a witch renowned for doing expert glamours. Today the witch was to work her magic on Vesper in an attempt to make Sharrua's shy, dowry-less, and rather odd middle daughter appear the perfect first wife to lead a nobleman's bevy of wives. Her guarantee had been encouraging: "For every girl I work with—she'll be someone's first wife, or she'll get a first-rate husband with wealth and power. One or the other or both or your money back."

Vesper was just as determined as her mother *not* to be there for the appointment. She'd left the house at dawn to go on a specimen-collecting field trip—for herbs, which she sold at a small profit, and insects, for her own personal study. Then Nim showed up…the one fellow who did want to marry her, first wife material or no. She'd refused his repeated proposals as kindly as she could manage, as she was fond of him and wanted him to be happy. Now the image of what he'd been doing was branded irrevocably onto her brain, and she didn't know if she could look him in the eye.

She made a dash for the stable. *Made it.* Standing inside, panting, she tiptoed to Jack's stall, patting the nose that pushed against the battered leather bag slung across her body. If the mule was in the right mood to run—or rather, since that mood hadn't struck him in all the years Vesper had known him, if he would at least walk quickly, perhaps Nim would be too preoccupied to notice, and she would be free.

You're a racehorse trapped in a mule's skin, Jack, and today you'll prove it, she thought as she saddled him, tied her bag across his back, undid his rope, and mounted.

If Jack could read minds, he didn't show it. He shuffled out of the stable and bent down to crop at a patch of grass. Vesper was prepared for that; she reached into her bag and pulled out an apple.

Just as she cocked back her arm to throw, though, Nim turned. Slightly protruding blue eyes widened, and his face broke out in such a smile that Vesper couldn't just dig her heels in and gallop away, even if Jack had cooperated. She sighed as Nim ran to her, arm extended, flowers bouncing with every step.

"Oh, Vesper," he cried. "You're awake! I brought you these...and I wanted to ask you something."

"Hi, Nim." She reached down and took the flowers, looking at the wilted blossoms to avoid the eager face turned up at her, a face that was itself like a freckled flower. "I'm in a bit of a hurry this morning... perhaps we could talk when I come back?"

Nim's smile disappeared. "It's important, Vesper."

She sighed. "What is it then?"

"Have you thought about my marriage proposal?"

Vesper bit her lip. "Nim...I already told you I can't."

"I don't need a yes now," Nim continued doggedly. "We could wait another year. You'd still be my first, and maybe my only. I just need to hear that there's hope for me, that someday you might want to...don't you think we're perfect for each other?" He paused. "What are you making those funny faces for?"

"I'm sorry, Nim. I just—I need you to understand that I don't think I want to get married." She fidgeted with the flowers, not knowing what to do with them, and she tucked them under the edge of Jack's saddle, out of reach of the mule's ever-questing mouth.

"But you have to," Nim protested. "You're already nineteen—you can't stay under your father's protection forever—"

"I know that," Vesper said. "But I can petition the mayor to have my own guardianship, just as soon as I can show I can support myself."

"But why, Vesper? It would be so much easier if we just married."

"I want something other than a life of having babies and running a household. I...I want to be a scientist, or a philosopher...something different." She felt herself blush; she felt stupid for her confession, and even more at the way Nim's lip curled in skepticism.

"I wouldn't make you have babies—not right away at least—and... well, Vesper, I don't think they let girls be scientists and philosophers. But I'd let you have hobbies and stuff. Whatever you wanted."

"I...I need to think about things," she mumbled, gaze skittering again toward the house. She could see signs of life stirring within; a shadow of a figure passed by the window. Then she heard it.

"VESPER!" Her mother's holler was unmistakable.

"Sorry, Nim," she said again, casting one more agonized glance at the crestfallen lines of his face, his brow furrowing from trying to think of the one thing that would convince her to change her mind.

She threw the apple, and the flowers fell from the saddle and scattered behind her as Jack lunged forward in the wake of the flying fruit.

***

One of Vesper's prized possessions was a magical compass that resembled any such ordinary device except, when pointed at an object, it caused that object to spring out of the way. Only with its help could she get off the road immediately and into the woods, trees, and brush alike, all parting for her as if an invisible hand were sweeping aside all obstacles. Jack, who had no problems moving once he'd actually started, passed through with ease, and within moments they were no longer in view of the house.

Vesper sighed in relief. She'd been horrified when her mother had first told her about the witch who did "makeovers." The changes the witch made were simply temporary, a glamour—and once a man had been caught and trapped into marriage, he would discover that her confidence, her seeming ability to manage a legion of wives and children and to support her husband's rise in society, had simply been an illusion. What he would be left with was a passably pretty, but socially dysfunctional female to take care of who wouldn't even make a good third or fourth or fifth wife—because she had nothing to offer in the way of domestic skills or entertaining company, but rather liked to waste all her time in strange, un-womanly habits.

On her end, she would rather die than enter a partnership under such pretense. If a man couldn't accept her as she was now, how would he even begin to see the real *her* that went beyond all appearances?

Nim's devotion, which didn't care that she was awkward and bookish and liked to dissect things, came close to giving her what she wanted, but still didn't make her feel...*seen*. To him, she was one of the few girls who was nice to him, the stodgy son of a poor alcoholic shoemaker with such little status that he seemed unlikely to even get one wife, let alone the three or more that designated a man of standing. He still wanted her to be a real wife; he would accord her the protection of his name and his livelihood, and she would in turn give him status—her time and energy would be his to direct. Since he didn't value her for her mind or her curiosity or anything else that was really *her*, she had no doubt that her time would be spent struggling through the domestic tasks she'd always hated.

Aside from Nim, Vesper had aroused no interest in the men of Pecktown. Like Aren, she had the lustrous brown hair and sable eyes that hinted at ancestry amongst the mysterious olive-skinned Egregians to the south, and her angular face and slender frame were in their way as pleasing as her sister's curvier shape. Still, the major difference between Vesper and her sister was that Aren wanted to be courted, and Vesper didn't.

She noticed Jack's pace was nearing standstill as her thoughts had drifted. If he stopped now, she wouldn't be able to get him to start again until he'd eaten and rested. So she pulled herself back to the present, clucked her tongue at him, and focused on the road ahead, leading away from town and into gentle woods.

She'd been quite clumsy with her first few batches of insects, but she was getting the hang of it—proper incisions, removal and the like, according to her newest obsession, a rather expensive book from Egregia. The book was called *Fortunetelling and Personality Analysis in Insect Innards*. From early experiments, it seemed her personality and future were quite messy and chaotic, but now she planned to get some really big insects whose innards would surely be more conducive to clarity.

When she arrived, the sun shone in full early-morning brightness, the air crisp and cool but with the promise of warmth to come. She suspected that the promise would remain unfulfilled here in the forest, where the damp and the shade created an insidious sort of cold, the kind that crept into the marrow and urged the spirit to leave. Vesper shivered, unable to stop her gaze from seeking the shadows.

After she'd wallowed in unease for a moment, she squared her shoulders. "Let the mysteries come, then! Perhaps I'll be the first to discover something and I'll write a book about it."

In the meantime, Vesper perused the flora around her. What had first struck her as dark and oppressive in panorama, had settled into a rich quietness, her gaze slowing to notice details of the vast trees with their hues of dark red-brown or gray or ocher. Around them the undergrowth lay as a thick carpet of brush and spiny branches, where passage would have been challenging without the aid of her compass.

She came to a place that looked promising. A small, dark clearing angled downward toward a stream. Several tall mounds of dirt rose up amidst the brush—telltale signs of large ants living in the area. After dismounting and removing the bag, she let Jack wander to the stream and the patch of grass beside it. Kneeling, shovel in hand, she began to dig.

The back of her neck prickled in subtle warning. Was she being watched? She glanced up and around, seeing and hearing nothing untoward. She continued to dig, but she couldn't dismiss a feeling that she wasn't alone, and she didn't like it.

A large-bellied ant the size of half her pinky finger poked out of the dirt. She reached into her bag to pull out a specimen container when she spotted another movement out of the right side of her periphery. to her rightUnder a fallen branch, she spotted a reddish-colored object resembling a piece of uncooked meat.

First she thought it was just that—some carcass left partially uneaten, only appearing to move as the wind shifted the grass around it.

No—the object itself was moving. Could it be a mole or a mouse of some hairless variety? No—its movement was more languid, almost wormlike. Vesper got to her feet and backed away, never taking her eyes from it. What *was* that thing?

Her first instinct was to get back on Jack and leave as fast as possible. Anything that looked that unnatural tended to be mixed up with magic in some way—as in curses and possessed objects—and magic tended to be contagious, to stick to its finder like dog manure on one's boot.

Then she heard tiny moaning noises coming from the direction of the object. It sounded almost human. She couldn't leave without knowing what it was.

She approached it, reached out, and lifted the branch. About as long as her hand and pink, it resembled a piece of flesh. She identified it immediately…after all, she'd seen another one just this morning.

It was a penis.

One side had a rounded end, bisected by a gentle indentation with a small irregular hole in the center. On the other end, it still bore its testicles in their dark red sac. Ic, and if it had ever belonged to a man, the wound had disappeared completely, as Vesper could see no place where it appeared hacked off or scarred.

Vesper recoiled, dropping the branch and drawing back.

The branch struck the penis, which shrieked and sat up, rolling onto its sac and growing taller and straighter.

"I was having a terrible nightmare," the penis said then, its voice high-pitched, but quite male. The small hole on the round end moved a little bit as it talked—could it possibly be a mouth? Then the head swiveled a little, directing the small hole toward Vesper. "Ooh, a female. Hello there, cute stuff."

"Oh...hello." Not attached to a man, it actually wasn't so intimidating. She leaned closer. How could something like that actually articulate sounds? Could there be a tiny tongue, vocal cords in there?

"Pick me up why don't you? I can tell you want to."

Vesper drew back again. She did admit an urge to poke it with her finger, but it was a detached talking penis, and that in itself made it suspect. Then something occurred to her. "Are you under a spell?"

"Not exactly," it replied. "But you can kiss me if you want."

Its tone was almost neutral, but it contained an edge of something that made Vesper uncomfortable—it was almost creepy. She noted the same sort of edge in the voices of men who sat in front of taverns calling at girls who passed by them. Those men always made her feel as if they saw her as public property, an object with nothing inside; the difference between her internal richness and their view of her made her want to scream and rip off the image they saw.

She considered putting the penis in her specimen container and taking it home, but she didn't trust it. Not only was it unnatural, but it could be demon-possessed. In real life, unnatural found objects such as these tended to be trouble, without the benefits of granting free wishes or turning into handsome princes like in the tales. Besides, Malland had no handsome princes for it to turn into except for King Bugger's only son Magnus, a reputed philanderer and wastrel.

Without engaging the penis in any more conversation, Vesper turned and headed straight for her mule.

Impolite not to say goodbye, perhaps, but Vesper understood that when one was toying with creepy magical things, sometimes the wisest course was to disengage entirely without giving it anything else to respond to—so nothing else could be tripped or triggered in the spell-work that had disturbed its natural functions. Better to go somewhere else and start afresh in her insect search. Vesper suppressed a surge of resentment against the penis and went to grab Jack's reins.

Only when she was astride and urging Jack into a walk did she see it.

The penis.

She'd been wrong to think it couldn't move, save for a little with that loose skin on top. It was mobile—extremely mobile, apparently, because it was hopping through the brush and grass to catch up to her.

Vesper felt a stab of fear. She dug her heels hard into her mule's flanks. Jack, startled, broke into a trot.

Well, he's no racehorse, but there's still no way a little hopping thing can catch me now. After a moment, she pulled back a little from where she'd hunkered down over her mule's neck to urge him to move a little faster. She glanced back.

She nearly toppled off in surprise. The penis was still there, all right, and no longer hopping—it was *flying*. If she hadn't been looking specifically for it, she might have mistaken it for a bird of some sort. It wasn't flying that fast—it rather pumped itself through the air with a weaving kind of motion, but it was definitely faster than the hopping, and it was gaining on her.

"C'mon, Jack," Vesper urged. She fished in her bag and pulled out one more apple. *This could either work or turn out very badly*, she thought as she pulled her arm back and threw the apple harder than she'd ever thrown any fruit in her whole life.

They surged through the fields they'd come from in the direction of the closest road, and Vesper was thankful that their earlier tramping had flattened enough of the flora to ease the return. Vesper clutched Jack, unused to this sort of speed coming from him–glad for it, but knowing it wouldn't last.

Just then, she thought of the compass. At the speed they moved, it was difficult to access her bag, but with a fortuitously timed lunge and a quick twist and pull, she had her bag in front of her. A few seconds later she had the magical instrument in her hand. She pointed it at the grasses before her—in a direction slightly off from where they'd come—right at a tree.

Jack was going too fast to stop, even had the tree not moved out of the way. Move it did, though—bowing to the side almost to the ground, so the mule barely had to jump to clear it.

Smack!

The penis must have hit the tree. Vesper didn't need to slow Jack down to confirm it, as he'd finally found the apple and stood by the tree, smacking and crunching.

She saw the penis on the ground on the other side of the tree. It quivered, then went still. Was it injured?

Now that it was down, it occurred to Vesper that this penis could make an interesting specimen. If it was already hurt and about to die, she'd have no qualms about giving it a quick death, and then opening it up to see how it could talk. If it seemed likely to survive, however, perhaps she ought to help it. After all, she was to blame for its injury, even though it had been the one chasing her.

She slid off Jack and took one of her well-padded glass collection containers out of the bag. She approached the penis one cautious step at a time until she was sure that it wasn't moving. It seemed smaller than before, and was no longer rigid, but looked like a curled-up dead worm—all soft and wrinkled.

"Hello? Are you alive?" she asked.

It said nothing.

"Yes!" she exulted. She couldn't wait to dissect it. She picked it up, noting that it was quite soft now, and popped it into the container. Fortunately the penis had shrunk, because it wouldn't have fit in her case otherwise. She screwed the lid on, wrapped the container in its cloth again, and packed it into her bag.

She would have to put off her insect collecting for another day. She was already far from the original site, or any other place where she knew of the giant ant homes. The sun blazed high in the sky; surely the witch had already gone home. Doubtless Sharrua was furious. Sighing, Vesper remounted and turned Jack to head back home.

CHAPTER 2

Vesper managed to sneak in through the kitchen entrance when she got home. The cook hired for the day was shouting out orders to the three kitchen assistants, one of whom was openly sobbing.

Aside from one irritated glance from the cook, no one paid Vesper any heed as she tiptoed through, eyes to the floor.

She had almost made it to her room when her luck ended and she ran into her older sister, Medalla, who was clothed in her second-finest gown. Medalla, whose husband was a merchant, had access to discounted fabric of high quality, and thus she and her sisters were better-dressed than their family's economics would otherwise have allowed. This dress was of dark blue satin with emerald trim around the bust line, high-waisted with medium-puffy sleeves, and it set off Medalla's red-dyed hair to her best advantage. The faint swelling of her belly was mostly hidden, so not even the baby-to-be could upstage Aren tonight.

"Mother is really upset with you," Medalla said cheerily, her voice several decibels louder than necessary. "You missed your appointment with the witch."

Vesper didn't need to try to look contrite, because she felt sorry that she was about to lie. "I forgot."

"Well, at least get the maid to do your hair and make-up. You know Ruben hired a maid for us, right? Take advantage of it. You're a fright, Vesper. Are those leaves in your hair?"

"Umm—I don't think so. I'll go find the maid." Vesper dashed to her room and slammed the door, leaning against it, panting.

She had no intention, actually, of finding the maid. If she had to spend the whole evening in public, avoiding people while trying her hardest to appear as if she was having a good time, she would enjoy every possible precious moment alone. Instead, after shoving her bag under the bed, she sat on her bed and did some deep breathing exercises she'd read about as being good for stress.

As she inhaled to the count of five, held the breath, and then exhaled to the count of five, she tried to think of positive statements she could make about the upcoming evening.

I won't say anything stupid tonight, she thought. No...that didn't sound right. She should rephrase it...*I will only say smart things tonight.*

That was partially the problem, though. She was terrible at making conversation about the weather or fashion or the latest gossip about the royal family. She knew that chemicals made up the sun and that rain was condensed moisture in the atmosphere, but she could never get beyond a "It's quite warm today, isn't it?" during discussions of the weather. Even though she could spend hours discussing her ideas about the purpose of life and whether souls existed (at least, she imagined she could—no one had ever wanted to do so with her), the witty banter about trivialities that was mastered by every other female she knew had always evaded her.

While she sat and breathed deeply, she thought about how nice it would be if everyone forgot about her and she just stayed sitting and breathing all night long. Except she was beginning to get that nervous feeling that someone, her mother or Medalla particularly, would soon come looking for her and would have a fit that she wasn't ready. Sighing, she got up, stripped off her day-dress, and donned her best gown. It was of eggshell blue with lace edging on the hem, and she'd picked this fabric and style because she'd thought the pale color and demure cut would help her blend in better. She brushed out and pinned up her hair in a simple knot. She stood in front of her vanity and stuck her tongue out at her reflection, then took three deep breaths and headed for the door.

"You have some explaining to do," Sharrua hissed as Vesper came to the front door to stand by her sisters, just as the bell announced the first guest. "You completely humiliated me this morning! Do you know how many months it took me to get enough money to pay for that session? I had to give her every penny still, you know!"

"Sorry, Mother," Vesper said. "I forgot."

"Forgot! Don't give me that. You remember every word from those ridiculous books you read. Don't tell me you *forgot*."

Then Sharrua's scowl melted away into a beaming smile as the door opened, and two well-dressed elderly women entered.

"Dearest Sharrua," said the first, kissing her on the cheek.

"And lovely Aren, radiant on your day," said the second.

"Medalla, with your budding baby to be," said the first. "Husband traveling again?"

"Yes," Medalla exclaimed. "He's meeting his second wife and will bring her home in time for the baby's birth."

"*Second* wife already! What a wonderful husband," cooed the old woman. "That's something to be proud of, Sharrua—*two* of your daughters becoming first wives, and without even having dowries." Medalla beamed, and Sharrua nodded with a tight little smile, acknowledging both the compliment and the insult.

As the two women came to Vesper, their eyes scraped over her hairstyle, her bare face, the lack of accessories, and the same dress she wore to every social occasion. "Dear Vesper," one of them said. "Not too sad about your little sister marrying before you, I hope?"

"I know an amazing witch who does magical makeovers," said the other. "If you have a session with her, someone will certainly want to marry you, too. The quiet ones make excellent second wives, you know. There's no reason why little Vesper couldn't make someone see that, with a bit of help."

Sharrua's teeth were clenched as she smiled. "Thank you for the suggestion."

"I'll leave you her direction later tonight, shall I?" She blew a kiss with a lemony pucker, and then she pulled her companion off into the milling crowd of guests.

So it went. The introductions and greetings lasted the next hour and a half. Vesper tried not to yawn. She'd woken up far too early that morning, and she knew she was going to suffer for it tonight. The party would doubtless go on until the wee hours. She wondered if anyone would notice if she snuck off early and went upstairs—if enough alcohol flowed, she thought she just might be able to.

Aren's fiancé, Ruben, arrived. A strong-looking, rather hairy man, he looked as if he might become heavy sooner rather than later. He'd been in the king's guard for some years and had performed well until his leg had been injured in a border scuffle on the Gorge side of Malland. Now he walked with a limp and he spent his time training a small militia for the region. Vesper had never understood Aren's attraction to him, but her sister was smitten.

"He...don't you think he drinks a lot?" Vesper had asked her. "And he's killed people...I don't think you can ever really be at peace if you've killed people..."

"I kind of like the fact that he's killed people. He's a real man," Aren said.

Vesper didn't think so, but since her ideas about what made a "real man" were based on fantasy, she wondered if her sister might be right. "But do you think you know him well enough? Most of the time he's been gone, and when he's been here he's only seen you in public a few times. How can he know anything more about you than that he likes your looks? And you, that you like his money?"

Aren's eyes flashed. "Not everybody is so complicated as you. And you ought to think of the family—Mother and Father can barely support us. If you want them to have any sort of good life, you'll get yourself married off too."

Vesper had flinched and grown hot at that, as she knew it was true. Still, she couldn't bring herself to lower her standards for what she found acceptable in a husband. She'd made excuses that she already made a little bit of her own money, and soon she would petition for self-guardianship...but when she thought of some of her more ambitious fantasies, such as becoming an advisor to the king, she felt so stupid she wanted to sink into the floor.

"Vesper," someone was saying repeatedly, and she started. She'd been nearly dozing off on her feet, eyes glazed as she nodded and smiled at the blur of faces and stifling wafts of perfume that passed by in an extended dream in which the same thing happened over and over.

"What? Oh, hello, Nim," she said. She smiled at him, feeling relieved enough at the sight of a friendly face that she almost forgot about what he'd been doing while he stared at her window this morning. "Are your parents here?" She looked behind him, but he was alone, wearing his church clothes—somewhat threadbare and slightly too tight on a figure that had broadened in recent years. His shoes, however, were stylish and new, dyed bright blue and with a clever fringe and tassel on the tops.

"No...Mother's not feeling well tonight and Father stayed to tend her," he said, but he looked down as he said it. Vesper knew he was lying, and he knew she knew it. Nim was the son of their closest neighbor, a poor shoemaker whom Sharrua had been trying to get rid of for years—"They're pushing down the value of the neighborhood," she'd complained, even though her husband, as town butcher, had no more social status than a shoemaker. "Status is as much behavior as birth, and at least we've got the former down," she would say. Nim's family had only been invited because they *were* the closest neighbors, and Aren had wanted everyone to share her joy.

Nim looked up again. "I had to come, because we'd already gotten a present for Aren...and I wanted to give you this."

He kept hold of the larger box, presumably Aren's gift—probably shoes, which was always the present his family gave—and out of his waistcoat he drew a smaller package.

"Oh—thank you, Nim. You shouldn't have. There is no occasion to give me anything." She smiled, though; she already knew what it was, and she tried to conceal it in the folds of her dress. It was a book, one of many Nim had gotten her, and it was precious to her—one more reason to forgive his behavior this morning.

"I hope you'll read it and think more about what I said this morning," Nim said, and Vesper felt herself blushing. While she read it, she hoped rather that she'd be able to forget what he'd been *doing* that morning.

"Tell that boy to stop giving you those dirty things, filling your mind with nonsense," Sharrua hissed at the next pause in receiving guests. "Give it to a servant—you're embarrassing me, being seen holding that thing. It's as if your sister is less important than a book."

"I'll just run and bring it upstairs," Vesper began, but her mother snapped her fingers and made to snatch the package away. Vesper avoided the grab, but handed it over to the maidservant who stood at attention in response to Sharrua's gesture.

"Put it by my bedside," Vesper said, before her mother could give alternative orders, and the maid nodded.

Finally, when the line of guests had slowed to less than a trickle, Sharrua decided that they had spent enough time in reception and she signaled for the musicians to start playing. That was the cue for the dancing to begin.

Vesper far preferred dancing to most of the conversations she would have there tonight. Unfortunately, she was given her least coveted job of circulating to keep guests happy, as Medalla had to stay seated due to her pregnancy, and Aren's job was simply to be beautiful and blissful, dancing within the meaty circle of Ruben's arms.

Although Sharrua had tried to make the numbers of male and females balanced, her husband Bobbin insisted on setting up a games room. Since Ruben was paying for all of it, he said, "Blast if I'll have to stand around chit-chatting with the town harpies." Vesper thought wistfully that she'd prefer playing card games to chit-chatting as well, but she wasn't allowed to escape. Half the men had flocked to that room, which Bobbin had stocked with barbecued appetizers, complimentary cigars, and gambling implements. Every so often, Sharrua would stick her head inside the games room and make angry clicking noises; she and Bobbin would have a low-voiced argument, during which the butcher would nod and apparently agree to everything she said (a trick Vesper admitted that she'd picked up)—but still, the men stayed. Thus the large male deficit in the dancing-room remained unchanged.

Vesper was supposed to be mingling and taking care of guests who looked lonely, but in her ambits around the room she was pretty sure she was the single person not talking to anyone else. She wandered closer to a knot of non-dancing females around her age, all of whom congregated near the drinks table. They were Aren's friends, or acquaintances at least, and thus they usually suffered the presence of the awkward older sister, even if all she did was stand there with a fixed smile on her face, nodding and laughing a second after everyone else did as if she didn't quite follow the conversation.

She actually wasn't listening most of the time because it took so much effort to pay attention to the birdlike chatter, let alone join it. By the time she'd thought of something innocuous enough to add without drawing undue attention, but interesting enough to not be disdained, the topic had usually shifted to the next bit of gossip.

Vesper wished she could get to know them better, but she had no idea how; it seemed incredible that she could know so many things but be so unable to think of a single witty thing to say in idle company.

She caught a drift of conversation from the group that sparked her curiosity, and she took a few steps more in their direction. She reached for a drink and stood there, sipping.

"I hope he doesn't die," said one of them.

"He's the prince. He's got the best doctors in the kingdom and all the magic the king can buy. There's no way he'll die."

"Maybe he's fallen in love, and he's reading poetry to the woman of his dreams all day long," said another, a wistful-eyed blonde who clasped her hands in front of her chest.

Her statement was met by raucous giggles.

"Oh, stop, Erryl," said the first. "That man will never fall in love. All he loves is an endless variety of p-u-s-s-y. The king has probably got him on lockdown to keep him from having to support so many bastards."

"I'd be happy to make a bastard with a man like that," said the second. "I saw him when he had his eighteenth birthday tour around the kingdom. He wore the tightest leggings—you could see *everything*."

Vesper found herself losing interest in the conversation, and she began to sidle away.

"What do you think, Vesper?" asked Erryl, one of the few who tried to be kind. "Would you want to be with the prince, even for just a night?"

"Oh—not really," Vesper replied absently. "The royal line's been inbred for centuries, so I'd be afraid of the genetics involved in procreating with someone like him. Maybe if I put some sort of a device on his penis that would prevent the sperm from entering the womb, then it would be possible."

The girls stared at her in silence; one of them snickered. Vesper blinked, not sure what she'd said wrong; she gulped her drink, but it ended up going into her windpipe, and she choked and spat punch all over the floor. It was a blessing in disguise. "Excuse me," she spluttered, fleeing.

After getting a glass of water, Vesper found the largest potted palm and hovered behind it. There, unobserved, she allowed her thoughts to roam. She wondered what sort of an illness could be preventing the prince from engaging in his favorite activity. Prince Magnus, who was said to be handsome and charismatic, wasn't someone Vesper dreamed about meeting like so many other girls did—someone like that would accumulate quite a number of wives, and not only would each one have to deal with competing with all the other wives, but they'd all be under dissection by every gossip in the kingdom. So many people would have expectations of him that he wouldn't have much time to devote to one partner, let alone five or ten. No...that would never be a partnership to foster being truly seen.

A part of her did like to hear the gossip, though. It spoke of things that fascinated her, but of which she had no experience. Royalty...sex...magic.

Although she'd never admit it to anyone, Vesper did fantasize about becoming a famous philosopher or inventor whose ideas would attract the attention of the royal palace. She would become a court scientist and advise the king on important matters, her tongue as glib as honey. She'd never again commit any of the social gaffes that she could never seem to help whenever she was in public.

Perhaps she'd never see the royal court, but she was determined to exercise her scientific mind. She recalled the penis-thing upstairs. If she cut it open, would she find that it had developed a tiny trachea and larynx, perhaps a small tongue? She could probably get some detailed anatomical drawings of human penises, but it would be best if she had a real one that she could lay by the talking penis' side so she could compare them. She could probably find an animal penis...she would have to ask her father whether he could spare one when doing his butcher rounds...but she couldn't see how she was going to find a human one unless she skulked around open-casket funerals and committed a crime when no one was looking. After rigor mortis had set in, it probably would be difficult to cut off, too. Although...if she was caught sawing off the penis of a dead man, that would definitely get rid of any suitors who didn't truly understand her. *Hmm...not a bad idea...*

Honestly, she was much more comfortable with a detached penis, dead or alive, than with the thought of dealing with one attached to a real man. Sharing such an intimate act, how could anyone avoid giving a part of themselves away—and taking on something of another?

The chimes for dinner rang, and Vesper, who'd been hanging around a dark corner lost in her thoughts, was relieved. Soon everyone would be merry with drink and food, and then she could make her way back upstairs and check to see if the penis was truly dead.

Then an ear-splitting scream rent the gentle babbling of guests as they sat at the table. It was coming from upstairs. Next came the sound of porcelain breaking.

Vesper jumped up. *Oh no...I hope that isn't...*

Half the guests were jostling their way to the reception area, and she followed.

The maidservant who'd been sent to put Vesper's book at her bedside came hurtling down the stairs. Ashen-faced, she pushed through the crowd of people and ran into the kitchens.

"What's going on?"

"What happened?"

The questions blended and rose in a clamor of voices. Then, with a horrified intuition, Vesper knew—and confirmed it an instant later when she saw the fully erect, dark pink penis hopping down the stairs with its thrusting, pumping movement.

She hoped and prayed that no one would see it. If she could just get through this gaggle of girls and reach it before it got down—she could just grab it—

Then someone pointed.

"What is that?!"

"A hairless mole—"

"Some kind of monster—"

"By the gods," screeched Medalla, her voice carrying as if she spoke with a magical enhancer, "it's a detached, self-propelling penis!"

Mayhem erupted. Guests screamed and ran for the door, some grabbing coats and cloaks without regard to proper ownership. Maids ran every which way, shrieking.

"Stop this! Order! Get back into position!" howled Ruben, trying to get in from the dining room—he'd not rushed over, as he'd already started on his appetizers by the look of the fried goodies he waved above the fray—and now the chaos of guests prevented his entrance. No one paid heed to him, and his face, bright with the sheen of an early start to the drink, grew even more florid with rage. Of Aren, there was no sign.

Vesper lost track of the penis. Somehow, the panic spread to the games room, and the cloud of smoke that emerged when the doors were thrown open soon gave way to rumors of a fire in the house. Vesper ended up pressed to the wall as people pushed and shoved their way toward the entrance. She imagined the penis being trampled underfoot…and she only felt a little bit sorry.

Soon enough, the press abated and then died as the stream of guests bolting through the door slowed to a trickle. As soon as Vesper could move around freely, she began to search anew for the penis—a few times she mistook barbecued sausages for the escaped member, but it was nowhere to be found on the stairs or in the main hall.

She found Medalla upstairs in her bed; the excitement had been too much for her. Bobbin remained drinking in the games room. Finally, she ended up in the empty dining room. She heard a strange noise—something like a moan. It sounded like it was coming from underneath the long covered table.

She heard the moaning again, repeating with an odd regularity that didn't sound quite like pain. Vesper bent down and lifted up the tablecloth.

Aren sprawled against a chair leg, her head on one of the chair cushions. Mouth open, eyes closed, the silk of her dress outlining legs spread wide, she squirmed and moaned. Arching her back, she grabbed the chair behind her, nails digging in.

"Oh…oh…oh…yes! Yes! Yes!" she screamed, and she slid down until she lay completely on the floor, panting.

Vesper dropped the cloth—but not before she'd seen, creeping out from underneath Aren's skirt, a pink worm-like object.

She started at a noise behind her, and she knew someone else had seen too—and turning, she looked into the red and horrified face of Ruben.

CHAPTER 3

"You're to marry Porter Gordo. Next month, if he can arrange the license on time," said Sharrua.

Standing before her parents, Vesper felt the blood draining from her face, even as she struggled to compose her expression. After the party, she'd done her best to convince them that it had been she whom Ruben had found in a compromising attitude under the table. She had assumed that besides the lectures she'd get and the cloud of disapproval under which her mother would regard her for a few weeks, she was beyond punishment.

She assumed wrong.

"Please—not him," she stammered. "He has five children and no wives to take care of them. And he smells bad."

Porter Gordo was one of Bobbin's most loyal customers; he'd been buying meat from her father ever since he'd started out in the butcher business two decades past. Several times, Vesper had visited his cottage on the edge of town to make deliveries with her father. Porter didn't like to leave his home if he could help it. This did not surprise Vesper. Despite a pleasant enough manner, Porter had a giant wart on the side of his nose that wiggled while he spoke and made her think of an egg sac about to give birth to hundreds of baby spiders. He also had the worst breath she'd ever smelled—what with the large quantities of meat he consumed. (Vesper suspected that he ate nothing else, and probably never cleaned his teeth besides) had .

"The fact that he has no wives is the thing! You'd be his second, but since she's dead, it's almost as good as being a first. And you'll take him, as he's the only man who doesn't care about your reputation. Do you know how hard I've worked to get us accepted into the better social circles? Your exploits these past years have made it doubly hard—but with your latest scandal, I wouldn't be surprised if we're all cut from every gathering for the next year. And if the only men who want you are the poor ones willing to pool their living to support one wife together...." Sharrua's eyes were black chips of ice as the implications of what she said hung in the air. Beside her, Bobbin dozed on the sofa.

"But I've already told you I'm not ready to marry," Vesper protested. "I don't know if I ever want to. I've been saving up, and soon I'll be able to leave the house—"

"Oh, your behavior tells us full well that you're more than ready for marriage," Sharrua said, a humorless smile touching her lips. "You should have been married the instant you were of age, and then maybe you would have saved us the humiliation of finding out you were an irresponsible wanton behind all those books. As for your rather pitiful savings, they'll go toward paying Ruben back for that party. He's demanded a full accounting, and he'll enforce it—to debtor's prison if need be. Porter has graciously agreed to pay off the balance of debt as a marriage gift."

"Debtor's prison?" Vesper repeated, her voice faltering. She hadn't thought Ruben could be so cruel. It did, however, fit with her theory that men who killed were never at peace.

"That's right," Sharrua said. "There'll be no riding off into the woods to avoid this. You got us into this mess, and you're going to get us out by marrying Porter. You'll take care of his children and warm his bed and cook and clean, and you won't have any more time for your nonsense with books or dead animals, and that will make a vast improvement in you, no doubt."

Vesper had nothing to say. They were right to blame her, and she would have to pay the price. She left the room feeling numb, cursing the moment she'd ever beheld the penis.

"I hate you," Aren said that evening, when Vesper came to visit her in her bedroom. Aren pulled the covers over her face.

"I'm not surprised," Vesper said, sitting by the bed. She placed the tea she'd brewed for Aren beside the bed, full of the most potent herbal contraceptives she knew of—although she didn't think the penis could actually get Aren pregnant, she thought it best to take precautions. "If it makes you feel any better, Mother and Father have engaged me to Porter Gordo."

The covers came off, revealing a face puffy and red from crying. "You can't be serious! You don't mean that old guy with the wart you told me about? The one with all of those brats?"

Vesper nodded. "I've got a plan though—if I can somehow pay off our debt, I wouldn't need to marry him. I'm going to go into town and see if I can make an agreement with Neela to collect and prepare more herbs, and maybe work in her shop with her as an assistant. If she'll loan me enough, maybe a portion of the debt paid off will be enough, and Ruben will accept the rest in installments." She didn't mention that the sum she received for the work she did was so paltry it would take years to pay off the debt—but maybe Neela would have come into a windfall in the week since they'd last met, and maybe she'd declare that Vesper was like a daughter to her and deserved a dowry...and then pigs would shoot from her ears and start dancing in the streets. She sighed. Her chances of escaping this marriage seemed less likely by the hour.

Aren frowned and glanced down at the blanket still clutched in her fingers, as if she was considering whether to pull it back over her head. "That's all well and good for you then," she said. "*My* life is still ruined, though. I tried to go into town this morning, and people were *laughing* at me. My supposed *friends* wouldn't even look at me."

"I'm sorry," Vesper said. "When I went to town, I told everyone it was me under the table...but no one believes me except Mother."

"Only Mother is blind enough to think you'd do something like that. And I heard that Ruben's been in the taverns the past few nights, raving about me. No one would doubt an eyewitness, even if it's a drunk one."

"The rumors will die down," Vesper ventured, praying that she was right. "And...to look on the bright side...maybe it's good to find out now that Ruben's not the right one for you. If he were a nicer person, he wouldn't have gotten so upset about such a little thing."

Tears began to slide down Aren's cheeks. "A little thing? He finds his fiancé under a table having sex with a detached penis. I think any man in the kingdom would find that objectionable, except possibly your mealy-mouthed Nim."

Vesper thought that it might possibly be true, except the part about Nim being hers. She never thought she'd actually wish that he were, but now, contemplating the alternative of Porter Gordo, she found that Nim didn't look so bad after all. *Don't think about it now. You're here to cheer up Aren, not feel sorry for yourself.* "Well...why do you think it happened?"

Aren swiped her eyes with the sleeve of her nightdress. "I guess I had a bit too much to drink. I was kind of nervous about everything, you know. I've never been engaged before. So when all that noise started, and Ruben got up and yelled at everyone, I stayed and drank some more...and then something was crawling up my leg and poking me and saying such nice things to me about how gorgeous I was. Then I guess—I got carried away."

Vesper took Aren's hand. Aren finally relented and allowed her sister's arms to come around her, and she sobbed.

Finally her crying slowed to occasional sniffles. "I can't believe it's over with Ruben," she said. "But...you know, I don't hate you. And I'll forgive you on one condition."

The fist around Vesper's heart eased a little. "Anything."

Aren looked at her, all big eager eyes. "Can I borrow the penis again?"

Vesper frowned. The penis had been under lock and key since she'd caught it that evening after the party; she'd found a bigger container for it and had hidden it away. No one except Vesper, Aren, and the maidservant knew that the thing hopping downstairs was truly an animated and detached penis; Medalla's shrieking announcement was attributed to being a pregnant woman's hallucination, and her own and Ruben's rumors all involved a sex toy.

Vesper's plans to experiment on the penis were no longer possible now that she knew it was alive. Since it was sentient, she felt some compunction about killing it outright, although she certainly wanted to that evening of the party, even more so after she'd caught it and lectured it back in her room.

"I ought to chop you into little pieces," she'd raged, holding it squirming in her hand.

"Mmm...it feels good when you rub me that way," the penis had said, using its skin to slide back and forth on her hand. "The drought has finally broken—it's been ages since I had seeeeeexxx...and I've decided that I want more. Lots more. Come on, girl, let's do it now. I can go on all night long."

Vesper wanted nothing more than to throw the penis against the wall as hard as she could—but she made herself hold on to it until she grabbed some metal tongs from near the fireplace—considering only briefly lighting a fire and threatening to burn it—but instead she just used it to hold the penis. "You're a disgusting piece of filth," she cried. "And you ruined my sister's engagement!"

"I rescued her from a man who won't satisfy her like I could," he said. "I could do the same thing for you, cutie pie. Not rescue you from a man, but from a life of boredom and no pleasure."

Did her life look so boring and pleasure-less, even to a brainless penis? She felt the urge to throw it again, but instead she put it in the container, closing it tight, and then, still clearly hearing its voice, wrapped a cloth around it.

"Oh, come on," the penis' muffled voice said. "I could make you feel so good. I don't like it in here—it's cold and dark. I mean, I like dark, but warm...wet..."

Vesper had stuck it under her bed. There it had stayed since that night. It had continued to make lewd or cajoling comments for a couple of hours, but then it had grown silent. She'd been too afraid to check on it, and part of her actually hoped it might suffocate there in the jar, thus absolving her of any responsibility for it.

She supposed lending it to Aren couldn't do too much harm. On second thought...considering what had happened at Aren's engagement party...it could. She'd given her word, though, and she wanted her sister to be happy again.

"I suppose so. If it's still alive. But just for a few days," she said, and Aren beamed. "And drink that tea!"

When Vesper felt around under her bed for the specimen container, her hand bumped against something. She took out the package that

Nim had given her—she'd completely forgotten about it. She must have accidentally knocked it under the bed. She put it on her bedside table for later.

Before bringing the penis to Aren, she thought she'd better have a chat with it. She removed the cloth, and the penis immediately started to hop up and down in excitement.

"Listen," she said, the container still closed. She steeled herself. *Be assertive. It's just a penis.* "My sister wants to borrow you for a few days. So you can come out and...and spend time with her. But I have conditions of my own for this. You aren't allowed to leave her room until I come and get you. If anyone comes to visit her room besides me, you hide and don't move or say a word. And you don't talk to Aren either. Behave and I might give you more liberties. Do anything at all outside of what I've told you, and I'm going to throw you into the fire."

The penis wiggled with excitement. "Sure, sure. That sounds good."

She wasn't so sure she could count on the word of a penis, but then again, if it did disobey she might just get mad enough to kill it without guilt.

Aren was just as happy to see the penis as it was to see her.

"If you could just hang on a minute and let me leave before you start that," Vesper said, face burning as she hastily backed toward the door. "And make sure you keep the noise down. I'm not responsible for keeping Mother from getting upset about this, okay?"

Aren nodded impatiently. "I know! Thank you, Vesper." *Now get out*, her body language said.

Vesper went back to her room and sat on her bed. Tomorrow she would go back into town and see Neela. She began her deep breathing exercises, feeling ragged from two days of more social interactions than she was used to having in a month.

After a few moments, her gaze alighted on Nim's present. Reaching for it, she unwrapped it and smiled down at the book inside. She ran a reverent finger along its spine, which bore some intricate scrollwork instead of a title. She noted the quality of the leather and tooling, despite the book's apparent age, and she blew a bit of dust off the still-bright gilt that edged each page and , .

She opened the cover.

"The Book of Offhand Truths," read the title page, with no author.

Curious, she thought. She turned to the next page.

A remarkably realistic illustration met her gaze. A handsome man lay in bed, fully clothed, his boots still on. He had longish dirty-blond hair, and a crown hung askew on his head, as if he'd forgotten to take it off before throwing himself onto the sheets. Filmy green fabric curtained a bed covered with silk sheets and blankets of rich green velvet. The man was the very picture of a prince: gorgeous, regal, rich.

Oddly, his face bore an expression of deep discontent—almost petulance...

She flipped to another page, not in chronological order. Another illustration covered the right-hand side of the pages. Here, the prince was sitting up in his bed, and he wasn't alone. A woman clothed only by long wheat-colored hair stood framed by the open bed curtain. Lips drawn back in a snarl, the prince had cocked his hand back as if to throw the glass of wine he held. From the surprise on the woman's face and the angle of her body, still half-poised in invitation, it had only just occurred to her that the prince was not interested.

Not very princely, Vesper thought. The plot was thickening—if the story was going in order at all. She flipped back to the first page.

The original illustration had disappeared. The setting had changed from bedroom to bathroom. The prince was relieving himself in a chamber pot, his face a grimace of annoyance. Vesper gasped—because the urine was trickling from a small hole in a smooth space of skin where his genitals should have been.

He had no penis.

She flipped to the next page and confronted blankness. As she scanned further, she found all the pages bare of both writing and illustration, except for the title page, still labeled "The Book of Offhand Truths."

She let the book fall, then brushed at her fingers as if its magic clung to them. The story contained in those three pages had delivered a message specifically for her: the detached, cursed penis belonged to the man in the picture—and now, remembering the conversation she'd overheard at the party, she knew that he must be none other than the supposedly sick Crown Prince Magnus. The penis belonged to him.

Vesper thought she understood the penis' obsession with sex a little better now. *Prince Magnus must be missing it sorely*, she thought. *Speaking of sore*...she wondered, *would it be sore at all, missing a body part?* She thought of the apparent cleanliness of its separation from Magnus' body. She put the book under her pillow. Perhaps she should ask Nim where he'd gotten it. If the book was telling the truth, she had one more headache to deal with—for the way things had been going for her lately, she wouldn't be surprised if someone showed up to arrest her for being in possession of stolen property.

Aren did not want to give the penis back. Vesper waited till the next day, wanting to let her sister have at least one night with it. When Vesper went to collect it, Aren burst into tears.

"But you told me I could have him for a couple of days," Aren sobbed. "Just one night isn't enough. He's just...just amazing. When I'm having sex with him, I forget all my problems."

"I don't need to know the details," Vesper said, holding up both her palms. Then, "I'm sorry to take it away from you. But I've found out who the owner is, and I think it should go back to him."

"Who?" Aren asked, her tears ceasing mid-flow. She clasped her hands to her chest. "The man who owns that penis already owns half my heart."

"What about Ruben?"

"Ruben, shmooben," said Aren. "He dropped me after the tiniest little mistake. He doesn't deserve me. Minimus told me so."

"Minimus? Who's that?"

"It's the penis' name," Aren explained.

It did make sense, Vesper thought, *that the penis would be Magnus' Minimus*. Despite this added personalization, she was even more convinced that she was right to take it away. "It—Minimus—broke its promise to me. It—he—told me he wouldn't talk to you. Since he's broken his promise, I have every right to take him early and...even punish him, if he's earned that."

"No!!!" cried the penis, poking his head out from underneath Aren's pillow. "You can't have me. I'm with my true love. If you separate us, I'll die!"

Vesper grabbed him with tongs from her pocket and wrapped him in a small towel, muffling the high-pitched shrieks he emitted. She shoved the towel-wrapped penis into the container, and then wrapped the padding-cloth around it. She could still hear his voice faintly, but that would have to do.

"Please tell me who the owner is," Aren begged. "That's the man I want to marry."

Vesper opened her mouth, feeling a sudden urge to share a rare bit of gossip—about the juiciest news she could imagine. Could she trust Aren to keep her mouth shut, or would her sister get them both into trouble? She decided that she'd better exercise some caution. "I wish I could tell you...but it's not my secret to share. I'm afraid he's not really eligible, though."

"If I wait to satisfy *your* standards of eligibility, I'll end up with no suitors and a forced marriage to a lump like Porter, too," Aren said, throwing herself facedown onto her pillow and pulling the covers over her head.

Vesper ducked her head and left the room, trying to ignore the muffled sobs coming from under the blankets.

She left a scrawled message in the kitchen for her mother saying that she was going into town to do some shopping. Then she put the contained penis into her bag, next to the book of truths. She decided that she would first go to Nim's, and she walked Jack to the tiny house which was the first stop on the road into town.

Nim's mother, Winne, was tending the garden. One large apple tree formed the centerpiece in a large and glorious spread of flowers and trailing vines. The house looked sorrier for its contrast with the lush greenscape; the plaster had fallen away in a number of places, only some covered with uneven patchwork, and an attempt at expanding a room on the side remained in a halfway stage—the same place as it had been a decade ago. Sharrua was right—this house did make the neighborhood look shabbier. Although Vesper's family didn't have money for dowries or other extras, at least they spent what they had wisely, and their house remained comfortable and well-kept.

"I'm glad to see you're feeling much better," she said to Winne, who shrugged.

"It makes me feel ill having to work my arse off taking care of a lying drunkard and never having enough to get the neighbors to stop looking down on me," Winne said. "Other than that, I'm just fine."

Vesper felt the telltale heat rising to her cheeks. She knew just which neighbors Winne was referring to, but when she opened her mouth to apologize, Winne looked up with such a baleful glare that Vesper thought she'd better not. "Is Nim at home?"

"Out back in the studio with his pa," Winne said, indicating with a jerk of her head.

Nim's father Oggen created his masterpieces in a shed little larger than a closet. Despite being an excellent shoemaker, Oggen spent every extra cent he earned on drink. Winne's resulting bitterness surprised no one.

Inside the studio, Oggen was working with intense concentration, bloodshot eyes fixed on the flap of leather he gripped with one trembling hand as he pulled a needle through. Sober for once, Vesper noted with surprise; Tthey probably needed to pay creditors. Nim cut leather, eyes bulging in concentration, while his father sewed.

Nim flipped his yellow hair out of his eyes and caught sight of Vesper. His whole face lit up, and he pulled out of his slouch and beamed. Vesper felt a stab of guilt. The only fellow in town who didn't care about her reputation ...but try as she might, she couldn't think of him in that way, and now it was too late anyway.

"Hi, Nim," she said. "Can I talk to you for a minute?"

Nim nearly leaped over the workbench. "Of course, Ves! Pa, I'll just be a second." Oggen didn't even acknowledge his son, but Nim didn't seem to care. "We can take a quick stroll if you'd like. My legs could use a stretch. I've been cramped up in there all morning."

Vesper tied Jack near a patch of grass next to the studio; she didn't want to risk him eating anything in Winne's garden. Vesper and Nim went over a gentle hill and walked through a dry field that crunched under their steps.

"I wanted to thank you for the present, Nim," Vesper said. "It's very interesting. Where did you get it?"

Nim laughed nervously and scratched his head, shooting her a sidelong glance. "Why…didn't you like it?"

"Yes, I did. Do," she said. "It's definitely a little different from the usual books. Have you looked at it?"

Nim sighed. "Actually, Vesper, I hadn't. You know that old witch-peddler who comes into town every so often?"

Vesper nodded. She was the one who'd sold Vesper the compass. "The one everyone says is crazy."

"Well…I stopped to chat with her…and she offered to sell me something that would…well, that someone I liked would enjoy."

Vesper frowned. "It doesn't have a love spell on it, does it?"

Nim's hair fluffed up as he shook his head, bright pink flooding visible skin. "You do have a way of stating things baldly, Vesper. O-of course I'd never try a love spell on you. But…she did say it would help you discover love. I didn't read it or even open it, but I thought…" His hand lifted in a half-hearted gesture that connected the two of them, and then his eyes dropped.

"Ah…I see." *A little too much.* "Well, Nim, I did like it very much. It's just a curious book—it's magicked." She took it out of her bag.

"How so?" Nim leaned close to look.

She held it open for him to read the title page. Then she flipped it to the first page.

She frowned down at an empty page. A quick perusal confirmed that she held a blank book in her hands.

"There's nothing there," Nim said, scratching his head.

"Hm," said Vesper. She closed the book and put it away. "I guess the magic's only meant for me. Anyhow, thanks. It answers a couple of my questions, at least."

"What's this about? What did you see in the book?"

"I'm sorry, Nim…I can't tell you," Vesper said.

They were heading back toward Nim's house. He stopped while they were still out of hearing range of his parents. "Did it…did you see something about us?"

Vesper suppressed a groan. "No, I didn't, Nim. It had nothing to do with either of us. I can't tell you because it's someone else's secret."

Venturing a glance at him, she found him frowning, looking as if he hadn't heard her at all. He spoke to his boots, a fine pair of glossy red-brown leather. "Vesper…won't you be practical? I know I'm not rich, but I know my pa's trade like he does himself. Most of the shoes that are coming out from us in town are of my make, not his. I'm saving up to buy a bit of land for my own cottage and studio, and since I know how to save money, it won't be long before I can provide a comfortable life for myself…and a wife. Maybe even two, after a few years."

Finally he blinked, and his mouth pursed with a determination that gave Vesper pause—she'd only ever seen that expression on his face once, the instant before he'd finished masturbating in front of her window. "There's one thing I haven't done to show you how good it would be for us…"

He reached for her, and Vesper, confused, moved only at the last minute. Nim tried to compensate, and Vesper's forehead slammed against his nose.

"Ow," she said. "What are you doing?"

Nim rubbed his nose. "I'm trying to show you something."

Vesper knew exactly what he was trying to do—she could see it in the pucker of his lips and the drooping of his lids over his eyes as he'd leaned forward. How could she avoid it without hurting his feelings? "I better get to town quickly—I need to catch Neela…"

As they ducked and moved from side to side, one trying to approach, the other deflect, Vesper had to suppress a bubble of hysterical laughter that arose—they must look as if they were performing an odd dance. It ended when Nim lunged forward and stamped a puckered kiss against the left half of her mouth. Vesper grimaced at the aftereffect of what felt like a having a cold rock bounced against her lips. Her first kiss—what an anticlimax!

"You don't like it?" he asked, his voice so mournful that Vesper, agonized by her own memories of multiple snubs, just couldn't tell the truth.

"Even if I did," she temporized, "it's no good, Nim. My parents have arranged a marriage for me, and I have to go through with it, because my fiancé will pay the family debt. If he doesn't pay it, my father may go to debtor's prison."

"Marriage!" Nim cried, his voice breaking on the word. "To someone else!"

"I'm sorry, Nim." Vesper watched as he appeared to age before her eyes. He sucked in a breath and gazed at her, a tremble shivering down his body until it reached his feet and he turned and stumbled back toward his house. Should she follow him, she wondered? No, she would just make it worse.

As she rode away on Jack, she found that she was trembling as well. She'd just badly hurt one of the few people who actually liked her. She tried not to think that if she managed to find some way of avoiding the terrible fate her mother intended for her, she would have to hurt him yet again.

CHAPTER 4

Shortly after her conversation with Nim, Vesper decided to take the long way into town. She would dispose of the troublesome man-meat once and for all. It was the lesser of her two problems, and she wanted it off of her mind; a part of her hoped that since her ill luck had begun once she'd encountered the penis, getting rid of Minimus would somehow influence the fates to get her out of her engagement to Porter.

She traveled a short distance along the route she'd taken in the woods that day she'd found the penis—just deep enough into the trees to ensure privacy. Not bothering to dismount, she allowed Jack to chomp on wildflowers while she took out the specimen container. She unscrewed the lid and dumped Minimus onto the ground beneath her.

"Ow!" he snapped, writhing like a potato bug on its back before rising atop his testicles. "That's not a nice way to wake up at all."

"I'm setting you free," Vesper said. "And don't follow me." She dug her heels into Jack's sides and clicked her tongue, but he didn't budge.

Minimus hopped back a few shaft-lengths and tilted his head forward to regard Vesper with his single eye. "But...I like you. Why can't I stay with you?"

Vesper slapped Jack on the rump. Still no movement. "I found out who you are. You're Prince Magnus' penis, and I could get in even bigger trouble if you're found with me. Why don't you just go home? I'm sure you're missed."

The penis wilted slightly. "I've been having fun with you, though. But if you don't want me, I know someone who does. I'll go back to Aren."

"No!" Vesper said, alarmed. "You can't do that. Can't you see how much trouble you've already caused? You ruined Aren's engagement to someone she loved, and now—to pay for the party, my parents have engaged me to someone so horrible—" She spluttered, unable to find a word to describe how repulsed she felt by Porter.

"I could help you end your engagement too," Minimus said.

"The same way you did with Aren's? I think not. And with the way things have been going, he'd probably want to marry me all the more! Please, I'm begging you, Minimus—leave us alone. Let me solve the problems you've created without you making more. Please—I wish you well, I really do. But if you like me at all, this has to be goodbye."

Jack finally consented to walk at this point—but he moved so slowly that Minimus didn't even have to fly to keep up; he hopped alongside them, sometimes springing from branch to branch to keep more at eye level with Vesper.

"Listen," he said. "I do like you. Even though you haven't been that nice to me and you haven't had sex with me, I still like you. I'll go away if you really want me to. I guess I could go back to my palace. But you know...if you took me back yourself, you'd probably get a reward."

Vesper swung her head to stare at him. "A reward?"

"A financial reward," Minimus said, nodding his head eagerly. "That party was nothing compared to what goes on at the palace every night. It can't possibly have cost that much—I bet you'd get several times the amount in return for accompanying me back safely."

Vesper thought for a moment, nodding slowly. "That might just work! I would still need to borrow enough for passage to Mallandina, but the fare for that would actually be manageable." Then her face fell. "But my parents will never let me go."

"Jin's balls! You're an adult. Why do you need your parents' permission?"

"They could disown me after discovering I'm gone, and then I could be arrested for having no guardian," Vesper said.

Minimus made some kind of disparaging noise. "Live a little, why don't you?"

She couldn't believe she was being lecturedto by a penis. But—he was right. She squared her shoulders. "I'll do it. I'll reserve a spot on a coach and pay in advance—and then I'll go to Mallandina and be back before the date of my supposed wedding. I'll pay the debt and cry off, with no harm done except to my reputation, which is already in tatters."

Vesper found herself in a much better mood as they headed into town.

Neela had set up her stall of herbs and potions on the border between the middle-class and the poor sections of town. There, she did excellent business. The rich had no need of herbs and potions, as they could pay for real magic spells and the best doctors; those who used magic often looked down on the herb-sellers as being witch-wannabes who trucked semi-magical plants rather than using human will to transform the nature of reality. Vesper liked herbs because they were predictable and one never had to put oneself in the power of a spell-caster and their personal abilities. She also felt that herbs were less of a crutch than regular magic—it seemed they only enhanced and complemented one's own natural abilities, easing the way toward getting something desired but not giving the actual thing on a silver platter. Although she loved her compass, it annoyed her that in more cases than not, magic complicated the natural order of things; for instance, Sharrua spent money on spells that persuaded vendors to give her discounts rather than simply paying that money directly to the vendors.

"Good day, Neela," Vesper said as she neared the stall, feeling a burst of warmth at the sight of the woman leaning over the counter. Brown curls that shone and bounced with every movement surrounded a round and rosy-cheeked face; she was a living advertisement for the success of her own youth tonics. Neela's small shop was one of the few places in the world that Vesper felt she could be herself.

"Vesper, how nice to see you! Have you brought me anything today?"

Vesper dismounted and tied Jack's rope to the side of the stall, and she shook her head. "Not today. I have some tinctures that need another week to cure. I went out for specimens the other day, but I was interrupted before I could gather any. I wanted to ask you for a rather large favor."

"You need an advance?" Neela asked, curls bobbing as she laughed at Vesper's expression. "Of course you can have one, my dear. I've got all my small change here. How much do you need?" She pulled out a purse.

Vesper had tried to estimate the largest possible sum she could ask for and not feel that she was asking too much. Even with that amount, she knew she would have to economize along the way, perhaps sleeping in stables instead of rooms whenever the coach stopped at inns, or asking if she could work for the evening in exchange for food. "Could you spare three silvers?" She bit her lip and forced herself to hold Neela's astounded gaze.

"Three silvers! Jin's balls, why do you need that much?"

Vesper's face flooded with heat, and she dropped her eyes. "I'm sorry," she stammered. "I shouldn't have asked for so much—maybe two would do—" She made rapid calculations. Two would definitely not be enough, but if she could even get to the first inn, perhaps she could stay a week and work…

"It's just such a large sum—are you in some kind of trouble, Vesper? This doesn't have anything to do with those rumors I've heard about you at that party, does it? I don't believe them, of course. You were covering up for Aren."

"Thanks, Neela." Vesper tried to smile. "But no, it's something else completely. Some would say it's not trouble, but a blessing. My parents have gotten me engaged to Porter Gordo next month in order to pay for the debt owed to Aren's ex-fiancé."

"No!" gasped Neela.

"I've got a plan for it not to happen, though."

Neela shook her head, lips set. "I won't condone your running away. It's too dangerous to go off on your own. Some women can make it out there, with no husband or father-guardian, but—well, you know what most of them end up doing. You're not tough enough for that."

"I'm not running away," Vesper said, suppressing her surge of annoyance at both Neela's assumption, and more irrationally, at the insinuation that she wouldn't be able to make it as a prostitute. Not that she ever would consider it—she suspected she'd have an awfully large learning curve in trying to be one—but it irked her that Neela would consider her not capable of something."It's complicated. I don't even know how to begin to explain—"

Neela held up a hand. She stared into Vesper's eyes for a moment, then nodded. "I believe you. You don't need to tell me more. I know you, and as much as you don't say, you're good for any loan. And you wouldn't ask if you didn't really need it. If you'll watch the stall for a few minutes, I'll run home and get it."

"Of course. Thank you."

Neela swung the stall counter open, slipping out and allowing Vesper to take her place.

During the next ten minutes, Vesper attended to a woman buying sage to burn in her house, and another who wanted syrup for her child's sore throat. She felt comfortable in this sort of interaction with people; she knew what to say, and few who'd come to a shop like this would inquire into her personal matters, curious though they might be about the stories about Aren's engagement party that were still spreading around town.

Another ten minutes passed while Vesper arranged bottles and jars into perfect rows. Neela lived only a few minutes away, so Vesper figured it would be any minute that she'd hear the patter of returning footsteps.

A shadow fell over the stall opening, and Vesper turned.

A woman dressed in black with a scarf covering most of her head and face stood there staring at Vesper, eyes sunken so deep in their sockets that, along with her attire, she could easily have passed for the incarnation of Death. Her strangely patchy skin sagged off her facial bones, but she had the mouth and eyes of a woman not over forty years of age; she looked somehow familiar, but Vesper couldn't recall ever having seen her before.

"You," the woman said. "I'm surprised you can show your face in public. Where is Neela?"

"She's gone for just a few minutes. Can I help you with something?" Vesper realized that this woman knew her, and she racked her brains—she thought she knew her as well, but from where? Surely she would have remembered such a woman.

"You don't recognize me, do you?" the woman said, stiff, poised for offense. "I'm Rena. Erryl's mother."

Vesper tried not to show her astonishment. She only knew Rena by sight, as the mother of one of the females her own age in town and a frequent customer of her father's. But the Rena she knew was beautiful and far more youthful in appearance than her age; she was often mistaken for Erryl's older sister. This person in front of her was, frankly, a hag.

"Oh, of course I know you, Rena—I was just distracted—"

"Don't lie," Rena snapped. "I know what I look like. I haven't been able to leave my house for a week. But I figured no one would recognize me, and I was right. I'm here to ask you for something, anything that might help me."

"Help you...with what?"

Rena glared as if affronted by such an intrusive question. For a moment Vesper thought she would turn around and leave. Then she sighed, and her shoulders drooped in defeat. "I suppose I can tell *you*, since you're a laughingstock and nobody would listen to anything you said about *me* anyway. Aside from the obvious things—I am no longer able to get a wizard to give me facelifts—there is a larger problem." She unwound her scarf slightly and displayed her right ear. Or rather, her lack of a right ear.

The organ was completely gone, leaving a hole in the side of her head, but no shell of an outer ear and no eardrum. Vesper stood there, blinking in shock. Rena wound the scarf back.

Vesper found her voice. "Would you like an herb to...improve your hearing?"

"Don't be stupid," Rena said. "My hearing is fine. I want something to grow back my ear."

"Did you...have an accident?"

Rena hissed through her teeth. "No, you idiot! I didn't have an accident! I lost my ear because all the wizards have gone insane! My regular wizard pretended he was going to do my facelift and instead he did this to me. He claimed it was unintentional, but I think someone who hates me paid him to do it. He simply refused to reverse it and bolted before I could call for him to be restrained and put in jail. Since then, I've gone to three wizards and five witches, and all of them have pretended their magic no longer works. It's a conspiracy against me!"

"A conspiracy?" Vesper repeated. "But how do you know they

were pretending? What if their magic really stopped working?"

"Don't be ridiculous," Rena said, eyes glittering slits within her hood. "What could possibly cause *all* the wizards and witches to lose their magic—at the same time?"

Vesper frowned. "Maybe a disease?"

"If you're going to spout nonsense instead of helping me, I'll go elsewhere—and the next time I see Neela, I'll inform her that you're responsible for her loss of business."

The barrage of threats and put-downs were having their customary effect on Vesper, who felt like cowering behind the counter. She forced herself to take a deep breath. "I'm—I'm afraid I know of no herb that can help you grow your ear back. Could you maybe just get it sewn back on?"

"It's gone!" Rena hissed. "That stupid thing told me it was sick of hearing me talk and it flew out the window two days ago. My servants have been looking for it since, and I notified all the neighbors. No one has seen it. I've even got a reward out for it."

"Your ear talked?" Vesper blurted. Something clicked in her head. Rena's ear had fallen off, talked, and flown away. Just like Minimus! "How about an herb for calming?" she asked, forgetting that this woman intimidated her even as ideas began to churn in her mind. "Or clear thinking?"

Rena glared at her. "I should have known better than to talk to you about it. Everybody says you're ridiculous, and I completely concur." She swung around and stormed away.

Vesper was too distracted to pay much attention to Rena's affronted retreat. Rena's wizard had claimed he didn't remove her ear on purpose, and then his magic no longer worked. The wizards she'd gone to afterward also could do nothing, although it seemed that they, too, didn't know until they'd tried. How could it be? Had something neutralized all magic? What did the body parts detaching and becoming animated have to do with it? Was there even a point to returning Minimus to the prince if Rena hadn't had any success getting her ear back on? Perhaps it could have been reattached if she hadn't lost it. It was a great mystery…and Vesper loved mysteries. Her hand went to her bag, half tempted to take Minimus out then and there to ask him some questions.

Her hand stilled. Who was she kidding to think that she could help solve this mystery? She needed to stay focused on her own problem.

Neela's sudden appearance interrupted Vesper's musings. "Sorry I took so long! I got caught up in the weirdest drama in the town square. I guess some witch or wizard thought it would be a funny joke to magic off some people's feet. Just imagine—half a dozen feet dancing as spry as you ever saw! Then a couple of men thought to mock them, and the feet ran over and started kicking and then—you should have seen it—the feet yelled back! Whoever would have thought that if feet could talk, they'd have such wit?"

"Indeed," Vesper said, still lost in her thoughts. "I—I should go."

"Don't forget your silvers!" Neela handed over the coins with a smile. Vesper took them, feeling a surge of guilt about repaying her benefactress with Rena's lost business—but then again, she doubted anyone in town could have made Rena feel any better. Something was definitely happening to the wizards and witches of Malland and anyone on whom they used their magic.

"When is the next passenger coach to Mallandina?" Vesper asked at the town inn, where all coaches stopped when passing through.

"Goes twice a week," said the flat-eyed man at the front desk. "Tomorrow's one, and then there's another in four days' time. Except this week the second one's not available, so if you want to go this week you have to go tomorrow."

"Why isn't the second one going?" Tomorrow was so soon—would she have time to pack and get ready?

"King's sent a commission here and that coach is on royal order now."

"Can't the coach be shared?"

The man shrugged. "Doubt it. It's not a public coach anymore. Do you want tomorrow's ticket or not?"

She had no choice, so she nodded. Although she blanched when the man told her the cost of the ticket, she handed over two of her silvers quickly, before she could change her mind. She left clutching the ticket, not quite believing she was doing this. Tomorrow felt far too soon, but she would be ready. She had to be.

Once at home, she closed herself in her bedroom and began to pack. The journey would take a week, possibly a day or two longer depending on the coach's speed and how many stops it made. She ought to bring at least one change of travel clothing, and then—what would she wear at the palace? She'd be seen by the prince himself, if not the very king! She felt paralyzed then, as if already pinned in place by hundreds of curious eyes. She'd be wearing her only nice dress, the eggshell blue, which was acceptable in a small town in which people were used to her lack of fashion sense. At the court, she'd be judged and found so wanting that they might throw her in the dungeon for insulting fashion so blatantly.

But, again, she had no choice. She took the dress out of her wardrobe and stuffed it in her bandbox. Over it went one travel dress, various smallclothes, and her hairbrush. Minimus, her compass, and *The Book of Offhand Truths*, along with her remaining silver, she placed into her battered leather bag, which would remain with her at all times.

One task remained for her preparations before leaving. She opened Minimus' container and upended him onto the bed, where he went from limp and listless to puppy-like eagerness in an instant.

"I'm bringing you back to your Magnus, but if I get any freshness from you, any attempts to make yourself known to the other passengers we'll be traveling with, or any trouble at all—then our deal's off, and you're on your own," Vesper said.

"I'll behave, I'll behave," Minimus said. He rolled and stretched luxuriously. His foreskin began moving up and down and he moaned. "Ah, the light and air is so nice! It's so good being touched. It's been so many days cooped up in that little box. Not even a friendly pat or a rub or a wash. I do wish I could sit beside you in the coach…or maybe deep between your sexy legs, hiding inside your luscious mossy grotto…nobody would even notice."

Vesper was ready for that. She took out a thin reed she'd prepared just for this purpose, and she whipped him across the side with it. He squealed and wilted, and he stopped masturbating.

"Why'd you do that?"

"No fresh talk," she admonished him. "Or there'll be more of that, and worse."

After he remained suitably chastened for a moment, Vesper said, "I've been meaning to ask you something. Do you know how you came to be?"

Minimus giggled. "Well, yeah. Don't you? My mother and father got together one evening and took off all their clothes. Then they—"

"That's not what I mean," Vesper cut in. "I'm not talking about when the prince was born. I'm talking about just you—how did you get like this, talking, and separated from the prince?"

The penis cocked his head in thought, and when he finally responded, he actually sounded serious. "I dunno. I feel like I always was separate from him. It was like I was dreaming for a long time, and then one day I woke up and found I was free."

"You sound like you really like it," Vesper said. "So why do you want to go back to the prince?"

"I'm not going with you to be brought back to the prince," Minimus said, and Vesper ducked as he spat the last word, a drop of liquid flying out from his "mouth."

"I'm being brought back to my rightful place as crown prince. To rule after my father."

Vesper couldn't suppress her chuckle, imagining a penis sitting erect on the throne. "You'll have to come up with a pretty convincing disguise."

"Make fun of me if you want. You'll see. I'll be the king someday and all the women—and men, too—will be begging for a night with me...all the diplomats and those stuck-up Herlanders will just lie down and spread their legs when I enter the room—"

He yelped as Vesper tapped him with the reed, ending the conversation. It was a new experience for her to actually be bossy with someone, and she found she rather liked it.

By the time Vesper went down to supper, she felt ready. The coach left at dawn on the morrow, which suited her fine; whenever she'd escaped the house, she'd done so at that hour, when no one else was awake. She would leave a note with her mother explaining that she was getting the money for the debt and not to let anyone know she was gone, as Ruben wouldn't demand payment until the date of the wedding.

But when Vesper sat down to table, Sharrua and Bobbin at each end, Medalla and Aren on one side, she knew something was wrong. Medalla was talking, which was normal, and Aren stared sulkily at her food as she pushed it around her plate –also consistent with her behavior of late. But Bobbin ate steadily, without looking up from his plate, when usually he had a warm smile for his daughter—and Sharrua stared at Vesper, lips pressed together and eyes narrowed, a sure sign of impending explosion.

What's going on? Vesper thought, confused; then Sharrua extended one bony palm, on which gleamed two silver coins.

Vesper's jaw dropped. "How...?"

"I thought you would try to run away," Sharrua said. "And sure enough, I learned of your little purchase today of one ticket to Mallandina by coach. I expected it, Vesper, but I'm still disappointed in you. I had hoped you wouldn't give in to your selfishness. But you'd rather imprison your father than make a sacrifice for your family!"

Vesper cowered in her chair, feeling so pummeled by her mother's rage that she wondered if maybe she had done something wrong and didn't know it. Unable to ignore the drama, Medalla had actually stopped talking, and Aren was sitting up and leaning forward with the fascination of one who liked to watch cornered prey. "No...I don't want him to go to prison," Vesper said, her voice whisper-thin. "But—"

"I don't need your excuses and lies," snapped Sharrua. "Your actions are enough evidence. You *will* marry Porter Gordo. And you're not allowed out of the house until the day of your wedding."

Vesper dropped her eyes, giving up on the hope of explanation. If she even touched on the truth, she would have to tell her mother about Minimus—and she couldn't even contemplate the sort of explosions and ear-ripping screams that would ensue. Anyway,

"Well?" Sharrua demanded. "Are you just going to keep staring at your plate, or are you going to eat your dinner?"

"I'm not hungry," Vesper muttered.

"Then go to your room and think about your mistakes, and consider what you'll do to atone for them."

Once upstairs, Vesper's first urge was to crawl under her bedcovers and cry. Out of the range of her mother's rage, though, she no longer felt the need to hide. Thus her next urge was to bang her head against the wall—she could have handled the situation a dozen different and better ways. Then she felt upset with herself for doing exactly what her mother had told her to do, so she ended up in bed, trying not to think, and finally fell into a deep and dreamless sleep.

In the morning, she tried to be practical. Maybe it wouldn't be so bad marrying Porter. She knew several herbs that could be put to good use...she could make a tea that would improve his breath, and perhaps he'd let her treat his wart. She could make calming tisanes for the children. Then, she could slip Porter something to minimize his libido. Maybe she could find that witch who did the glamours and hire her to make him look like the prince.

She shuddered. He'd still be the same repulsive person underneath the illusion. She couldn't imagine any situation in which marrying him would be bearable.

Her eyes fell on her leather bag in which she'd packed *The Book of Offhand Truths.* Would it confirm her worst fears? Or would it show her a more palatable future?

Unable to resist, she reached for it and flipped it open. She saw a traveling coach, herself looking out the window. The next page showed the inside of a coach, her leather bag propped up against the side, and Minimus' head just peeping out from the top. The third page showed a hazy view of the spires of a palace. As before, only blank pages followed those three images.

Her heart beat faster. She was still going to go—but how? Even if she managed to find another two silvers for her passage, the coach had left already.

She found no more answers in the following two days. Sharrua kept her word; she locked Vesper inside her bedroom except during mealtimes. The book continued to show images of Vesper traveling, so hope remained, although understanding eluded her.

Aren visited once, demanding to know—--if Vesper was going to run away—--why hadn't she invited her sister to come along? "You were going to leave me here in this horrible little town where everybody hates me now, weren't you? While you went off to Mallandina. Do you have any idea how much I've wanted to go to Mallandina?" She clasped her hands and gazed heavenward. "Imagine the dresses, the parties…the *men*! And everyone so rich, it would make Ruben look a pauper."

"But I wasn't running away," Vesper said. "It wouldn't have been a fun trip at all, because I was just going there to get enough money to pay off the debt, and then I'd come right back."

"How would you get the money?"

Vesper felt low enough that she didn't care to keep it a secret any longer. So she told Aren about Minimus and the prince and the potential reward. Aren looked speculative, but before she could voice her reaction, Sharrua burst inside.

"Aren—out! No one is to have contact with this little traitor unless under my supervision. I won't have you carrying her secret messages in and out to plan another escape."

Alone with her thoughts again, Vesper mulled over the book's insistence that she would travel. *But how? What do I need to do to make this happen?*

The book gave her no answer.

It came not half a day later, though. Several hours before dawn, Vesper awoke to someone shaking her by the shoulder. "Come on, Vesper. Get up!"

"What? Aren? What are you doing here?" she asked, blinking in the dark. Aren held no candle, but she'd pulled the curtains open so they could see dimly by moonlight.

"We're escaping! Did you unpack your things from before? No? Just this bandbox? All right. Get dressed and let's go! And don't forget Minimus!"

Vesper staggered into her dress, cloak, and boots, threw her bag across her body, and watched in surprise as Aren threw open the shutters. She tied a long rope of torn sheets to the bedpost, throwing the length of it outside.

"Go down first, and then you'll have to catch the box, or it'll make too much noise," Aren said.

Vesper's state of mental stupor prevented her from questioning the strength of the rope. It seemed as good an idea as any, and before she knew it, she'd shimmied down the rope with just a few scrapes on her palms and a bang to one knee.

By then she felt plenty awake, and she caught the bandbox Aren tossed down and then helped steady her sister when Aren dropped to the ground.

"Now what?" Vesper whispered.

Aren cocked her head, a motion to follow. Grabbing the bandbox, Vesper complied, hoping they didn't have to go far.

They didn't. They stopped in front of Nim's house where a two-horse coach waited, door open, and coachman already atop and nodding to them in greeting.

"What—who—" Vesper said.

Nim stuck his head out the door. "Fear no longer, Vesper. I'm here to rescue you!"

CHAPTER 5

The coach Nim had hired offered minimal comfort. The inside consisted of two bench-like and barely padded seats facing each other, the backs so hard and vertical that passengers had to sit ramrod straight and were in danger of giving themselves concussions whenever the coach hit a rut in the road. Only one person could lie down at a time, in a curled-up position, while the two others had to sit up and make the best of it by leaning against walls whose padding bore stained circular imprints that spoke of the passage of many prior heads.

For the whoops of excitement and exclamations of triumph that emerged from the coach's cabin during the first half hour of its journey, though, they could have been riding in the king's own carriage. Nim and Aren kept interrupting each other in their gleeful explanations of how they'd arranged Vesper's escape.

"I didn't know that *you* were the person who got the commission from the king," Vesper said. "Now that I do, the rest is easy to understand."

"I knew about it," said Aren, smirking. "There's quite a lot of use to gossip if you know what to listen for. As soon as you told me what was going on—you should have told me before, you know!—I went straight to Nim's house and told him that you were locked up and if he didn't help us get to Mallandina to return the prince's lost jewels, you'd be forced to marry that horrid Porter. The timing was perfect, really, that he had that coach all ready to go for today."

"The prince's jewels?" Vesper repeated.

"That's right. The ones you found in the woods," Aren said, and she winked.

So my sister does have some discretion, Vesper noted in surprise.

Nim practically bounced in his seat with pride at the part he'd played. "It was my pa who was commissioned, actually. He's the best shoemaker in the region, and everybody knows it. But he didn't feel up to the trip and he wanted me to have the chance. Since we've the same last name, no one will know the difference, and I'll also prove myself by the quality of the shoes I make. They're to be for the king's wives."

"Everybody knows King Bugger has this huge foot fetish," said Aren, pointing to her own shapely foot and nodding.

"I'm so glad it was me, and that I'm helping save you from this awful marriage," Nim continued. He leaned closer to her, eyes a warm, liquid blue in the growing dawn light.

Vesper pretended she had an itch on her neck to give her the excuse to turn away. Now Nim saw the path to their own marriage as unimpeded, and she was back to her old problem of having to reject him. Not that she wasn't grateful—she was one step closer to her freedom from Porter, and she also felt a surge of excitement knowing that she would soon see the palace—a, place that had figured in so many of her fantasies.

They traveled all day, stopping only at a watering station to relieve themselves, stretch their legs, and give the horses something to eat and drink. Vesper could hardly keep still the first few hours, looking out the window until the town grew to a pinpoint in her vision and then disappeared entirely. She'd never gone this far before or had so much potential for adventure and change in her future. Out here, she couldn't help but feel that of course she wouldn't be stuck marrying Porter or being hounded into some other marriage she didn't want—now her dreams of having a life beyond her small town, one in which she actually fit in and felt comfortable expressing herself, felt within her reach.

The coachman, a bland-faced fellow named Dispo, had the sort of unremarkable face that one would immediately forget until the moment he next appeared. discourseAfter their initial grunting introductions, he spoke not a word until just before darkness descended. "Inn coming up in an hour," he called down to them.

Vesper was still wide awake and excited about seeing the countryside by moonlight. "Can't we just change horses and switch Nim with you for driving? We could save half a day by riding through the night," she called outside.

"Nope. Bandits," Dispo said as the coach slowed.

"We really need to stop," Aren said, grimacing. "I could use a hot meal, if not a bath."

They found themselves at the Hoarse Neigh. After a quick inspection of the available quarters, Aren pronounced it satisfactory. The main taproom also felt cozy enough, although Vesper did look askance at the number of rough-looking men scattered about the room.

"Perhaps we could order food sent up to our rooms," Vesper suggested. She and Aren would be sharing quarters, and they got Nim a space in a room with three lone male travelers.

"Costs extra," said the innkeeper. He named a price that made Vesper stare at him, certain he was about to start laughing at his own joke, but he didn't laugh.

"And how much to eat down here?"

It would save a little money, but not much. Still, they ended up taking a table in a corner and ordering three servings of the food. The barmaid brought bowls of starchy stew with chunks of pork and some yellow root vegetable, a hunk of brown bread, and ale—hearty fare, if plain.

Nim frowned at the ale. "Don't you have anything non-alcoholic?" he asked the barmaid.

She laughed in his face. "This is a tavern, not a nursery," she said.

"Well, how about milk? You have a cow here, I presume," Nim said, lips pinched.

The barmaid made a face, but she turned. "I'll see what I can do. Might cost you extra though."

"Nim," Aren said in a low voice. "You shouldn't drink milk here. People will think you're not manly and that you can't protect us."

"That's ridiculous," Nim said, his face turning mulish. "People shouldn't judge others by what they're drinking. Or if they do, perhaps they would think me strong for refusing alcohol, and drinking something nutritious instead."

Aren rolled her eyes and downed her ale in one draught.

Vesper ate and people-watched. She thought that this tavern must be a regular haunt for the locals; far more patrons ate and drank here than could occupy the six rooms above.

Most of the men and the few women here sat in groups, but here and there a man drank alone. Near the hearth sat one who caught Vesper's interest. It wasn't the breadth of his shoulders, encased in a black tunic of obvious high quality, or his height, or the silky bronze waves of his hair, nor was it the perfect symmetry of his face, or the intensity of deep-set eyes. He had a rare sort of beauty, but she found it far more interesting that he was reading a book.

She almost never met others who loved reading, and certainly they would never do it in public. It bore more stigma than a grown man drinking milk in public—which Nim was now doing with a look of feigned indifference. The nobles had made reading unpopular, as it showed that one couldn't afford to buy spells or magical devices, since one had to get knowledge to do things the ordinary way; even if this view held little logic, the king himself was known to insult readers as "bookfaces" or "unable to think for themselves, so they need to spout what others have said," and these opinions became popular, as did most views expressed by the king or his son.

No one was pointing and laughing at the fellow by the fire, though. He made reading look like a manly pursuit. He was even clever enough to do several things at once...sipping his ale while he flipped a page, or reaching out to swat the bottom of the barmaid...Vesper frowned upon the gesture. Well, perhaps they knew each other already—old friends or flames...or perhaps he'd just seen a spider there...

She admonished herself: she had no interest in a stranger's behavior with maids. She did want to know the title of his book, though. Something philosophical...perhaps a scientific tract...she suddenly imagined herself curled up on a window seat next to him, discussing a book they'd taken turns reading. He would be impressed that she actually read more than books of recipes and fashion, the usual fare for women considered literate in Malland. *I never would have imagined a woman could be so brilliant as well as so lovely*, he would say. She tore her eyes away from the man as she blushed, toying with her food, allowing her dark hair to fall forward like a curtain.

"Vesper," Nim said, and the tightness in his voice made her turn immediately. "Your sister is a disgrace."

Aren had left her dinner half untouched and now sat at another table, talking and laughing with three of the locals. Of these beefy young men—all permutations of Ruben—the hand of one was creeping perilously close to Aren's leg. Vesper watched, fascinated, as the hand made contact, and squeezed.

And Aren? She glanced at the leg-squeezer sidelong and smiled. She continued chatting with the others. The hand underneath the table began to move up her thigh.

Vesper hesitated, concern for her sister warring with irritation with Nim for judging Aren. "I wouldn't really say she's doing anything particularly disgraceful," she said. "But maybe not very safe, either. I don't think they'd listen to me if I went over there—could you go over there and get her, Nim?"

Nim turned white. "I can't," he said in a strangled whisper. "If they want to fight me…I don't know how to."

"They won't want to fight you. Just say we need an early night's sleep. Come on, I'll go, too."

They got up and approached. Nim was trembling, and he stood there, lips pressed together, eyes staring, saying nothing.

Vesper wished she could disappear. Then no one would help Aren, who'd already done so much for her and who wouldn't be here if it weren't for Vesper. She cleared her throat. "Aren, come on."

Aren flicked an irritated glance toward her sister. "I'm busy, Vesper. You two go on upstairs. I'll be there soon."

One of the men sitting across from Aren gave Vesper the once-over, flicked away, then back. His expression said it all—*You're nothing much, but you're a female, and that's good enough.* "If you want to stay, Vesper, you're welcome to join us. Drinks on me. Your brother there can go upstairs and order some more milk. Maybe warmed in a bottle." The others laughed uproariously, slamming the table with open palms; Aren giggled.

"That's not funny," Nim burst out, hands balling into fists. "You want to fight? Let's go outside."

"No, no, that's not necessary," Vesper said, standing in front of

Nim. She struggled to think of something to defuse the situation. "Aren, if you come with us now, I might let you borrow something tonight—you know, the *thing* you like so much. Here in my bag." She patted the bag slung over her shoulder, and Aren stared at it in growing comprehension. Her eyes lit up.

"Really? Oh, Vesper!" She jumped up and threw her arms around her sister. She smelled of ale, the slight weave of her body that of an infrequent drinker being drunk.

"Hey, come on," complained the man who'd been sitting next to Aren. "What's she gonna give you that's better than our company?"

"Oh, it's nothing," Vesper mumbled, pulling Aren and pushing Nim toward the stairs. "Never mind us. Good night."

Suddenly the complaining man rose and grabbed Aren by the other hand. "You can't be a tease like that and not give me a little something in return," he said. "How about just a goodnight kiss, then?"

"Oh...I suppose that would be all right," Aren said, turning toward him.

"He just called you a tease, Aren!" Vesper whispered, trying to warn her sister with her eyes—which didn't work too well since Aren wasn't looking at her. When the man started pulling Aren closer, Vesper interposed herself between him and her sister and, in an act of sheer desperation, used a tip she'd garnered from a book about human anatomy. She rammed her knee into his crotch.

He howled, doubling over and grabbing himself between the legs.

His two companions stood, murder on their faces. One of them leaped forward and twisted his arm around Vesper's head, pulling her against a fleshy body that smelled of sweat and ale. "You can't do that sort of thing here, bitch," he said. "We protect our own here. Clem, let's take this slut with us and give her something in return."

"Yeah, and I wanna see what she was going to give that other girly," said Clem. "Lemme have that bag." He reached for Vesper's bag, and she struggled as she watched him undoing the flap—and then her vision began to go black.

CHAPTER 6

Aren shrieked. Nim shook, fists now up and close to his face, imitating a fighting stance. He swung a fist and missed, the force of his movement sending him stumbling.

Vesper's captor suddenly let her go, and she sprawled on the floor, from where she saw events unfold in a blurry, semi-conscious haze. Had her captor's hand actually fallen off, or did she only imagine the sensation? She saw the hand then, flying around the room, and its former owner chased it. Although the hand moved much faster than the man, it found itself hemmed in by closed windows, and the man made a flying leap and trapped it against the wall.

Vesper sat up. The other two men screamed in that high pitch men reserved only for true horror. One man was missing his nose, and the other's lips were strangely sunken, as if he had no teeth.

The room crackled with magic—like lightning in the air, but more subtle, and with a note of wrongness to it, or insanity. Vesper had never felt the like.

Then she saw its source.

The man in black, the one who'd been reading by the hearth, stood facing them. Although he'd approached only a few steps closer from his spot halfway across the room, Vesper had absolutely no doubt that he'd done this thing to these men. He'd left the equivalent of footprints—an aftereffect of energy, a charge that connected him to his crime.

Their eyes met, and the lightning shock connected into Vesper's body, bringing every part of her skin into hyper-awareness. She felt the blueness of his eyes like a cool sizzle.

Aren's continued shrieks now blended into the uproar in the tavern. "Settle down, please! No fighting here! No—stay and have a drink—" the innkeeper yelled, flapping his hands as he tried to get people to sit down again as they surged toward the door. Vesper saw a nose and a few teeth fly out along with the crowd.

Then the man in black stood before Vesper, stretching a hand out to her and pulling her to her feet with a grip both warm and firm. "Are you all right?" he asked.

Vesper nodded. Her throat hurt, and she didn't quite trust herself yet to speak, but she could tell that it was only her nerves that had been rattled.

"Look here, wizard," said the innkeeper. "You can't just go around doing magic in my establishment. I expect you to pay for the damage you've done, and to put those body parts right back on those fellows."

The man who'd caught his flying hand was trying to hold it onto his stump of a wrist, as if by sheer pressure it would meld back into place. The man without a nose was trembling, eyes wild, feeling his face and looking close to a nervous breakdown. The man without any teeth sobbed in sunken-mouthed terror.

"I've done no damage," said the man in black. "And what I did to those men prevented them from molesting, perhaps even killing these young ladies. I'm afraid I can't reattach their parts, as the magic doesn't work that way."

The innkeeper's face darkened. Then the man in black opened the purse slung along his side and took out several pieces of gold. "That ought to cover your injury," he said. "If you like, you can share it with those men."

The innkeeper's demeanor rapidly shifted to subservience. "Oh, thank you, great lord," he said. "You are very generous." He turned to the distraught men. "You three! Get out of here! You've made enough trouble here tonight. I don't want to see your faces here for a week. If I hear any complaints, I'm going to the constable to report you for brawling."

When the men hesitated, the innkeeper called for reinforcements; a burly fellow built like a blacksmith came out the back and tossed the three out on the street, one at a time.

Vesper was still shaking, but she paid no attention to it. She was trying to absorb what had just happened. This man—a wizard—had used his magic to cause body parts to detach and animate. He'd done it on purpose, but from what he'd told the innkeeper, it seemed this was the *only* thing he could do now with his magic. The spell had horrified her...but he'd done it for her. As feeling began to return to her traumatized body, her heart felt almost uncomfortably full. *He might have saved my life.*

She was afraid she'd betray something—in the flush of her heated face, naked admiration in her eyes. She had to collect her thoughts, alone.

"Let's go to our room," she said to Aren, whose shrieks had been replaced by snuffling and a trickle of tears.

She turned to the man in black, gazing at a point just over his shoulder. "Thank you," she muttered, feeling once again the lightning shock seeingat just a glimpse of those blue, blue eyes in her periphery—even though the magic had long since dissipated.

"You are welcome," he said.

His voice was a masculine thrum along her spine. She grabbed Aren and pulled her toward the stairs.

Nim walked them to their room. "Good night, Nim," Vesper said.

"I almost hit him," Nim blurted, as she was closing the door. "Did you see, Vesper? Did you? If I'd connected, I would've taken him down."

She held the door open, focusing on him for the first time since before the whole incident downstairs had taken place. Guilt creased his face, and his shoulders hunched up nearly to his ears with tension. "Yes, I saw, Nim. You did very well." She smiled at him with genuine warmth and watched the creases relax as he soaked in her approval. "I've got to lie down, though...goodnight, Nim." She closed the door.

Inside the room, Aren threw up in the chamber pot. She shuffled to the bed and collapsed onto it. "I feel better," she said. Vesper, searching for her nightdress, grabbed a water skin instead and handed it to her sister in silence.

Aren took a swig of water and made a face. Then the corners of her mouth turned up, just a little. "You mean it? You'll lend me Minimus again?"

Vesper paused, then shook her head. "I'm sorry I misled you about that. I didn't want Nim to get beaten up for your irresponsible behavior. Also, not only do I never want to sleep in the same bed as you while you're having sex with Minimus, but have you even thought about what would happen if he got you pregnant? What if he's not the prince's penis after all? You'd never even know who the father was. Go to sleep."

"You could go over and sleep with Nim," Aren said, slanting a glance at her sister through long lashes. "He could make up for his lack of manliness from earlier, perhaps."

"That's an even more disgusting suggestion than having Minimus leaping around our bed the entire night," she said. "*You* could sleep with him—and if you got pregnant, you could marry him too."

"Oh, he's never been interested in me," Aren said. "He's yours completely."

"I don't want to hear any more of that, Aren. I'm not interested in Nim."

Aren heaved a sigh, but she lay down without undressing, pulling the covers over herself. "I don't think I could sleep a wink tonight. Too much excitement. Did you see how that fellow beat those three guys? Wow. He was dreamy."

Something closed inside Vesper as she realized Aren had noticed him too. Of course she would—when it came to good-looking men, her sister never missed anything. "I hope you don't actually *like* this sort of excitement, Aren."

Aren, already asleep and gently snoring, made no response.

It turned out that Vesper was the one who couldn't sleep a wink. She lay there, thinking about the man in black. She tried to keep her thoughts logical, to wonder why he was here and where he was going, and how the magic he'd used was connected to the greater phenomenon of detaching body parts...but she kept remembering instead how her body tingled when he gazed at her with those blue eyes, and how she'd wanted to run her hand through those bronze waves while he read, and how his voice had thrilled her. She thought of the way its masculine tones tingled along her spine, almost making a squeaking noise...

She stopped. The squeak was coming not from her spine, but from the door. Lifting her head, she saw the handle turning, the door making a faint knocking sound as it hit the limit of the latch.

She shot up in bed. It just figured—someone was coming to kill them in their beds while she fantasized about some man. *Weapon*, she thought, scrabbling through the muck of guilt in her head for any useful idea. What could she use?

Grabbing the glass specimen container out of her leather bag by the bed, she tore the cloth off it and ran on tiptoe to stand behind the door. Holding the container ready over her head, she waited.

She held her breath as the latch slid to the side and fell, and then the door opened.

A shadow moved inside. Vesper could make out the tall, broad shape of a man, one who moved catlike, on silent feet. He headed unerringly toward the bed—and reached for the leather bag, cast on the floor.

With all her strength, Vesper slammed the specimen container onto the intruder's head. Glass shattered.

"I'm free!!!!" Minimus cried as he flopped to the floor. "Ow! There's glass all over here!" He shot into the air, did an acrobatic flip, and flopped onto the bedside table.

The intruder wavered on his feet, then toppled to the ground.

Aren sat up, sucking a breath in to scream. Vesper rushed over and clapped her hand over her sister's face. "Quiet," she hissed. "It's all right. Someone's tried to break in, but he's down. Get a candle lit."

Aren's eyes had widened with fear, but she obeyed, grabbing the candle by the bed and bringing it into the hallway to light, then returning and lighting one more. She turned to look at the intruder on the floor.

"It's that dreamy guy who saved you," Aren gasped, peering down at him. Then, with accusation, "He's all bloody. You've killed him!"

Vesper went to the door, closing and latching it again. She cast a wary eye at Minimus, who was doing a little dance on the bedside table and singing, "I'm free—as free as a penis can beee—"

"Shut up, you," Vesper snapped at him. "Unless you want me to get the switch again."

"No! Not the switch." Minimus tucked his mushroom head back in his foreskin and flopped back on the table, curling up like a turd.

Aren looked at Minimus, then at the man on the floor, and then back at the penis. "Hmm," she mused. "I think I might actually prefer it attached to a man."

Minimus poked his head out again. "How dare you! After all we shared." He began to sob loudly.

Vesper knelt down next to the man. He was still breathing. Still gorgeous, too—but probably dangerous. "I need something to tie him up," she said.

Aren got up, and they both began digging through the boxes they'd brought in from the coach.

"How about this?" Aren asked, holding up a cord she used to cinch a robe.

"I think that'll work," Vesper said. With some difficulty—he was heavy!—she got the man's arms behind his back and tied them with the tightest knots she could manage. She couldn't drag him away from the glass-strewn area of the floor, but she tried to sweep up the glass with the discarded cloth. The man had fallen on a few pieces, but it looked like the cuts were only superficial.

"Now what?" Aren asked.

"We wait for him to wake up," Vesper said. "Ask him some questions, and then we call the innkeeper to get the constable."

Aren knelt next to him and ran her hand down his chest. "Mmm," she said. "I love these muscles."

"Traitor!" Minimus muttered.

"Aren, stop that!" Vesper snapped. Aren pouted and flounced onto the bed again. "He's a criminal," Vesper continued. "He just broke into our room. He was probably trying to steal all our money, and then he would have murdered us in our sleep."

"He probably wanted to steal me," Minimus piped up.

"I doubt that," Vesper said. "Nobody knows you're here. And what would a man like that want with someone else's detached penis?"

Minimus moved his foreskin as if he was shrugging. "You'd be surprised how many men don't care about the genders of their partners. My person did, but I sure didn't. In fact, if you'd take off this guy's pants and let me at it, I'd stop trying to seduce you gals, at least for tonight."

Vesper frowned. "I told you what would happen if you keep talking lewd." Then something struck her. "Minimus—when you 'woke up' from being attached to…to the person you were attached to, do you recall anyone having just cast a spell on him?"

"I don't recall any spell. But I do remember waking up. It was goooood," he purred. "I was doing the wild thing with this hot witch-woman. I would've liked to continue, but *he* started screaming and trying to grab me. So I had to pull out and run. When I finally got ahold of myself, I was out in a field in the middle of nowhere."

"You ran all the way from the royal palace to that field where I found you?" Vesper asked, eyebrows raised in disbelief.

"You don't believe me?" Minimus asked. He stood, growing long and erect, pumped in place a few times, and then shot into the air. He began to whizz around the room, so fast he was almost a blur.

"Wow, that's fast," Aren said, her eyes round.

"Okay, okay. I believe you," Vesper said. "Could you stop that? You're making me dizzy."

The penis stopped in midair, flopping to the ground, then hopping onto the bed to sit next to Aren. He rubbed his head on her hand, and when she petted him a little, he hopped onto her lap and began to purr.

Vesper paced. "So, you don't remember a spell. But that doesn't mean there wasn't one. You say that *he* was having sex with a witch. Maybe she—maybe all the other witches and wizards—have some kind of disease that's affected their magic, so whenever they try to cast a spell, this body-part-detaching thing happens."

"That's the silliest thing I've ever heard—" Aren began.

They were distracted by a movement from their captive. His eyes opened, assessed his situation—pausing only an instant longer on Minimus—and came to rest on Vesper standing next to him.

Only then, with a stranger's eyes on her, did some of Vesper's self-consciousness return, and she folded her arms to hide her sudden urge to fidget. No one here was going to take control of the situation, so she would have to marshal her courage and do so herself. She took a deep breath.

"Explain," she said, proud that her voice only trembled a little. "First tell us who you are, and why did you break into our room?"

He sat up, folding his legs in front of him, as graceful as if he didn't have his hands tied behind his back. "My name is Garth," he said, and he paused, almost as if he expected them to know who he was.

"I'm Aren," Aren drawled, her voice husky and openly inviting.

"And you're here because...?" Vesper prodded, with a glance at Aren that implored her silence.

"I came here to take back something that was taken from me."

"I told you!" Minimus crowed.

"This is yours?" Aren asked, sitting up straight.

"It's yours?" Vesper repeated, pointing at the penis, brows climbing.

"Of course not. What would I do with a detached penis that's crawling with split-magic?" he asked. "No, you have a book that was stolen from me."

"A book?" Vesper asked. "I don't have a—oh, wait. You mean—*The Book of Offhand Truths* is yours?"

"Yes," he said.

"My friend got it for me from a peddler," Vesper said. "So I didn't steal it."

"The peddler must have gotten it from the thief, then," Garth said. "It's no fault of yours, but you are in possession of stolen property."

"Couldn't you have just knocked on the door and asked for it instead of breaking in?" Vesper said.

Garth's lips turned up at the corners. "I suppose I could have. I'm not used to such direct methods being successful…and I wanted to minimize having to give extended explanations."

Vesper got the book out of her bag. "I guess we should untie you," she said.

Garth showed his hands—they were free, the cord hanging loosely over his palm. "Here you go. This looks like it belongs to a female outfit of some sort." At the look on Vesper's face, he laughed outright. "This cord is made of very slippery fibers. You'd want something with more friction to tie someone up effectively. Your knots were fine, Vesper."

The sound of her name on his voice sent the shivers running along her spine again, and she admonished her spine to stay still and behave.

"I believe you that this book is yours," she said, "so I won't ask you to prove it to me. But…would it be all right with you if I looked at it once more, to see if it has a final message for me?"

He inclined his head. "Of course, but I believe it will only give its message in private," he said.

He had to be telling the truth, Vesper thought. How could anyone lie about a truth-telling book, anyhow? Unless the book was lying…but Garth seemed like a trustworthy sort. And she told herself it wasn't just because he oozed sex appeal *and* he'd possibly saved her life, her virtue, or both. "Should I go out in the hallway, then, or…"

"You can use my room," Garth said. "It's two doors down, across the hall. It's unlocked."

"Thank you," she said. She glanced at Aren, then at Minimus, who oddly enough seemed to be behaving; Minimus was sitting on Aren's lap and simply observing the proceedings—if that little hole on the top of his head had any optic properties, that was. It seemed to serve an awful lot of purposes anyway.

She lit one candle and left them. After finding Garth's room easily, she went in.

At a glance, he'd left few signs of his presence in the room; it was neat, the bed apparently not slept in, and little in the way of belongings, save a cloak draped over the bed and freshly cleaned boots beside it.

Well, she hadn't come here to snoop about Garth. Setting the candle down on the small table, she opened the book to the first page.

She could see the vague outline of shapes on a dark background, a suggestion of texture, dimension. She brought it closer to the candle to see more clearly. The illustration showed the inside of a darkened coach—a coach traveling in the late evening, perhaps. She could see faces now—her own, an angry-looking Nim, Aren across from him—and beside Aren, was Garth.

"That can't be right. What would he be doing in our coach?" she muttered, turning to another page.

The next one was much, much clearer. It was herself and Garth locked in a passionate embrace—his lips on hers, her arms about him, clinging.

She slammed the book shut. Her heart was suddenly hammering, and she passed a hand over the back of her neck, which had broken out in a sheen of sweat. "It's lying," she said. "The book must be lying!"

It could very well be. She had no proof that it told the truth other than its self-declared title. The reason why she preferred science was because of its predictability—one knew what one dealt with, instead of fiddling around with the unreliability of anything that had been touched by magic. This book—it was making her angry; she should be glad to give it away so she wouldn't be tempted to look in it any longer.

Like the temptation she was feeling this instant. She picked up the book again. Would it have anything else to say, a final message? She opened it slowly.

This time the picture showed only Garth's face, his eyes looking straight at her, an odd expression in them—questioning, intelligent, and almost caressing.

She forced herself to look at him and not slam the book closed again. She had to admit she found him attractive. *Even more than attractive: he's perfect*, came the unwanted thought as her eyes traced the masculine line of his cheek and jaw. She noticed an odd unfurling inside her belly, and she felt lightheaded all of a sudden—as if a tightly closed bud had suddenly softened, recognizing the existence of sunlight. All rationalizations about why she never wanted to be with a man fell away.

If such a man owned her, obliterated her identity with his own purposes…would that be so bad? Shame flooded her at such a traitorous thought. She found she was afraid—not of him, but of herself, of the reactions she was having to him, the fact that she would have gladly accepted a glamour if it would cause him to find her more appealing. Insidious voices in her suggested that all the things she'd ever said about the unimportance of appearance, and how if she wasn't loved for herself she would rather not be loved at all, were just empty words from someone with no experience or maturity, the type of female who wouldn't be at all appealing to a man like Garth…

She gave in to the urge, and she slammed the book shut again. Enough! She was thinking herself into self-torture. She didn't dare hope that Garth would see something similar in the book. If he did, she didn't think she could bear it…but if he didn't, maybe she couldn't bear it either.

She returned to the room she shared with Aren, avoiding meeting Garth's eyes.

"Anything interesting?" he asked.

"Um…well…" she said. She could, at least, tell him she'd seen him coming with them. She saw no harm in that. Then she glanced at him and did a double take. He was looking at her exactly as he had been in that third illustration—down to the angle of his head, the expression in his eyes, the gaze that was like a caress…

She could say nothing for a long moment. Even if she could choke the words out, if she told him, everyone would think she was chasing him. If it was going to happen, it would happen no matter what she did or said. Better to let fate take its course…even if she vastly preferred one course to another.

"Nothing interesting. Just…sights," she finally mumbled, handing the book to him.

"Thank you," he said. He moved to the door. "I'm very sorry I disrupted your evening. There's still a few more hours before light—you should get some rest. Will you be moving on in the morning?"

"Yes, we're going to stay at the royal palace. Isn't it exciting? The king himself invited us," Aren said. She reclined on the bed, Minimus on the pillow beside her—*my pillow*, Vesper noted with slight horror—she hadn't ever cleaned him after he'd been with Aren.

"Well—he didn't exactly invite *us*," Vesper said. "But he did invite one of our party."

Garth nodded. "Mallandina is quite beautiful. I, too, will depart on the morn, to continue my own quest. It was good to meet you all."

He nodded again—glancing once more at Vesper—then closed the door behind him.

The lingering sense of Garth's presence affected Vesper like a drug. She felt lightheaded, off balance, perhaps even a little nauseated. She shook her head and tried to focus on something else. She took an extra specimen container from her box and approached Minimus.

"Noooo!" he cried, jumping up. "I'm not going back in there. It's so dark and cold and I just have nightmares all day long. If I'd known you'd stick me in there the whole time, I'd never have suggested you accompany me back."

Vesper lowered the container, feeling contrite. He was right, and she was rewarding his saving her from a dreadful imprisonment in marriage with another sort of imprisonment. "I'm sorry," she said. "You're right. But would you try to be discreet, then? I still think it would be dangerous for people to know we've got the prince's penis with us."

They agreed that Minimus would travel in Vesper's bag, and he could peep his head out when he wasn't asleep. Aren found a handkerchief from her box and wrapped it around Minimus like a swaddling cloth.

"So you'll be more comfortable," Aren cooed, and she placed him back on the table by the bed. Minimus looked as peaceful and harmless as a penis could possibly look in such a situation, and he made a few inarticulate sounds of contentment.

"This is nice," he said in a sleepy voice, growing more soft and limp by the second.

Vesper made her way back into the bed, flipping the soiled pillow over. She yawned. It would be dawn soon.

She drifted off to disturbing images of body parts that attacked her while she was kissing Garth, who turned into Clem, and then Nim... in her dream she fought desperately to hold onto the image of Garth, and finally she managed some semblance of him—but he looked different, a thinner, somewhat distorted version of his perfection, a shadow...

and then the shadow consumed them both…

A pounding on the door awakened Aren and Vesper. "Come on, you two! Open up! Can you hear me?"

Vesper sat up, feeling like she'd slept about ten minutes and needed ten more hours. She rubbed her eyes and staggered to the door, unlatching it to reveal a fully dressed and disgruntled-looking Nim.

"It's late morning, and the innkeeper wants us out unless we're going to pay for another night here," he grumbled. "I've already had breakfast and I've been waiting around for you two for ages. If I'd known girls took this long for their beauty sleep, I mightn't have brought you along!"

Aren groaned and covered her head with the pillow. Minimus, unnoticed by Nim, still lay on the table wrapped in his handkerchief, faintly snoring.

"All right, Nim. We'll be ready to go in fifteen minutes."

"I know what that means," Nim growled. "Pa told me. When a woman says five, she means thirty. So I guess I'll be waiting for another hour."

"No…it means an hour and a half," Vesper blurted, and she slammed the door in his surprised face. *What's wrong with me? I never thought anything would get me riled up enough to be rude to Nim…*

She dragged the covers and pillow off Aren. "Time to go already, sleepyhead."

Aren groaned, but once she got up, she moved quickly enough. Vesper helped shove her things back in her box, and with a minute to spare before fifteen they were downstairs in front of the coach.

"Aren't we going to eat anything?" Aren asked.

"We'll eat in the coach. We have plenty of food still from yesterday."

Aren made a face, but she didn't complain.

"Ready?" Nim said, exiting the inn and closing his purse.

Aren got into the coach. Just as Vesper was about to follow her, Garth came out of the inn and approached them.

"You!" Vesper blurted, feeling suddenly short of breath. "I mean… good morning." What did he want?

"I suppose it's my fault you're off to such a late start," he said. "All the luckier for me. I had some purchases to make in town, but now I'm ready to go."

"What?" Nim and Vesper said in unison.

Nim was the first to recover. "You can't," he said. "There's no room. And I'm on a very special commission to the king, very important. We aren't a passenger coach."

"No," said Garth. "You're in a coach hired by the king. I work for him, so by rights I can travel in this coach or commandeer it for my use. You see, I am the king's court wizard."

CHAPTER 7

A soft snore escaped Aren's nose as her head lolled against a wadded-up cloak pressed against the wall. Nim glared at Garth through half-closed eyes. Garth was looking out the window, and Vesper pretended to sleep, although every pore of her body could sense him sitting across from her. Now the first and third images of the book had come true. When would the second take place, and what would it mean?

Nim had resisted for some time after Garth made his revelation, but the man had been convincing.

"If you find out that I'm telling the truth, and you don't allow me to come, you'll be in a great deal of trouble," he'd said. "In fact, I am quite sure the king would be put out enough that you would lose your commission—and perhaps be forced to pay your own expenses to get home."

"If you're a court wizard, why don't you just...fly there, or something? Or magically force me to let you come?" Nim was a study in contradiction—bluster belied by hunched shoulders and quivering lower lip.

"My magic has been compromised by the split-disease," Garth said. "So I can no longer compel you by normal means. I could, however, cause one of your body parts to fall off and run away from you—I don't know you well enough to guess which. Would that be compelling enough?"

"If you were really honorable enough to work for the king, who is an honorable man I'm sure or he wouldn't be our leader, you wouldn't be slinging rude threats," said Nim, spittle flying in all directions.

Garth sighed. He opened his purse and fished around, finally pulling out a gold chain on which a token, stamped with the king's seal on one side, bore the inscription "Official Court Wizard Garth Biggens" on the other.

The token did not fail to impress Nim. His eyes seemed almost as if they might pop out of their sockets and touch the precious thing. Finally he looked back up at Garth and his chin jerked up and down. "I suppose you could come. But it's still just not nice the way you ordered us and assumed it was going to happen. You could have asked politely."

"I suppose you're right," Garth said, slanting an amused glance at Vesper, who blushed, remembering she'd said something similar to him the night before. He entered the coach, followed by Nim; Aren's look of surprise transformed into a sultry smile as he sat next to her.

The coach rolled into motion. "To honor the idea of being more open, I'll tell you why I've been traveling, and why I'm returning now," Garth said. His gaze met Vesper's. "You were correct in your hypothesis that it is a sort of disease that's affecting wizards all over the kingdom."

"A disease," Vesper repeated. "You called it the split-disease, didn't you?"

"That's what people have been calling it—not a very scientific designation, but it definitely does create splits. It takes over the use of magic so anytime we try to cast any sort of spell, the person we're directing the spell to will lose a body part—which will, as you've seen, be able to talk and move on its own."

"And you've got this disease!" Nim crowed, looking almost happy for the first time since Garth had joined them.

Garth nodded. "Unfortunately, yes. It's been spreading very quickly. No one knew for a while how it was passed. Now we've concluded that anything or anyone can carry the disease if split-magic has touched it, and whenever a wizard tries to cast a spell on something that's been infected, that's how they'll become infected as well. I caught it trying to mend a broken plate with magic. Since then, the only thing I'm capable of doing is causing people's body parts to fall off, and spreading the disease further."

"But you put it to excellent use already, saving our lives," Aren said, turning her dark and worshipful gaze to him.

"From across the room, where it was nice and safe," Nim muttered, scowling once again. "Doesn't seem so heroic to me."

"I did what I could," Garth said modestly. "I am happy I was there to help—it makes my trip not such a waste after all. I've been traveling for the past few weeks in search of a cure for my infection, and when I stopped at the inn I'd just come from a town nearly on the border of Egregia where I spent some days with a renowned specialist on magical disease. But he could do nothing. I didn't know what to do next, except to track down the book that Vesper returned to me yesterday—and so I've been led to you. The book has always been my way of finding the next steps in situations such as these. And now it has informed me that I should travel back with you."

"What? Vesper's book? You mean—" Nim turned to Vesper, eyes accusing. "You gave *him* my book?"

"I'm sorry, Nim. The book was stolen," Vesper said. "I can't keep stolen property."

"My present to you," he half-moaned, then turned to the window, his back a wall of damaged pride.

Vesper stared at the floor, overwhelmed by a surge of guilt. Garth had such a presence that sometimes she forgot that Nim was even there, despite the snippy comments he kept inserting into every conversation. Half of her wanted to make it up to Nim for ruining his trip and the other half—or maybe a bit more than half—wallowed in a feeling that if she didn't do everything just right to get Garth's attention, she would lose her chance with him.

Aren sensed no tension; she was smiling in undisguised appreciation of her new traveling companion. "I think these signs...these urges...must always be obeyed," she said, voice husky. "Maybe the cure has already been found where we're going."

Garth shrugged. "Perhaps, but I doubt it," he said. "Scientists have been working on it for months, ever since the disease was first discovered. My intuition says that it's something more—something that has, perhaps, to do with one of you. As a catalyst of a discovery." His eyes rested on Vesper for a moment, just short of significance.

"Really?" Aren said, scooting a little closer to him. "Wouldn't it be amazing if the cure turned out to be something really simple? Like fevers—they're supposed to burn out infection. Maybe you just need to get your body heat up." The way she looked at him, there was no doubt she'd be willing to help him with that particular experiment.

Vesper turned away and gazed out of her window, the image of the kiss from the book springing unbidden to her mind. She'd looked at it only for a second—it occurred to her now that perhaps she had been seeing Aren with Garth. His face had been unmistakable, but of the woman she'd only seen dark hair that resembled her own, and she'd automatically assumed it was herself, but it could very well have been Aren and Garth.

As they were two consenting adults, and Vesper had no connection to Garth beyond admiration, she had no right to feel the slow burn of jealousy that threatened to give her indigestion. She tried to suppress it by admiring the landscape, although the dry fields or even drier combinations of sand and rock that they'd been passing all day long gave her little to work with. She almost wished for Minimus to distract them all with more of his antics, but he had chosen today of all days to do a penis' equivalent of navel-gazing.

She dozed off, waking only in the late afternoon when the coach stopped at a watering station. They took out their food from the day before; their rations had even less appeal after sitting for hours in the heat. Vesper chewed on a stale roll and a piece of jerky.

Aren sipped water and wrinkled her nose at the food. "You could've turned this into a feast if your magic was working, couldn't you, Garth? I would give anything for a roast and a glass of white wine."

"I could have done so, yes," Garth said.

"What happens if you use magic on an inanimate object?" Vesper asked. "Or an animal?"

"Nothing at all," was the reply. "In those cases, it's as if I have no magic at all. I've been reading this—" He opened his own small pack and took out a book, handing it to Vesper. The title read *On Consciousness*. "Do you ever wonder where souls come from, Vesper?"

"I—well, not really," she said. Part of her exulted that he'd asked her, out of everyone in the coach, this question; he must think her intelligent. The rest of her, though, wanted to slap herself for disproving his thought. Here was her opportunity to have her fantasy of a deep philosophical conversation come true with Garth, and all she could say was *well, not really*. Idiot!

"Everybody knows that," Aren said. "The gods make them, and they pop them into new bodies as they're born."

"That's one way to put it," Garth said, "but in this book, it suggests that souls are simply aspects of ego splintered off from Mae and Jin, the two original gods. They began with no ego at all, you know. But as they gained awareness of themselves, each affirmation of something they *were* created a denial of something they *weren't*. This created a polarity, a split between themselves and something that became a new 'soul'—an un-being that gave that shadow voice. One god, declaring himself to be good and denying that he was evil, split into two parts—one good and one evil—because each god is both good and evil. Each part, as it gained awareness of itself and declared itself this or that but denied that it was the shadow of each new identification, split into more and more pieces—creating an exponential birth of new souls."

"So you're saying that souls aren't discrete units—or even units at all," Vesper said, nodding thoughtfully. "They're more like...reflections of consciousness in a fractured mirror..."

"Blithering nonsense," Aren said. "That would mean *my* soul is a piece of someone's rejected soul. I don't think so."

"It's sacrilege," Nim muttered at the window, shaking his head. He'd pronounced the word wrong, but Vesper decided not to mention it.

Garth shrugged. "It's just a theory."

"You think it's what the split-disease does," Vesper said. "That it somehow causes new 'souls' to be born—new separate consciousness to form in some physical part of a person's body, which then splits off." She found the idea fascinating, and immediately she began pondering how such a thing could possibly be tested.

"Exactly," Garth nodded, and all thought became paralyzed beneath the force of his bright blue gaze—approving, admiring. "It follows that if a person has nothing in themselves that they're denying, no shadows or conflicts within themselves, they would not be affected by a spell cast by an infected wizard or witch. But that seems to me near impossible."

"Well," said Aren, tossing her head, "I don't think it's that impossible. I haven't got any issues of self-conflict."

Maybe we should have Garth test that theory. Vesper immediately felt guilty for the thought.

A part of her did mean it, though. She'd love it if Aren's tongue would fly out so she would shut up...provided it would come back after another hour or so, she amended. Oh, why was she being so horrid? Of course she wanted nothing bad to happen to her sister, but it was frustrating because this conversation was the first time all day that Garth had expressed interest in something about her, and Aren was ruining it!

You're being ridiculous, she admonished herself. *Doesn't Aren deserve romance since I was the one to steal it from her last time?* Somehow, though, she couldn't feel happy for her sister, and her insides twisted into knots as she hated herself, Aren, and Garth in turns. Minimus and Nim didn't fare much better in her barrage of abusive thoughts.

The direction of her musings only darkened further. As the day wore on, to stave off probable disappointment Vesper forced herself, over and over, to imagine her sister and Garth kissing. She would get so used to the image that her heart—and her pride—would be in no danger of breaking.

Despite her efforts, the idea of stopping at another inn and lying there agonizing about or notexactly when the book's image would come true rankled her. So later, when the sun had gone down and Dispo announced an approaching inn, she felt herself tightening up in apprehension.

Surprisingly Garth repeated her suggestion from the day before. "Can we continue, Dispo? I'd rather not drag the journey on. We can exchange for fresh horses and supplies at the inn, and I'd be happy to drive while you sleep inside."

"Bad idea," came Dispo's voice again, just as he had warned yesterday. "Bandits in this area, you know."

"One thing my magic is still good for is defense," Garth said. "We'll be all right."

"But I want to sleep in a normal bed," Aren said, twisting sulky lips. She reached out and ran a finger down Garth's shoulder. "Don't you?"

"I do," he said, and Vesper couldn't tell if he insinuated an extra layer of meaning in his words and glance. "But the situation with this disease is worrisome. I've seen a couple of clues that tell me the king's policy toward carriers of the disease is becoming harsher than it should be. I think we should get to Mallandina with all speed."

Nim agreed to continue as well, so Dispo exchanged the horses while everyone got down to relieve themselves and stretch. Within a half hour they were ready to go again.

Aren pouted the whole time they were stopped, but when Garth climbed up to the coachman's seat, she brightened. "I'll sit up with you," she said, "to make sure you don't fall asleep up there."

Vesper found that an adequate arrangement; she would be relieved to have a break from looking at the two of them nearly cuddling right in front of her all day long. Nim continued to ignore her, and Dispo fell asleep almost instantly upon entering the coach and inserting his head into the oily circular imprint on the wall. Only her thoughts kept her company now, but she found them far less stressful without direct visual stimulation.

She only realized she'd fallen asleep when she woke several hours later; the coach had come to a stop. Aren and Garth re-entered the coach, and Dispo resumed his post. Vesper closed her eyes again, but not too soon to see Aren yawning and leaning against Garth's side as if they'd been a couple forever. Was the front of his pants open? What had those two been doing up there anyhow? She jerked her gaze away. *Stop!*

She couldn't go back to sleep. That was why an hour later, when the sun was just beginning to lighten the edge of the horizon, she heard the *thump*, as if something—or someone—had been hit. She looked out the window in time to see Dispo's body sliding down to hit the dirt, rolling once and then lying still.

The coach rocked. Someone else was mounting the post to take the coachman's place. The horses slowed, and Vesper could tell they were being turned. Who was sitting on top, and where were they headed?

CHAPTER 8

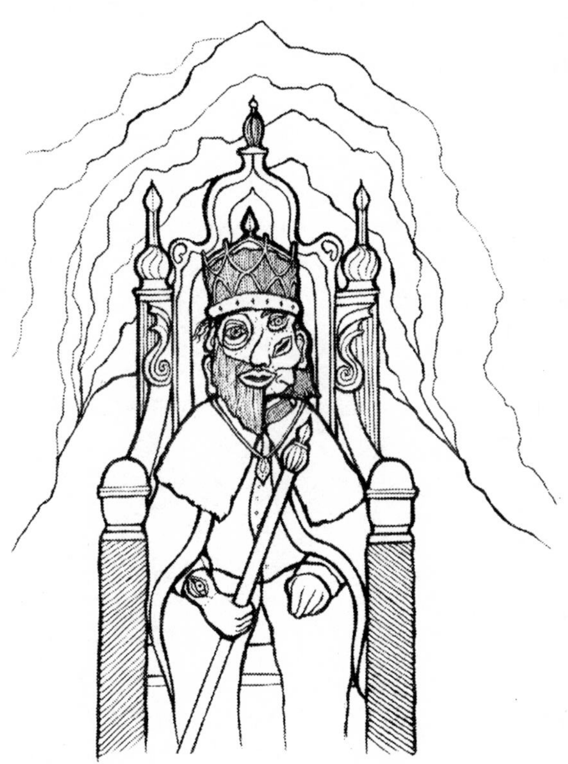

"Garth!" she hissed. "Nim, Aren—wake up! I think we've been hijacked."

Garth awoke immediately. He moved to look outside, but swiftly drew back, his retreating face followed by the point of a sword. A horse whinnied just outside the coach, and the blade wavered dangerously, then withdrew. Vesper caught a glimpse of an olive green cloak, but in the dimness of early morning light, she could see little else of the man riding alongside the coach.

"Stay inside. No funny business or you're dead." The voice spoke in a growl, directly outside the coach.

Garth sat back and lifted a hand.

"Should you—" Vesper began.

"They've threatened our lives. They deserve whatever they get," Garth said, and that crackle of magic Vesper had felt in the tavern flickered to life again.

He cast a split-magic spell, she could tell—but the only sound that greeted them from outside was laughter. Garth frowned and tried again. The man outside seemed to be unaffected.

"Why doesn't it work?" Vesper asked in a low voice.

"I don't know. I suppose we'll find out soon enough," said Garth.

Tension paralyzed those within the coach; every so often a gasp broke the silence—the sound of air drawn into lungs that had forgotten to breathe.

Twenty minutes later, the terrain became rockier; they'd gone off the road. Soon the horses slowed and halted. They'd entered a stretch of shallow woods, and the coach would no longer travel between narrowly spaced trees and over roots and brush.

Vesper became aware that more than just the olive-cloaked man rode around them. Her thoughts turned to Dispo, who had paid the ultimate price for their foolhardy decision to travel at night. He had warned them of bandits in the area, particularly at night. Vesper could hear them gathering around the coach. They were talking and laughing, but their voices were too muffled for her to make out what was being said.

The door swung open. Vesper gasped and drew back as she saw the face of their hooded guard—it was a patchwork of broken and mismatched pieces—eyes of different colors, one of them unmoving; a nose too large for his face, and of a darker skin color than his cheeks and forehead; a piece of chin that grew no beard, even though the rest of his face was darkly stubbled. Apparently, many of his original parts had been replaced by pieces from other people's bodies. He smiled horribly, exposing gaps where half his teeth should have been.

"Welcome to our home," he said, slurring, the words nearly unrecognizable. "We are so happy to make your acquaintance. Please exit your vehicle so we can greet you properly."

Garth scooted toward the opening. He lifted a hand and blasted the fellow full in the face with magic. The man grinned and spat out another tooth, which gave a small shriek and fled. Vesper understood then why the magic hadn't seemed to work. It did, but the fellow had been subjected to it so much that he had become inured to it. Perhaps eventually, he'd even have nothing left in the way of internal shadows and denied pieces of self to separate out—although she somehow doubted it.

The man's fist slammed into Garth's jaw. Garth reeled back against Aren, who shrieked twice—once as she tried to keep herself from being crushed and again as Garth spat out a bloody tooth.

"Wizards are my favorite for harvesting parts," he said, grinning. "Go ahead and hit me with some more. Everything you make me lose, I take from you. Lucky for you it was just a tooth. The last wizard got rid of my liver, and I had to take his too. Sad to say he didn't survive the... extraction." He cackled, and the bandits behind him laughed with him. "Now come on out, or I'll kill this young lady here." He motioned to Aren with a hand full of mismatched, sewn-on fingers.

Garth exited the coach without further ado. Aren followed. Vesper noted the corpselike pallor of Nim's face—any minute he would certainly faint. She drew back her hand and slapped him as hard as she could before pulling him, blinking tears, out after her. She tried to reach into the coach and grab her bag, but one of the patchwork men blocked her way. Minimus had to have heard what was happening—would he be able to escape?

Vesper's own prospects didn't look promising. She didn't know what she'd been hoping for, but her heart sank as she observed the circle of bandits surrounding them. Their giggles and grins did not bode well. All of them had the same horrid patchwork quality about their bodies—and not all of them had replacement parts. Some of them were missing huge chunks of what Vesper could see of their bodies. The nicer the clothing, the more whole the bodies, as a rule; some of the more ragged ones among them could barely even be distinguished as human.

The bandits tied their captives' wrists behind their backs. Vesper winced as someone wrapped a blindfold too tightly around her eyes and then pushed her until she lurched forward into a walk. She could tell they were going deeper inside the forest from the depth and sound of the ground underfoot and the cold of the trees that grew thicker, blocking the emerging light of dawn.

They walked for some time. Vesper lost count of distance as she concentrated on not tripping. She heard Nim fall once. The proceeding sounds of boots kicking flesh, and the shouts and curses that accompanied, more than convinced her that she was best off moving as they told her, with the least disruption to their plans as possible. These people were frightening—no ordinary bandits, even though they might once have been. Their guard had spoken of harvesting body parts, and she wondered if her adventure would end that way—being chopped up into little pieces. How ironic that she'd been so obsessed with wondering whom Garth would kiss that she'd agreed to a course of action that meant neither of them would kiss anyone ever again.

The air around them grew cold and still, and beneath Vesper's feet she felt rock, which made her think that they must be inside a cave. Then her wrists were cut loose, the blindfold torn off; what looked like a human-sized bird cage loomed before her and her anonymous captor pushed her head down, forcing her to duck as he shoved her inside. The door clanged shut behind her.

Vesper had been correct about their being in a cave. She had no idea, however, that a place like this could exist—an enormous naturally-made space, possibly twice the size of her entire home, but open and undivided. Some shallower entryways bled off from this main room, which appeared to be the main hub of activity. Several other bandits joined the twenty-odd from outside; on a makeshift throne made of slices of an old oak tree sat a bandit she'd not seen outside—someone with so many parts from different people replacing its own that she couldn't even tell if it was male or female to begin with. It wore a cloak of as many patches as its body—all of the finest materials, silk and velvet sewn with pearls and gemstones and thread that looked spun of real gold. Together, it created a fascinating but gruesome effect.

Plenty of torches lit the cavern, but that much light gave it an ominous aspect. A number of objects of varying size, ranging in color from off-white to peach to dark pink, blood-red, and brown, flew about the cavern—and Vesper realized that they were body parts.

Cages lined one end of the cavern—she located her companions; Aren, and a man who she supposed must be Garth, had been placed close to each other, and she caught a glimpse of Nim's yellow hair at the far end of their row. Three others of the dozen cages were filled, leaving five empty. Although she could see only vague shapes in them, Vesper guessed that those three people were male. She shivered, wondering how long an imprisonment those other prisoners had already suffered, and what horrors they had witnessed.

In worker-ant formation, the bandits ferried in the boxes and belongings from the coach, dumping them into a pile of loot on the side. Then they set up a table festooned with restraints for the wrists and ankles. One of the bandits sat beside it, sharpening a knife.

Things were not looking good at all.

The bandit on the throne stood and approached the cages. It paced in front of them, stopping in front of each of the new captives to stare at them a long time.

"Women," he said—for he had a man's voice, after all. "It's been a while since we've had some. And now we have two. Although I have very little in the way of morals, my heart—one of my few original parts—says that killing women is wrong. Especially such young and lovely ones as you two.

"As you can see, despite efforts to bring our group down with this split-disease, we have survived many months, and we have learned to gain from it. We take what we need in terms of parts, and we sell the rest for excellent profits. We have need of some lady parts for a client who has suffered ill fortune with this disease—but only one of you need fulfill that role. The other is welcome to join us for a little while. You will have the great honor of being a First Wife—and to not just one man, but many.us all" He chuckled, and the bandits behind him echoed the sound. Some of them began discussing the merits and faults of both Vesper and Aren.

Vesper would have blushed if she'd had any blood left in the outermost inch of her skin. She faced two alternatives: a horrible death or a horrible life. She couldn't see Aren's face, but she could hear noisy sobs, punctuated by unintelligible curses, coming from that direction.

"So, who shall it be? What do you choose?"

"I choose for you to go to hell!" Aren yelled.

The bandit king turned calmly to Vesper.

Vesper swallowed, praying her voice wouldn't shake when she spoke. "Why do you need our parts? There's so many here." She indicated a few of the parts flittering nearby.

"Useless," he said. "All useless. They've got their own minds now. They'll rip themselves right off if you try to sew them on. And most of them won't shut up either. No, it's nice quiet cooperative parts we're looking for." He leered.

"But...won't they rot?" Vesper asked.

"We use special preservatives and sealants. They won't last forever, but we've got enough of you people coming in that we can always replace any that are getting un-fresh. But this is getting boring. What is your answer?"

What should she choose? She wanted to live, of course, but to say so in front of Garth—and Nim, her only friend, and Aren, who would die by her choice—could she live with that? What sort of a life would she have? She'd not wanted to marry any of the men of her town, had objections to the erosion of her identity through becoming intimate with someone—and if she lived, it would be at the cost of everything she valued in herself. Come to think of it...she'd rather die.

What if that would have been Aren's preference, too? Could she subject her sister to such a terrible existence? She craned her neck, trying to see Aren's face, to get some kind of a clue what her sister would want her to say.

No. As the elder sister, she should make the decision for both of them. Her gut told her that Aren would mind the fate of becoming a sex slave a little less than Vesper would. Perhaps, too, Aren would find a chance to escape. "I'll take the death," she said, although her voice petered to a gasp at the last word.

The bandit king wandered over to Aren's cage. Aren spat at him, and his lip half-curled in an expression which might have been a sneer.

"Actually, I think this one will be better for parts. I dislike killing women, but I dislike high-maintenance bitches even more."

Vesper fought down a wave of nausea. She could try to throw a fit or something, to show that she could be just as difficult as Aren—but would that result in both of them dying? She had to buy some time. "Then can we have until tomorrow at least? And in the same cage? She's my sister."

"Awww....how sweet," the bandit king said. "I *am* in a good mood. So I think I'll agree. No one ever said I wasn't generous. Our client has waited long. She can wait another day. Put those two in the same cage."

One of the bandits opened Vesper's cage, took her arm, and yanked her over to Aren's cage. She reached an awkward hand out to touch her sister's arm, receiving a violent elbow for her efforts. Aren folded her arms and fixed her glare on the bandit king standing in front of their cage.

"Doubtless you asked to be with your sister so you can plan escape," he said. "So plan away, my dears. Or not. You have until the morning. But you know that if you do anything that makes you troublesome, you'll both die instead of only one of you. So think on it well."

They watched him saunter away back to his throne.

"Aren, I'll figure something out," Vesper whispered. "Don't worry. We have a whole day. I'll think of something."

"Shut up," Aren muttered. Her sobs had receded into hiccups. "Just shut up. Your brain can't get us out of *this*. Just leave me alone."

Vesper had nowhere to go, but she turned away, trying to think. ButDismally, she just went in circles around what Aren had said. *Your brain can't get us out of this...*

Stop it, she told Aren's voice. *There has to be a way*, she thought. She tried to breathe deeply, even though her first few tries had her almost choking. She had to ignore any feelings that weren't helping her and think: what could possibly save their lives?

Could she call for help somehow? Maybe...if she could get Garth to cast a spell on her, she could grab whatever body part came off herself and convince it to go for help. Although most of the parts she'd encountered displayed little more than a rudimentary intelligence, she had to admit that she believed that a part coming from herself might be smarter than the norm. Anyway, a plan full of holes was better than no plan at all.

She looked over at the next cage, where she'd thought she'd seen Garth earlier. She did a double take.

How could she have mistaken this scruffy, dirty fellow for Garth? The resemblance ended with the shape of his face, the deep set of his eyes. He certainly had none of Garth's extraordinary good looks. This man's beard lay in haphazard tangles over a face more angular than Garth's, with an enormous bird's nest of hair that was likely several shades darker than bronze, although its current condition prevented any definite conclusion. His nose, broken at least once, was not set quite in its proper place. And rather than that brilliant blue, light brown—perhaps almost amber—eyes gazed at her in an almost familiar way—not an admiring look, but one that seemed to peer into her soul, and perhaps found it amusing.

She wished he would stop looking at her as if something were funny. *Does it look like something fun is about to happen here?* she thought. Glancing at the bandits, she saw that they had built a fire and were preparing a stew in a large cauldron. They'd opened a bottle of something and were passing it around, each taking a swig or two. Some of them had started opening boxes from the coach. Garth had carried little with him. Nim's threadbare clothes, still an improvement over what some of the bandits wore, caused a small scuffle, and the shoes he'd packed became the center of a five-minute brawl. She wondered what would happen when they got to her bag. She hoped Minimus had already escaped; she dared not fantasize that he might come to her and offer assistance. No, she couldn't rely on the penis' wit to save them.

The bandits looked busy enough not to overhear, so she turned to her neighbor, leaning closer and trying to talk without moving her lips. Now what should she say? "Stop staring at me," she whispered, then covered her mouth—had she actually said that? She'd been thinking it, but it wasn't like her to be impolite.

The man's eyes crinkled at the corners as he smiled, looking as if he held back a laugh. "Why should I?" he whispered back. "I haven't seen anything so nice to look at in weeks."

Vesper felt herself blushing. Flirting never failed to render her stammering or speechless, but she couldn't afford to be either now, so she concentrated on that other tickle of an emotion—an anger that burned red-hot and pushed through the paralysis of her fear. She clenched her fists and glared at him. "This is a rotten time to flirt," she hissed. "I need to concentrate. I have to think of a way out of here."

"We could flirt while we're thinking of a way out."

Vesper furrowed her brow. "What's this 'we' business? From the looks of it you've been here for a long time, obviously without any successful escape attempts. Quiet and let me think!"

The man shrugged, still smiling, but after a moment he turned away, humming under his breath.

Not being stared at didn't help—Vesper still couldn't think of anything. Garth certainly must be planning escape—a man like that wouldn't sit around with his companions in danger.

She couldn't even see Garth, though. She craned her neck, trying to make out his shape through the dimness of the cave and across the row of cages.

"Who are you looking for?" her neighbor whispered.

"Someone who was taken prisoner at the same time as me. Oh, please won't you move your head back? Your hair is directly in my line of sight."

This time he did laugh, but without sound, and then he reached up and held the mass of his hair down, lifting eyebrows in silent question. Vesper couldn't maintain her scowl; she felt the corners of her lips quirking up, and she sighed, giving up peering through the shadows to find Garth.

"I suppose *you* aren't a wizard," she whispered, mostly to herself.

His smile faded as he lifted his shoulders in an apologetic shrug. "Sorry. I doubt I could do anything even if I were, though. Everything in this cave and within miles of it is infected with the split-magic. Any magic would just make a few more body parts pop off those guys. They wouldn't even notice."

Vesper sighed. She didn't bother telling him she'd had a different idea, as it dead-ended without a wizard—and she had to admit that it had little chance of success. This irreverent fellow would probably laugh at it, at least. He'd probably been in here so long he'd been driven half insane; how else could anyone make such light of their situation?

She checked on an inert Aren, and then began to examine the lock surreptitiously. Not that she knew anything about locks, but it gave her something to do besides having a hysterical fit, and she wanted to look too busy to talk more with her disconcerting neighbor.

As she furrowed her brow at the contraption, a pair of lips flew into Vesper's cage, smacking her on the cheek. On instinct, her hand came up and grabbed it.

"Lemme go!" it said. Vesper noticed that the sound came from around the lips—not between them, as if the voicebox had become part of all the external skin of it. The lips' movement corresponded to the words that emerged only as if from afterthought or habit.

This could be the chance she'd been waiting for—but what could she possibly do with it? She had to think fast—to do *something*—

"I need you to help me," she whispered urgently.

The lips squirmed between her fingers. "Ow! You're hurting me! Yeah, sure, okay. Stop that—I'll do anything!"

The man in the neighboring cage was staring again. Vesper refused to let that calm, curious gaze unsettle her as he waited for her next move.

She had no idea what that might be.

She could threaten the lips—or torture them into submission—but no. Her stomach knotted even just imagining it.

Perhaps bribery? What sort of things would a detached mouth crave?

"If you do what I ask, and we get out of here alive, I'll give *you* something," she said. "We'll take you with us and search for the person you got detached from—"

"But he's right over there," the lips said, jerking a lip in the direction of the bandits around the stewpot. "Don't much like him. Almost miss my teeth so I could go over and bite him when he's sleeping."

So much for that idea.

"Food, then. They probably don't feed you anything. When we get out, we'll give you a feast—any kind of food you want, and as much as you want. How about that?"

The lips pursed. "Do I look like I can eat food? Digest it? Where would that happen? I remember food. Every day, passing by, hour after hour. Making me work all the time, but no reward. What would I do with more of that?"

"Then what's something you want?" Vesper asked, despairing.

"Kisses," the lips said, smacking one into the air. "I want those. In fact, I never got any, my whole life. Not even from my mom."

Kisses! She...she could do that. She ignored the wave of revulsion at the idea, tamped down her resistance, and nodded. "Okay. I'll give you ten kisses in return for helping us get out."

"Ten! Are you cheap or something? A hundred."

"Ten from each of us," she countered. "There's seven of us, so that would make seventy if all of us get out, and you'll get more variety."

The lips pursed as if in deep thought. "Hmm...I guess that sounds all right. But it really depends what you want me to do. If it's too hard, I won't do it."

"If you could fly out of the cave and locate someone to tell them there are captives here—and show them the way—"

"That's too complicated," the lips said. "I'm just a pair of lips. I was born last week. And what you're saying sounds scary."

Vesper exhaled through her teeth. Out of ideas, she lifted the lips to toss them out the cage when her neighbor held up a finger. "Wait."

He opened his fist, revealing something lumpy that was wrapped in a piece of dirty ripped cloth. "Have the mouth dump the contents of this in the stew when no one is looking." He moved the cloth-lump forward, to the edge of his cage.

Vesper glanced at him, suspicious of his sudden seriousness after all that unhelpful banter,. bBut he was looking off in another direction, mouth pursed in a soundless whistle as if he hadn't said or done a thing except sit there looking like a dolt all day. "Lips," she said, "In the cage next to me is a small pouch of something. Can you get it and bring it back to me?"

"I guess I could do that," the lips said, slowly. "You're nice. No one's been nice to me since I was born."

"Good," said Vesper. "That man in the cage over there is nice too. Go to him and get the pouch, please."

The lips did as they were bid; they fetched the pouch and brought it back to Vesper, dropping it in her lap.

That achieved, she began to feel a tiny spark of hope, more so when she saw her neighbor take out a small pin from up his sleeve and hide it in his palm—a lock pick? She had no idea of the contents of the pouch, but something in her gut told her she could trust this strange man—and at this point, she had nothing to lose from acting on any plan whatsoever.

She watched the bandits. Because the cauldron sat exactly in their midst, someone was always looking in theits direction of the cauldron. She began to think that the lips would be unable to find a moment to slip the contents of the pouch into the stew undetected. Just then, someone began to build up the dying fire underneath the cauldron, piling on two logs and a quantity of smaller sticks. Vesper watched as the steam rising from the cauldron thickened.

"Up high above the cauldron, where that big plume of steam is coming up—float over there, stay high, and dump the powder in. Try to get as much into the stew as possible. Go!" Vesper whispered.

The lips drifted over to the ceiling above the cauldron, then descended into the smoke. So far so good——-no one was looking up there. Vesper mouthed a silent prayer as the lips upended the contents of the pouch; it came out in a fine powder, and it blended in nicely with the steam.

Had anyone noticed? Vesper held her breath. No one said anything. Had enough of the powder gone in? Perhaps it had been dropped from too high up and diffused into the air instead of going into the stew.

Two of the bandits grabbed ladles and bowls, serving and passing stew until everyone got a bowl and began to eat. Vesper watched and waited. She glanced at her neighbor, a question in her eyes—what was going to happen? He shrugged slightly, that smile again turning up the corners of his mouth.

Then, one by one, the bandits began to sleep. They staggered over to pallets on the other side of the cavern; some, less ambitious, remained where they sat and allowed their heads to droop down to their chests or to fall back against the wall. Within ten minutes, the thunderous sound of thirty-odd men snoring filled the cavern.

All except for the bandit king. His eyes, one of them green and one brown, both of the sclerae bright red, were trained on Vesper.

He limped toward her. "Not a bad escape attempt at all," he said. "I'm impressed. But you know I have to kill you now. It's a shame—I rather like you. What did you put in the stew, by the way?" he asked.

"I—I don't know what you're talking about," she said.

"I hope you haven't killed them," he said. His hand whipped out and grabbed an ear that flew by. He tossed it in his mouth and bit down with a crunch, abruptly stilling its scream. He burped. "That's to answer your unasked question—why I'm still awake. I don't eat dead food. And now that I have a spare body that needs to be killed, I might as well make a little feast out of it, don't you think?" Half his mouth turned up in a dreadful smile as he opened her cage door and grabbed her by the arm, dragging her out. With his free hand, he drew a long and wicked dagger from his belt sheath. "What shall I eat first?"

He didn't fear her at all; he barely had hold of her. She twisted out of his grasp and rammed her knee into his crotch. It contacted nothing but bone, and she yelped, pain shooting through her knee.

He grunted, then half-smiled at her again. "I never replaced those troublesome parts down there. Some have said I'm less of a man for it, but I just kill them," the king said laughed gleefully. Now, my dear. As I was saying?" He waved the point of his dagger and giggled.

Then, "What about my kisses?" said the lips from behind the bandit king. As he turned, a cage door swung open, and her scruffy neighbor jumped out, his arm coiling around the patchwork man's neck. He shoved something deep into the right nostril of the bandit, whose face turned patchwork-splotchy, all red and white, as his body convulsed once, twice, and toppled.

Vesper gaped, frozen in a moment of shock. She'd recovered by the time her rescuer located a key off one of the sleeping bandit's belts and moved toward the other cages. Drawing in a shaky breath, she made herself breathe; he'd just saved her life, and she owed it to him to not fall apart. She turned to the still-hovering lips. "You deserve every kiss," she said, "but we need to get out of here first." As her neighbor began to fiddle with a lock, she asked, "How can I help? Is there another key?"

He shook his head. "Only this one," he said. "Go and help your companions get up, as fast as you can, and then get your things—only what you need. We don't want to stay very long. The men are only asleep, and I don't know how strong the powder was. They could wake any moment." He smiled again, softening the impact of his words, and Vesper felt her spike of fear recede.

Aren, who had fallen asleep curled up on the floor, came awake with a curse when Vesper shook her. "Shh," Vesper said. "I told you we'd figure something out. We're escaping—quick!"

Aren got her head back quickly. The same could not be said for Nim, who wouldn't respond to his name being called.

"Someone will have to carry him," Vesper said. She glanced at her scruffy new acquaintance as he opened the final cages. She noticed only now the unsteadiness of his gait, the stiffness of his legs, as if he was unused to them. But of course—sitting in that tiny cage, he'd had no opportunity to stretch them out for weeks. She didn't think he could manage carrying Nim, let alone himself. She spotted Garth in the final cage, emerging rumpled but as gorgeous as ever.

"Garth, can you—" she asked, but he wasn't paying attention—he was staring at the man who'd just released him. He had the oddest look on his face, as if he'd just sucked on a lemon.

"Jules," he said. "Fancy you being here."

"You know each other?" Vesper asked, looking from one to the other. Of course they must—now that they stood facing each other, that resemblance had appeared again, and even through the excess layer of grime and the reduced layer of flesh on Jules, the two looked alike enough that they must be…

"He's my brother," Jules said.

CHAPTER 9

Garth was magnificent when angry: a lion defending his territory and none the worse for wear for his brief stay in the cages. His eyes had deepened to storm-blue, and they flashed a mixture of intense animosity and some indefinable discomfort as he tried to stare down his brother. The shiver of electricity in the air made Vesper think that he held onto his corrupted magic and the injury it could inflict by the merest hair. His very stance marked him as predator, and dangerous.

The contrast between him and Jules was almost laughable; the latter, thin and dirty and standing as if perched on wooden legs, scratched at his beard while he looked off to one side. His thin, mobile lips pursed as if whistling in silence. He looked so vulnerable that Vesper just restrained herself from interposing her body between them to protect him from Garth's wrath.

But it was Jules who broke the tension first. "We'll have to put off our happy reunion for later," he said, flashing his grin to include both Vesper and Garth. "We need to get out of here."

Spurred back into action, Vesper turned to Garth. "Can you carry Nim?"

Garth frowned. "I suppose...but that fellow doesn't like me."

"I'll do it," Jules said.

"But your legs—" Vesper said, but he was already shouldering Nim with a heave and a popping of his joints. He tottered for a moment and Vesper lunged forward, preparing if not to catch Nim, to break his fall—but then Jules' legs firmed, and he strode toward the opening of the cave.

Of their belongings, Vesper grabbed her leather bag. A quick look confirmed Minimus' absence. *So much for the entire purpose of my journey*, she thought. No time to dig through these piles for her clothes, but she found some of their food and water provisions and took as much as she could carry. Aren, unused to carrying her own things, took nothing and would probably be upset later when she discovered no one had grabbed any of her boxes—although out of immediate danger, they were close enough to it to feel nothing but gratitude for still having their lives and their bodies intact. As well as some riches—she could see Garth, purse recovered, sifting through the bandit's haul. Something flashed in his hand before it disappeared into his purse.

The seven escapees picked their way amidst snoring bandits. Several dozen animated parts accompanied them toward the entrance, more like flies following a scent than from any sense of purpose; the lips, too, smiled at Vesper from midair before turning and whizzing ahead.

They found the horses at the front of the cavern. They'd been tied to a tree, with a little grazing available but no water. Jules perched Nim in a sitting position against the tree and took one of the water skins from Vesper, and he sliced it open wide enough for the horses to slake their thirst. While the horses drank, Vesper tried to find an orientation in the forest; the uniform thickness of the trees around them confused her direction sense beyond redemption. She had no idea which way to go, except away from whence they'd come. "How do we find the coach?" she asked.

Jules tossed the empty skin somewhere behind him and pointed in a seemingly random direction. "The edge of the forest is that way, so no doubt we'll find the coach there, and then the road."

Vesper frowned. "How long are those men going to sleep? If they wake soon, and you're wrong, we're dead."

Jules shrugged. "We've already beat much slimmer odds, so fifty-fifty doesn't sound too bad to me."

"He's usually right about these things," Garth said. His arm snaked around her waist, possessive, pulling her close as if the movement were natural—as if he knew her intimately. *Oh Mae I can't believe he's touching me!* part of her shrieked. Her burst of hormonal enthusiasm made her aware of her body, which was shaking. All the fear she'd suppressed came surging into emotional existence, and she suddenly couldn't bear being touched. She moved to follow Jules, and Garth's arm slid off.

Sure enough, the coach appeared after a short walk. The two emaciated rescuees, who gave the names of Philler and Iness, could have fit inside with the four original passengers, especially now that no one had any baggage. But Aren, who seemed fully recovered from her experience, put her foot down. "Anyone who hasn't taken a bath in the last month has to ride up top," she said.

Jules took the coachman's seat, and Philler and Iness sat next to him. Despite their reticence and their dour faces under their beards, they had developed an obvious closeness from being neighbors in the cages for who knew how long; after a mumbled conference, they asked for a ride only to the nearest town where they would figure out what to do together.

Vesper sat next to Nim, thinking to comfort him, but she didn't know how and ended up giving him awkward pats and a few words of sympathy here and there. He finally began to respond when spoken to, although every so often he would pause in the middle of a sentence, stare in front of him, and give a tremendous shiver, as if reliving some moment of an incredible nightmare. It *had* been a nightmare—the most frightening experience of Vesper's life—but now that they were free, and every moment more surely so, giddiness soon replaced the aftereffects of fear, and she felt pride at the part she'd played in their escape. Self-conscious as she still might be, she felt that she actually had something to say now.

"Isn't it the oddest coincidence that we found your brother there, of all places?" she asked Garth.

He shrugged. "A wizard's life is full of synchronicities," he said. "As for Jules being there, it's not that surprising. He's a criminal and a coward, just like those bandits."

Jules had killed the bandit king by stuffing something into his nostril. He'd met Garth's fury with calm bordering on indifference. He hadn't seemed cowardly at all. Also, not that she truly considered taking from bandits stealing, he hadn't helped himself to any of the bandits' treasures, either—unlike Garth. "You mean literally, he's a criminal as his line of work?"

"More or less," Garth said. "Have you heard of the Children of Mae?"

"The cult?" She knew of a religious group whose members went door to door, preaching the benefits of self-discipline—abstinence, celibacy or monogamy, vegetarianism—pretty much anything fun was prohibited. They had never come to Vesper's house because her father was a butcher and probably pretty low on their list of possible converts. Jules belonged to them? How could that be possible? She'd thought those cult members were crazy. Certainly, he had been oddly amused in the face of having his parts harvested, but his behavior still seemed a far cry from being a Child of Mae.

"Yes," Garth said, mouth set in a grim line. "And they are criminals, as any people are who eschew any societal responsibilities and who speak against our government."

"Really?" Vesper asked. "What do they say about it?"

"They masquerade spirituality but preach anarchy—that there is a law above that of our king: an internal law that somehow magically emerges if you impose self-discipline and material deprivation. With this hogwash, his group seeds and feeds discontent and undermines the king's authority and collective agreements toward reform. Honestly, I'm embarrassed that he's my brother."

Vesper was intrigued. She'd read about anarchy, and she'd dabbled a little in books on politics that questioned the value of monarchy, but she'd never heard of open defiance of the government in the form of a religious organization. "But if they preach a law above the king's, it's not really anarchy, even if it is a little hard to know what the law is," she pointed out.

"Don't argue about something you don't know anything about," Garth said, and Vesper drew back as if slapped. Then he looked at her and his tone softened. "What I mean to say is that the self-governance they preach simply isn't possible, because people are too immature. So it amounts in practical terms to anarchy."

Vesper stayed silent. Garth's snapping at her had reminded her of her habitual behavior with him—tongue-tied and self-conscious and too aware that he certainly had a different "type" of woman. So when she felt something soft and wet brush against her cheek, she felt gratitude, rather than annoyance. The lips pulled away shyly and hovered there, parted, waiting. "And how about my kisses now?"

Aren had been unusually quiet, but now her eyes fixed readily enough on the lips and her upper lip curled in distaste. "You're going to kiss those lips? You don't even know where they came from!"

"All of us are going to," Vesper replied, although she could tell she sounded unconvincing, and she had the blush to match. "I promised ten kisses from each of us, in return for these lips helping us. They saved our lives."

"Well, I have to be in the mood, and I'm not right now. Especially not with those. They probably belong to one of those men back there who tried to kill us!" Aren said. Vesper's face burned. The lips waited, drooping a bit at the corners—whose wouldn't, having people right in front of them saying they didn't want to kiss you? But, aside from Nim's impromptu attempt before their trip began, Vesper had never kissed anyone before. What if she messed up? She didn't want her first tries witnessed by her sister, Nim...and Garth.

But the worst thing to do would be to make a big deal out of it, bringing more attention to her self-consciousness. She steeled herself and nodded. "All right, lips. Twenty from me."

She leaned forward, puckering just a little, almost closing her eyes. The lips were just as tentative. The first kiss was a butterfly's touch, the following several applying more pressure, but still as chaste. *This isn't so bad*, Vesper thought; then she made the mistake of opening her eyes to glance at her companions.

Nim had sat up out of his stupor and he stared, his own lips puckered as if he were imagining himself in the lips' position. Aren had crossed her arms and rolled her eyes skyward as if she'd encountered such ridiculousness that she'd forgotten to point them back down. And Garth leaned forward, elbows resting on his knees, head tilted, too-blue eyes studying this fascinating scene unfolding before him.

Vesper jerked back, causing the lips to shriek and free-fall for an instant before they shot back up. "Hey, that's only seven!"

"Could you all stop staring?" Vesper snapped. "It'll be your turns soon enough."

"You have a very…interesting kissing technique," Garth said.

Vesper couldn't possibly blush any harder, otherwise her head might explode. "Why don't you do your ten and demonstrate how it should be done? Lips, Garth is ready for his turn. I'll do the rest of mine later."

The lips turned obligingly and moved toward Garth. He didn't hesitate, meeting the lips with an open mouth and a flick of his tongue. His mouth responded to each movement of the lips, and as he pulled away to end the first kiss, he did so lingeringly. The second kiss was slower and hotter, and Vesper found herself holding her breath, her heartbeat accelerating, wanting to look away but unable to do so.

Aren was just as mesmerized. Mouth open, she practically panted, and as Garth continued his kisses the coach became so stuffy with pheromones that Vesper had to stick her head outside to clear her head.

"Mmmm," said the lips. "You're good."

"It's my turn," Aren said, voice husky, crooking a finger at the lips.

"I thought you didn't want to," Vesper said.

"I do now."

Vesper mostly didn't watch Aren—although she couldn't help but notice that her sister knew how to kiss. *She must have done it plenty with Ruben*, Vesper thought. *Or had she with Garth…?*

When Nim's turn came, the lips kissed him once, receiving his grandmotherly peck with a moue of distaste. "I'll pass on the others with him." Vesper recalled her own kiss with him and felt no surprise; she tried not to look at him, but she could feel the embarrassed heat emanating from him.

Vesper had just called an explanation of their debt to those on the top of the coach, and sent the lips up to collect, when a loud "Wheee!" sang into Vesper's ear and Minimus sailed through the window, delivering an inadvertent blow to Vesper's face as he went by.

"Ow," she said, sitting back and rubbing her cheek.

"Wow, what's been going on in here?" Minimus asked. "Smells like sex!" He appeared to grow taller and straighter, and his one eye peered about as if he might find an orgy if he looked hard enough.

"Don't you ever think about anything other than that?" Vesper asked irritably, crossing her legs. "I forgot—I'm talking to a penis.

Never mind, Minimus. I'm glad you're safe."

Minimus danced on Aren's lap. Aren laughed and stroked him when he butted against her hand. "So nice to see you!" Then Minimus jumped over to Vesper's lap and waited expectantly until she, too, gave him a quick pat on the head.

Garth shook his head. "I never thought I'd see the prince's cock be a loyal friend to a woman."

Nim sat up straight, suspicion animating his face. He had returned to his bad mood since the lips had rejected his kisses, although he no longer seemed traumatized. "That—that's the penis that was at your party! And you've had it all this time—probably using it every night, fantasizing that you're having sex with the prince—"

"I hadn't even thought of that," said Aren, excited. "Wow, I've had sex with the prince!"

"Listen to that! She's had sex with the prince—but it's been in your bag—you've been having sex with him, too?" Nim turned eyes full of accusation on the object of his unrequited longing. "Back there when I thought we were going to die, all I could think about was the fact that the two of us would die innocent, neither of us ever tasting the fruits of our love—" He began to sob.

"I haven't been having sex with Minimus," Vesper shouted, trying to make herself heard over Nim's blubbering. "And yes, he does belong to Prince Magnus, so I'm returning him to his owner, which is why I'm here."

"I thought you were here to free yourself from that old guy so you could marry me," Nim said, voice still shaking, although at least he wasn't crying any longer.

"I am here to free myself from Porter, but I already told you my answer about marrying you." She winced as she said it—she wouldn't have chosen this time or place to have this conversation.

"But I thought all women say things they don't mean. You have to read between the lines, interpret what their eyes are saying, not their mouths. Pa told me so," Nim said.

"Your pa is an alcoholic and a business failure," Aren said. "You shouldn't listen to anything he says at all. If Vesper says no, she means no. You ought to know better—you've known her her whole life."

"Oh, I hate this trip. This is the worst day of my life," Nim said, turning to face the wall.

Minimus had been watching the exchange with intense interest. "No means no," he repeated in a thoughtful tone. "I don't think Magnus knows that. I'll be sure to tell him."

"I'm sorry, Nim," Vesper said, cringing at the uselessness of her apology.

Awkward silence dominated the coach for the next few hours, except for happy chirps from Minimus, who flew in and out of the coach talking about things he saw. He confessed that he had snuck out of the bag earlier and had been wandering about, exploring when they'd gotten waylaid by the bandits.

"Otherwise I would've helped you!" Minimus said. "I can't believe those people wanted to make dead body parts and sew them on others. That's two big crimes! How did you get out?"

Vesper explained her accosting the lips, and then Jules' contributing the sleeping powder which the lips delivered into the bandits' dinner.

"I like the sound of those lips," Minimus said. "Maybe I'll see if they're still around... I'd like to give 'em ten kisses, for sure." He flew out the window again.

Once outside, Minimus was the first to spot a group of body parts ahead, blocking the road.

"Trouble up ahead!" he called, hurtling back in through the window. "Rowdy body parts!"

CHAPTER 10

The coach slowed.

"Not more bandits!" Aren groaned.

Garth was looking outside. "This is different," he said. "Not bandits—but possibly the bandits' missing body parts."

Garth descended from the coach, Aren trailing after him. Vesper, curious, got down as well. Even with the advance warning, she could hardly believe what she saw. Eyes, ears, noses, teeth, chins, fingers, toes, larger limbs—feet, hands, arms, and legs—along with a variety of genital parts and unidentifiable organs or other pieces floated above the road before them. They were arranged in a loose circle, calling, cheering, and placing bets while a hand and a foot brawled in the middle.

The hand seemed to have the advantage, as when it got a hold of the foot, the foot couldn't dislodge it. It punched the foot with a series of quick jabs that left the foot in a stupor. Then the crowd parted, distracted by the arrival of the coach; the hand turned to see what was taking away its audience.

The foot delivered a tremendous kick to the hand, sending it hurtling to the ground. Foot jumped on hand, and the hand struggled but couldn't escape.

"Winner!" cried a bloodshot eyeball. "The foot wins." It turned toward the newcomers.

"Welcome," it said. "You may pass, of course, but first one of you must defeat the champion."

The foot rose in the air to hover next to the eyeball. "Bring 'em on!" it growled.

"This is ridiculous," Garth said. "Fight a foot?"

"I'll do it," said Jules.

"You? Fight?" Garth's sneer showed what he thought of that. "I'll go." He strode forward before anyone could stop him.

The body parts formed a larger circle, shifting back to include the whole people from the coach this time. Garth faced off with the foot in the center. He lunged.

And missed. The foot danced just out of reach, then landed a kick straight in Garth's eye.

Garth reeled, shook his head to clear it, lips drawn back in a snarl. He tried another grab, but missed. The foot laughed.

No matter what Garth did, he couldn't get a hold of the foot, which was landing a series of solid kicks to his head. After twenty minutes of this, Garth was beginning to wear down. Finally, with a stomp to the top of his head—exactly in the same spot Vesper had brought him down with the glass jar at the inn—he wavered on his feet and came crashing down, unconscious.

"Winner!" the eyeball yelled, over the cheers of the body parts. "Next!"

"What happens if none of us can beat the foot?" asked Vesper. She did not look forward to getting kicked into unconsciousness, but of course it could always be worse.

The eyeball jiggled as it chuckled. "Well...you'll just have to stay and keep playing our games until you can. If you get bored...you could always try to escape." More laughter.

That was worse.

Jules frowned. "I don't have any of my powder left," he said. "I'm not sure I can bring it down without injuring it pretty badly."

"I could go," said Philler. "Pretty useless for much else. I might as well tire him out, and maybe I'll get lucky."

Vesper glanced at his bony chest. Even she and Aren would last longer than him. She had no compunction about killing the foot, but Jules' obviously dampened spirits moved her to try something else. "Wait," she said. "Don't go yet, either of you. I have an idea."

She ran over to the coach, where, as she hoped, Minimus still lingered. She found him rolling around on the plush cushions of the seat, just starting to masturbate.

Vesper leaned in the window. "Minimus!" she hissed. "We need your help."

Minimus sat up. "Aww, I was just getting comfortable."

"Those body parts out there want us to fight to the death. I don't think any of us can beat their champion—it's a foot, and it's too fast and strong. It already knocked Garth out. But you—I think you can beat him. I've never seen anyone as fast as you."

Minimus swelled up in response to her compliments. He jumped to standing. "I will defeat this foul-smelling, cheese-ridden foot for you, my lady!" he cried, and he flew out past her shoulder. The eyeball danced midair in front of the foot, calling out, "Who'll be next? Come on, are you humans or chickens?" The rest of the crowd clucked like chickens, and a few of them who had bony edges to use pecked at the ground, laughing.

Minimus barreled toward the eyeball, which jumped out of the way with a squeal. "I, Crown Prince Minimus, shall deliver your doom."

The foot fell down and laughed so hard its toes shook. Then it stilled and crooked just its big toe, beckoning. "Come on then. You're just a stupid penis. No digits, no bones, just a useless piece of meat."

Minimus began to whizz around the foot, springing in and slapping it roundly whenever he found an opening. The foot laughed and waited.It gave its signature kick. Minimus went down, and the foot stomped, grinding Minimus into the dust. The crowd roared. Then the penis went limp and soft, rolling out from under the foot, then erect again and began to batter the foot, slapping it left and right.

Vesper bit her lip. Perhaps this wasn't the best idea. How was a penis possibly going to knock out a foot? Or a foot a penis, for that matter? They could be here for days.

Then Minimus swelled even more and enormous gobs of sticky white liquid spurted out of his mouth-hole, covering the foot from ankle to toe. Before everyone's disbelieving views, the foot disintegrated—exploding into a mass of bones, ligaments, pieces of muscle all squealing newborn body parts drifting midair, then flying off to hide in the nearest trees and beyond.

A collective hush fell over the body parts. Only after a moment, the eyeball turned to Minimus. "Uh...winner? But...you killed our champion!"

"I haven't," the penis said. "My magical sperm has helped liberate his parts into further parts. None of whom can beat me. So he is no longer your champion. I am! And I demand that you let my people pass."

A mutter of discontent shivered through the mass of body parts.

"Cheating!" grumbled a middle finger.

"You shouldn't be hanging out with them," said an ear. "You're a body part. You're one of us. Those people are the enemy."

Minimus turned his head from side to side, looking at each of the body parts. They fell silent, some bowing the head-like portions of each of their parts in a semblance of respect, many who floated in the air descending several inches, unable to meet the force of his gaze..

"You ought to be ashamed of yourselves," he said. "You all came from people--and you're the best parts from them, the first to be freed. And now you're just a useless bunch of brigands. You shouldn't think that you're worse off now that you're not part of a greater body—think of it as you earning your freedom, your independence! You're no longer connected to all those inefficient parts who weren't good enough to separate from the body. You ought to be out discovering the world and sharing its joys with others like you—not giving body parts a bad name."

The parts stared at Minimus, confounded; any that had the means to gape were doing so. The penis' speech surprised even those from the coach—he'd never talked like this before. *Why*, Vesper thought, *he actually sounds intelligent and somewhat revolutionary*—she could finally see that he could be the penis of a prince. FMinimus turned back to the eyeball. "So have we earned the right to pass?"

"Uh...I guess so," said the eyeball, still stunned.

The humans, including a groggy Garth, got back in and on the coach, and Minimus hovered above it, overseeing as the body parts parted and let the vehicle go through. Still, none of the coach occupants could relax, even after the body parts were out of sight; they'd experienced too many traumas that day, not to mention the witnessing of Minimus' strange new power. The penis stayed on watch outside, but whenever he whizzed past the coach, anyone looking out the window would flinch as if sperm might come shooting in his or her direction.

They breathed a collective sigh of relief when they saw the lights of an inn by the side of the road before sundown, on the edge of a small town.

Philler and Iness thanked the coach occupants for the ride.

"But what will you do?" Vesper asked, concerned. "Do you need some money?" She eyed their attire, or lack thereof—the men wore no shirts or shoes and little more than rags as pants.

"Got that covered, miss," said Iness, and he dug in his pocket and held up a gold watch—he and his companion had taken a few things from the bandits' cave. The two ambled away, and Vesper watched them for a while before she became distracted by her own hunger and desire for a bath.

Garth took charge at the inn. Within minutes, he'd gotten the innkeeper to produce fresh clothing for all of them, in more or less their sizes. They each agreed to meet in the tavern after taking turns at the bath. After Vesper took her bath and put on the clean, rather shapeless brown dress she'd been provided, she went to the tavern where she found Garth facing Nim and a strange man who looked oddly familiar. Garth was arguing with the man—and then, coming closer, Vesper realized that she was looking at Jules.

The bird's nest on his head had disappeared, replaced by silky shoulder-length brown hair still wet from the bath. He'd shaved his beard as well, and her gaze flew to a rather finely-shaped mouth below that several-times-broken nose, then up to eyes identical to Garth's save for the color and their far calmer expression. *He doesn't clean up half bad*, Vesper thought; his face hadn't the perfection of Garth's, but he was pleasant enough to look at.

Not ordinary, though—no one who could face such wrath as his brother's with such equanimity could be called ordinary. Now he was insisting, quite pleasantly, ever-smiling, "I'll be happy to drive us to Mallandina."

"I've plenty of funds to hire a different coachman," Garth said. "I'll not have you and your unlawful speech around the gentlewomen in my company. You know that association with the likes of you could get them in trouble."

"We've had plenty of trouble already without him along," mumbled Nim, belligerent. He glanced at Jules and straightened, glaring at Garth, raising his voice. "Actually our trouble started when we met *you*. This fellow is obviously useful. He saved our lives from the bandits."

Nim's unaccustomed bravado surprised Vesper as much as Garth losing his unflappable charm. An unhealthy red tinged the golden tan of his face, and perfect white teeth clenched together as his fists balled at his sides.

Vesper moved in. "Please let's not fight. I…I don't mind if Jules stays with us. I think we owe it to him."

"I'm in charge of this expedition," Nim added. "You butt in on our coach and ordered us to take you—but that doesn't mean you can dictate if anyone else can or can't come with us. I say he stays."

Garth took a deep breath, visibly calming himself. He nodded stiffly. "Fine. Don't say I didn't warn you, though." He spun on his heel and went to join Aren at a table; she was talking to the barmaid, ordering what sounded like half the food in the kitchen.

Vesper went to go sit with Nim and Jules, who were both drinking mugs of milk while they waited for their food. "Milk for you too?" the barmaid asked Vesper, perfectly serious.

"I think I'll have ale," Vesper said. After the day she'd had, she could use a little alcoholic buzz.

"I've been telling Nim about why I stayed alive so long in the bandits' cave," Jules said after the barmaid placed a foaming mug of ale before Vesper.

"How many of you were there?" Vesper asked.

"I was waylaid with two of my spiritual brothers. We joined seven others in the cages, and a few more came and went before you arrived. I think it's been an ongoing operation these past few months."

Two of his spiritual brothers, Vesper thought. Since Philler and Iness had no such connection with him, Jules must have watched them die. She gulped down ale. Then she thought of something else. "Months? Has the disease been around that long?"

Jules shrugged. "I suspect longer than that. Odd, isn't it, the sheer number of missing body parts those bandits had? We've seen most people missing one or two parts, but those fellows looked as if someone—or more than one person—has been using magic on them with the purpose of dissolving them into little pieces."

"Maybe an angry penis came and shot sperm all over them," Nim said darkly.

"I don't think Minimus would do that," Vesper said.

"Who said I was talking about him? Maybe it was a *different* penis."

Vesper ignored him. "Maybe they were purposely attacked by a wizard living nearby—someone who wanted revenge against those bandits for some reason."

"I'm thinking they were purposely attacked, for sure," said Jules, "but not by a wizard living nearby. I'm thinking they may have been targeted...and then released, to create chaos."

"Who would do that?" Vesper asked. It sounded like a conspiracy theory, a product of paranoia.

Jules shrugged again. "I can only speculate. But I do know that whenever you get more chaos in a society, people are more willing to give up their autonomy and allow someone else to control them, in the name of protection."

Vesper glanced around, wondering if anyone could hear them. So this was the sort of thing Garth had warned her about—Jules was going to say that it was the king who'd purposely infected these bandits and then set them up so they could kidnap people and cut their parts off. Although she saw no one around who might accost them for speaking against the government—not that anyone would take their discussion seriously—better not to discuss it in public. SSo she changed the subject. "So, how *did* you stay alive so long in there? What was in those powders—and where were you keeping them, anyway?"

Jules reached into his mouth and popped one of his teeth out—but then she saw it was just a hollow covering over his real tooth. "Fake tooth with a pocket. Pretty standard," he said. He snapped it back on. "The powder was a very effective poison, which in very small doses produces sleep. As for the first question—that's a little harder to explain. I used a lot of psychological tricks. In my training, we try not to objectify others, and that encourages others not to objectify us. It's necessary to objectify people in order to kill them. So I did small things to make them prefer to kill someone other than me, whenever they made a choice."

"Small things—like what?"

He shrugged. "Like not finding them disgusting to look at. Looking them in the eye at the right moments—and not looking them in the eye at others. It's more something I do out of instinct now. There are no hard and fast rules to it."

"Is that an idea from your cult?" Vesper asked.

"My spiritual group, yes," Jules said.

"Then why did the bandits kill your companions?"

Jules finally dropped his eyes, and Vesper felt, for an instant, oddly bereft. "I suppose luck had a large part in it as well. They would have killed me eventually, object or no."

Nim's eyes shone, round with rapture as he drank in every word. "No, I bet it wasn't just luck. I bet they wouldn't have killed you. They'd have let you go. I would have."

"Thanks, Nim. You're a good guy." Jules clanked his refilled mug with Nim's, and they both swigged down their milk.

"Speaking of letting people go," Vesper said, "all those bandits are probably awake now, hunting for more travelers to kidnap and cut up. Why didn't you kill all of them?"

"Maybe I should have. I try to make choices to minimize casualties. I killed that one who was attacking you, as he seemed particularly dangerous, and men like that usually want vengeance if you beat them once. As for the others, I've already reported the presence of that cave to the authorities, and when I meet with my brothers again we'll do some work to inform those traveling through the area to take alternate routes...and hopefully we can get the bandits some help so they no longer feel compelled to commit crimes."

She'd have felt more comfortable if the bandits had all died—it was delusional to think they could be helped. Her saying so was interrupted, however, by their food arriving. Vesper and Nim got plates with thick slices of beef drizzled in gravy, and Jules received an enormous serving of green beans.

After Vesper finished her meal, she started a second mug of ale while she watched Jules surreptitiously. Where Garth radiated confidence, Jules was more contained and grounded; despite his odd reluctance to harm people who'd had no such compunction about killing any of them, Vesper had to admit that she felt safe around him—she experienced none of the girlish giddiness that made her forget herself and her words, the self-conscious anxiety that she couldn't help but feel around his brother.

Vesper only realized that she was staring at him, lost in thought, when she jumped at the sound of Nim's chair scooting back. He grabbed his empty mug and walked—almost strutted—toward the barmaid.

"Where's Nim going?" she asked.

Jules grinned. "I've been encouraging him to go seek his heart's desire."

Vesper blinked at her yellow-haired neighbor; he was conversing with the barmaid. His shapelessly stocky body slouched in a semblance of grace—he'd lost his usual awkward twitch, and the easy way he was now chatting, lids half-closed to disguise the usually unnerving intensity of his gaze, made him about as attractive as Vesper had ever seen him. She looked down at her ale and then back up at him. Was she imagining this? She watched, astounded, as the barmaid nodded and smiled at something Nim asked, and then they went up the stairs together—holding hands!

"That's his heart's desire?" she asked, eyebrows climbing.

"Of course he'd rather it be you. But I pointed out that you're not interested in him, and he's beginning to understand that you wouldn't make him happy, anyway. He hasn't really *seen* you, not as you want to be seen, but he's starting to, a little."

Vesper nearly knocked her mug over in her start of disbelief, at which point she decided she'd better finish it, so as to not lose her ale. She drank down, then regarded Jules in bleary surprise. She'd never spoken to anyone before of this business of being seen, loved for who she was; to have it voiced by this man she'd just met sent chills down her spine. She wondered all of a sudden if she could talk to him about her feelings for Garth, which had grown less clear as his temper had eroded...but no one was perfect, and she should welcome knowing that. At the same time, she felt that at this moment, she'd rather talk about Garth with Jules than actually talk with Garth.

But Jules was already scooting his own chair back. He nodded at her. "I think my own heart's desire is calling to me—a nice soft bed and sweet dreams all night long." He grinned and headed for the stairs.

Vesper stayed a few moments longer, lost in thought. She recalled the look Nim had cast in her direction as he was going up the stairs with the barmaid—*you didn't save yourself for me, so now it's your turn to suffer*, his look said.

Suffer, she would not. She had had too much to drink to be suffering tonight. Or to be thinking about Jules or Garth or Nim or anyone. Her greatest issue of the moment was ascending that great mass of stairs looming before her.

She achieved the task, although it did take a long time. She had no candle, but the one in the hallway lit her way just enough to find her room. Once there, she felt her way along the wall until she got to the bed, patted it to make sure she wouldn't fall on top of Aren, and then collapsed onto what felt like the downiest, softest surface she'd ever contacted. She felt as if she were sinking down into its depths, and then she slept.

She snapped awake shortly after—or a long time after; she had no idea. Had she imagined a clicking noise, as if a door had been closed softly? Was it the door to their room, or one in the hallway? "Aren! Did you hear that?" she whispered. Was someone already in the room? Maybe Jules' talk of conspiracy was making her excessively paranoid. "Aren!" She reached over to shake her sister.

Aren was gone.

CHAPTER 11

Vesper sat up. The ale had burned through her system, leaving her blood clear but her head feeling as if it had been trampled. Eyes adjusted to the darkness, she managed to get to the door without tripping more than a couple times. The hallway had a tinderbox and a spare candle. She lit it, then reentered the room. No signs of struggle…had Aren left of her own free will? Or maybe Aren had never come to bed…

Immediately she thought of Garth, who was right next door—how convenient! Her mind flashed over Aren's closeness to Garth the last few days; they'd had dinner together, and talked and laughed throughout. Vesper hadn't seen them afterward—perhaps they'd been up in his room the whole time, having a secret assignation.

She put her candle down and paced. Her head ached. She shouldn't care if Aren was with Garth. But…what if it wasn't true? What if Aren had met someone else—like one of those dangerous fellows back at the other inn? Shouldn't she go and find out, make sure Aren was all right?

After agonizing about it for a good five minutes, she decided she wouldn't sleep a wink just waiting here. She saw that Minimus was snoring in the towel she'd wrapped him in. Taking the candle, she slipped on her boots without tying them. She opened the door again, then tiptoed to the room next door and put her ear to the wood.

Nothing. If they were busy having sex, shouldn't she hear something? Maybe they had finished and lay there relaxing in each other's arms. Maybe they were just quiet at it. Maybe…

She gasped as the door opened, and she fell inside.

Straight into Garth's arms.

He caught her neatly and pulled her inside, shutting the door. He took the candle from her, placing it by the bed. Then, before she could even react, he'd turned and his mouth descended on hers, warm, and as luxuriantly sensuous as it had been on the lips in the coach. One strong hand cupped her head, winding fingers into her loose tresses, and the other was inching down her back.

Her first thought was that she liked this much more than Nim's attempt. Garth definitely knew his way around a woman's body, and she felt something in herself responding, a slow opening from her core, her skin suddenly aware of each place the rough cloth of her dress brushed it, every spot bared to the candlelit darkness. Adjusting to her tentative response, the kiss deepened, Garth's tongue flicking into her open mouth.

I'm being kissed by the man of my dreams, she thought, and it thrilled her—even though she didn't know if it was the kiss itself, or just the idea that she was kissing him that thrilled her more. Part of her felt so excited by what was happening that she wanted to stop him so she could go write it down, to make a record of this moment and exactly how it had come about. But if she stopped him, she might miss out on what came next...she'd read a number of romantic stories and they talked about feelings of melting, time stopping, explosions, maybe even divine inspiration. She couldn't wait!

"Vesper," Garth murmured, lips moving down her throat. "Relax."

She stiffened. She was doing this wrong. He must think that she was the worst kisser in the world. Where was she supposed to put her hands? They hung uselessly at her sides; she put them on his arms—felt the sweat of her palms against the muscular bareness of his flesh—so snatched them off, and clutched her skirt instead.

She found her hands tangling with Garth's, as he was also grabbing her skirt—he was backing her toward his bed, fistfuls of cloth creeping up her legs. Was she ready for this? Panic mingled with excitement. She couldn't decide...she could barely make her legs move how he was encouraging them to move, one step back at a time...

Then came a sharp rap at the door.

Garth muttered a curse under his breath and withdrew, slowly enough so Vesper wouldn't topple over. She still wove on her feet for a moment, head spinning.

Garth opened the door, and Jules stood outside, holding a candle. His rumpled hair was the only indication he'd been sleeping at all; his easy stance, the brightness of his eyes, that ever-present smile made him appear as alert as he'd ever been. He regarded Vesper next to the bed, and Garth bare-chested with his lips flattened into an angry line, with no surprise.

"What do you want?" Garth snapped.

"I'm sorry. Have I interrupted something? I've been hearing doors opening and closing all night," Jules said. "I just came by to see if everything was all right."

"You have interrupted. Everything was perfectly all right until you did so."

"Terribly sorry," Jules said, with no trace of apology. "I'll just get on back to bed."

"Actually—everything isn't all right. I was looking for Aren," Vesper burst out. "She's missing from my room." Although she didn't know why, she felt she needed to explain to Jules that she hadn't been secretly meeting his brother. She had never yet felt judged by him, but after that talk of being seen, she wanted him to know that this wasn't normal behavior for her...but that was so stupid. What was she thinking?

"Aren, missing?" Garth asked. "You didn't tell me any such thing."

"I—well, I—" Vesper stuttered.

"Let's have a look," Jules said. He strode to the room next door and opened it, shining the light of his candle inside.

After their eyes adjusted, the three could see perfectly well that Aren lay in bed, a comfortable lump, dark hair spread across the pillow.

"Oh," said Vesper, heat flaring in her cheeks. "She really was missing! I'm not lying. I thought Garth might know about it. I didn't want to try Nim's room yet because, well, you know."

"And you didn't want to try my room?" Jules asked with an exaggerated sigh.

"Mine is the obvious choice," Garth said, glaring at his brother.

Vesper had no objections to the fighting for once. She would rather them focus on each other rather than ask her more questions about what she'd been doing in Garth's room. Mumbling something about *that Mae-cursed ale* and *this isn't happening* and then *so sorry*, she dashed inside her room and shut and latched the door.

She made her way again through the darkness into the bed. She lay down next to her sister, pulling the sheets up to her chin. She must have been so drunk she was imagining things. She'd been stupid to suspect Aren. She'd been stupid to go to Garth's room. Jules was stupid for barging in on them, even though she had to admit some relief at being interrupted—she wasn't ready to be with Garth, not yet! She had to study more, or something...prepare herself a little bit so he wouldn't think her such an incompetent innocent. How had Aren gotten so good at kissing anyway? And how could Vesper get in a little more practice before the real thing came along again?

"Aren, are you awake?" she whispered.

Aren did not reply, but something in her breathing told Vesper that she was feigning sleep. Had she been missing after all, then, or had drinking brought out Vesper's paranoia as well as dulled her sight? Vesper sighed. Nothing could be solved by lying here thinking in circles. Perhaps it was just best if she slept.

Nim took a turn first at driving the coach the next day, which left Garth and Aren sitting on one side of the coach, and Vesper and Jules facing them. After the depth of last night's conversation, an odd distance in Jules' attitude toward Vesper made her give up after a few attempts at conversation.

Although sweet and solicitous when addressing Vesper, Garth focused his attention on Aren at his side. Vesper tried a few times to engage him in more intellectual subjects, hoping to impress him, but Aren would draw him relentlessly back to her own conversation, and Vesper had to give up on that as well. She had to comfort herself with a few meaningful glances exchanged and held with Garth—the promise of what it might be like one day if and when they were openly bespoken to each other...

"I think I'm going to see if Nim wants some company," Jules announced. He reached a hand outside the coach and rapped. He didn't wait for the horses to completely stop; when they slowed to a walk he'd already climbed out the window with a fluid swing and clambered up to the top like a monkey.

Vesper wished for an instant that she could go with him, but he didn't seem to want to talk to her today. The coach felt claustrophobic. Vesper would have liked to see the road from up top and breathe fresh air. She sighed and tried to tune out Aren's exclaiming over some explanation by Garth of fashion trends in the palace.

They passed three towns without stopping, eating food they'd purchased from the inn the day before. Still, in each town the road traveled straight through the middle, and Vesper noticed an increase in the amount of people who lacked body parts. Some of them wore prostheses, while others covered unsightly holes in their bodies with scarves or veils. Peddlers hawked creams "guaranteed to numb and reattach your parts," and Vesper actually saw two prostheses-selling stalls in the last town they went through.

Then, the checkpoints began.

Here, two days away from Mallandina, the road that had shot straight from Pecktown began to split off into other main thoroughfares. At the second multiple fork they approached, Jules, who was up driving the horses, slowed. "Group of soldiers up ahead," he called down. "I don't know what they want, but I think they're going to stop us."

"I'm so tired of being stopped," Aren said, pouting. "The past two times were just awful. What's it going to be now?"

"I could get us through," Minimus announced, head peeping out of Vesper's bag.

Garth looked outside. "Better to stay out of sight, Minimus, to avoid any uncomfortable questions. These men bear the king's colors. They cannot mean any harm."

The face of the soldier who stopped them said otherwise. "Everyone in the coach, out, and get in a line," he snapped. "You, get down from there."

"Why the checkpoint? Just tell us what you're looking for," said Jules, but he climbed down anyhow.

"Silence!" the soldier shouted. He took out a small round object—a crystal embedded in a rock, wound with metal wire. Holding it in front of him, he walked down the line from Jules, to Nim, Aren,

Garth, and Vesper.

When he reached Garth, the rock glowed red. The soldier stopped and looked up into Garth's face. "You're a wizard," he said, spitting the word as if it were a curse.

"That's correct," Garth said. "I am King Bugger's court wizard, actually." He reached into his purse and flashed his official medallion with a confident snap of the wrist.

The soldier's face reflected indecision. "I have orders to detain all wizards and witches for questioning..."

"Why is that? It's not a crime to be a wizard."

"Actually," said the soldier, with bravado back in place, "it may now be. By order of the king, all wizards and witches are to be collected and tested for split-disease. Those who are found to be infected are to be quarantined at a location in Mallandina."

"What?" Garth said. "That's preposterous."

"You will come with me," the soldier said, signaling with his hand. Two more soldiers stepped up to assist. One of them put his hand on the hilt of his sword.

"I am certain the edict does not apply to me," Garth said. "I am headed to Mallandina myself, on official business with His Majesty."

"I was given no instruction as to any exceptions."

"Since when do you ever arrest the court wizard?" Garth continued. "And I have no disease. I guarantee that. My word should be enough, and the word of my companions."

Vesper looked down, hoping very much that no one would put her terrible lying to the test, oOr weigh Nim's dislike of Garth against a desire to protect his companions.

"That can be confirmed easily enough," the soldier said. "Use magic on one of your companions. We will see then if you're free of infection or not."

Garth considered. Then he lifted a hand; Vesper felt the crackle of magic being marshaled, as did everyone else. *What's he doing?* Vesper thought, alarmed. Was he actually going to do as the soldier bade? Why was his hand aimed in her direction? She tried to sidle off to the side.

Then the energy dissipated. "I cast a spell on an object in this young lady's bag," Garth said. "A compass. You will find it bears magical properties now."

"Let me see," said the soldier.

Vesper reached into her bag, avoiding a suggestive wiggle from Minimus inside, and she removed the compass. Had Garth done something to it? She could sense no difference. She handed it to the soldier, and he turned it this and that way, watching objects bend out of the way wherever he pointed it. "Interesting," he said. "I'm sorry I doubted your word, Sir Biggens. You may travel on." He passed the compass back.

Nim took the coachman's seat when they continued.

"You lied about the compass!" Vesper said. Somehow, it bothered her watching Garth's charm directed so effectively at another. Could he convince *her* so easily of an untruth?

Garth shrugged and smiled. "Soldiers aren't hired for their intelligence here."

"I doubt that trick will always work," Jules said. "Do you really think it's a good idea for you to go on to Mallandina?"

"The book says I should," Garth replied shortly.

"But what do *you* think? Aside from what the book says?"

"I'm older than you. Don't patronize me," Garth said. "The book's never been wrong before. And I think it's time I returned to Mallandina. This whole quarantine business smells of someone else's power play. It's too subtle to be all Bugger."

"Well, that may be," Jules said. "But I still think you got lucky that time. Not everyone's going to be intimidated by your credentials."

A shade of uncertainty had settled into the lines of Garth's face, and after a moment he stood.

"Aren, get up," he said. Surprised into obedience, Aren moved to the small space between Jules and Vesper. Garth began to pull at the cushion covering his seat. "Some of these are made hollow," he said.

Sure enough, the seat pulled up, revealing a coffin-like space just large enough to hold Garth—although by no means comfortably.

"I'll get in when we see the next checkpoint," he said.

"You don't think they'd search there?" Vesper asked dubiously.

"They're made with magic to put off the casual observer," Garth replied. "It should be safe enough."

So when Nim called down that a checkpoint was coming up, the passengers did a quick shuffle and Garth got in, curled up, the cushion coming back down. Vesper hoped he wouldn't suffocate.

The soldier in charge at the checkpoint asked them to exit the coach, and a quick check with a rock-sensor found no wizards among them. He allowed them back inside, and within minutes they were on the road again. After they could no longer sight the soldiers, the travelers let Garth out.

"Perfect," he said. "We'll simply do that for every checkpoint, and I should arrive with no problems."

But at the next checkpoint, the soldier in charge didn't ask them to come out; he simply opened the door and leaned in with his rock-sensor. He passed it over Aren, went across to Jules—and the crystal grew red.

"Wizard!" the soldier said. He passed the rock over to Vesper's side; it glowed more brightly than ever. "And a witch too!"

Then Vesper realized that she and Jules were sitting on the cushion under which Garth was hiding. The rock sensed him—but how could they admit that?

"Don't try anything," the soldier said. "The two of you—out. Now."

"This is a mistake," Jules said. "We don't do magic. Your rock must be defective." Still, he and Vesper descended from the carriage while Aren gaped and Nim chewed frantically on his lower lip.

"You're allowed to prove you don't have the disease by casting a spell on one of your companions," the soldier said.

"But we don't have magic—so we can't cast any spells!" Vesper cried.

The soldier glowered, pulling his head back on his neck so far he formed a triple chin. "Don't try to pull that one on me," he said. "The rock doesn't lie. If you won't prove your innocence, you'll have to come with me. You two—" he gestured to Nim and Aren—"can go. Witch and wizard, you are both under arrest."

CHAPTER 12

To his credit, Nim protested vigorously as additional soldiers bound Vesper and Jules' wrists behind them with manacles of a blue metal that felt oddly numbing on the skin. "We'll stay and wait for them here," he'd said, "since I know they can't do any magic, and they definitely don't have this disease you're talking about. Don't you think I'd know? I've lived next door to that girl since the day she was born!"

"Wait if you'd like," the soldier had said with a lipless smirk. "But then we'll be forced to arrest you as well, for loitering. But it's your choice."

Vesper hadn't stayed long enough to hear what Nim's decision had been, but doubtless they would leave—they couldn't keep Garth inside that coffin-like seat for much longer. She half-hoped that Minimus might come bursting out to save them, but caught no strains of his piping voice as soldiers escorted her and Jules into a tent and strung a chain through their manacles to attach them to one of the tent poles.

Why hadn't Garth done anything? He'd had to have heard what happened outside the coach—that she and Jules were arrested on his account. But…it would be stupid to think he'd leap out and protest, or offer himself in her place. He wouldn't need to, because once the officials discovered their mistake, she and Jules would be released and allowed to rejoin their party.

"Vesper," Jules whispered. "See if you can reach inside my shirt and get my lock pick."

"Inside your shirt? Where?" She maneuvered herself so her back was to him, fingers against his abdomen.

"You're already close. It's on the inside hem in the front. Tucked into my pants."

Her fingers fumbled with the cloth behind her, and she began to pull on it. The cloth bunched up and snagged, and she tried to wiggle underneath. She found her hand squeezed against a warm, taut stomach that shifted against her skin as he breathed.

Then she became aware of the rest of him standing behind her, his breath against her neck, a tightening in his stance that told her that he, too, was responding to her proximity.

She managed to find the hem of his shirt and yanked out the pick. "Here," she muttered, and he turned to take it from her. When their fingers brushed together, she felt it in her entire body.

"Turn around again. Quickly," he said.

The urgency in his tone startled her, and she turned. "What—"

Her question was stifled as his mouth caught hers.

Their hands were still manacled behind their backs, but Vesper felt as if he were holding her nonetheless—she found herself on tiptoe, leaning into the strong, solid column of him, kissing him back as thoroughly as he was doing with her.

Desire flared up in her. Silly of her to think she couldn't kiss. Of course she could—this was all she had to do, it was so easy, and so good...and she couldn't get enough—if only she could get rid of these stupid manacles—

Then Jules ripped himself away. "Back," he said softly. Vesper was reeling, but she tried to compose herself, and an instant later the soldier who'd arrested them re-entered the tent.

He was followed by a man dressed in the same uniform, but with general's stripes on his sleeves. The uniform of the general barely contained his flesh, but Vesper found more distracting his ear-to-ear mustache and temple-to-temple eyebrows pinned onto an oyster-like face, flat and shiny. He looked Jules and Vesper up and down, and his small, pearl-pale eyes lingered on Vesper.

"General Perrin, these are the two," said the arresting soldier.

"So they are, eh?" said Perrin. "They look guilty to me. You can go, Pion." The soldier saluted and left the tent.

"Guilty of what?" Jules asked.

"Bad things," Perrin said, shaking his head. "Very bad." He took out a pad of paper. "Now, tell me your names, and explain in detail when and how you got infected with the disease."

"But we're not infected," Jules said. "We can't even be, because I'm not a wizard, and she's not a witch."

"Vesper," Perrin wrote on the pad. "Last name?"

"Maven," she replied after a pause.

"And you." He pointed to Jules.

"Jules Biggens. But you need to let us go, because our arrest was a mistake—a misunderstanding. Just use the sensor again and you'll see—neither of us has a drop of magic."

He spoke in a reasonable tone. Everything about him emanated harmlessness; *I'm just an ordinary fellow*, his expression said. Vesper could not quite follow what he was doing, but she began to feel a spark of hope—maybe Jules could talk them out of there.

Perrin harrumphed. He took out a rock-sensor, holding it first in front of Jules, then Vesper. He came closer, tried again. He went behind Vesper and placed the rock directly onto the skin of her exposed palm, then did the same with Jules. Then he glared at them and put the rock into his pocket. "I don't care what the rock says. If my men say you made the rock turn on before, they wouldn't lie about it. So you must have cast some kind of spell for me not to see it now. And I won't let you slither your way out of it, you little snakes."

Jules sighed. "If we were able to cast a spell on the rock, then that would prove that we weren't infected, and you'd have to let us go. Anyhow, you know that this law is only in order to prevent the infection from spreading. It's not because the wizards and witches have done anything wrong. So why are you treating us like criminals? We don't have any reason to hide anything from you."

Perrin narrowed his eyes and began to pace around them, hands and writing pad clasped behind him, his stomach swaying slightly as he moved. "You wizards think you're better than us normal people. Always have," he said. "Think you're above the law. Think you can go around making people's bodies fall apart whenever you feel like it. I'll have you know that *feeling superior* is a crime in itself, even if you don't exercise a whit of your infernal magic—a crime of pride. And it's time you pay for it."

He stopped in front of Jules. "You, I am certifying as infected," he said. "You're to be sent to quarantine where you'll have plenty of time to reflect on the errors of your ways. You," he said, turning to Vesper, his mouth a red oily gash beneath the bristle of his moustache, "I believe I need to test for the infection. Pion!"

The other soldier appeared at the door.

"This wizard is infected. Been so for a long time. He's been going around everywhere spreading the disease out of spite. Needs to be locked up, maybe whipped as well! I'll keep this little lady for testing for the next few hours, and I'll report the results then."

"Yes sir," Pion said, taking Jules by the elbow and yanking him out between the tent flaps. Vesper stared after him. She hadn't even had a chance to say goodbye, let alone a number of other things that had suddenly come up for her in the last ten minutes.

"You—Vesper," said Perrin, lingering over her name. "Come in." He opened the flap leading into the main tent chamber, motioning her inside.

Wary, Vesper entered.

The luxury of the inner chamber struck her as excessive, for the tent of a general. A low bed dominated half of it, and mosquito netting draped from the ceiling had the appearance of a canopy. No sun from outside came into the windowless chamber, but lights burned in glass bulbs, and Vesper had no idea what they were made of—because they weren't fire, but something that glowed as bright as flame nonetheless.

An L-shaped sofa of plush dark fabric dominated the other half of the chamber. "Please, have a seat," Perrin said, indicating the sofa. "Oh—one moment." He came forward and unlocked her manacles. He didn't release her hands right away, but stroked across her palms with sticky hot thumbs until she snatched them out of his grip and crossed her arms in front of her body.

Vesper waited for Perrin to sit first, and then she chose the farthest possible point from him on the sofa. Perrin got up to fetch a small tray from a table that had appeared at the entrance to the room. On the table sat a bowl of glazed nutmeats and plums that had been soaked in some marinade, and a decanter of some golden liquid. He placed the food on the table before the sofa, sitting down next to her, knee almost touching hers. So much for trying to avoid sitting near him… she scooted more to the side until she was almost hanging off the edge.

Perrin poured two glasses of the liquid. "Drink," he said. "Have a snack. It's all perfectly safe. And very expensive quality, I might add. I don't suffer, not with my salary."

"No, thank you," said Vesper. "I'm not thirsty or hungry."

Perrin took his glass and sipped. "Ah, so polite," he said. "You'll be more comfortable if you have a little drink, at least. Please."

Perhaps shel should humor him, Vesper thought; maybe he was just being friendly, and if she cooperated she'd be gone that much sooner. She wet her lips with the liquid. A drop went down her throat; it tasted like fire and perfume. Immediately she felt her muscles loosening, and she became aware just how tensely she'd been holding herself.

"Better, eh?" said Perrin. He edged closer. "I'm going to test you for the split-disease. If you relax, it won't hurt…it may even feel good. Very good." He put his hand on her knee.

She froze for an instant, and then she pushed his hand onto his own knee. "If you believe I've done something to change the results of the rock-sensor test, why wouldn't you think I'd do the same thing with this other test?" She concentrated on looking at his ear, wanting to avoid those pale smoldering eyes, that quivering mustache with the drop of liquor standing just on the left tip.

Perrin chuckled deep in his throat. He took her glass from her and put it down, then moved closer. "Once you experience the test, you and I will know it's the real thing," he said. "It's something not even the most experienced witch could hide from. It's something basic and primal, something that will go deeper than the deepest witchcraft training and reduce you to simply a lush, desirable woman, capable of giving and receiving pleasure."

Vesper tried to breathe shallowly, to avoid the stink of Perrin's armpits and breath. He unbuttoned his uniform, revealing a tight white shirt underneath that accentuated his man-boobs. Now she had no doubts about his intentions.

"Please don't," Vesper said, her voice small. "Can't you just give me a test…a real test, and let me go?"

"All right," said Perrin. "Hungry for it, aren't you? You look so innocent, but you're all sluts underneath those fresh faces and that snotty reserve." He pushed her further down onto the sofa, beginning to drag up her skirts. "Test coming right up," he breathed, unbuttoning his pants, releasing a bulbous erection that waggled like a chastising finger.

"No," Vesper said, twisting, kicking out, but too wildly to connect. "You know I'm not a witch. Get off! Help!"

Perrin slapped her, hard, and she stilled, breathing hard. "You won't leave till we're finished," he said. "Remember, I need to certify that you're disease-free before you can leave here. Or the other alternative is I mark you as teeming with split-disease, and then you'll be put in a barred wagon and sent to the capital, where there is a newly built dungeon waiting for you." He laughed, and bent to cover her lips with his.

This time he made contact. He smelled of urine and sweat, and the slobber from his mouth it was tasted just as bad. After that other kiss she'd just received, that oh-so-lovely meeting of lips that had gone straight into her soul, this one violated her utterly. "Now let me just check you for the disease with my special sensor here..." He giggled, fisting his erection and moving into position.

Then he froze, his face going clammy.

"Let me go!" someone cried in a high voice—but not Vesper's. Perrin sat back; he still held his penis, but now, no longer connected to his body, it struggled in his hand in front of him. He screamed. Just then, the penis gave a mighty lunge and freed itself, flying straight through a rip that was forming along the side of the tent.

Vesper felt that *wrongness* crackling through the rent—but not like that other time, with the men in the tavern. If that had been a pinpointed attack, this was an explosion of that energy—what she now knew to be the split-magic.

Perrin's body began to fall apart. One of his eyes, then the other popped out. His nose and lips came off, then his fingers, one at a time. He tried to run blindly, but then he had no feet. More pieces flew off, all of them shrieking and trying to escape, some colliding in midair, landing on the floor to twitch and crawl. Blood splashed onto Vesper's face and dress, and she turned to avoid a wad of entrails that flew her way. It squelched against her back instead.

Then—Garth came through the rip in the tent.

Grim-faced, he strode to the sofa and grabbed Vesper's hand with one of his, pulling her to her feet. "Let's go," he said, and she gasped where his hands, still tingling with magic, touched her. She had a flash of horrified imagining that her skin might break off under his touch, fly away shrieking and leaving great bloodless chunks missing from her flesh. Then Garth broke the contact. She tried not to look at the torso that writhed on the floor—the remains of Perrin—or at the dagger Garth unsheathed and threw into the heart of those remains. The steaming pile of flesh made no sound.

A horse waited outside. People streamed in every direction, although mostly away, spurred on by multitudes of Perrin's body parts fleeing along with them. "Split-magic," and "infection," and "run!" traveled in shouts and panicked shrieks through the mayhem.

Garth threw Vesper onto the horse and leaped up behind her. Now that they had turned and were running, the soldiers regained some sense of purpose and tried to organize. Shouts and then arrows followed them, horses neighing as soldiers mobilized for pursuit.

A few backward glances, a few more of those electrical-magical surges directed from Garth to the soldiers closest behind, cleared their wake. Still, they rode until their horse was winded, only then slowing to a trot.

The land began to rise and fall in hills of rock and clay, where before it had been flat sand.

"Where are we going?" Vesper asked. She felt it strange to be holding the man she'd thought she wanted, but his waist beneath her fingers felt wrong—and only because of a moment's embrace with someone else.

"First, to get away from those soldiers," Garth said. His voice softened. "Then, to rest a bit, and perhaps to clean up, before we decide what to do next."

"We need to rescue Jules," she said. "He was certified as infected—they're sending him to the quarantine dungeon."

"Jules can take care of himself." Garth's voice had hardened. "He never fails to find a way out of any situation he gets in."

"But he didn't get out of the bandits' den on his own."

"He's got the luck of demons. I'm not even sure he didn't manifest us showing up there, just to get him out. He doesn't need rescuing. Even if, by some minute, nearly impossible chance, he didn't, I might just want to leave him there—the world is better off without a fellow like that taking the law into his own hands. He's a revolutionary, you know, and in the worst sense. He opposes authority for its own sake."

Vesper felt too tired to argue. Jules would have to wait...but she would find out what happened to him...after she got her head together.

One more thought nagged. "Nim and Aren?"

"I told them to go on. That I'd catch up to them at the palace when I found you," he said.

"Then you're thinking we'll go to the palace?" Jules would be in the palace dungeons. Surely she could speak to someone, get him released...

"I'm not sure it's necessary," he said. "After all, the book told you you'd go on a journey, but did you actually see yourself in the capital city? When we stop, we'll consult the book and see. But I'm inclined to stay away—it seems all witches and wizards are being treated as criminals, and I don't want to end up in quarantine. My priority right now is finding a cure for the disease."

Vesper frowned. Although grateful for Garth's rescue, she couldn't help but feel that they shouldn't be riding off to rest, and if Garth wanted to find a cure, this wasn't the place to seek it. But what could she say? He obviously had a place he intended to go, and she felt she had no choice but to stay with him. At one point, that thought would have overjoyed her. So why did she feel such trepidation?

CHAPTER 13

They rode for several more hours, although they traveled slowly. The footing up these hills was unsure and deceptive; in some places the land ascended so steeply that they had to make long circuits round to find a place flat enough to cross. In other places, clay resembled rock and their horse would slip, and several times Vesper thought they might fall. Her own horsemanship couldn't have handled today's ride alone.

Gradually, the foliage thickened to forest. The air grew colder, although the position of the sun said they had a while to go before dusk. "Are we almost there?" Vesper asked, glad of the heat of Garth's back behind her.

"Just a little longer," he said, his breath against her temple.

Vesper realized that she had been holding herself vice-tight for hours, as if gripping something deep in her gut. She tried to relax back into the circle of Garth's arms, but there she felt awkward, and she couldn't stop wondering if he could sense her tension. A little longer, and then what? She was alone with this man, this perfect man—she shouldn't let one desperate kiss with a brief acquaintance spoil this opportunity to get to know him better.

After a while, she found herself dozing, drifting in and out of sleep, a nightmare of Perrin's body falling apart causing her to jerk awake every so often, just to find that Garth's body behind her was a hulk of bloody, faceless meat...and then she would know she still slept—or hoped that she did—and scrabble toward an oblivion that always hovered just beyond her reach.

"Vesper, we're here," Garth said, and she blinked, sitting up. Her entire body felt pummeled, but she so preferred reality to her dreams that she didn't care. She allowed Garth to clasp her about the waist to help her down, and she swayed on her feet, then stopped, captivated.

Vesper gazed at the strangest and loveliest place she had ever seen. They stood in the heart of the forest, beside a round cottage of earth that had been built on the side of a gentle slope. Its roof extended directly from the hill—covered with grass and wildflowers and vines that crept over the roof and wound down around an archway leading inside. Two round holes had been dug out for window-spaces.

"What is this place?" Vesper breathed, walking through the archway, feeling enchanted. Inside, the light streaming through the window revealed a nook that had been dug out to form a sort of shelf for sleeping. In the same way, benches and a table had been formed, a hearth, and shelves in the walls—some of which had pots and pans, cups, and plates, and others which held books and odd objects—carvings of animals, twists of metal forming symbols. The walls bore art of a sort Vesper had never seen—the pictures, although they were of simple subjects such as trees and flowers, were formed of such intricate lines and layers that she felt she might fall into them if she looked long enough. Although a stillness permeated the place as if it had not been inhabited in some time, neither dust nor mold had touched it.

She sighed, and with that sigh she exhaled out tension she'd been holding for hours, and she realized that she felt safe here. The nagging sense that she needed to be somewhere else, looking frantically for a cure, petitioning someone for Jules' release, finding someone to explain the horrible circumstances of General Perrin's death—all of that dissipated.

"It's my retreat," Garth said, and he went inside, crossing to the bench and sitting down. He watched Vesper as she walked past the walls, fingers stretched out—not quite touching, but almost. "When I first showed signs of having magic, my parents petitioned to excuse me from my obligation as a noble's firstborn to serve in the militia. They bade me follow my destined path. I found a teacher, and we lived here in the mountains, and when he died, he left this place to me. He was from Herland—the architecture and art is in that style, and within its walls are built in sacred geometries that ground the place and its inhabitants."

Vesper thought for a moment. "Jules is your younger brother, is he not? So the obligation to serve would next fall to him, wouldn't it?"

Garth's face darkened. "Yes," he said. "And that was where he showed his true colors to me. I knew he'd always been jealous, unable to ever be anything other than second best, but in this regard he showed true selfishness."

"He didn't do the service?" She ran her fingers over the spine of an old book, and she wondered if Garth had read all of these. Her fantasy of sharing books with him, having intellectual discussions and listening to his praise, seemed like a childish dream she'd had a long time ago in the face of what they'd gone through in the past day.

"He did, for two out of the six years that he should have," Garth said, nostrils flaring. "And then he deserted! Refused to do it any longer. It was a disgrace. The obligation actually reverted back to me—even though I was here, busy doing important things. Finally, I was able to avoid it by agreeing to become a wizard for the court."

"So that's why you dislike him?" Vesper looked at Garth, whose anger made him seem not a part of this place of peace. "Did you ask him why he deserted? Maybe he didn't like what he was fighting for."

"It was his duty," snapped Garth. "To our family and to our kingdom. It isn't for him to question the king's policies. Why do you keep wanting to talk about Jules, anyway? Is it him you want to be around, or me?"

Vesper turned so he couldn't see her face, to hide her confusion. She had to admit to herself that just this moment, she didn't want to be here. Something terrible could be happening to Jules—something for which Garth could be blamed—and relaxation or enjoying a retreat in the woods felt impossible. Only she couldn't bring herself to say the words, to criticize him when he'd just rescued her, and when he was finally giving her what she'd wanted from him since the moment she'd met him—a chance to get to know him better.

She didn't feel quite ready for that, either, though. "You said I could clean up. Have you a tub for bathing?"

Garth took a deep breath and exhaled through his teeth, eyes closed. Then he composed himself and looked at her. "I'm sorry," he said. "My brother has always brought out the worst in me. Of course you can bathe. And I have something better than a tub."

He took her elbow and gave it a gentle tug, and she followed him outside. Obscured by weeds at first, stepping stones emerged and wove around the hill until they reached the opposite side of the home in the hill. After descending for a bit, Vesper heard it. "Water," she said, tilting her head to try to catch the sound—not fast, but moving, a pleasant trickle.

"A stream," he said. "Small, but adequate. No mosquitoes. Tastes clean." They walked amidst thickening trees until they came upon a course of water about three times Vesper's height wide, running clear over multicolored rocks.

"I'll leave you to clean up," Garth said. "You don't have to wash your dress. I'll heat water in a cauldron at the cottage and we'll boil it, otherwise I doubt those bloodstains will come out. I'll fetch something else for you to change into. I'll leave it there, on the rock." He pointed to a large one by the stream, which in a short while would be fully warmed by the sun.

Vesper nodded, eyes already mapping a pathway over the rocks.

Garth left and Vesper continued to contemplate the stream, waiting for him to move far enough away to suit her modesty. She berated herself for the thought—of course he wouldn't hang around to snoop. A man like him didn't need to do that; he could see nearly any woman naked for the asking.

Stupid train of thought. Stripping off her dress, she kicked it to the side of the stream and stepped in. A fish darted away from her foot.

The sun had warmed the shallows of the water enough to make it pleasant. She waded to where the water came midway up her thighs, at just the depth that she began to shiver. There, she ducked, gasping at the cold, and thrashed her arms about with vigor if not grace until the water began to feel warm against her skin.

She submerged again, scrubbing her hair, came up for air, and repeated several times. Long after she felt clean, she floated in the water, enjoying the sensation of sun on her breasts and belly as the water caressed her around her back and sides.

After some time, she remembered to look at the rock Garth had pointed out earlier; sure enough, a small pile of clothing lay there, neatly folded and stacked. She felt herself blushing halfway down her torso. When had he come? While she washed her hair, fully submerged, or while she lay on the surface of the water, fully exposed, eyes closed against the sun? She bit her lip and waded to the rock.

He'd left a cloth atop the pile. Stepping onto the bank, shivering, she dried first her hair, then the rest of her body. Then she picked up the rest of the items one at a time.

He had brought smallclothes, and a dark green dress, short-sleeved, with a cord to tie it. She smiled at that, remembering the cord she'd used to try to tie Garth's wrists. Everything fit perfectly. Although she liked the feel of the heavy fabric against her skin, she frowned. Why did Garth have female clothes at his retreat? Just how often did he bring women here? Maybe he had an entire closet hidden in the hill, full of cast-off clothing from an enormous harem.

On the bottom of the pile he'd placed a wide-toothed wooden comb, which made a pleasant weight in her hand. She began to comb her hair, yanking as she tried to work through her confusion as much as her tangles.

Garth was in so many ways the man of her dreams. In looks, he certainly fit her fantasy in every way, and his kissing showed he had skill in the arts of physical love. Intelligent, worldly, and literate, with about the most fascinating occupation Vesper could imagine, she was certain they could enjoy hours of stimulating conversation. That was, if she could ever get over feeling not quite good enough for him. Because something about him made her conscious of her inadequacy, she found it hard to break free of her habitual social awkwardness.

She didn't feel like that around Jules, who never triggered any issues of inferiority or superiority. With Jules, she found it easy to be herself.

She still felt the wonder of that kiss with Jules, the phantom of that pleasure still tingling across her skin at the memory. Maybe the danger they'd been in had distorted her experience—fooled her into thinking the kiss something extraordinary; maybe it would have gotten worse if it had lasted longer. Or maybe Garth's would get better. She sighed. Why did Jules have to come along and spoil everything anyway? She had been so sure that she wanted Garth before. Now… she thought of silken brown hair, of a smile that quirked at the most inappropriate moments, of ridges of abdominal muscle shifting underneath the pads of her fingers. Her senses clamored for the source of those memories, craved that touch and to feel that calm gaze invading her being…*Stop it*, she told herself. She had to focus on the present. She would react the same, or more strongly, if Garth just had another chance to sweep her away.

Her hair had almost dried by the time she finished combing it; she tucked the comb in the towel and began the climb up the hill.

Garth smiled to see her. "It suits you," he said. "Did you know, the book showed me the dress to buy you?"

"What?"

Garth nodded. "That was what I was doing while you were sleeping in the next morning at the inn, and delaying your leaving. I had to go to half a dozen tailors before I found the dress—ready-made, but with time for some customizing."

"I thought it was a cast-off from an old mistress you'd brought here," Vesper blurted.

He turned and looked at her. "You are the only woman I've ever brought here," he said, and she squirmed under the intentness of his gaze.

She felt herself blushing again. Was she going to spend half her time in his company with too much blood in her face? She dared not look down to check, but she had an awful fear that the blush showed on her chest as well.

His smile grew wider. "You look lovely, in either green or red," he said.

"Can you read my thoughts?" she asked, horrified. She'd never thought about just what it meant to be a wizard.

"Right now your facial expression is about as open as if you had words printed on your forehead," he said. He tapped his knuckles under her chin. "Don't worry. I can't read your thoughts. Come and eat."

He'd cooked a pair of fish with mushrooms and some greens. When had he had time to fish? She sat down at the table. When she tasted the fish, she felt a twinge of surprise that he could cook; in fact, she had to resist the urge to close her eyes to savor the tender meat that fell apart at the touch of her tongue. the meal She took a sip of water from the mug he'd provided.

They ate in pleasant silence. Afterward Garth cleared the plates. "Do you want to rest, or shall we look at the book?"

"Rest...you mean together, or by myself?" Suddenly she felt breathless.

He grinned. "Either one."

She became aware of her heart beating, its reverberation suddenly loud in her ears. Her body clenched—*I'm not ready*, it said. "The book," she said, out loud.

Garth inclined his head. He fetched it from the shelf. "Do you want to go first, or shall I?"

"You go first, since I went last time," she said. She exited, grateful for the excuse to be alone. She clambered up a rock, delighted to discover a lovely view of the horizon beyond the mountain. She watched the sky deepening from pink to mauve.

Several moments passed before she heard Garth's step. "Your turn," he said.

"What did it show you?" she asked, taking his outstretched hand and hopping down.

"You look first, and then we'll both share."

He'd left the book on the table. She sat before it, taking a deep breath. Was she going to see more images of herself with Garth? Kissing, or perhaps more? She squared her shoulders. She wouldn't let a book control her actions, but she could still look.

She turned the page, took another inhale at the title page, and exhaled as she turned again.

For a moment she could make no sense at all of the picture. Yellow ocher filled the page, with bits of green here and there, and near a thicker mass of green bloomed an ellipse of dark blue. Then she realized that she was looking at a view of land as seen from high above.

It told her nothing at all.

She turned the page again.

It showed a picture of a pedestal of marble, with a small bronze gargoyle sitting on top. Somewhere indoors—walls of smooth white in shadow, and the gargoyle grinning at her with teeth poised to bite.

She shivered, and turned once more. This time she saw Garth out in stark white daylight, in a strange sort of courtyard with structures of earth and crystal—but he on the ground, bleeding, eyes closed, and pale as she'd never seen him. Unconscious, or dead?

"No," she said. "It can't be!"

She shut the book. Although she felt part disappointment, part relief that no complicated things like kisses appeared in her immediate future as seen by the book, this was far more serious. What did it mean, then? That Garth would die if they went back to the palace? Or if he stayed away from the palace? Or was he dead because he'd not managed to find a cure? She'd hoped to see something that would show her a clear next step, but the book had given her nothing but a few cryptic images and an ominous warning about Garth.

Walking to the archway, she ran straight into Garth, who was just ducking slightly to enter.

His arms folded around her, and without a pause, his mouth descended and met hers. He kissed her, his lips wet and full, tongue flicking out to lick at her still-closed mouth.

She had to warn him, not kiss him! She pushed at him, and his arms fell to his sides. "Garth, we need to talk—I can't do this—you can't! In the book, I saw you dead or dying—"

Garth kissed her on the nose. "Maybe I was just asleep," he said. "Shall I tell you what I saw?"

His eyes shone, and he was smiling, unfazed by her revelation. Vesper calmed, curious despite herself. "What, then?"

He drew her closer until he'd pressed her against the warm breadth of his chest, and she could hear his heart beating. "You and I. Married."

Vesper drew back, confused. For such a long time she'd objected to marriage, so as a knee-jerk reaction, she resisted the idea. But this was *Garth* saying it. "But how could that be?"

He shrugged and smiled, a wry twist of his mouth. "You know, I'm not really sure. I hadn't really thought of marrying someone in Malland before—all this first wife, second wife business and setting up a household with a wife who rules with an iron fist. It's not really my thing. But that's what the book showed me. So I'm open to it."

"Oh," Vesper said. "Oh."

She couldn't think of anything to say, but her mind whirled. Married...to Garth! She couldn't say she hadn't imagined it, because she had, regularly, since the moment she'd met him. But the feeling she had for him seemed to be more based on fantasy than on any real interactions between them. She hardly knew him. Of course, many marriages had far less of a foundation...*I can't believe I'm actually considering it!*

She shook herself. "But what about what I saw?"

"What exactly did you see?" Garth asked, his tone all reasonableness. He pulled her down to sit on his lap.

She closed her eyes, the vision indelible, as if painted on the backs of her lids. "You were bleeding and lying on a gray stone floor outside."

"Well, the book only ever shows things for a reason. And sometimes, it's so you can change the future."

Her brow furrowed. "Then perhaps we won't get married."

"Do you want to?" he asked, his tone uncertain, but his expression unshakably confident of her answer.

She thought of Jules...he did understand her better, and that kiss he'd given her still made her toes tingle. Except as a a member of a cult, little more than a traveling priest, Jules' sort of life didn't include romantic partners. She could see her fantasies of what she'd wanted for herself meshing seamlessly with the trappings of Garth's life. Although they'd never talked about her aspirations to work at court, advising the king on matters of science or philosophy and advancing the cause of women, he'd shown respect for her views, and could be a powerful ally in introducing her to court.

Perhaps more understanding between Garth and her would come in time. She liked his kisses too; she only disliked her awkward reaction to them, and that, too, would certainly shift after a while.

"Yes," she blurted. "I do want it."

Garth's face broke out into such a smile that Vesper felt that her decision must be the right one. His hands cupped the sides of her head and he bent to kiss her again, first her eyes, then her cheeks, and finally, her mouth.

"I ought to give you something, to officially betroth us," he whispered against her lips. "But I think I'd rather just show you how much it means to me, to have your commitment."

He started slow, and she tried to follow his lead. *I'm doing this wrong*—but then he obliterated that thought by doing everything that needed to be done. His lips grew hungry, passionate, and she began to feel consumed, swept up in a maelstrom of desire in which she couldn't tell where hers ended and his began. Her legs collapsed, and he held her up, body and an obvious erection firm against her. He lifted her into his arms as if she weighed no more than a feather and strodeiding the four steps to the bed, which he'd outfitted with several thick blankets. Then he lowered himself onto her, mouth traveling across her collarbone as he slid the dress off her shoulders, then ripped off her chemise with an impatient grunt. His knees separated hers, and she gasped as he licked her nipple; she felt him kicking his trousers off, and then the hairs on his legs were tickling the smooth skin of hers.

One clear thought emerged from the haze of passion. "Garth," she gasped. "I don't want to have a baby—not right now, at least."

Garth paused, looking somewhat pained. "My dear...you needn't worry. I'll take care of you, whatever happens." He covered her mouth with his again, and she felt his cock brushing her inner thigh.

She placed an open palm on his chest, pulling her mouth away, trying to clear up this nagging worry before she jumped back into the storm. "It's important," she said.

He began to plant slow, soft kisses along her temple, gentling his touch, desire banked but not extinguished. "Trust me," he said. "Will you?"

She wanted to. How she ever wanted to! She didn't even know exactly what that meant, though. She supposed he was saying he wouldn't get her pregnant by pulling out before depositing his sperm. She should ask...but his kisses were already becoming more insistent again, his hands touching her more surely, and she was lost...couldn't find a single coherent thought anywhere in the tatters of her brain. Garth moved onto his elbows, and she felt his manhood notching between her thighs, and she gritted her teeth as she felt him easing into her until he'd reached the inner barrier. He pulled back, then surged forward, sudden sharp pain taking her breath away.

A woman screamed. Vesper wondered for a brief instant if that noise had come from herself. Then, Garth looked up, and Vesper saw him turn white.

"Allegra!" he said, pulling out of her as he jerked himself upright.

The broken contact, the sudden absence of connection, hurt her as sharply as the pain she'd just experienced, but in a different part of her anatomy altogether.

Vesper watched as Garth stood, grabbing his pants and pulling them on so fast he stumbled. She could see that he gave no thought to her lying there, so stunned it took her a moment to close her legs and pull a blanket over her bared chest, the streaks of blood on her inner thighs.

"You'll pay dearly for this," the woman said, voice trembling with tears, or rage, or both. Then Vesper saw her standing several steps inside the entrance—a woman with hair like red silk cascading around a face like a flower. She was dangerous—Vesper could feel it, that hum of magic summoned and held at bay. A part of her screamed a warning to move, but her dazed body refused to obey.

"I told you never to come here. This is my private sanctuary," Garth muttered, and within a few strides, disregarding whatever spell she was about to let loose, he'd taken Allegra by the arm and propelled her outside.

Vesper got up slowly; she found she was shaking. She pulled on her dress, wincing as it touched skin still sensitive, still buzzing with the ghost of Garth's touch. She found she didn't want to go outside. She would wait for the woman to leave, and then she'd hear Garth's explanation—doubtless Allegra was some jealous old flame of his, stalking him. Doubtless, she assured herself—except she knew she lied to herself.

Closer to the cave opening, Vesper could hear raised voices outside—Garth and Allegra were arguing about something. Sidling closer, craning her neck to hear, she just peeked out her head—

And shrieked, as Allegra bore down on her, red hair flying, angry face practically right in Vesper's. Vesper took a step back and Allegra filled the entrance, her petite body haloed by the outside light and looming far larger than it ought to be possible.

"I suppose I should feel sorry for you," Allegra spat. "But right now I hate you too much. I just wanted to let you know that we are leaving, Garth and I, back to my father's house. He's attending the horses as we speak. I suppose you have a way to get home yourself, but if not, I don't really care."

Allegra turned to leave.

"Leaving? But—we're engaged." She shouldn't admit that, Vesper thought—she shouldn't say anything to anger this woman...but this woman was taking her fiancé from her!

Allegra twisted to face Vesper, and her lips curled in a sneer. Vesper took a step back despite herself. "Engaged? Oh, yes. I forgot that your country has that barbaric custom in which men can marry more than one woman. Well, in *my* country it's not legal. And as his one and only wife, I won't allow him to have you, too."

Vesper flinched as if she'd been struck. It couldn't be true! "You're lying," Vesper blurted.

Allegra smiled. "Why do you think he jumped off of you so quickly when he saw me? And is perfectly willing to leave you here to come with me?"

"You've bewitched him somehow. There's no other way he'd just pick up and leave like this." Vesper could hear how naïve she sounded. She barely knew Garth—how could she know what he would and wouldn't do? Or how many wives he felt entitled to marry?

Green eyes fixed on her, and suddenly she couldn't move or breathe—her throat had swollen into something so hard and huge that it blocked the entry of air altogether. She felt her skin burning, but only on the surface; everything inside was rigidifying into frozen cold.

Then Allegra sniffed and tossed her hair, and the moment passed. Vesper bent over, coughing, as heat regulated itself in her face and throat, and air rushed back into her lungs.

"That's for calling me a liar, *liar*," Allegra said, voice now honeyed and warm. "And of course Garth would leave with me. He loves me. When he realized that I came for him, he could barely remember your name, let alone spare you a thought. He's all impatient to go back with me to Herland where we'll make love all night long, to make up for all our months apart."

Herland, Vesper repeated to herself, bewildered. He was going to Herland. Then, with dawning horror, she recalled the image of the courtyard where she'd seen Garth dead in the book—earth and crystal…patterns similar to the ones in this very retreat. She felt certain that that courtyard was located in Herland.

"Wait," she said, struggling to straighten as Allegra turned to leave. "I don't think Garth should go to Herland. He's to die there, or to be hurt badly—*The Book of Offhand Truths* said so—"

"Oh, did it?" Allegra said. She went to the table and picked up the book that lay there. "You mean this thing?" She ripped it in half and threw both pieces into the dying fire; Vesper uttered an inarticulate cry and sprang for them. Before Vesper could reach them, Allegra pointed; a tendril of magic crackled and the fire exploded to life. Vesper still made a grab for the book, pulling a piece of it out, stomping on the flames. Unfortunately the effects of Allegra's magic lingered, slowing her, and the blackened pages crumbled to ash beneath her bare feet.

Allegra watched her, scorn etched in the narrow lines of her face. "I've done you a favor. That book is full of utter nonsense. He used it to get me in bed, too. Garth is a wizard, remember—so it will show whatever he wants you to see. And he can use it to pretend he saw all sorts of things about you—did he see you kissing, naked? Did he see that dress you're wearing before he found it in a tailor's shop, ready-made? How convenient that it's actually one of my dresses that I left here when I lived here with Garth."

Vesper's head swam. What was this hateful woman saying? That everything Garth had said to her was a lie? It couldn't be. He was… they'd just nearly.... "I need to talk to him," she said.

Allegra shrugged. "He's a free man," she said. "Despite his being my husband. And he continues to prove his freedom every single day." She stomped out, and Vesper hurried to follow her.

Garth stood outside—he'd been waiting for her, she realized, the constriction around her heart easing just a little. He glared at Allegra as she swept by him, but when he turned back to Vesper, his expression shifted back to the charming, and now loving, Garth she knew.

"I'm so sorry," he said, gathering her to him, embracing her so tightly she almost couldn't breathe. She had an uncomfortable recollection of what Allegra had done to her inside the cave, and pushed him a little until his grip relented.

"Why are you sorry? You mean you're going with her?" Vesper asked, trying to keep the hurt from her voice.

"Allegra's informed me that King Bugger has ordered all wizards and witches to be imprisoned. I can't go to Mallandina and I think it's too dangerous for me to stay anywhere in Malland. I had thought I could find a cure here...but Allegra's right. Herland's wizards are uninfected and they will certainly cure me. It's also the best place from which to pressure King Bugger to behave—he's only ever held in check by Herland's magic, and it's time they start exerting their authority.

"You'll be safe without me to trigger the rock-sensors—best you get back to the palace and rejoin your sister and Nim. I will come for you as soon as I can."

"Oh," she said. "But...how will I reach you? How do I leave this place?" The questions she really wanted to ask remained glued to her tongue. "Are you really married to her?" she managed, in a whisper.

Garth snorted. "She told you that, did she? Well, I was. But in her country, even though men are not allowed to marry more than one wife, marriages only bind a couple for a space of two years. After that, they can choose to renew their vows, or not. Our two years are up in a couple of months. So, I'm basically a single man.

"You and I, we're destined to be together." His burning eyes met hers. "Remember that. We just need to do what we need to do, and bide our time. As for leaving—just keep going north. You'll run into a caravan or cart heading for the capital. You can easily pick up a ride. You're a resourceful girl—one of the reasons why I like you." He kissed her then, a hard, perfunctory pressure that released as quickly as it began.

Allegra, already mounted, had turned, her head held high as if she couldn't care less what they said behind her—but she cared enough to remain so close that she could hear all. With one vicious kick, her mount surged onto the path. Garth glanced toward the redhead, and then back at Vesper, apology in the hunched line of his body as he strode to his own mount. "Be safe, my love."

Vesper clenched her fists, not sure whether she fumed or grieved.

She watched as Garth turned and disappeared down the hill. How much of what Allegra said about him was true?

CHAPTER 14

The earthen cottage no longer calmed Vesper. She stood inside, leaning against the door, with *what do I do now?* echoing through her mind in a broken loop. As evening turned to night, she sat in front of the fire, eating bits of leftover fish, not because she was hungry but because she was numb.

Most of what Garth had said made sense. Of course he ought to go to Herland, if that was the place that could best cure him and safeguard him from the king's actions. The part that bothered her was his not telling her he was already married. He'd said the marriage was going to end...but Allegra didn't seem to think so. Allegra had also implied that Garth had a habit of doing this sort of thing—that he'd actually applied some kind of a tried-and-true seduction method on her. Vesper couldn't help but believe the woman at least a little, since in her brief acquaintance with Garth she had observed his consummate skill as a flirt. Except he'd also seemed so earnest in his affection and his intention...he'd kissed her in front of Allegra, there at the end...

Thinking about it made her head hurt, which bothered her almost as much as the ache in her chest.

Her eyes fell on a scrap of paper that had survived the burning, her heart beating a little faster as she realized that it was a piece of the book. This particular page had a bit of an illustration on it: something mottled red-orange in color...a mushroom of some sort. It grew in the sparse shade of a yellow grass plant.

When she tried to pick up the scrap of paper, the last of the book crumbled in her hands.

Allegra had claimed that the book was full of nonsense—just saying what Garth wanted it to say. If this were true, why would Garth want it to show a picture of mushrooms? Perhaps the book told the truth after all—or perhaps only sometimes? Although she could never know the answer to that question, one thing for sure was that it had given her a message. Could it be trying to give her the cure for the disease? If so, why couldn't it have just told her where to find it?

In the meantime, she would continued her journey to the palace. Jules...she could hardly bear to think of him now, not with Garth still practically imprinted in her flesh, but she still had to find him and free him, if necessary. She should put Garth from her mind—he'd said they were destined, anyway, so it shouldn't matter what she did, as regardless they would meet again.

She tried not to think about the image *she* had seen of Garth's ending.

She had nothing to stay for here—the sight of the walls and the bed, which previously filled her with such contentment, now only made her aware of her isolation, and that she had been abandoned before the culmination of something that she'd longed for.

Best to stop thinking about him and to leave as fast as possible. She would do so directly at dawn. Pulling the blankets off the bed, she made herself comfortable in front of the fire and fell asleep for a few fitful hours.

She woke before the sun rose, just when the sky began to lighten. After filling a water skin and packing a sack full of whatever bits of food she could find, some spare clothes, a rope, a dagger, and a blanket, she left the cottage and began to walk.

Fortunately for her awful sense of direction, she could clearly see the path down the hill. She remembered the precarious surface and the rocks, but only from the vantage point of being mounted, so it took her much longer than she anticipated making her way down.

Soon she could see that Garth had been wrong about how easy it would be to get a ride to the capital. After she got to the road, a few caravans and riders did go by, but all of them were coming from the capital, not going toward it. "You're crazy to go there," a rider told Vesper when she told him where she was headed. "It's pure chaos. The closer you get, the worse it is. Weird stuff flying around everywhere. It seems to be attracted to the city, for some reason."

Enough of those riding in the opposite direction gave Vesper something to eat, or a drink of water, so she only needed to forage very little. However, no one gave her a ride, so she walked and she sleptep on the side of the road at night. When she walked, she wished she'd brought less, but at night she would have given much to have another blanket. She was able to build a fire, but it took so much effort that she usually just went without.

Then she started to understand what the rider had warned her about. Every couple of hours she would see a body part flying or running by—knees or balled fists cartwheeling by like tumbleweeds, butt cheeks slithering across the dust, tongues dripping drool as they leapt from one scenic protuberance to another. They all painted, through the sky and in dry prints or broken brush, an obvious path to the royal city.

Most of the body parts ignored her, so Vesper returned the favor. She did wonder at their single-minded silence, their arrowing toward some goal, because she had thought them aimless creatures who talked too much and made little sense.

Then, two mornings after she'd started her journey, a punch to the side of her head woke her up.

"Ow!" she cried. "Stop it!" She rolled to her feet in time to avoid a swing that would have rammed her full in the face.

The fist swung at her again. It literally was just a fist on an arm, cut off just past the bicep, and it was trying to beat her up.

It had considerable force behind its punches, being a beefy man's arm, muscles flexing in its forearm and a wealth of dark hair covering it from knuckles to elbow. Still, without the weight of a body behind that arm, the blows lacked force; Vesper managed to avoid getting knocked out. Then the fist grabbed her by the throat.

She struggled, gasping, raking her nails across the arm. Her fingers tangled in the arm hairs and yanked; the arm grunted in pain, its hold loosening slightly. It gave Vesper just enough of an edge to roll on top of it and, with a spark of intuition, jam her elbow into a spot in the crook of it that Neela had taught her was a pressure point for releasing stuck emotion.

The arm spasmed and let go. Vesper dove for her dagger, which she'd kept under the sack for easy reach during the night. In a flash she was holding the point of the dagger against the arm's wrist.

"Don't hurt me," the arm grunted, its voice low and slurred, almost unintelligible.

"You want me to let you go, so you can try killing me again?"

The arm turned its fist back and forth, as if shaking a head it didn't have. "Won't try killing you. Didn't want to kill you...I just was flying along, and I saw you there sleeping so peaceful, and it made me mad so I hit you. Ow!" Vesper had pressed the dagger in a little bit, and a drop of blood appeared beneath the dagger point.

"Why would seeing me make you mad?"

The arm's voice grew slow and mournful. "My wife cheated on me," it said. "She ran away with a wimp of a fellow. An artist. I found them and I...I killed them. Beat them to a bloody pulp. I've been in prison since then. When I saw you, I thought you were her again, here to haunt me. To tell me I didn't deserve to be free. Thought I'd have to kill you again."

Repulsed, Vesper resisted the urge to pull away. Firming her grip on the dagger, she wondered if she would have to kill the arm after all. "Your—person whom you belong to—is still in prison?"

"Escaped," was the reply, "since the magic in the fences is all funny now. It used to zap us good when we tried to get out. Now it just makes pieces of our bodies split off, but we can get out."

"And you're going where now?"

"Dunno. Thataway—I want to go thataway. Something good over there." The arm motioned vaguely in the direction of Mallandina.

"Is someone…calling you there, do you think?" Vesper asked.

"Dunno," it repeated, and she could get no more from it.

All those parts flying in one direction couldn't be a coincidence. Was someone doing something to attract them there? A witch or wizard? Someone conspiring against Malland?

Glancing up in the sky, she had a sudden recollection of the page in the book that had shown her the view of the land from up above. She had an idea then—crazy, perhaps, and certainly not safe—but it snapped her out of the lassitude of days of wandering, and she felt determined to do it.

"I won't kill you," she said, and she felt the tiniest easing of tension in the arm. "But you'll have to do me a favor. I'd like to get a ride from you. Any funny business, I'll cut your wrist. If you drop me, I'll take you down with me. But bring me safely there, and you'll live."

The arm remained silent for a long moment. "I know you're not my wife," it said. "I did a wrong thing, trying to hurt you. I promise I'll do better: bring you safely there."

Vesper slung her sack over her shoulder, clasped the arm's hand in both of hers, shook it to seal the bargain, and took as firm a hold as she could manage. The arm rose into the air. They flew fairly low and didn't go very quickly, but after a few minutes Vesper knew she couldn't maintain the grasp for long. "We have to come down," she said, and the arm descended, depositing Vesper gently onto her feet.

"We'll have to take a lot of breaks, or I won't be able to hang like that," she said, despairing. It would be far more dangerous than walking, and maybe it would save no time at all.

"Or you could rig something to sit on," said the arm. "I could carry that just as easily."

She looked at the arm, wishing it had a face to read. Did it wait with an unnatural sort of stillness—an anticipation? Or was her imagination being overactive? The thing truly seemed solicitous now, with no more attempts at escape. If she could trust it, its suggestion would certainly save her a lot of time and agony.

She took out her rope, studying it for a moment. Then she made various knots, loops for her legs, and came up with a contraption somewhat like a swing, but securing her legs.

"That'll work," the arm said, approving. Vesper knotted the rope around the arm, winding it around several times and knotting again. If the arm tried to drop her, it would take some effort, and Vesper might just have enough warning—to what? Scream before she plummeted to her death? She didn't know, but she had committed to it and would see it through.

They ascended again. The sling-swing chafed, and she tried not to squirm. It would bear her in safety if she could stand the discomfort. The arm ascended higher than before, to twice the height of the trees—and it sped up.

In any other circumstances Vesper might have enjoyed the scenery. They were passing over Malland faster than most people would ever see it; wooded grasslands turned to plains, and then to unbroken fields. They skirted along the edges of a village, and more than once Vesper had to speak sharply to the arm when it slowed at the sight of a young woman doing the laundry or tending sheep. They continued to fly.

They had been flying for a good two hours when they reached the edge of another town. This one was larger than the last. Vesper tried to calculate distances in her head; after a while, she gave up, but she thought that perhaps they were nearing Mallandina—they could be just a town or two away, given that they'd been only a town away where Vesper had been arrested, and traveling this way was much faster.

Then the arm slowed down and began to descend.

A young woman walked away from a farmhouse holding a young man's hand. They basked in their love for each other, oblivious even to a rut in their path as they stumbled and fell against each other, laughing. The man picked a flower and handed it to the woman.

Vesper could feel the tension in the arm transmitting through her sling. "Arm, it's not your wife," she said. "That man isn't the one your wife left with. Stop looking. Let's go on."

"She left me for a man like that," growled the arm. "A wimp. An artist."

"He's a farmer!" Vesper cried. "He doesn't look like an artist at all."

"You can just shut up," the arm said. "I'm sick of you and your managing and nagging. Thinking about him reading you stinking poems and giving you roses while you look down your nose at me. A man's driven to drink by a woman like you!"

Vesper caught her breath. He wasn't talking to her anymore; he continued to rant, some angry speech he'd given a long time past, to another woman. "Let me down, arm," she said, keeping her voice even, calm.

"Sure, I'll let you down," he said, and then he laughed, a terrible manic sound that ripped out of a memory of lungs. The arm plummeted straight down into a tree. Vesper screamed as the branches ripped her skirt, scratched her legs. The arm shot back up, and then flew higher and faster. Vesper struggled to free her legs from the loops—although she could see nowhere to jump that wouldn't break several bones, if not kill her.

Then she saw it—they were approaching a small pond. A hedge of nasty brambles stood on its opposite side. They would shred her skin to bits, and she could bleed to death just hanging here.

She lifted her dagger and slashed at the rope loop around her right thigh. It came free, but now she dangled dangerously and off balance.

"No you don't!" screamed the arm, and he descended, straight toward the hedge.

She had no time to free her other leg, not the way she was hanging. She only had a few seconds until they were over the pond and into the brambles—so she allowed herself to fall out of the loop, slipping her foot in and standing up, where she could just reach the arm and slash.

Blood spurted, and they fell, splashing into the pond just shy of the brambles. Vesper gasped and flailed, kicking to free her foot of the rope. She felt the deadweight of the arm as the rope slid from her foot, and as she swam to the non-brambled edge of the pond, it wriggled after her, fingers reaching—but then it slowed and came to a motionless float, slack, pale, and thoroughly dead.

As she pulled herself out of the pond, she nearly put her hand straight into a patch of yellow grass that clung to the exposed roots of a tree.

She knew that this was the grass she'd seen on that one burned leaf of *The Book of Offhand Truths*.

From her forays for Neela and her own personal study, she knew all the species of grasses that Malland grew, by description if not by sight; this particular strain seemed to fit the description of a rare and poisonous mycorrhizal plant, thought to live only in partnership with even rarer species of fungi.

Hands trembling, she sat up and emptied her sack of water, seeing what she could salvage from the sodden mess inside. She wrung out a cloth and laid it to the side of the roots, and then she used her dagger to start scraping the grass off.

Sure enough, mottled red-orange mushrooms lay nestled among the yellow fronds.

The grass burned her fingers wherever it touched her skin, and angry fluid-filled blisters formed almost immediately. Her hands would be unusable if she tried to separate the mushrooms out, so she simply took the grass along with them, removing everything onto the cloth, then wrapping it and securing it with a bit of rope. Although she wouldn't have passed a specimen-collecting test this way, it would have to do.

The outskirts of a town took shape around her—shacks and small farms arose next to manicured fields and a semblance of a dirt road. Fortunately, no one witnessed her walking around in a damp dress, cursing as she tried to air out things in her bag. After she gave it up for useless, she stopped and fashioned a makeshift belt with the rope, tying the water-skin to her side with a loop for the dagger in its sheath. The slim package of mushrooms she tucked inside the top of her dress, along with her trusty compass. The sack, she tossed into a bush.

A body part whizzing by confirmed the direction she needed to go.

By the time her dress dried, she'd found the road. She guessed that she still had a ways to walk, but she felt encouraged at how much ground she'd covered in such a short time—even at the cost of the additional trauma.

As evening fell, farms gave way to inns and more modern houses. She must be in Mallandina now. A question to an old woman sitting on a rocker outside her house confirmed this. The woman had looked askance at Vesper's odd clothing, with several chunks missing in the skirt, and ragged gashes showing legs striped with scabs. Still, the woman answered readily enough.

As dusk turned to evening, Vesper entered the true city. Coaches rattled through cobbled streets, horses shuffled past, and enough pedestrians wandered about that Vesper felt safe enough. She did notice that, in line with the increasing amount of missing body parts she'd seen in the towns before, many people—perhaps a good twenty percent here, which meant more, as many parts simply weren't visible—wore prosthetic parts or simply went without an ear or a hand or a lip. No one seemed to think it strange. In fact, some people had decorated their prostheses to make the difference more visible—noses gilded with silver and encrusted with gemstones for the rich, eyebrows or hands replaced by flowers or ferns for the poor.

Parts continued to fly by her. They arrowed toward the highest buildings in the city, towers of gray and white stone: the palace.

When she reached the gates, black iron under a great stone archway, she found them barred closed. She peered through the bars. Torches burned beside the walkway leading to the palace, and she saw lights and music coming from inside.

A guard dressed in black, with red stripes across his shoulders and the hems of his uniform, stood and looked at Vesper through the bars, frowning. She saw then that he wasn't alone; another guard sat to the other side of the gate, but he was busy eating a sausage stuffed in a roll. Vesper's stomach growled.

"No entry to the public," the first guard said.

"But my party's in there," she said. "I got arrested—improperly—and separated from my companions a few days ago. I'm—the assistant to the official shoemaker for the king." It sounded even more stupid than she felt for saying it, and she felt grateful for the darkness that covered her blush as both guards broke into laughter.

"It's such a dumb excuse I almost believe her," said the guard eating the sausage, voice muffled by meat and bread.

"Listen," said the first guard. "You look like a nice girl. But hardly a night passes we don't get one of you coming here on some pretext, trying to slip into the festivities here to snag yourself a prince. But I gotta tell you—the prince isn't looking right now. So unless you've got a hankering to be Wife Number One Hundred of our great king, you wouldn't even have a chance to get what you want, even if we let you inside. Especially when you haven't even bothered to comb your hair."

Vesper thought of the wooden comb by the stream, pain battling with frustration. "I have no interest in snagging anyone," she said. "I do need to talk to the king though—I—I might have a cure for the split-disease."

The guards laughed again. "That's an even better one! Does it have to do with getting naked?"

Vesper bit her lip. She wanted to ask about Minimus, who would certainly vouch for her—but had he even made it back to the prince? After a moment of being unable to phrase any question about the penis that wouldn't make her sound even crazier, she decided she couldn't. "Is the public ever allowed inside the gates?" she finally asked.

"Petitioners in the morning, line up at dawn, doors close at noon," he said. "First come, first served."

"Then I'll wait here, and be first in line."

"No loitering." His mouth firmed into an uncompromising line.

The other guard, finishing his meal, cast a sympathetic glance at Vesper. "Here, girlie. Go buy yourself a drink, on us. Get a good night's sleep and come back in the morning." He threw her a copper.

Vesper caught it, but she still stood there, thinking. She could try to leave a message—but she didn't even have a place she could be contacted, if Aren or Nim received it. No, the best thing would be to come back at dawn as the guards suggested.

At least she had a copper now. It wouldn't go far—but perhaps she could get something to eat, and warm herself as the night got colder. She wandered through the streets until she found a tavern that looked clean and not too seedy, and went inside.

Soon she was sitting in front of a fire, eating a bowl of soup. It cost more than a copper, but the barmaid had taken pity on her. The tavern wouldn't be open all night long, so she'd have to sleep on the street, but at least she could put off worrying for another couple of hours. So she enjoyed her soup, and afterward nursed a mug of mulled wine—also courtesy of the barmaid—and she tried to organize her thoughts.

She could do so easily, because her thoughts had only two themes: Garth. And Jules.

Garth, because she could still feel him, his lips and his hands branding her skin, her body printed with bruises that went deeper than physical. Because she couldn't forget the image of him lying pale in the Herland courtyard, and now he seemed fragile to her—diseased and possibly on the edge of death.

And Jules, who'd just escaped one cage to be thrown into a dungeon. How she wanted to talk to him now! About what, she didn't know...since they hadn't actually had many successful conversations in real life. Within their brief interactions, he'd just startled her time and time again by saying something that made her feel as if he understood her. She also couldn't forget that kiss...

Being understood and being wanted were so new to her. She'd wanted both her whole life; why was it that experiencing them both had to confuse her so?

"Ale," someone cried. "A round of ale for all the soldiers outside. We've got us another ten wizards in the wagon. Got to fortify ourselves against those wily bastards—the night's far from over."

Vesper froze at the familiarity of that voice. She let her hair fall over the side of her face as she turned to look.

She recognized Pion, the soldier who'd been working for Perrin. Ten wizards—she wondered if the soldiers had actually found real wizards or just more unfortunate people who'd offended the soldiers at the checkpoints.

Men filled the tavern when it had been nearly empty moments before. Lone female travelers were uncommon enough that she was certain to attract attention, and Pion was one of the last people whom she wanted to encounter. Was he looking in her direction already? Cold prickling her spine, she stood and made for the door. Almost there...

three more steps...two...

An arm snaked around her, holding her arms pinned, her back against a hard chest. She felt manacles that numbed her skin tighten around one wrist, then the other. "Going somewhere, young lady?"

At least I won't have to worry about finding a place to sleep, she thought, as Pion dragged her outside.

CHAPTER 15

Outside the tavern, Pion patted Vesper down, swiftly discovering her sheathed dagger and confiscating it. He took her water-skin as well, but he missed the mushroom-packet; she breathed a sigh of relief and resisted the urge to look down to confirm its presence. Perrin would have found it.

"After what you did to General Perrin, you're going to pay," Pion hissed. "No doubt he thought you too innocent to kill, so he freed you from the chains that hamper your magic. I will make no such mistake."

He dragged Vesper toward a closed iron wagon, four horses standing hobbled before it. The door of the wagon opened in halves; Pion opened only the bottom half and shoved Vesper inside. Someone grunted as she tripped over a pair of legs and crashed into someone standing, who shoved her aside with a curse. The door slammed shut.

Vesper could see nothing in the pitch darkness inside. With one sense compromised, the smell and heat from unwashed people overwhelmed her all the more. The top of the wagon bore some air holes, each so tiny it looked as if little more than a finger could fit through. Vesper struggled to her feet—with her arms behind her she could barely find her balance—and finally found a free space to stand, but then she stepped on someone's hand.

"Ouch!" he said.

"Sorry," she said. She backed up and bumped into someone else.

"Watch it!"

She heard others scuffling, and it seemed someone was moving through the mass of people toward her. Lots of *ows* and *heys* could be heard—then someone had her by the arms, tugging her to a corner.

"The corner's not for newcomers!" a nasal voice complained. "Newcomers have to sit in the middle."

"I've been here longer than anyone, so I've got a right to my corner—and I'm taking the newcomer with me," said the person who had her by the arm.

"Jules," she gasped, and then his arms folded around her. Suddenly she didn't mind the heat and stuffiness so much; at least for a moment, everything was all right.

She thought he was going to kiss her, but then she felt his hands at her wrists. He was picking the lock on her manacles. Within a moment she heard a clicking sound, and they opened; Jules took them and put them somewhere.

He ran his thumb over her wrist. The touch soothed the soreness, brought it back to life from the numbness, but that wasn't all it was doing; Vesper felt a slow uncurling of arousal beginning in her belly. "Glad you're alive," Jules said. "I was pretty sure you wouldn't be released. I don't have any of my powder left, so I haven't been able to escape. I'm glad I didn't now. What happened after we separated?"

"I—Garth rescued me," she blurted. They kept their voices soft; unnatural quietness surrounded them as curiosity from the others in the wagon felt almost palpable in the hot darkness. "He took me to some place in the hills. Then—some woman came and took him to Herland—to cure him, she said—and I had to travel back by myself."

Jules' hand stiffened almost imperceptibly, and with it, she felt a distancing from him. Or was she imagining things?

The hand fell, as if by accident, and Vesper felt as if her lifeline in this dark stuffy place had suddenly been withdrawn. "Garth took you to his retreat," he said, only a hint of a question in his tone. She knew then that she wasn't imagining it—she'd offended him by having been with Garth.

She wanted to protest that all because she and Jules had shared a brief kiss, it created no ties or promises to be violated—but then again, he wasn't obligated to be warm or kind toward her either. She stood there in silence, unable to deny his question, part of her wishing she could undo what she'd done, but only because it was hurting so many people—Allegra, and Jules...Nim, no doubt...and herself.

The wagon lurched as someone climbed on top of it, and more men jumped on and clung to the sides; the murmur of prisoners talking died down as horses neighed and the wagon began to move.

A lurch of the wagon sent Jules careening against Vesper. He pulled himself away, but his hands remained flattened against the wall to either side of her head. She could feel his breath on her forehead. She shivered and half-wished he'd careen against her again.

"I'm sorry," he said, and now that the wheels were crunching on stone road and the horses' hooves clopping, they had some measure of privacy. "I don't know why I'm acting like this. I know you don't owe me anything."

Vesper stayed silent for a long moment. No, she didn't owe him anything…but she couldn't help but feel that she wanted to give him something. A reassurance, perhaps…or maybe another kiss. Rather than listen to that treacherous inner voice, which wanted something that was bound to end in heartache, though, she changed the subject. "They're taking us to the quarantine dungeon," she said. "What can we do?"

"Short of looking for more flying mouths to bribe? Not much. Even the real wizards and witches in here can't do magic, since they've all got the disease *and* this wagon's been built with that magic-blocking metal even if they could do more than just make people's body parts fall off."

Vesper reached into the top of her dress and touched the cloth that contained the mushrooms and grass. She had never tested the mushrooms; they could be as poisonous as the grass, for all she knew, or they could be harmless but ineffective against the disease.

Should she suggest that she had something that might help, or would it be a mistake—perhaps a fatal one?

"Jules, I need to tell you something. I found something on the way here. Something I believe might be a cure for the disease. I saw a picture of it in Garth's book, and then I found it...so I'm not sure, but I rather think it is."

She felt him lean closer. "What is it?"

"A mushroom," she said. "But I had to harvest it with a bunch of grass that I know is very poisonous, so I don't know how I could separate the mushroom out in the dark to give it to people to try."

"Give it to me," Jules said.

"I told you I can't separate them—"

"All of it," he said.

Vesper took out the cloth and handed it to him. She couldn't see what he was doing, but after a few minutes he handed her the wrapped package again.

She had no time to ask him what he thought, or say anything at all, because the wagon ground to a halt.

The bottom half of the wagon door creaked open. Vesper blinked; even the night appeared bright compared to the darkness inside the wagon. "Come out, one at a time," someone yelled from outside. "Move one hair the wrong way, and you'll get a special treat, made just for impudent wizards and witches."

The prisoners began to emerge. At one point, Vesper heard the sound of someone grunting, as if he'd been punched in the belly. Footsteps slapped pavement, running away—then the steps halted as a man screamed, and to the accompaniment of a horrible buzzing noise, he screamed again.

When Vesper's turn came and she shimmied out of the hole, she saw what had been a man on the ground—face contorted in agony, eyes rolled up to show only a sliver of pupils. Dead. He must have tried to escape. Eight guards ranged around the wagon; four of them handled the manacled wizards who'd already exited the wagon, now strung together by a chain. That left four attending the prisoners still in the wagon. One of them took hold of Vesper's arm, lifting the chain to wind through the edge of her manacles. His brow wrinkled in confusion as he stared at her empty wrist.

Casting a panicked glance behind her, she found her gaze arrested.

Jules emerged from the wagon, sliding out in a smooth athletic move, a frighteningly blank look on his face as he uncoiled, arm flying out and throwing something that flashed bluish-black in the air at the head of one guard—her manacles, Vesper realized—and flicking something else into the eyes of another. As the first guard recovered and opened his mouth to yell, another flick and the man went down, body going into convulsions. The men clawed at their own eyes and screamed.

Jules threw an arm around the neck of one of the screaming men, twisted his head with an awful snap, and grabbed something that fell from the man's hand—a long baton of metallic blue.

"He's got the wand!"

"Call for reinforcements!"

"Don't leave those prisoners! Secure the wagon!"

Before Vesper had time to speculate about the wand's purpose, Jules had pressed something on its base and swung it to connect with a guard's sword. A buzzing noise burst from the wand, and the guard shrieked and dropped his sword, then fell to the ground. Vesper smelled burned flesh.

Other guards had drawn their swords, but they were backing away from Jules. He grabbed Vesper's hand then and pulled. The chain clanked as it fell out of her manacle.

They ran.

CHAPTER 16

Even a person with a better sense of direction than Vesper would have had trouble remembering which way Jules led her. They took a bewildering set of turns, running down small streets, over fences and even through someone's house, until they ended up in a part of town where the streets were engulfed by rickety structures and the smell of trash and sewage. Women in tight-bodiced dresses shivered on the corners or leaned out of windows as Jules and Vesper passed, auras of sweat and stale perfume repelling as much as their hands beckoned. Men fell into step beside or behind the fleeing pair every so often, remaining until Jules flashed the blue-metal baton or even a bit of that blank look he still wore. Either would be enough to trigger the men's disappearance into the shadows as quickly as they'd appeared.

It seemed that, for now, Vesper and Jules had lost their pursuers—if any of the guards had even thought to pursue. Jules had been intimidating enough without that baton; with it, he radiated invincibility. As if he could feel Vesper's eyes on the baton, Jules glanced at her, a hint of his usual mellow calm surfacing in his expression, and then he tucked the baton away in the waistband of his trousers—where it couldn't possibly be comfortable, but Vesper could pretend, a moment here and there, that she hadn't seen what he could do with it.

Finally Jules knocked on the door of a building on a narrow street. Vesper felt the crawling sensation on the back of her neck that told her someone observed them; she glanced above, where darkened window-spaces obscured all within. Then the door opened, and a squat man with a clipped gray beard, dressed in the most shapeless, unattractive gray top and trousers Vesper had ever seen, stepped aside for them to enter.

"Burl," Jules said, nodding to the man, who closed and bolted the door.

"Jules," Burl replied. He pinned Vesper with a gaze that felt almost intrusive, assessing her, judging her for all the sins she'd ever committed and was likely to commit in the future. "Who are you?"

"She's a friend," said Jules.

"Oh?" Burl asked, eyebrows rising, insinuating. "Have you been doing anything that might disqualify you from membership in the Children, Jules?"

"Shut up, Burl. We were both wrongly arrested by the king's soldiers. We've just escaped and need sanctuary for a short while."

"You did what!" Burl yelled. Jules shouldered past him, and Vesper skittered past Burl with an apologetic smile. Burl followed them, slamming the door. "You know, you're already wanted for questioning over that business with those body-part bandits. Why'd you have to tell anyone at all about them? You should have just gotten rid of them, with no one the wiser. You gave them your real name! They've identified you down to the last hair, and point to you as the murderer of their leader. And now you've come *here* after escaping arrest? How do you know you weren't followed?"

"I wasn't," said Jules. "Look, we needed to come here. I wasn't sure before, but now I am—someone in Mallandina, I suspect the king himself, is using the split-disease as a weapon. It's on his order that all of the wizards and witches are being systematically infected and then imprisoned. I suspect his plans go further than that, though."

"All right," Burl said grudgingly. "I'll call a meeting for directly after morning meditation. You can leave her in your room." He poked at Jules' arm. "What happened to your hand?"

Jules lifted his right hand—he'd been holding Vesper's with his left—and turned it over. Blisters and open sores covered his fingers. He shrugged. "It's nothing. I'll clean it up in a minute."

Vesper gaped at it in horror. No wonder he was so unlike his usual self! Before she could say anything, Jules was moving again. She followed him into a large room roughly divided into two sections by the arrangement of sparse furnishings; in the first section, a number of people sat on the floor, dressed in those same shapeless gray clothes. Eyes closed, hands resting on their folded knees, they sat in absolute stillness even as she and Jules walked in their midst.

In the second section, six men in gray clothes stood in pairs. They looked as if they were dancing in slow motion, bodies curving and meeting in —movements that had no logic, but infinite grace, responding to the other almost like a mirror. She thought of Jules with his baton; this had been his training ground, she realized.

Most of the people ignored Jules and Vesper as they passed, although she could feel attention fixed on her, curious.

They entered a hallway and climbed two flights of stairs, to the last room on the right. Although as clean and spare as the rest of the building, this room was little more than a closet. A single mattress, a small table where Jules lit a lamp, a wardrobe. One window looked out onto the street. The ceiling angled too low on one side for a person to stand up straight.

"Let me see those wounds," Vesper said. "How did you get them?" She examined his hand—it looked like raw meat. The blisters reminded her of something—and, then she knew. "It's from the yellow grass."

Jules nodded, then winced as she probed, looking for signs of infection.

"I'll get something to clean it," he said and left the room, returning a moment later with a flask and a clean shirt.

The flask contained alcohol. "This won't help much," Vesper said. "I wish I had my herbs..."

"It's okay," Jules said. "One of the things we learn here is pain management...and good dietary practices. It'll heal."

Vesper sighed and opened the flask. She ripped off a piece of shirt and used it to soak up the liquid that ran off Jules' hand. His face didn't even twitch, although he did grow several shades paler. She tore off another strip of cloth and bound the hand.

"I didn't know the Children of Mae actually had a headquarters," Vesper said as she worked. "I thought you all just traveled around proselytizing...Are you really wanted now for murder?" she burst out.

Jules moved his hand in its binding, testing the hold. "Thanks," he said. "It's not really a headquarters, but a bunch of us were living here, and when we started growing we just did everything from here. I'm part owner of this house, which is probably the only reason why they haven't kicked me out of the organization yet. So yes, I'm probably wanted for questioning about that bandit's death. But it's just an excuse for the government to bring down the Children of Mae."

He got up and endeavored to build a fire in the small grate, his right hand only slightly stiff as he placed the wood. "Malland is a dictatorship. That wouldn't be so bad if the dictator's policies were halfway fair, but Bugger is greedy and wants power only for its own sake. As a man, he's one of the less observant and conscious people I've seen, and as a leader—well, to put it bluntly, he isn't one. I haven't seen any care of his people in his actions. The only thing that's kept him in check is Herland's magical defenses. But Herland, too, lacks balance—there is too much emphasis on being positive, to the detriment of being real."

"So what is your goal? To get rid of Bugger?"

"To get rid of the entire monarchy," Jules said. "Preferably, to get rid of all government. Under the theory that each person, guided by internal self-discipline and the need for compromise in order to live in society, will behave more ethically than if given rules from the outside."

"That's crazy," Vesper said, shaking her head. "You've been sitting in meditation too long, I think. Speaking of not being real—you've lost touch with it completely. Maybe Bugger is doing some things that are wrong, but I don't think the best way to defeat corruption is to get rid of the whole corrupt thing."

"It's a goal to work toward," Jules replied. "For now, we make pinpointed strikes against those in power—be it person or system of control. And then we educate the oppressed so they can keep the power we give them. They can choose their own paths, because they'll have liberty. Space." He had finished with the fire; light and warmth cheered the room, making it cozy rather than closet-like. He took a broom from the corner of the room and began to sweep the floor. Vesper sat at the table, hugging her knees to keep her feet out of the way.

"You can't be right about the split-disease being caused by the government," she said. "It seems it's benefiting your group more than anyone. Lots of pinpointed strikes against those in power—and the king has lost all of his court wizards and witches."

Jules snorted and shook his head. "Those aren't pinpointed strikes. They're pure chaos, which is always a method to establish more control."

"Even if the king's behind it—which I doubt—there'll be people in his employ—advisers and officials—who aren't. Instead of taking power from those in charge and destroying everything that works along with what doesn't, we should work through the system first to see if we can get the changes we want without disrupting everything. We can bring the cure to the king and see how he responds. If he's not interested, that might be more evidence of his complicity. If he is—well, things will be a lot easier than organizing pinpointed strikes and trying to bring down a government that might not be all—or even a little—bad."

"Better we free those in quarantine and give them the cure personally instead of trying to 'work through the system.' Who knows how long that would take?"

Vesper shook her head. "Those people are in quarantine for a reason—to stop their spreading the disease while the officials control it and find a cure. Which we might now have, and if we do, it should be tested and refined, made more efficient. So the best course would be to keep them there and for us to do everything legally, in cooperation with the king's scientists and physicians, who I think are the best in the kingdom. As soon as the cure is found, perfected, and administered, I'm sure there would be no problem releasing everyone."

"You've been unjustly arrested *twice*," Jules said. "It's near impossible in this kingdom for anyone to find the narrow space where you can be yourself and do what you really want to do without triggering a person to want to shut you down, or arrest you, or control you. You haven't had the practice—with your honesty and forthrightness, they'll eat you alive at court. Look at how easy it was for Garth to manipulate you."

Vesper glared at him. "How dare you change subjects like that! You have no idea what's between him and me, so you shouldn't be sitting there making assumptions—and judging me!"

Jules' mouth twisted in a mocking smile. "I know he took you to his retreat and seduced you."

"That's what *you* said, not me," Vesper retorted.

"Didn't he?" He looked at her, and she crossed her arms and refused to answer about something that didn't concern him.

"I know you don't know me very well," he said, "but won't you trust me on this? I don't want you to go to the palace. I'm not sure if it's for personal reasons or for the good of all, because my decision-making skills seem to be a little off when it comes to you. But if you stay here with us, you can learn with us, train with us, and we can work on testing the mushroom together. It can't be that hard to make a rough substance we could use, and then even easier to find a volunteer to take it. There are still wizards and witches on the loose, and my group has the contacts to find them."

All argument went out of Vesper at his appeal. Without her anger, she noticed tension he still held, particularly in his face and shoulders. He'd killed the bandit king, and now several more were dead or badly injured on account of him. His colleagues still blamed him for not killing more, to cover his tracks. *I don't think you can ever really be at peace if you've killed people*, she'd told Aren. He'd done so…it seemed at least partially because he felt compelled to protect her. Had it been against his better judgment? She wasn't sure. One thing she knew was that she did trust him, killer or no, inner peace or no.

"Okay," she said. "Maybe you're right. I'll stay." Garth would probably be furious when he found out—but he would have to deal with that, she decided.

Jules' face relaxed the slightest bit. "Good," he said. "Can you wait a little while to eat? You can rest. I'll meet briefly with the others and then bring you something to eat."

After Jules left, Vesper tried to rest, but after lying awake on the bed for a while she got up and paced the perimeter of the room instead. She stared out the window, although she could see little in the darkness. When Jules had been gone a half hour, she wandered to the door and opened it.

A drift of raised voices reached her, and she tiptoed halfway down the stairs to hear better.

"You made vows, Jules," someone was saying, an angry voice.

"We shouldn't be focusing on my personal business," Jules said. "The issue is not Vesper. It's those innocent people being kept in a dungeon—and figuring out why Bugger wants them there."

"We can try to break them out," another voice said.

"No. First we focus on this girl. Because we've said, time and time again, that if we want to make changes outside, we have to be true to our disciplines first. No meat, no drink, and no sex."

"I haven't had sex with her," Jules said.

"Not yet. It's obvious how you feel about her. Get rid of the temptation. She's compromising your judgments."

"But I'm not going to," said Jules. His voice was tired, edged. "She's with Garth. I'm just trying to protect her."

Silence. "You know what we've talked about with your brother and the competition he makes you engage in. If she's connected to Garth, and if she's bringing you back into your old feud with him, it makes it even worse having her here. Everything is too sensitive now, after the mess you made with those bandits. You got two of our own killed, too. If you bring the king's men down on us, you'll get more of us killed and we won't be able to do a thing about this stuff you tell us is happening now. I say get rid of her, and as fast as you can."

"All right," Jules said, utter resignation in his tone. "All right, I will."

She heard footsteps, and she dashed back up the stairs and into the room, heart pattering rapidly. Sitting on the lone chair, she tried to look as if she'd been there a while even as her mind raced.

Had she heard correctly? What did Jules feel about her? What was this talk of competition with Garth, and her attracting trouble? Although getting the answers to her questions would probably do little to ease her worries, as Jules entered the room, she couldn't help but stare at him, trying to read his face. His expression was pleasant as usual, but devoid of any answers.

He bore a loaf of brown bread and a large chunk of cheese. Vesper wondered if he could sense she'd eavesdropped, but he simply smiled at her and began to divide the food in halves, only a little awkward as his bandaged hand tried to hold the bread as he tore with the other.

"Let me do that," Vesper said, and she took the loaf from him and continued the tear he'd started, handing him the half when she finished.

"Thank you," he said to the floor.

They ate in silence for a few moments before Jules spoke again. "Look," he said. "I'm sorry. I've spoken with my colleagues, and we agree that it's best you continue on to the palace and rejoin Aren and Nim. Once you're with your party, I don't think you'll have any more trouble with being taken for a witch, and in fact you'll probably be safer as you'll be under the king's protection. But I would suggest that you not tell them that you think you have the cure for the disease. Just say you would like to work on it, and then when you test it, do so without letting anyone know it works. If that's too hard, I'll try to stay in touch with you somehow. If you let me know your progress, I could test it for you here on the outside."

Vesper would probably have argued with him again, even though just two hours ago she'd been arguing the opposite; based on what she'd heard, though, she found herself tongue-tied. She managed to choke out an assent.

"I'll take you there in a few hours, after we get some sleep," he said. Brushing off crumbs of food, he stood and divided the blankets between the bed and the floor. "I believe they accept petitioners until noon or so. You'll be there in plenty of time." He lay on the floor and closed his eyes, ending the conversation. Or the non-conversation, rather, with its unasked questions and unsaid answers.

Vesper finished a few more bites of food, then, not knowing what else to do, she followed his example. Dim light outside signaled that morning had come, so she had to sleep now or never. She slipped underneath the bedcover. Even after the exhaustion of nights of sleeping outdoors, the last of which she'dnight spent in one great sleepless misadventure, she couldn't relax. She was hyper-aware of Jules on the floor not six feet away, and unable to repress memories of their kiss. How she wanted to climb out of bed and put her arms around him and make everything right! Only nothing would be made right by such an action. She had to remember her engagement to his brother...even though that situation involved feelings even messier than the ones she suffered now.

Talking about it wouldn't help. If talking could have solved anything, surely he would have said something. Her thoughts continued to go round in circles for hours, and finally her fatigue dragged her into oblivion.

Jules was kind to her when he woke her several hours later, although he wasn't any more open; he brought her a pail of warmed water and a small washcloth, and a pot full of porridge. She ate in silence, feeling a bit bedraggled and a lot confused, but staying longer would change none of that.

"Shall we go?" Jules asked, standing.

Vesper nodded, suddenly blinking back tears she didn't understand, and they were off.

Jules and Vesper parted ways before they reached the palace. By then, though, she knew which way she needed to go; she'd made the trip before, and by daylight the spires of the palace towers stretched out in white relief against the sky. She followed them through streets where people bustled about, focused on their daily activities.

Although it was the tail end of the hours in which the palace received petitioners, the line still stretched down half a block from the open gate. More arrived even as Vesper drifted to the back of the line, and they came on horseback and by coaches far more luxurious than the one that had borne Nim and his party. Along both sides of the gate, a dozen or so men and women carrying signs stood, martial expressions pasted on their faces. Vesper squinted to read the signs:

"PARTS ARE PEOPLE TOO"

"PARTS' RIGHTS"

"LET PARTS SPEAK FOR THEMSELVES"

None of the protesters were allowed inside the gates, Vesper noticed. Now she saw that others were being turned away as well. She glanced down at her clothes. Jules had given her a long black cloak back at the house they'd stayed in, and it covered the worst of the ravages the green dress had gone through. However, she still feared that she looked a beggar or a servant wearing her mistress' cast-off clothing.

A doughy bald man, dressed in the dark red tunic and trousers with black piping that denoted an upper-level court servant, questioned each petitioner about their purpose, rejecting a good one-third of them.

Of course they had to let her in. She had a purpose here—she belonged in there, with Aren and Nim—she could mention Garth's name; perhaps that would carry some weight…but as she watched the doughy man's face, she could tell that he reacted to what people wore just as much as what they said. Worry gnawed at her insides.

By the time Vesper's turn came, she'd practiced what she would say in her head enough times that she had almost convinced herself of its plausibility. She surreptitiously stuck an elbow in the velvet-encased belly that kept bumping up against her from behind and moved forward when her turn came.

The doughy man barely gave Vesper the once-over, his eyes dismissing her as inconsequential and coming to rest somewhere over her left shoulder. "State the purpose of your petition."

"I'm actually here for another reason," Vesper began.

"Then you are in the wrong line," he said. "Next!"

The velvet belly bumped, and Vesper caught a whiff of fetid breath. "Excuse me," a nasal voice said.

Vesper completely forgot her planned speech. "This is ridiculous. The purpose of the petitions is to hear what the people have to say, and if you won't even listen to me—let go of me!"

The doughy man didn't even have to signal the guards; one of them hauled Vesper to the side. She recognized him as the one from the night before who'd tossed her a copper; he caught her eye and shrugged as if to apologize, gentling his removal of her with a small quirk of a smile.

Then, "Out of the way!" and more guards streamed out, pushing the line to the side. The other half of the gate opened.

A group of riders on horseback approached from within the palace grounds. Two guards in front, and then an oddly familiar-looking young man, handsome, with a mane of blond hair and teeth so white they almost looked unnatural against the tan of his face. He was followed by an elegant young lady with dark hair piled atop her head, and four guards behind them.

Vesper stood there, lost in her dejection, when suddenly the dark-haired woman on horseback turned and looked straight at her. "Vesper!" she cried, voice piercing through the crowd like the blare of a war horn.

Only then did Vesper recognize that face.

"Aren?" she said, blinking.

CHAPTER 17

Even with the voice, the familiar face, Vesper could hardly believe the woman was her sister. Aren had never worn anything so fine as this: an aqua dress embroidered with what looked like real sapphires and pearls, and strands of the same woven through her hair. Nor had she ever applied her cosmetics so liberally—her eyes smoky, brows darkened, lips and cheeks rouged. A girl from the country, the daughter of a butcher, didn't hold herself as if she were one of the royalty herself.

"You—guards, let go of my sister!"

Immediately the men holding Vesper released her. Aren smiled then, a lazy curl of her lips that showed her awareness of her own power. "I'll have inquiries made later about your treatment of her," she continued. "Vesper, I'm going for a ride, but I'll be back soon. You'll be treated well—or else—and we'll catch up then." She glared once more at the doughy man and the guards, then beamed at Vesper and waved as her horse surged out of the gate.

Vesper remained speechless for a moment, watching with the others as Aren rode away with the man. Then their gazes turned to Vesper.

"So…can I come inside?" she asked.

"Yes, of course," said the doughy man who'd rejected her plea earlier, his tone now deferent, even groveling. "You should have told me you knew the king's fiancée. But of course, you shouldn't have to. My deepest apologies."

Both guards bowed as she walked by, so they didn't see her stumble or note the stupefied expression on Vesper's face. The king's fiancée? *Aren?* Had some magical twist of time occurred that made months pass by here while Vesper experienced just half a week?

A guard accompanied Vesper to the main entrance, where they were met by a fellow whose long face was made even longer by the addition of a manicured black beard combed to a shiny downward arrow. He wore the dark red servant's uniform, but everything about him shouted that he belonged to a higher class of servants—from the way he held his chin so his beard pointed nearly horizontally, to how he flourished his hands as he talked. The guard held a hurried conference with him, bowed again to Vesper, and returned to his post.

The arrow-beard swiveled to point at Vesper. "A friend of Aren's?"

"Her sister. Vesper."

"Her sister. How delightful. I am Nevin, the royal steward. You are most welcome here, madam."

Nevin led Vesper down an enormous entryway of white marble, up a winding staircase with a crystal-encrusted golden railing, down two hallways decorated with the thickest rugs and the longest tapestries Vesper had ever seen. He opened two doors wide to reveal a sumptuous apartment decorated in green and gold. "These rooms are right next to Lady Aren's," the steward said, indicating another set of doors far down the hall. "You can rest here. Would you like a bath and refreshment brought up to you?"

"Oh yes, please," Vesper said.

She passed the next couple of hours in pure bliss. Silent servants brought up a silver tub and multiple pails of both hot and cold water; they mixed the water to a perfect steaming temperature and left a variety of scents on a tray beside it, along with a selection of soaps and salts. As Vesper relaxed in her first warm bath since the inn, which felt like ages ago, a female servant brought in a tray laden with exquisitely formed pastries, nutmeats, exotic fruits, and a decanter of a golden-orange liquid. The tray was placed on a small table and brought to stand next to the bath; Vesper snacked while she soaked, and then she got out of the bath, dried herself on a thick cloth, and donned a wraparound robe of such soft green velvet that she wriggled just to feel it brushing her skin. She sat down in a chair before a gentle fire and ate the tiny pastries both sweet and savory, sipping on a peach wine and trying to keep her eyelids from drooping so she could enjoy these moments all the more.

She was dozing when the door opened. She started awake to see Aren sailing in; her sister sat on the bed with a dramatic sigh, and then grinned at Vesper.

"What took you so long to get here?" Aren asked.

Vesper frowned. "You know, I was arrested," she said. "Don't you remember?"

"Of course I remember. But you aren't a witch, and I figured that once they realized their mistake, they'd let you go. And you're here, aren't you?"

"Well, yes. But a lot has happened."

"To me too! Guess what—I'm engaged to the king!" Aren clasped her hands to her heart and fell back on the bed, giggling. "I've never been so happy."

"That wasn't him you were riding with?" Vesper asked, more a statement than a question, as the man had been far too young, and the guards too small in number for a king.

Aren giggled again. "Of course not, silly. That was Magnus. He's ever so nice. He was so grateful we brought Minimus back."

"Ah," Vesper said. So that was Magnus—she should have recognized him from the book's pictures she'd seen, but without the look of agony on his face, he seemed a different man. "Did you ask him about a reward?"

"Silly! I'm going to have so much money I won't know what to do with it. I'll make sure that debt is paid off. It was my fault anyway."

Vesper smiled in relief. At least there was that one problem taken care of. "So you like Magnus," she said. "Why not him instead of the king? Isn't he a lot closer to your age?"

Aren rolled her eyes. "I'm not so superficial as to pay attention to things like appearance and age," she said. "Besides...they sewed Minimus back on him, and even though the prince is up to all his old activities, I hear the sex is just too weird. He's always shouting at his dick and they don't agree about anything."

"He seems quite nice," Vesper ventured. "It's hard to imagine him angry."

"You'd be surprised. He's got a split personality or something."

Vesper shook her head, trying to free it of the image of the prince having arguments with his penis. "I guess so long as you're happy...but didn't it happen a little, um, fast? You met him a few days ago, right?"

"Love at first sight," Aren sighed. "We passed by each other when I first got here and was being taken to some nasty room in the servant's hall. He stopped me...and we've barely been apart a moment since. We've already spent months' worth of time together. He asked me to marry him after our first twenty-four hours together."

"Oh," said Vesper, unable to help smiling at Aren's enthusiasm. "Um...how many wives does the king have already?"

"I'm going to be number twenty-nine!" Aren said. "But he hasn't taken a new one in five months. So I'm special. Definitely his current favorite—I'm the only one who's been going to dinner with him these past few nights. I just wish Garth hadn't gone haring off like that, so he could be here to see what he's missing out on."

Vesper's mouth went dry. "Garth?"

Was Aren watching her for her reaction? She found her sister's expression unreadable beneath all those cosmetics. "Yeah, that bastard. So sleazy. I ought to tell you—he told me he liked me. A lot. I even thought he was going to propose to me. But then, after I slept with him, he started talking about you, and how you were so different. He made it obvious I was just a fling. He's got a terrible reputation with the ladies at court—almost as bad as the prince's. I just wanted to warn you that once he's had you, he loses interest—fast. After he slept with me, he only kept talking to me to make you jealous. Now he's probably already moved on to his next interest—otherwise he'd have tried to rescue you, at least."

Vesper sat in silence and hoped the flickering of firelight hid her expression, which never failed to show how she felt. Garth and Aren—they'd been lovers. She remembered that night back in the inn, when Aren had been missing—and Garth had been awake in the next room, and so passionate right when Vesper had entered. He'd probably just been having sex with Aren. A terrible reputation with the ladies at court...but he hadn't actually proposed to Aren; wouldn't that mean he really did think Vesper was different, someone worth committing to?

She could not base her hopes on so little. "He did rescue me," she said woodenly. "But now he's gone. He left with his—his wife, some kind of noble person of Herland."

"His wife!" Aren spat. "I should have known. He's one of those types who pretends he's loyal to just one woman, and it gives him an excuse to have sex and leave dozens of others. I've half a mind to tell her..."

"I think she already knows," Vesper said.

Aren brushed nonexistent dust off her dress, as if flicking Garth away. "Anyway. His loss. Of both of us! I'm glad you didn't fall for him after all—there's plenty of more eligible men here at court, anyway. Do you want to borrow one of my dresses for dinner? Magnus and my Bugger want to meet you, and hear about all your adventures."

Relieved to change the subject, Vesper put the mess of her Garth-feelings into a small compartment in her mind for later musing. She met Aren's eyes and made herself smile. "I suppose I will have to borrow something," she said. "I wish I'd just grabbed my eggshell dress from the bandits' cave—"

"You couldn't wear that!" Aren nearly shrieked. "This is the royal family we're talking about. You are *lucky* you lost that old thing. It's decades out of fashion! Bugger's own tailor has been fitting up a storm for me. They're cut to my figure, but yours is close enough they should do with few adjustments."

Aren took her sister to her apartments, a sprawling set of rooms that eclipsed the guest suite in size and luxury. The two then spent the next hour arguing over dresses. None of them suited Vesper's tastes; she refused to wear anything ostentatious or uncomfortable, and all of Aren's gowns fell in one category or the other—most of them low-cut, so tight in the torso as to prevent proper breathing, and so stiff in the skirt that knocking over precious works of art became a fashion risk.

Finally they agreed on a pale purple dress, short-sleeved and somewhat looser and plainer than the others; the tailor had sewn in several panels of darker purple silk to give the illusion of a more elaborate design.

Dinner was not to be a cozy affair. Vesper and Aren entered an enormous hall that glittered with chandeliers, gold-paneled walls, and plenty of mirrors. All the nobles either living at or visiting the court used dinnertime as their main social gathering. Ten long tables took up the main floor, and a raised mezzanine area held the king's table, at present unoccupied, where Aren and Vesper were to sit.

Vesper sat down, and she took the glass of wine a servant brought to her and sipped.

"Where's Nim?" she asked, looking around the room for the telltale yellow hair and stocky torso. People occupied only about half the seats, but there were a lot of seats.

Aren wrinkled her nose. "He eats in the servants' hall—where we'd be if it weren't for *me*."

"But he's our friend. Isn't that prestige enough to get him an invitation to eat with us?"

"He's *your* friend, Vesper. As for me...I think he *ought* to eat with the servants. To see him fawning over the king's wives, you would think he wasn't just a servant—you'd think him a slave."

In all honesty, Nim's absence relieved Vesper. He'd been such a help to her, and she had repaid him only with rejection. She promised herself she'd make good with him soon...but not tonight. Tonight she wanted to relax a little and enjoy an unfolding fantasy of herself at the royal court!

"I just love sitting here and watching people come in," Aren said. "Magnus definitely started some trends—look!"

As lords and ladies began to trickle into the dining hall, taking their places, Vesper saw the same phenomenon she'd noted in town, only more pronounced—many people here wore prostheses in place of missing body parts, but they'd chosen materials and manner of attachment to highlight the difference. Vesper saw limbs of beaten gold or silver, wooden or fabric ears decorated with lace and feathers, and scalp-pieces set with gemstones or dyed garishly.

She also noticed an even more disturbing, yet smaller, group of people who kept their detached body parts on leashes or trained to sit on their shoulders, or sewed them back on their bodies but allowed them to speak and struggle and behave independently, yet still remain attached. Aren had said that Magnus had had Minimus sewn back on him—this latter trend must have started just the past few days, then, explaining why it had not yet fully taken off.

The thirty-something woman who sat on Vesper's other side sported hair dyed bright red and piled high on her head in a mass of sausages. She had one bright blue eye, and the other socket bore no eye at all, but something glasslike, with a sapphire winking out from its center. Vesper felt glad she sat on the side of the real eye, as whenever the woman turned to look at her with both the good eye and the one of glass and sapphire, she had to suppress a shudder.

"What part have you gotten freed?" the woman asked, with one blue eye beady and disapproving as it roved over Vesper's plain gown. The other eye of sapphire remained still, but it winked in the torchlight.

"Freed?" Vesper asked. "You mean, by the disease? Oh…none of them," Vesper said.

"Tut tut," the woman said. "You shouldn't call it a disease. It's not, you know. More a 'liberating force.' You really ought to get a part or two freed. Everybody else has. If you don't, you won't ever really fit in here in court. Besides, people will think you're selfish."

Vesper was mystified. "Selfish? Whyever so?"

"Why, because there's a part or two or three waiting to be born and freed from you—a living, conscious thing. Haven't you heard of the burgeoning Parts' Rights Movement?"

"Uh, no."

Sausage-curled hair bobbed as the woman shook her head. She looked as if she was about to deliver a lecture, when a man entering the room to a fanfare caught her attention.

Magnus marched in with the confidence of a man who looked good and knew it. He lived up fully to his reputation as the perfect prince package—from the tousled golden locks, bedroom eyes, and sensual lips, to his broad chest and height. Yet he had an easygoing, carefree demeanor that put people at ease–so carefree, in fact, that he'd walked in with Minimus sticking erect out of his pants, gently bobbing as Magnus walked by the tables. The penis called out greetings as he passed each table, which people and people's sewn-on body parts responded to with enthusiasm.

Once Vesper got over her innate tendency to not stare at people's crotches, she noticed that someone had dressed Minimus for the occasion—he wore a small cape of dark blue velvet lined with a bit of ermine, exactly like the one Magnus wore, and on his head he even had a small golden circlet to match the Prince's.

"Glorious," Vesper's faux-eye neighbor breathed, clasping her hands together as Magnus approached. "I must get myself a companion part as well. My own eye is long gone—Jin-cursed thing—but I've got the resources to adopt someone else's—and it'll probably be a lot better behaved." Red lips curled at the thought, while in her head, Vesper went over the argument she still imagined with Jules about why she believed she'd rather work with the current system than support overthrowing it. She had to admit that her arguments sounded less and less convincing.

Bugger's entrance followed soon after, to even bigger fanfare. Although at least twice Aren's age, the king was easier on the eyes than so many people at court because he hadn't lost any obvious parts. His curly bright red hair (Vesper was getting an inkling of the inspiration for her neighbor's hairdo) lent him a youthful air. Still, some indefinable lasciviousness about him made Vesper uncomfortable. When he kissed Aren and stuck his hand down the front of her dress to fondle her breasts in plain sight, and when he ordered several women to lift their feet for him to kiss, instead of their hands, she began to understand her reaction. She tried not to wince each time a woman tripped and fell because Bugger greeted her feet with too much enthusiasm.

Then, Vesper had to change her opinion completely about the king being easy on the eyes when, during the first toast, Bugger reached up and picked his head off his shoulders and lifted the whole thing up into the air to tremendous applause and cheers.

"To the head of the kingdom!" he shouted. Aren, flushed and smiling, clapped along with the others.

When the head settled back onto King Bugger's shoulders, he caught sight of Vesper. "The sister of my beautiful bride-to-be!" he boomed. "Welcome, my dear. Aren tells me you took a little detour to get here. Had a little misunderstanding with my soldiers, did you? They're commendable folk, to be sure, but a little too thorough sometimes. Easy mistake to make." He grinned.

Vesper thought about Perrin and suppressed a retort. She smiled back, although the muscles of her face didn't want to cooperate. She could feel Dame Sausages by her side, avidly listening, curls quivering with anticipation for every word spoken, which would surely be gossiped all around the court by the next day. "Yes, just a misunderstanding. It was corrected."

"Good, good," said Bugger. His head moved the other direction; he'd finished their conversation.

She weighed things quickly. If she spoke now, she would have many witnesses, and any promises or commitments made would be more likely to be kept. "King Bugger," she said. The head came swinging back, the eyes a little less twinkly, but still intent. "I...I have a great interest in this split-disease, and some...strong theories about its cure. Might I be able to confer with your scientists about it?"

Suddenly the whole table quieted. Vesper stumbled on, wondering if she'd made a mistake—maybe she didn't need *this* many witnesses—she could have asked Bugger just in front of Aren. "I thought—I thought that if I could help find a cure, you could give it to those in quarantine, and they could be released. Because when I was arrested improperly for being a witch, I knew what that was like, to be taken against my will even though I'd done nothing wrong, and I believe everything should be done to release these people as well, who are guilty of nothing except being victims of a disease."

Silence, except for a whispered "liberating force" from Vesper's other side, as the whole table waited for Bugger's answer.

Bugger regarded Vesper over steepled fingers. "A woman, working with my scientists?" He chuckled. Then he began to laugh harder. His head tipped back, so far the space between it and his neck gapped open. A heartbeat later, the court joined in, howling with laughter—men and women alike rocked in their chairs, slapped their knees, and pointed at Vesper. Even Aren giggled a little bit, although she did cock her head in sympathy at her sister.

Vesper couldn't feel her face anymore—she only sensed heat everywhere, as one giant blush. Her worst nightmare, being mocked in front of the king and the entire court, had come to life.

In that most humiliating moment of her entire life, though, she realized something: she had nothing to lose by pressing her case.

"And why not?" she asked, pitching her voice high and loud, so it would be heard above the din. "I could bring a fresh perspective to the discussion. All I'm asking for is a chance. If you feel women are so incapable, but you never test or challenge them, you'll never know if it's the truth or just an assumption."

King Bugger's laughter had died at her first words, and by the time she finished, she was speaking into silence. The court lay poised to ridicule her again; the barely restrained sneers, the snickers and whispers would start at the slightest signal from their king, but he nodded then, slowly.

"You know what, young lady, you're right. I ought to give you a chance. I would let you confer with my scientists, except I don't happen to have any at the moment—they've all run off on me. But what do you think of this: I'll give you your own laboratory, and you may confer with yourself about the cure to your heart's content. If you find it—I'll grant you your self-guardianship that instant, and you'll be free to own your own property and travel my kingdom at your leisure." Red lips curved in a magnanimous smile, and Aren beamed at him, clinging to his arm and smacking a kiss on his cheek.

Vesper thanked him, stammering a little. Attention dispersed from her, and she tried to still her shaking hands. She'd done it. The shift in her status could not have been more extreme. Now, when people looked at her, they cast only approving looks—even Dame Sausages. Magnus eyed her with interest, and when the music started, he bounded to her side, offering his arm to dance.

Thankful for an opportunity to get away from the table, Vesper accepted.

"Hi, Vesper," Minimus piped up, waving his whole self so that his cape swirled.

Magnus grabbed her, pulling her close enough that she could no longer see the penis, saving her from conversation with the prince's crotch.

Still, once they began to move, the pace of the music ensured that Vesper had to see Minimus bobbing around to the intricate and somewhat frenzied steps of the dance. She found it so distracting that she stepped on Magnus' toes twice and lost most of her usual coordination. "Sorry," she muttered at Magnus' expletive, and she almost tripped again when she heard Minimus laughing at Magnus' discomfiture.

"Don't mind him and his smart mouth," Magnus said, when they came together for a slower part of the dance. "Part of me—ha ha!—actually would like it if you'd work on a cure to reattach the parts, just so I could shut him up once in a while."

"Couldn't you just—tuck him away then?" Vesper asked.

The dance ended. Magnus gave an exaggerated shrug. "The people love him," he said. "They seem to have forgiven all my earlier indiscretions—I've a great fondness for women—because my discretions were mainly, well, committed by him," Magnus laughed. "My father thinks it's wise, too, to celebrate our detached parts in public, to get everybody used to it." The music began again—a slower tune, and Vesper moved unwillingly into his arms for a waltz. She tried to hold herself far enough away that a giggling Minimus wouldn't keep rubbing against her.

"I would think it would be better to find a way to unite the parts back with their owners," Vesper said.

"I couldn't agree more," said Magnus. "But my father has plans...

and until I'm king, I have to at least look like I'm listening to him."

Vesper couldn't help but like Magnus for his easy, boyish charm and his sunny looks, even though he seemed neither particularly intelligent nor with much of an ability to stand up to his father. She also had to admit that Magnus' attention, along with the sudden new respect from everyone at court after the king had granted her request, flattered her in a way she'd never before experienced, with her history of being the strange one and the wallflower at every party.

She had accomplished much today. She had the cooperation of the king, the admiration of the prince, and soon she'd have her own laboratory. Still, she couldn't forget the way everyone had laughed at her; their blindly following the moods of the king added to a sense of unease. She tried to dismiss it—but she kept wondering: what if Jules was right?

CHAPTER 18

King Bugger stayed true to his word. The next day, a red-liveried servant brought Vesper to her new laboratory—a room in a far wing, away from any apartments, large and filled with all sorts of strange equipment she'd never seen before. Egregian supplies, the most advanced in the known world, stocked the shelves. She found chemical substances both natural and manufactured, and equipment to analyze, separate, and combine in any way she saw fit. She didn't know the purposes of any of the substances or how even to begin to test her mushroom, but she found plenty of manuals and books that explained the equipment, whose magical properties facilitated experimentation.

She wondered, perusing the supplies, what had happened to the other scientists. Was this their equipment? King Bugger had said that they'd all left him—was that true, and if so, why would they? She'd just have to keep her eyes open, and not get too caught up in her experiments.

Fortunately, Vesper didn't have to figure out any of the actual science at this point, so her plans would remain simple. She only needed to see if these mushrooms would cure the disease, as she hoped. That was a large *if*, though.

The mushrooms, with the few remaining strands of yellow grass, had already wilted somewhat. She could dry them and grind them up to make capsules, or she could make alcoholic tinctures. She opted for the latter, as that would extend her pitifully small supply, and it would guarantee their preservation. She divided her mushrooms into three partsallotments. The smallest sectionlot she would use for making an experimental tincture. She would try to find a way to cultivate more of the same mushrooms with another sectionlot. The third and largest partlot she stored in a cellar dug into the side of the wall.

She had made plenty of tinctures in the past; the process was simple enough—let the substance sit in a strong alcohol for at least two weeks, and then find the weakest dilution that would still work to destroy the infection. She placed the mushrooms in a beaker and poured the purest alcohol she could find in the laboratory, covering the fungi completely, then adding an inch more. After sealing the beaker tightly, she put it aside.

Now she had to wait the two weeks until the tincture was ready. In the meantime, she divided her time between attempts to cultivate a mushroom colony from the few she had, and reading the books in the laboratory—anything that had to do with disease, infection, viruses, and how to test it using the equipment here.

She knew a little about how to grow mushrooms, but not enough. Afraid to deplete her supply too quickly, she was more comfortable researching first. Soshe read until her eyes hurt. *Perhaps I need a break*, she thought; she could pick up some food from the kitchen and then do something different—she'd like to interview some of the magical practitioners in the quarantine. Perhaps she could learn something useful about why people lost particular body parts...she could explore some of the psychological issues Garth had brought up about souls fracturing.

After she ate, she found Nevin and asked for directions to the dungeon. He frowned. "I don't think you should go there. It's dirty and cold—not the place for a lady."

"But the people in there aren't criminals. They shouldn't be in a place that's dirty and cold."

He smiled, although the expression didn't reach his eyes. "Of course. I misspoke. I thought you meant the dungeons for criminals. Nevertheless, you shouldn't go near those who are quarantined. They're diseased and thus just as dangerous as if they were murderers and thieves."

"But I heard the dungeons are made with a metal that prevents the use of magic inside," Vesper argued. "It couldn't possibly hurt just to talk to them."

"Who told you that?" Nevin snapped.

Vesper's mouth gaped. "I...don't really remember...I think I heard it when I was mistakenly arrested. Inside the wagon. It was dark—impossible to know who was speaking."

She actually remembered quite clearly that Jules had told her, but she also remembered his caution. No need to share information unless absolutely necessary.

"That proves my point that the wizards are dangerous," Nevin said.

"The king said I'm to have the freedom of the court," Vesper said, crossing her arms over her chest.

"The court does not include the dungeons. Now if you'll excuse me, I have things to do."

"But—"

"You can take it up with the king. He's holding court at the moment with the daily petitioners." He pointed down a hallway, then turned and walked away to forestall more argument.

Vesper found the main receiving hall several turns off from the passageway Nevin had indicated, drawn to it mainly through the noise—a steady hum of voices, interspersed with a loud baritone announcing each petitioner.

Vesper emerged from a hallway to the foyer, which she recognized as the place she'd entered the palace. Now she saw where the line of petitioners ended—it stretched from the entry into the palace all the way to two enormous gilded doors, open and flanked by two guards on each side. Beside the last guard on the right was a sign:

"NO BODY PARTS ADMITTED WITHOUT OWNER"

She'd arrived early enough the day before that she hadn't gotten much of an impression of the petitioners, except as a blur of expensive clothing.. In today's much larger group, she noticed that many of the petitioners carried cages or leashes that held organs or limbs.

She tried to bypass the line and nearly slammed into a palm on a leash that suddenly zoomed before her face. "No cutting, ferret face!" it yelled.

"But I'm not a petitioner. I just need to ask the king something—"

"Then you're a petitioner. Get to the back of the line!"

Vesper tried to duck around the hand, but it anticipated her move and dropped to block her path again. One of the guards intervened, pulling Vesper away. "Stop trying to do our job, hand," he said, then turned to Vesper. "Young lady, he's right. You need to wait your turn."

The crowd of petitioners radiated enough animosity toward her that Vesper saw no use in arguing, although she was thoroughly sick of waiting in lines to be heard by people who probably wouldn't listen. She tried to breathe deeply, to think about what Jules might advise in this situation. *Treat them as you want to be treated*, maybe. *Pay attention to their problems rather than only your own*, maybe. She would try.

About twenty minutes passed before she'd moved up enough in the line to see into the receiving room. An odd sight greeted her; Bugger's head had come alone to hold court, and it hovered above the throne or came to rest upon a blue velvet pillow by turns. Aren sat on his right side, her posture rigidly upright, as if she were trying to force herself to stay attentive. but Her glazed eyes betrayed her.

Magnus sat on Bugger's left, and he wasn't even trying to fake his inattention. Fully asleep, he slumped in his throne, head on his hand and long eyelashes resting on his cheeks.

Aside from the petitioners, a number of nobles slouched about the room in comfortable seats. Most of them held quiet conversations amongst themselves, but a few listened to the petitions and offered advice when they felt moved to do so. She thought many of them looked familiar—she'd seen them at the dinner last night, and she stared at each one in turn, trying to put names and tidbits of information to faces and missing or prosthetic body parts.

The most vocal input came from the nobles who defended "parts' rights," and they had plenty of chances to speak, as most of the petitions had something to do with issues regarding the body parts. To whom went the responsibility for a crime committed by a body part—did the former owner have to pay restitution? If a part decided to take up residence with another person, did the former owner owe anything for the part's upkeep, or was he owed anything by losing the command of that part? Did the king bear responsibility for helping find and return lost parts?

Many people had lost their parts, and those who noticed mentioned that for some reason the parts all seemed to be flying in the direction of the palace. Parts that had been questioned expressed an inexplicable draw to come here—and then, no one ever saw those parts again. Vesper's concern grew upon hearing that despite the checkpoints that sought infected wizards and witches, the disease was still spreading rapidly. Some people claimed that officials were allowing it to spread intentionally—that they'd been threatened with infection and the loss of body parts unless they paid tithes.

Two secretaries took notes as the king's head nodded, made concerned noises, and said "I'll have my people look into it," to each petitioner.

In cases of two parties showing up to resolve a conflict, Bugger took obvious pleasure in creative adjudication. Along with assessing fines and payments or determining disputed property, he usually tossed in a requirement that the two parties exchange embraces or massages, or, on random occasions, sexual acts.

Before Vesper got to the front of the line, Aren had spotted her, her gaze refocusing and blinking, her frozen face coming back to life. "Vesper!" Aren waved her over.

Bugger's head turned to Vesper as she clasped her sister in an embrace.

"Ah, my bride's sister," he said, with a smile that spread like ruddy grease across his face. "Having a pleasant stay so far? How's the cure coming along?" He turned back to the crowd. "This young lady is working very hard to find a cure for the disease," he announced.

A light patter of applause filled the room, as if no one was quite sure how to respond.

"It's fine," Vesper said. "I just wanted to come here and ask if I could speak with some of the wizards and witches in quarantine. Strictly for research purposes, to understand the disease better."

Bugger nodded. "Of course, of course. Anything you wish. I'll speak with my advisors and something will be arranged for you shortly."

Vesper hadn't expected it to be so easy, and she smiled in relief. "Thank you."

Bugger's head bobbed up and down a few times in a strange, detached-head nod. "You didn't need to listen through all these boring petitions. Stuff for us men. You should have come to me straightaway. Magnus!"

"Wha—what, Dad?" Magnus sat up, blinking.

"Why don't you take Vesper out for a picnic lunch? Show her the palace grounds. She's been working too hard and is exhausted from all that thinking. I bet she'd like the gardens—girls love their flowers, eh, Aren?"

"I don't really—" Vesper said.

"Nonsense. Don't make me make it a royal order for you to have fun now. Do it!"

Magnus rose and held his arm out; not knowing what else to do, and uncomfortable under the speculative gazes from all corners of the hall, Vesper took it, and together they left the room.

She glanced up at him as they walked through a hall that had an animal theme—leopard print rugs, tapestries of forest scenes with wild animals peering through the trees, life-size statues of predators about to leap on their prey, interspersed with a number of smaller animals observing the scenes from marble pedestals. Magnus himself resembled a beautiful animal. With his tawny hair, his muscular swagger, and his broad, leonine face, he certainly looked the part of a prince of predators. Oddly enough, though, she felt no attraction to him, assessing his beauty as an artist or poet might, rather than as a woman.

"Where are we going?" she asked.

He turned bright blue eyes—the same eyes as his father's, but far more attractive in a head that remained attached to his body—on his companion. "Dad said a picnic. Show you the grounds. We can do both at the same time."

They stopped in the kitchens. "Picnic," Magnus announced, and an assistant cook produced, within moments, a large closed basket. Magnus tucked it onto one arm and took Vesper's hand with his free one. Then he pulled her back into the passageway with the animals. Stopping in front of a gloomy raccoon on a marble pedestal that stood before a tapestry of a tree dotted with bright birds, Magnus dropped Vesper's hand and touched the base of the raccoon's tail.

Vesper heard stone scraping across the floor, and she stared at the tapestry from which the noise had come.

Magnus laughed and pulled the tapestry up by its side to reveal an open doorway. "Secret passageway," he said, eyes alight. "There's all sorts in this palace. Let's go." He nodded at the empty dark space.

Curiosity won out over caution, and Vesper stepped through. Magnus followed, and then the door slid closed.

"It's dark," Vesper said, her voice almost a squeak.

Then she felt Magnus' arm snake around her, pulling her back against him. His lips nibbled at the back of her neck.

"What are you doing?" she shrilled, pulling away.

Magnus whistled three sharp notes. One torch, then many more flared to life, illuminating a narrow passageway that stretched straight as far as her eye could see.

In the dim light, Vesper could see the smirk on the prince's face. "Sorry,. I forgot myself. You're not even my type, you know. I like girls with curves. But in the dark, sometimes I can't help myself. It's like I have the thought, and before I know it I'm already doing it."

"Well, please don't do it again," Vesper said. Somehow, the double insult, first of being groped and then being told he didn't find her attractive, canceled each other out. She couldn't stay angry at plain stupidity.

"The good thing about me is I usually don't make the same mistake twice," he said cheerfully. He held out his arm, and after a pause and a glare Vesper took it again.

After a length of straight passageway, they began to ascend stairs set in a narrow, winding spiral. Vesper became glad of Magnus' arm when her footing became less sure in the flickering torchlight.

At the end of the stairway, Magnus pushed open a door ; they emerged on the top of a tower. Vesper caught her breath. She felt she could see the entire city—from the green gardens surrounding the palace, to beyond the gates at the city center and the buildings built in rows beyond it. She watched as a leg from the knee down flew through the air towards the palace, then disappeared from view somewhere below her. Then, at a more leisurely speed, came a breast, large and white with an enormous brown nipple.

"Where are those parts going?" Vesper asked.

Magnus had set his basket down on a lone bench of stone that furnished the tower-top. He dug through it and pulled out two small round pies. With a flourish, he opened a napkin and set it on top, handing it to her. "Eat," he ordered.

Only after Vesper sat down next to him and both started munching on the still-warm pies, which were and filled with meat and leaking a savory sauce, did she repeat her question.

Magnus shrugged. "Who cares? Good company, good food, and a gorgeous view—what more could we want? This is a boring city, but there are some fun things to do if we make a little effort. Tomorrow I'll take you hunting, if you'd like."

"Hunting?" Vesper repeated. "Where is there anywhere to hunt around here?

Magnus grinned. "It's a special little hunting place right here on the palace grounds. I won't tell you more—that would ruin the surprise."

They ate the rest of the food with relish. Along with the meat pies, they snacked on a selection of fresh fruits and sweet pastries, and Magnus produced two wineglasses and poured them a tart, sweet bubbly wine. Magnus chattered lazily as they ate, recounting adventures he'd had as a boy in this place or that place, pointing out the locations from their roost on the tower. Vesper found her thoughts drifting, wondering what Jules was doing—and then, on a guilty tangent, thinking about Garth, her maybe-fiancé. She found she didn't like thinking about Garth so much, because when she did she thought inevitably of that witch Allegra...perhaps she should confine her thoughts to Jules, with whom a relationship was a dead end...although nothing about him felt dead...

"You're tired," Magnus said, and Vesper snapped awake. She hadn't realized she'd dozed off. "Let me take you back down. You can nap and you'll have plenty of time to prepare for the festivities."

"Festivities?" Vesper repeated. "Again? What's the occasion?"

"Dinner," Magnus said. "Every night we celebrate dinner with festivities. Dad insists on it. It's a great way to keep the women at court happy—you know how they love parties. And Minimus, too. I really can't stand how much he talks, you know, so I stick him in a sleeping potion in the mornings and he stays quiet all day, thank the gods. But at night he wants to socialize, so I let him out for a few hours and it keeps him cooperative enough."

"Oh," Vesper said, nodding. Magnus tossed the wine bottle and glasses into the basket and opened the door that led to the passageway. He whistled those three notes again and torches burst back on; they descended, and it seemed shorter going back than arriving. Magnus walked Vesper back to her bedroom and kissed the top of her head after she opened the door. "See you tonight," he said.

Vesper had been meaning to seek out Nim, but her dozing off in Magnus' company hadn't been entirely from boredom. She slept until Aren came to her door to wake her for dinner.

Thus the rhythm of Vesper's days was set. She spent mornings in the laboratory; it took only moments to shake and check the tincture, but then she worked on isolating spores from the mushrooms to try to grow more. Her attempts were time-consuming and entirely futile; most of the mushrooms produced no viable spores, and when she finally managed to get some of the precious dust, one batch grew contaminated fungi and the others refused to grow at all.

She felt less impotent with her other work in the laboratory. As she read through the manuals to the equipment and the substances on the shelves, she began to analyze the mushrooms.

Using small crumbs of mushroom, she watched its reactions with various substances that the manuals claimed would expose the properties of any test sample. She noticed something odd about the mushroom: in substrates of inert chemicals, it did nothing. Bbut when she placed pieces of it in any remotely reactive substance, it became almost aggressive, coating everything around it with its spores. When she looked at the substances under an Egregian magnifying scope, she saw that they had been broken down and transformed to resemble the mushroom structures, complete with the ability to spread more spores.

The mushroom behaved just like the split-disease, Vesper realized. It broke down substances into forms that could bear its spores. She began to question the efficacy of a tincture to treat the split-disease—how could a fungus with the same properties as the disease cure it? Wouldn't it just make it worse? She had to study this more.

She could spend years here, easily, and still explore what the laboratory had to offer. To her delight, she found that much of the equipment had magical qualities. She discovered a metallic box that cleaned anything put inside it, to the point where rusty objects looked new, and even old bloodstains or ingrained dirt would disappear from cloth. She found a stick that, once it was "attuned" to one substance, glowed whenever it encountered the same substance. She was particularly fascinated by a machine that balanced poisons with antidotes—with the poison on one end, the machine had a meter that turned colors according to what was placed on the other end, and a perfect antidote would cause the meter to glow blue.

She became so immersed in the laboratory's offerings that she would have skipped lunch more often than not had Magnus not shown up every day to take her out to "have some fun," as he called it, or to "keep her from turning into a man," as his father called it. He took her out riding, for picnics on the tower, walks to the city market where all sorts of exotic goods were sold. He also took her once to the private hunting grounds he'd told her about—but after seeing it once, she refused to ever go again.

A giant net enclosed a portion of the palace grounds. Within it grew a small bit of cultivated forest, the spacing of its trees too even to have grown that way naturally. Vesper soon discovered, when Magnus took her there and shot his first arrow to the response of a human-like squeal of agony, that they weren't hunting animals.

"Got it!" Magnus shouted, and he ran to a tree and picked up the thing pierced by his arrow and squirming on the shaft. It looked animal-like, but Vesper needed only a moment to identify a human scalp—a young woman's scalp, covered with long brown hair that resembled her own.

"You can't shoot those!" Vesper cried. "They're—they're just as conscious as real people. And intelligent. You should know that more than anyone, with Minimus and all."

Magnus shrugged. He pulled out his arrow and tossed the no-longer-twitching scalp into a bush. "Yes, they're like real people. But people can be good and bad, and these parts are bad. Zinfel puts them in here for me—the ones who are like criminals, or uncooperative, or whatever. They'd be killed either way. But this way, I get to hone my archery skills, and to have some fun besides. Do you want to try? I've got a slingshot I could teach you to use, too."

"Get me out of here," Vesper said.

That ended Vesper's experience with the hunting grounds. She tried to avoid Magnus after that, but he kept showing up at the laboratory or knocking at her bedroom door, and his big-eyed puppy-dog look always broke down any resolve. When she asked him why he wanted her company so often, he sighed. "I think you're the only person I've ever met who doesn't want anything from me. I didn't mind the girls who all liked me because they want to be my queen, or because they think I'm handsome, but since this thing happened with Minimus...I...well, I can't really do the things I used to do. Sometimes I can, but only if he cooperates, and then I don't even enjoy it. So I like being around you because I don't feel any pressure."

Vesper felt a wave of sympathy for Magnus. It was the first time he'd ever said anything to her that showed that he might be more than a superficial and immature young man, and from then on she resolved not to avoid him and to actually be his friend.

Anyway, few in the palace had time for her. She sat next to her sister at dinner, but during the day Aren sat with the king while he held court or stayed closeted in his quarters. When they did speak, Vesper found herself listening more than speaking, which had always been their pattern anyway.

She saw Nim only once during her first two weeks at the palace.

After a few cursory questions about Vesper's rescue by Garth, and a slightly lengthier probe about Jules' safety, he got to the real reason for his visit. He wanted to share his happiness and his pride at being the official shoemaker. Plus, another reason grounded both of those emotions. "I think I'm in love, Vesper," he said. "I wanted to tell you that—about how sorry I am for those things I said, and how I know you were right about us. Now that I'm truly in love, I understand that what I felt before was just a crush."

"Mm," Vesper said, looking away so she could roll her eyes unnoticed. "Who is it? One of the servants?"

Nim looked aghast. "Of course not. Do you think my future wife would be a servant? No—it's Number Seven of the wives. Her name is Begonia."

"Oh, no, Nim," Vesper said. "You can't fall for one of the wives! She's married. And to the king, no less. That's illegal. Maybe it shouldn't be, but you'll still probably be arrested if anyone finds out—or worse."

"I knew you'd say that," Nim said, turning away. "You're such a prude, Vesper. Love is above things like rules. And the king has so many wives and mistresses—he doesn't even remember all of them."

"No, Nim—" she protested, but only to a slamming door.

Despite her lack of company, Vesper discovered an unaccustomed contentment living at the palace. She wished everyone in her hometown could see her now—spending time with the prince, working on the cure and interacting socially with some of the most important people in the kingdom. Her mother would actually smile at her, and her father would grunt and look pleased. Beyond her town, she wished Garth and Allegra could see her. Garth would see how well she fit into his world, and Allegra—she'd have to eat her words and recognize that Vesper wasn't just another in a line of conquests, but someone who might just be a partner for life, rather than just for two years…

And Jules, if he saw her? He probably wouldn't be impressed… but with him, her "I told you so" moment would come more when she showed him that the problems in an existing regime could be solved and changed from within. That sense of unease from her first day had dissipated until she could push it to some corner of her mind and dismiss it as paranoia.

Two things did nag at her, though, living at the palace.

Firstly, court as King Bugger ran it was odd, to say the least. Vesper could never have imagined such excessive waste of food, the opulent decorations that changed every night during the festivities, or the ways court life could change to accommodate the presence of body parts either freestanding or as talking accessories. ButNevertheless something else bothered her much more—a loyalty to whatever King Bugger said that bordered on hysteria. She began to understand why book-reading had become unpopular, and why in a modern society such as theirs no one questioned the treatment of women as property; the king held all these opinions, and even though his views changed as often as the court décor, people followed them and instituted them as social mores. Bathing habits, sexual habits, fashion, relationships and roles—nothing was off limits for King Bugger's opinions.

Did people follow the king out of fear? Vesper didn't think that the mass conformity was inspired by anything good he had done, but since she herself could never gauge social acceptability, her she doubted her ability to judge the court trends as being wrong or off. Instead, she simply tried to avoid the court beyond the obligatory dinners and focus on what was working for her. Because so much was working here in the laboratory, in what she was learning and in how right she felt in this role of scientist.

Then that brought her to the second thing that bothered her. So far, she'd been unsuccessful in making her visit to the quarantine dungeon. "Soon," Nevin told her, or "perhaps the day after next something will be arranged," and his beard would swing up and to the left, dismissing her. She thought about how the king made those same assurances to petitioners, and she'd yet to hear of anyone taking action against town officials accused of taking bribes, or doing anything to find all the lost parts disappearing into Mallandina. Perhaps she needed to have more patience.

After two weeks had passed, she decided that the tincture could be tested. If she could scrape off some cells from an infected wizard or witch, she suspected that the poison/antidote balancing machine would give her the answer about the tincture's efficacy.

"Do you think you might help me to visit the quarantine dungeon?" she asked Magnus when he came by the laboratory that afternoon. "I want to test the tincture, but arranging my going there has been impossible. I don't suppose *you* would be refused."

"It's ready?" Magnus asked, blue eyes wide. "Test it on me first!"

"But you're not..."

"I'm infected, too," Magnus said. "If the cure works, it should work on me."

"Well," said Vesper, dubiously, "I don't want to just have you drink it. It might be poisonous. How about I scrape off some of your skin cells and use this balancing machine to check it?"

"It'll be quick, right? And if it works then, you can give it to me right away?"

Vesper nodded.

"All right then. Scrape away," Magnus said.

Vesper took a small file and swiped at the skin on Magnus' shoulder, then placed the file on the right end of the poison-antidote balancer. She placed another file on the other end, and used a dropper to place one drop of the tincture onto it.

The meter glowed red.

"What does that mean?" Magnus asked, looking from the meter to Vesper and back.

"I don't think it works. It's supposed to turn blue if it balances," she said, heart sinking.

"Well, I don't trust those machines. You need to test it on a real person," Magnus urged. "Come on, give it to me. Just a drop. I can't stand this stupid talking dick. I'll do anything to have him return to normal."

"No," Vesper said, shaking her head. "Absolutely not. It could make things worse if I can't even get it to pass the machine's test..."

"As your prince, I order you to give it to me," was his answer.

Vesper pursed her lips. She supposed one drop couldn't harm him—it was just a mushroom, after all, and not poisonous like the yellow grass.

So she gave him a drop on his tongue, and then one more she put directly on a sleeping Minimus' head.

"Do you feel anything?" she asked, biting her lip.

"Not yet," Magnus said. "Hey, you! Wake up!" he yelled, giving Minimus a violent shake. The penis remained limp and unresponsive. "I did give him the sleeping potion. Maybe I won't know until tonight. I don't feel anything, though—not more...connected, or anything."

"Ohhhh..." groaned Minimus. "I feel...pretty good, actually." He perked up and stood erect, then without even a rip or a snap, he popped right off of Magnus and began a leisurely pump-and-sail through the air.

"No," Magnus said, clapping a hand to his forehead. "It doesn't work!"

"What doesn't work?" asked Minimus. "Whatever it was you just gave me, it feels great. Kicked that nasty stuff ole' stupid here's been giving me right out of my system."

"Shut up. Shut up!" Magnus shouted, and he grabbed Minimus out of the air and slammed him against the table.

At the same time as Minimus shrieked, the penis hit the edge of the poison-antidote balancer, and it wiggled on its base. The drop of tincture that sat on the file spilled onto the machine.

It went crazy. The meter shifted to yellow, then orange, pink, purple. It settled at red, but when Vesper moved, it shifted back to purple. What had happened?

"Oh...sorry, Vesper. Did I break it?" Magnus' anger was gone as quickly as it had arrived.

"I bet you did, you oaf," Minimus grumbled.

"I don't know," Vesper said. She wiped the machine dry, which sent the colors into another round of shifts. She frowned at it, then glanced at the prince. "I'm sorry, Magnus. I think I should stay and figure this out. I'll see you at dinner, all right?"

Magnus shoved Minimus back into his pants, with some difficulty, as the organ remained fully erect and complaining loudly. "All right. I guess it doesn't work after all...what a disappointment."

"Well, it does have an effect, and it's not entirely negative," Vesper said. "It did make Minimus feel better. I guess I'm back to the beginning on curing the disease, though. I'm sorry. I know I got your hopes up."

Magnus stopped pouting at his obviously struggling crotch. "It's okay, Vesper. You've done more than anyone else has so far. I'll see you at dinner, all right? I'm going to go get this thing sewn back on again." He blew her a kiss and left.

Vesper focused on the machine, which she noticed continued to shift colors whenever she moved anything, including her own body, in the room. She began to experiment—scooting a stool to one side, transferring a stand of vials to a higher shelf, pouring substances together into beakers to initiate chemical reactions. The colors didn't shift dramatically until she began to actually put objects into cold storage, or to take them out of the room entirely. It almost seemed as if the meter's sense of what it balanced had extended beyond the scales to the entire room.

Maybe the tincture had somehow strengthened the magical properties of the machine.

She confirmed her theory when she tested small drops of tincture on the other magical devices in the laboratory, which responded similarly—the cleaning-machine now had the ability to disintegrate cloth or metal, and the sensing-device became so sensitive under the tincture's influence, that it glowed continuously.

The most impressive demonstration of the unique properties of the tincture occurred when she tried it on her magic compass. It normally only bent things out of the way that had some flexibility to begin with, but with a drop of tincture it began to bend even the hardest substances. The effect did not last, though—after just a few minutes the compass' magical properties lost their enhancement.

The Book of Offhand Truths had shown Vesper the mushroom. She still felt that the mushroom must be the key to the cure—but this discovery, although fascinating, was not it.

She recalled her analysis of the mushroom under the Egregian scope, how it had transformed any live substances into smaller versions of itself. The disease did the same thing, and treating it with the tincture made something about it stronger instead of neutralizing the infection. Why would the Book have shown her a substance that so resembled the disease? How could that cure it?

She'd read something else she could try, she realized. A book that claimed that *like cures like*...and that she could make a remedy with the energetic imprint of a similar disease to the one she wanted to cure, one that would stimulate the same healing mechanisms in the body that the true disease needed.

Taking a crumb of mushroom, she placed it in a beaker of water and shook it. Then she proceeded to dilute it and shake it a number of times, each time testing it against the file of Magnus' infected skin cells. The machine shifted colors, to green, then aqua, and finally, after the tenth shake-and-dilute, it glowed a bright blue.

She'd found the cure.

Part of her couldn't wait to tell the king—to have her self-guardianship become official. With her discovery proclaimed round the kingdom, to spearhead the recovery of hundreds of wizards and witches, she would not only be able to support herself doing more scientific work, but she could possibly lead the change of how women were treated throughout the kingdom.

No. Wait, something in her said. The voice in her head sounded like Jules'. She scowled. Since when had her conscience, or intuition, or whatever it was, started taking on his features? She didn't know why she'd want to keep her discovery from general knowledge, but something told her to have at least a little caution before revealing it.

Very well, Jules, I'll wait, she said in her head. *But not for long*.

CHAPTER 19

"I'm ready to test a possible cure on someone in quarantine," Vesper told King Bugger the next day, in front of the entire court. She'd showed up mid-morning, when the crowd of petitioners was at its peak, and no one had objected this time when she passed the line and cut immediately to the front. "Arrangements haven't been made yet for me to visit the quarantine, but now that I want to do more than just interview a wizard or witch, I'm sure I will have your approval to go there as soon as possible. Right now would be great."

Now, in front of the whole court, Vesper felt uneasy at her bravado. Perhaps she should have sent another message in private...but no. Nothing would have happened, and she also feared that without witnesses, she wouldn't get her declaration of self-guardianship. She had to push the king's hand, but the way he stared at her now made her want to squirm. His eyes were cold, corpse-blue...

Only his mouth smiled. "Wonderful," he said. "You have proven my views of the capability of the female mind completely and utterly wrong. I am your servant with regard to anything you ask of me."

"Visiting the quarantine, then...?" Vesper prodded.

"Of course," Bugger said. "In lieu of visiting the dungeon, I'll have one of the infected wizards brought to your laboratory. How about that? Say, in an hour?"

"Oh—yes, that would be perfect," Vesper said, not sure if she felt more relieved or unnerved.

Back in the laboratory, Vesper got everything ready. She checked the remedy she'd made from the crumb of mushroom; the meter on the poison/antidote machine shifted slightly greener, so she shook the remedy and diluted it once more until the meter glowed blue again. While she waited, she poured the contents of the beaker into smaller vials. Then she spent a quarter of an hour just arranging and re-arranging her chair and writing materials for recording what happened.

In two hours exactly, someone did come to her laboratory. It was Court Advisor Zinfel, whom Vesper had seen at dinners and the occasional other nighttime functions she was pressured into attending. In public, he could always be found somewhere near the king, but he blended easily into the shadows, a short and hunched fellow with a narrow, triangular face. Now, Zinfel was here...but he came alone.

Her gut clenched in terrible premonition.

"You understand we are only trying to protect you," he began. He stood at the door of the laboratory, his fingers perpetually massaging a piece of his clothing, eyes just as restless as they traveled about over the neatly organized supplies, to the stark and well-lit edges of the room, skittering over Vesper's plainly clad person and back to his fingers. "We think you have gone as far as you need to, and we can handle the rest, the dangerous parts. We are, of course, very pleased with your work, and for your part in bringing our dear prince's penis home. You will be amply rewarded for both, and given a ride back to your home in such pomp as is sure to impress your parents and friends. A coach has been reserved for your use tomorrow morning."

"What? You're sending me away *now*? But—we don't even know if what I have is the cure! And what about my self-guardianship?" Vesper felt as if the ground had been ripped from underneath her. She'd been so secure in her position, and now to have some disagreeable rat-faced fellow telling her to go the instant things were going to get interesting—she wouldn't stand for it. "I need to talk to the king."

"Of course," Zinfel said, lips stretching across his teeth. "Tonight, you shall be the guest of honor at the nightly festivities. King Bugger will wish to thank you personally for all you've done, and I'm sure he'll grant your petition then. And dear Magnus will be so sad to say goodbye to his little companion of these weeks."

Vesper crossed her arms in front of her, feeling, as she always did in front of this particular advisor—on edge. Unlike most everyone else in the palace, he seemed to have all his parts connected; still, despite his being whole, he made her flesh crawl. The king had chosen him for her to reason with, though, so reason with him she would have to. "I see no danger in my staying to oversee the testing. The wizards and witches aren't criminals, so we don't need to treat them as if they are. They'll want to be cured, just as much as they want to be freed, so I'm sure they'll cooperate with us in order to achieve both ends."

Zinfel shook his head. "I understand your belief, as uninformed though it might be," he said, ignoring her outrage. "But you don't know the minds of these folk like I do. Most of them are certainly harmless, but a few—you never know. Some actually want to retain this split-power as a weapon. They would not hesitate to use it to harm the one who is trying to take it from them. Others—well, studies have shown that wizards attain a higher degree of insanity after being kept in a small space than people without magical abilities."

"What you're saying has a high degree of insanity!" snapped Vesper. "That's a ridiculous argument. It doesn't even make sense."

Still, try as she might, Zinfel denied her. Murmuring apologies, he finally left, saying he would do what he could, but without any further messages from him, her departure was planned for the morrow.

She stood there, fuming, staring at the vials of super-diluted mushroom remedy lined up on the laboratory counter. She supposed she should be grateful that she'd been given so much more than initially expected—and after tonight, she'd have what she needed to go home, pay off the debt to Ruben, and start a new life free of Porter Gordo. Still, she'd gotten invested in the project and she badly wanted to see it through, and to see the imprisoned wizards and witches released.

Maybe just her ego had wanted all this—tthe prestige of her fantasies, to continue rubbing elbows with the most powerful people in the land. Her ego needed to accept that if the king told her she was done, then she was done. What else could she do? He'd been good to her...perhaps what Zinfel said had been correct, and she should just ensure as easy a transition as possible for whomever took over the next phase. If she cooperated, who knew what the future would bring? She could still help change women's roles in Malland. The king might want her help again if she left him with an impression of intelligence and a cooperative nature.

She wrote a brief explanation of the tincture's properties, trying to emphasize its possible uses for healing and noting that it still needed experimentation. Everything to do with the cure for the split-infection she labeled more carefully, writing down in detail how to make the remedy and her guesses as to dosage and what might be expected in terms of results—if it worked. She swept the laboratory a final time and took her remaining tiny store of mushrooms along with one vial of remedy and one of the orange tincture, to be packed with her belongings.

Back in her room, she arranged what she'd take with her. She'd accumulated a few more items of clothing in her days here. As the sister of the king's fiancée, she'd been discouraged from being seen in public in the same dress twice. She'd thought of borrowing more of Aren's gowns, but she'd hated them all so much that she'd allowed several of her own to be made at her direction. After bathing, she donned one of them for tonight, a confection of green lace over a silk white lining, which, like all the dresses, revealed more skin than anything she would have chosen. She supposed that being the guest of honor would mean she'd be the object of a few drunken and embarrassing toasts, and she didn't want to look a complete dowd even for those brief moments of attention.

Aren waved when Vesper came into the dining room. "I haven't seen you in ages," she complained, as Vesper sat down next to her. "You've been stuck in that laboratory for days on end, and now you're already leaving."

Vesper looked at her sister. As usual, Aren fairly glittered; today she wore a gown of deep blue embellished with sapphires. But had she painted her cosmetics too heavily, as if to hide late nights, or anxiety? Did her smile look a little forced, not quite reaching her eyes? "Yes, I suppose I've worn out my welcome," Vesper said, remembering Bugger's initial statement that she could stay as long as she wanted. "But you—are you all right? Will you be okay here when I'm gone?"

Aren lifted a creamy bare shoulder and looked away. "Of course. I've got lots of company. The other wives will accept me once I'm married. Everything will be perfect then."

"Have they not accepted you so far?"

Aren's lower lip trembled. "They…they keep trying to get rid of me, honestly. They've made up all sorts of things about the king to try to convince me that he's crazy or something. I know they're just jealous—trying to scare me off because they don't want more competition." She glanced about nervously. "I don't think I should talk about it here…"

I should have made more of an effort to see Aren these past couple weeks, Vesper thought. She'd been so caught up in her fantasy come to life that she'd thought only of herself. Only now did it occur to her that Aren's inability to listen to any of her concerns might have meant that Aren's own were too worrisome. Now Vesper could no longer rectify her inattention.

"At least—I'll be back for your wedding, I'm sure. When is it going to take place?"

Aren sniffed. "I'm not really sure. We got engaged so quickly after I met him that he thinks we ought to wait a little while, give the court and his wives some time to get used to me. But I don't know, Vesper. I don't feel like anyone is getting used to me."

"I think we should talk more before I go," Vesper said. "After dinner, let's meet—"

She was interrupted by the fanfare, announcing the entrance of some royalty. Bugger appeared, accompanied by a young blonde whose décolletage fairly spilled out of her crimson dress.

"Who's that with the king?" Vesper asked, at the same time as she heard a catch in Aren's breath, and she bit her lip.

"Oh…that's Daisy. She's the niece of one of the nobles who stays here at court," Aren said. "I know it looks strange, but Bugger tells me he's just being kind by showing her around, since she's new here, and her uncle is infirm…she doesn't mean anything to him, of course."

But Aren's nervous demeanor showed the lie, as did how she hunched into herself and cast longing glances in the king's direction, behaving as unlike her normal kittenish behavior as Vesper had ever seen. Even Aren's flirtations with her dinner companion on her other side lapsed at odd moments into sullen silences.

Bugger's treatment of his new companion confirmed the lie—the way he put his arm around her to guide her to the seat next to him at the table, and then the frequent touches at any excuse—then, no longer even excusing, but outright fondling her in front of everyone. Chatter continued at the table all around him, everyone steadfastly ignoring the king's activities, and continued more intently than ever as he pushed down on Daisy's head until she got off her seat and went under the table. As did everyone else, Vesper averted her eyes, but no one could quite drown out the sound of Bugger's grunts of pleasure, the silverware clinking as he gripped the tablecloth.

"Disgraceful," Aren hissed. "That woman is such a strumpet."

An image of Aren sprawled out under the table at her engagement party flashed through Vesper's head, and she thought, with a flicker of amusement, that perhaps she understood a little of Aren and Bugger's attraction. Still...the man was living proof that being royalty didn't automatically grant class.

"He's got so many other wives already," Vesper said. "Didn't you know he would want more?"

"I didn't think it would be so soon. We haven't even married yet. I'm afraid he'll be sick of me before it even happens." Aren's voice breaking coincided with Bugger's finishing with an especially loud grunt, and Daisy emerged from under the table, wiping her mouth and giggling.

"Not bad," Bugger said. "I might have to keep you around! Maybe I need another fiancée, eh? Got twenty-eight wives, why can't I have two fiancées, and marry 'em at the same time? What a wedding night I'd have!" he shouted, laughing, and the woman simpered.

Aren stiffened further. After a moment, she pushed her chair out and strode down the length of the room, shoulders held high in affronted pride.

Bugger laughed even harder.

"I envy you, Bugger," said a duke halfway down the length of the table. "All these gorgeous gals at your beck and call—providing such entertainment for you even at dinner."

"You like it, Stuffen?" Bugger said. "Daisy, get back under the table and give our dear duke some entertainment! A queen of my kingdom is a servant to all!"

"Oh—that's not necessary—" Stuffen protested, turning bright red, and then his eyes bugged out as Daisy began to minister to him under the table.

Bugger swigged down the contents of his glass. "More wine!" he shouted. "Anyone else? Want a turn on her dance card? First come, first served!"

Magnus swaggered in, with Minimus for once tucked away into tight brown leggings. He dropped into the chair Aren had vacated. "Good idea, dad. Just the thing for a pre-dinner appetizer, eh?"

Vesper had been on the edge of going after Aren already. Magnus always became a little less kind, a little more unpredictable around his father, and Vesper found that more than enough of an excuse to leave. Perhaps she could speak with Nevin about arranging her payment and certificate of self-guardianship. She scooted her chair back—and then uttered a small scream as Bugger's head whizzed off his body and hung in the air, directly in front of her. He grinned, wet red lips setting off yellow-splotched teeth.

"Not so fast!" he boomed, and Vesper shrunk back from the spittle that flew. "As the guest of honor, you must stay the entire evening. Have a drink, get comfortable. You're entitled to a favor from Daisy before my whore of a son gets one. He gets 'em all the time."

Vesper tried to calm herself. Only diplomacy could get her out now. "Thank you, Your Majesty," she said. "You are very generous. I wasn't leaving; I was just getting up to dance a little, as this is one of my favorite tunes—Magnus?" She turned to the prince, eyes pleading.

Magnus sprang to his feet. "Of course!" he said, and he held out his arm. Vesper took it, nodding to Bugger's head, whose eyes continued to follow her as she moved. She almost glanced behind to see if those bright blue orbs had popped out of the head in a further disintegration, but she steeled herself, pasted a smile on her face, and moved into a dance with Magnus.

"I'm so sorry you're leaving so soon," Magnus said as they whirled. Vesper caught a glimpse of Bugger, whose head hovered above Daisy, cheering as she worked on yet another diner.

"I was sorry, too," Vesper said, "but considering things…perhaps it is a good time for me to leave." She tried not to glance at the king's raucous head, although she couldn't block out his shouting. "Would you do me a favor and dance me over to the exit?'

"Of course," Magnus said, and they whirled their way across the room.

"Thank you," she whispered as he released her near the archway exit.

But Bugger's head blocked her way, blue eyes blazing, teeth bared.

"Tsk tsk," he said. "Pretty thing like you, cooped up in a laboratory for weeks, and now you're trying to leave without having any fun! If you don't have fun, what good is it being a woman? So you don't want Daisy—you don't swing that way, eh? How about a man then—the one every woman in the kingdom dreams of? How about a favor from my son?"

His breath smelled of alcohol and sourness, as if he'd not brushed his teeth in days.

"No, thank you," Vesper said, and she reached out and pushed Bugger's head aside.

"How dare you!" he screamed. "How dare you touch the royal head with such disrespect! When I was just trying to get you to have some fun! Well, you're going to have fun if it takes all night long! Guards! Hold her down. No, carry her to the table. There, there. Magnus—give her her favor!"

A reluctant twist of Magnus' lips marred his handsome face. "Dad, I don't think—"

"Yeah, that's right! You don't think! Sometimes I wonder if fucking my cousin was such a good idea. No, I take that back. Fucking her was great. Marrying her—that was the mistake. Gave me the most inbred heir on the entire continent. If only those damned Egregians would give me a potion to increase intelligence rather than all this weird shit! Do as I say, you stupid whoreson."

Magnus looked as if he was trying to come up with a protest, but he shook his head, sighed, and unbuttoned his leggings, popping Minimus out.

"Whew! Hard to breathe in there," the penis complained. "What's going on? Oh, hi, Vesper."

The guards had pulled up Vesper's dress. Her drawers disappeared somewhere, and she could feel vice-like hands gripping her legs, pulling them apart. Vesper twisted her head about, seeing if anyone in the room could help her—but all the guests were going on as usual, pretending a rape wasn't about to happen on one of the dining tables. Magnus wedged himself between her legs, and Minimus bobbed gently up and down. Bugger's head, satisfied with the proceedings, flew back to the table onto his body, where he began to swig wine directly from a bottle.

"No! Minimus—don't!" Vesper shrieked.

Minimus' head was poised to enter. "Hey, I remember something. No means no," he said thoughtfully. Then he shrank and went completely limp just as Magnus started to push him in.

"Damn you, you stupid prick," muttered Magnus. "Don't embarrass me now!"

Minimus didn't respond, either verbally or physically.

Magnus stood up and tucked his penis away. "Well, that's that," he announced, flashing a smile. "I've decided I'm not in the mood after all."

Bugger's face turned an ugly shade of purple. "Ridiculous!" he shouted, voice slurred. "That's no favor! I need a volunteer..." His head lifted off his neck a little bit. Then his eyes rolled, and the head fell off, landing face first in the pot roast that sat before him.

The guards holding Vesper let her go, rushing to attend to the fallen king's head. Vesper struggled to her feet and fled.

CHAPTER 20

Vesper didn't stop running until she got to her room. Only after she'd slammed the door and leaned against it did she give way to the trembling that seized her body and a brief but violent storm of sobs that left her drained but determined.

She couldn't stay in this place even one more night. She would leave now—she'd find an inn, and in the morning she'd get her own coach. She had no money—but her gowns had enough gemstones embroidered on them that she could probably pawn them, or perhaps sell the gowns themselves. Certainly the gems would be enough to cover her family's debt. She would have no certification of self-guardianship, but she could still petition for it at home with the mayor.

Without a bandbox or satchel to pack anything in, she tried throwing a few of her gowns onto a sheet and tying them into a package. She surveyed the lumpy, overly large results with dissatisfaction. Should she cut the sheet and sew it into a sort of bag? Just as she grabbed needle and thread, though, she heard a noise outside her room. Were those footsteps? Had Bugger woken up and sent soldiers to drag her back to finish her rape?

Leaving the gowns, she tiptoed to her door and opened it, peering outside. She saw no one, b. But panic had set in—they would find her here. She had to leave now.

She could notNot leave without some small part of the work she'd done here, though—something far more precious than gemstones. She took nothing but the needle and thread she still held and made her way to the laboratory, poking her head around corners and dashing down hallways with her heart pounding in her ears.

,By the time she reached the laboratory, she knew how she would do this. Remembering how Jules had secured his supplies on him, she attempted to imitate it—she found needle and thread and, as quickly as she could, sewed two rough pockets under the flounce of the dress. Into them she tucked a well-padded vial of the remedy, one of the tincture, and one mushroom. She put her compass, which she'd stored in the laboratory as well, in for good measure.

She left the laboratory and moved down the dimly lit hall, thinking to exit the palace from the kitchen.

Then she heard a noise—voices coming her direction.

She panicked, running the other way, then up some nearby stairs and hid in the dark until the voices passed. When she tried to backtrack, though, she found she was lost.

Calm down, she told herself. If she could find a window, she could orient herself. Taking a deep breath, she moved into another passageway.

A lion blocked her path, and she suppressed a shriek. No, not a lion—a statue, in the room with the animal-themed decorations. She could hide in the secret passageway, she realized, reaching toward the raccoon—then pulling her hand back. What use would it be going up to the tower? Also, Magnus might find her there.

She glanced at the other animals on the pedestals. A squirrel perched on one...a harpy...and here, a gargoyle.

Seeing the gargoyle triggered recognition. Where had she seen it before?

Then she remembered. *The Book of Offhand Truths* had shown her a picture of it on the page after the illustration that had foreshadowed her ride through the sky across Malland, .

The gargoyle was about as large as her torso, and a bit dusty—all except for a spot on its hind paw.

She touched the spot, and a door slid open soundlessly behind it.

The pitch darkness framed by the doorway repelled her. Still, the book hadn't led her astray yet.

She stepped through.

Even when the door slid closed behind her, she could see the shape of the walls around her, and up ahead...a light.

Then, she just caught the edge of a squeak through the stagnant dark. Was that a voice—a cry? It sounded like someone in distress.

She heard it again, more clearly—someone whimpering first, then shrieking as if being tortured. Vesper stood, half poised for flight. *No. I'm here, and it's not a coincidence. I need to look.*

The cries continued, making it easy to guess which direction to go. Flashes of light illuminated the walls in flickering intervals, and Vesper had to blink away the afterimage that grew brighter as she approached a room that had no door.

A piece of someone else's nightmare greeted her eyes—not her own, for she never could have imagined anything like this. Hundreds, if not thousands of body parts filled the room, all of them pinioned on rows of metal wire strung from one end of a long room to the other. Some parts writhed and whimpered, and others appeared to be dead. Garish light flickered on and off. A strange buzzing noise accompanied the lights, and when Vesper ventured to touch one of the wires, she pulled her finger away instantly as she realized that the buzzing noise indicated electric shocks that traveled down each wire.

Someone had been torturing these body parts. Who—and for what purpose?

She focused on the nearest part—an ear hanging by its lobe on a wire, moaning softly and twitching. "Who is doing this to you? And why?" she asked.

It moaned and twitched with a little more vehemence, but did not respond otherwise.

The back of her neck prickled, and she whirled.

An eye hovered in the air, staring at her. "Who are you?"

Vesper gasped, but recovered quickly. "No one," she said, heading for the door. "I made a mistake."

She began to run down the hall.

"Intruder!" the eye screamed. Before she got halfway down one hallway, two-dozen hands had seized her, lifting her into the air. She shrieked and struggled, to no avail.

The hands carried her past the flickering room to the one beyond.

An army of parts occupied this room, organized into categories—ears there, feet there, larger parts there. Each hovered at attention. The hands brought her to a closet-sized barred cell, tossed her inside, and locked the door.

Vesper lay where she'd been deposited until she could move again. She felt bruised all over, wincing as she sat up and scooted close to the bars. She looked out.

Five eyes stared back at her. Five ears hovered, listening. Hands waited to seize her if, by any chance, she managed to escape. The other parts beyond remained in their ranks, waiting for an order—to do what? Did the king know of this, and if so, why was he building an army of parts?

Vesper's heart dived. Jules had been telling the truth. Something horrible was happening here, and she suspected now she had worked so hard to find a cure that would never be used. She'd been utterly deceived.

Now what would her fate be? One couldn't speculate on a madman's moves—and she feared that all the evidence pointed to Bugger being quite mad.

For hours, she pondered what the king's strategy might be. Now she understood that the body parts that she'd seen flying towards the palace, during her journey to Mallandina and after she'd arrived, had been called here somehow—by someone who was torturing and training them…but for what? When petitioners had spoken of their problems with a disease that couldn't be quelled no matter how many wizards and witches were quarantined, no one had realized that it wasn't meant to be stopped. It had been planted intentionally. People were falling to pieces…and the king didn't care, because his own insanity had caused it all.

After some time, she tried and failed to sleep. She huddled against the back of the cage, as much out of sight of the ever-watching parts as she could manage. Her thoughts collapsed into an exhausted blank.

She lay curled up in a corner until she finally heard a foot fall in the room. She straightened, hope and dread tangled into an indigestible ball inside her belly.

"Why, hello again," said Zinfel. "Discovered our little training ground, have you?"

Oh, no, Vesper thought. *Anyone but Rat-Face*—but she said, as politely as she could manage, "Please let me out. I came here by mistake. I'm supposed to be leaving in the morning from here—I'll be missed if I don't show up."

"I don't think so," Zinfel said. "No one will look for you. Everyone will assume you've left already if they can't find you. Your belongings will be easily disposed of."

She felt as if a fist squeezed around her heart, because she knew then that he did not intend to set her free.

"What are you going to do with me?"

The advisor's nose wiggled as he laughed, *sniff-snort-sniff-snort*. "Well, I don't think I'll kill you. Not today at least. I think we'll just keep you safe for now. First, however, I'll give you a little tour. It's so seldom I get to show the genius of my work to someone who understands. Hands! Release her, but contain her. And follow me."

The mass of hands, which had been standing at attention, unlocked the cell and grabbed Vesper by whatever handholds she presented—elbows, skirt, and hair. When she squirmed, they clung all the tighter.

Zinfel turned and led the way.

They stopped first at the room with the flickering lights, full of the body parts pierced by metal wire. A collective mass of cries and shrieks sounded at Zinfel's entrance. He giggled. "They love me," he said. He took a stick with a pointed metal end from the wall—Vesper recognized the same kind of lightning-stick as Jules had stolen from the soldiers—and poked at a squirming beer-gut belly. "Whom do you serve?" he shouted.

"Bugger and Zinfel," the belly cried. Zinfel jabbed the stick against it and pressed a button. A loud zap of electricity sounded, and the belly screamed.

"Wrong answer! Try again."

"Zinfel and Bugger!" the belly gasped.

Zinfel smiled and nodded. "That's better. It's funny how these people who profess to know about science—"" he gave the belly another vicious poke, eliciting another yelp—"don't know anything about order." He sidled a glance to Vesper and giggled. "You were wondering where the other scientists went, weren't you? Now you know. They've joined the ranks of my other volunteers, ready to serve our kingdom in a more useful way than piddling around in those laboratories."

Vesper stared at the rows of body parts, so horrified that she could say nothing. She watched Zinfel wander down the rows, hands clasping the stick behind him. "Every day I kill one of them. Pain and fear are the best tools for creating an army. They know that one of them will die, one who is a little bit behind in his training, so they hasten to obey." He turned and stabbed a breast with the stick, then pressed the button. The breast jiggled and screamed, a high-pitched keening wail that died out as the smell of charred flesh filled the room.

"Stop!" Vesper cried.

Zinfel turned backing so he could watch both the burning breast and Vesper's face at the same time. She tried not to react, knowing instinctively that he was enjoying her horror, but she couldn't stop herself from feeling faint. Even as her knees buckled, though, the hands held her in place, anchoring her head to keep the now-dead breast well in her view.

"This one didn't come from a scientist. Imagine that—a woman as a scientist! All she is is a collection of useless body parts, like these tits," he said. "Women have used them as instruments of control for centuries. But by themselves, what are they? Just subcutaneous fat. Can't fight, can't pick up objects, can't even credibly threaten anyone. Better off dead."

Zinfel hung the stick back on the wall, but Vesper should have known that he was far from finished with his "tour." He commanded several contingents of the army of parts to follow, and then they went down the hallway and through a door that led to winding downward stairs. The hands pushed and pulled Vesper, holding her up when she would have stumbled.

They arrived at a door made of a strange metal—Vesper recognized the same metal that had been fused into her chains—the kind that could block magic. Zinfel snapped his fingers, and a hand flew forward with a key, opening it in a smooth, oiled motion.

Vesper could tell it was a dungeon from the smell. A waft of human waste and unwashed bodies made Vesper want to cover her nose, but she didn't want to give Zinfel the satisfaction. She lifted her chin and walked in before him, not allowing herself to be dragged by the hands. She stiffened as the smell grew worse. She could see little, but as her eyes adjusted to dim light that came through several small barred windows close to the ceiling, she observed that they were going down a long aisle lined with narrow cells, each with one tiny grate looking in at eye level.

They stopped in the middle of the aisle, and Vesper found herself in a living nightmare, endless doors stretching out behind and before her, to the left and the right. Although she could see no movement except for the flutter of body parts and, to her side, Zinfel's endless massaging of his clothing, Vesper sensed life teeming behind the doors, of a horrible near-insane kind that had lost all hope.

"Time for games!" Zinfel cried, his voice echoing shrilly through the darkness. As the prisoners could certainly hear him, Vesper didn't think she imagined the feeling of despair and near-insanity going up a notch in frequency.

Zinfel turned to Vesper. "Since you're still the guest of honor, you may choose who is to play today. Any cell. Any witch or wizard who takes your fancy. Shall I open them up, have you take a look? Or do you want to just spin and point at one?"

Vesper shook her head. "No. I won't be a part of this."

"Even if you are the default choice if you don't choose someone else?" Zinfel asked. The darkness didn't quite obscure his wide-eyed leer.

"You're going to do whatever you want anyhow, so just do it."

Zinfel paused, one finger to the side of his nose as he contemplated. "Tempting…but I think not. It wouldn't be very entertaining, since you have no magic." He paced before the cells, humming as he walked ten down, then five back up, peering inside one grate, then the other. "Ah. I don't like *you* very much," he said. "Hand, open this cell."

The hand with the keys unlocked the cell, and more hands flew through the opening and emerged again, dragging out a grizzled old fellow who looked more warrior than wizard.

Zinfel passed something to the hands, and they held the man and forcibly opened his mouth. Vesper gasped as the hands poured in the contents of a small, familiar-looking vial. They'd given him the split-disease remedy—the very one she'd prepared this afternoon!

But why? They weren't doing it to set him free, that was for sure.

As a group, their next destination was a medium-sized room adjoining the halls lined with cells. Enough torches illuminated the space that Vesper had to close her eyes for a moment to adjust to the brightness—and then she thought that perhaps she might have preferred darkness, to avoid seeing a room full of what looked like primitive instruments of torture. This place had been—or maybe still was—used for interrogation and possibly execution. The hands dragged the grizzled wizard to the empty center of the room, where the hundred-odd body parts ringed around him. Severed hands released the wizard's manacles and dragged them away.

"You—wizard," Zinfel said, "Whatever your name is. Now you will have your chance at freedom. You fight my body parts and win, and you go free. And to make it easier for you, you've been given a cure for the split-disease—courtesy of this lovely lady here, who will no doubt cheer you on. So you have your magic back. For now."

Vesper didn't know if she wanted the remedy to work or not. After a few moments, she knew it didn't matter.

The man lifted his hands, going into a crouch, but the body parts were already attacking. Unlike the brawling bandits' parts that had blocked the road on the coach's way to Mallandina, someone had trained these parts to fight, and they also had no compunction about using anything available to further their ends—seizing scalpels, rusty nails, pincers.

The wizard cast a spell that paralyzed ten body parts at once. They fell to the floor in a concerted thump. He barely had time to lift up his hand to marshal his magic again before a foot kicked him in the eye, and a hand brandishing a blade slit his throat. Blood sprayed. The wizard gurgled once and toppled to the floor.

"Just as I thought!" Zinfel crowed. "Even against magic, my parts are far superior as a fighting force. They will have no trouble at all, my great army."

"Did you take the cure and test it on your own?" Vesper asked bitterly. "You knew it worked, so that's why you wanted to get rid of me. You never intended to distribute it. You were never going to release these innocent people from their prison. You're going to let the disease keep spreading."

"Perhaps, perhaps not. There's only so many body parts wizards and witches will make for our army before they just stop trying to use their magic. But soon we won't even need them to spread the disease, as we are perfecting methods that will give us complete control over it. That tincture you made, with the thoughtful comments you wrote about it, will be quite helpful, I believe. There is a certain type of force field our enemy is able to use, and I think your tincture might be the answer to my difficulties with it. I also do thank you sincerely for the cure to the split-disease. You're correct that we won't distribute it widely, but we will use it."

"If you turn everyone into a bunch of body parts, you won't be able to control people anymore—because there won't be any people left!" Vesper burst out. She recognized the futility of arguing with him, but she couldn't help it.

Zinfel looked at her with an expression almost of disappointment. "Don't be small-minded," he said. "It's called evolution, my dear! Solving conflict by separating everything out from us that is conflicted."

"Put her in the dead wizard's old cell," he directed the hands. "Tomorrow you can watch the games again; perhaps we'll be able to come up with a more entertaining fight. Maybe we'll use *two* wizards. Sweet dreams!"

The hands dragged her back into the aisle of cells, opening one, tossing her in, and slamming the door shut. Two seated bodies at the far end of the cell broke her fall. "Ow. Get off!" one of them said.

Vesper knew that voice. Her eyes didn't even need to adjust for her to confirm it. Even as the sound of body parts rustling through the air subsided, and the clank of the closing door left them in silence, she recognized one of the men who sat on the floor and shared her cell.

"Nim!" she said.

CHAPTER 21

"Did someone find out?" Vesper asked. "I mean, about you and… you know." She glanced at the two other men who shared their cell, both of whom watched the reunion with undisguised interest.

"Begonia," Nim said. "My sweet Begonia. No, no one found out—or, I guess everyone already knew. Nobody cared about that. I could have—I could have had intimate relations with her in the middle of the morning petitions and the king wouldn't have cared. No. I was thrown in here because of something else—something I saw that I wasn't supposed to see. That I really, really didn't want to see."

Vesper leaned forward. "Me too, Nim—I wonder if we saw the same thing? The training of all those body parts into an army—that room of tortured parts—"

"No, I didn't see that, although I'm not surprised," Nim said. "It was something different. Something worse. I…I was going to the king's rooms to show him the newest shoe designs I'd made, and I stumbled on his private…foot room."

"His what?"

"A room—full of detached feet—like hundreds of them. Maybe thousands! And I saw the king in there. He was having an orgy with them. It was the most horrible thing I've ever seen. Like a bunch of insects crawling all over his naked body. Except they weren't insects."

Vesper thought of Daisy at the dinner table. "That doesn't sound like something the king would care if you saw, from what I know of him."

"He wanted me to join them," Nim said miserably. "He ordered them to—to attend me, and they started running over to me and sticking their toes into everything. I've never told you this, but I've had a nightmare of that happening ever since I was a kid—of being attacked by feet. When it happened in real life…I just cracked. I couldn't deal with it. And I guess I threw a few of the feet and maybe injured one of them—and the king got really mad and ordered me thrown in the dungeon."

"Bugger's insane," said one of the cellmates, whose round, cheese-like face nodded so eagerly that Vesper wondered about his own state of sanity. "It runs in the family, because they keep marrying their first cousins. Gets worse every generation."

"He's insane, but not stupid," said the other, a bare-chested emaciated fellow with a great nest-like mass of hair that reminded her, with a nostalgic pang, of the first time she'd seen Jules. "He's been wanting to build his empire for ages—but Herland and its wizards always stopped him. If he's managed to get the disease to spread there, they won't be able to use their magic to keep peace on the continent, and he'll do whatever he pleases. Sounds like he has the manpower to take on all the neighbors by force now."

"So he's going to use this army of parts to create his empire," Vesper said, the missing pieces of Bugger's strategy falling into place. It all made sense now. "Zinfel said that they were developing some way to spread the disease without the wizards and witches—that way, his army will be unlimited in size. And I've seen those parts fight—they're ruthless."

"Imagine what it'll be like when Bugger has unlimited power," Nim said. "We'll all be a bunch of separated body parts, all slaves to that head of his."

"But that can't happen!" Vesper looked from one gloomy face to the next. Their slumped shoulders and hanging heads spoke louder than words. They didn't even think they were going to get out of these cells—why be optimistic about the state of the kingdom? "I found the cure for the split-disease—at least it can stop any new parts from detaching. There must be a way to get the detached parts re-attached. There are already people working to undermine Bugger, if only we could send them a message, get the cure to them to be distributed—"

"You're really smart, Vesper," Nim said mournfully. "But you can't break out of a dungeon. The best wizards and witches in the kingdom are all here—if they couldn't get out, neither can you." He sidled closer to her until she could hear him breathing through his mouth. "You know…it's kind of selfish of me, but I'm glad you're here with me. It'll make the days easier."

Vesper got up and moved away from Nim's gradual creep closer, too preoccupied to feel annoyed. She had no room to pace, but she did so anyway—two steps in one direction, a spin just short of stepping on Cheese-face's foot, and back the other way. "What has anyone tried, in terms of escape?"

Nest-head replied, after a long pause. "We've been here for many days," he said. "We've tried many things. We can't use magic because the cells are entirely made of stone, reinforced with the metal that suppresses our magic. Even if we could use magic, most if not all of us are infected with the split-disease, so all we can do is make more body parts, which wouldn't help us escape."

Vesper thought about that, and she had an idea. "But say you could somehow use your magic—if infected wizards turned all the prisoners into parts, they could fly away and escape, and maybe later we could figure out how to put everyone back together."

She knew even as she said it that it was a terrible idea.

"The parts can't escape," Nim said. "Begonia told me—the king has some kind of a magical device that makes the parts have this obsessive urge to come to the palace. That's why they're all flying here."

Nest-head continued to tick off reasons why escape was impossible. "Our food is brought to us once every day by body parts who push it through the slot and take out and empty our waste pan. Our door is never opened—except for today, twice, once to bring our colleague to his death, I assume, and once to put you in here. There is no way out. I'm afraid the only kind of creativity that is our option is to find ways to euthanize each other painlessly, whenever any of us is ready to go."

Vesper paced, not wanting to match their despair. Then she remembered the ace up her sleeve, or rather, under her gown, and reached under her dress to remove her compass and the two vials—one, the remedy for the disease, and the other—the orange mushroom tincture. The others watched her with interest as she opened the vial of tincture and tipped it over the compass to spill just a drop of orange liquid. She didn't know if it would work in a dungeon made of magic-blocking metal, and if it did, if it would last long enough...but she had to try. She capped the vial carefully, then stood and held the compass toward the door.

The metal didn't even squeak as an enormous rent appeared in the center, clean-edged, but with a tremble as if under great strain. "Quick," Vesper said, and she motioned for the others to pass through.

They needed no more bidding. The three men jumped up. Nest-head went first, then Nim. As Cheese-face went through, the trembling rent snapped back to wholeness—so quickly the poor fellow made no sound at all as his body was cleaved in two.

She ordered herself not to throw up as she watched the dark pool of blood spreading from the bottom half of Cheese-face's body. She tried to focus, to count seconds in her head as she re-imagined what had just happened. About seven seconds per drop, she estimated.

Her hand shook as she got herself ready—one drop on the compass, and then a leap through the rent—trying to avoid stepping on the bloody torso fallen on the other side.

Nest-head and Nim waited on the other side, or at least, Nest-head stood staring at the fallen piece of his companion while Nim bent over against the opposite cell, retching.

"We have to get the others out," Vesper said. When neither of them responded, she went to the closest cell and stood on her tiptoes to look through the grate.

"Get ready to jump out of your cell when it opens," she said. "You'll have seven seconds to get through the hole. If there are four of you, you'll all make it if you don't dawdle."

Vesper had doubts that this escape attempt could actually succeed. Thankfully the four wizards in that cell all came out with two seconds to spare, and to Vesper's surprise, Nim was already going down the row and murmuring through the grates, warning each cell of what was coming and what they'd need to do. As Vesper continued putting tincture on the compass and opening cells, the freed wizards and witches joined Nim, making the whole process go much more smoothly than she could have anticipated.

Only one more mishap occurred. At the end of the first row of cells, a witch had gone insane and refused to leave. One of her cellmates tried to drag her through, but too slowly—he lost one of his hands, and since she'd been leaning forward, legs dug into the floor, the closing rent shaved the top half of her skull cleanly off.

Vesper made a decision then, which was disseminated through the grate by the prisoners outside their cells, who now numbered twice that of those still inside—"If someone doesn't want to come, leave them. We don't have time to deal with them."

The final prisoner freed, she turned to the wall. "Which way goes outside? A place where there won't be guards," she called out.

Fortunately, with that many wizards and witches in one place, a few still had a functioning direction-sense. A smooth-faced woman with eyes coated over with a white film pointed at a wall without hesitation. Vesper looked at her store of tincture; less than half remained. She had no better ideas. "Line up. Get ready to go," she said.

She tipped a drop of tincture on the compass and aimed. The wall parted, and light shone through, momentarily blinding Vesper so she didn't even see the first rush of prisoners streaming outside.

She had not planned it well. Perhaps no one could have, but she felt control slipping in the wake of mayhem. No one counted seconds, but desperation drove all to be the first—and people pushed, shoved, kicked their way to get through the hole, leaving at least three cleaved through and thoroughly dead with the first closure of the rent. Horrified, Vesper paused before putting the next drop onto the compass, despite a rising clamor to do so from the crowd, and a tangible wave of desperation that felt as if it was about to get mean. Someone would try to take both compass and tincture from her in a moment.

"Everyone will have a chance to get through," she said. "Don't risk each other's lives. Line up and go through, five people at a time, or I won't open the wall any longer. And any move to take it from me, I'll spill the whole thing."

It worked for a while, more or less; a few times six or seven went through, but no one else died. Then, when about two score prisoners remained, they all heard it—the tell-tale sound of the lock turning.

"They're coming!" someone screamed. Two score made a break for the rent; several made it through, but the re-forming wall maimed or killed many more.

"Hurry—open it again!"

Vesper's hand trembled. She had to plan her own escape too. All too quickly the door to the cell swung open, and the body parts streaming inside screeched out an alarm even as flying hands reached to claim the remaining prisoners.

She had barely any tincture left, but it would be enough to get her through. Someone jostled her elbow, knocking the dropper from her hand. No matter—she upended the bottle over the compass...but right at that moment, a hand grabbed her elbow and pulled. The remaining tincture spilled onto the floor.

More hands took hold of Vesper, clamping onto all her limbs, immobilizing her. Flying body parts thickened the air, and she couldn't even see who remained with her. Had Nim escaped? She thought so. There was that, at least. But for her...she had to look forward to more of Zinfel and his games...

The hands dragged her toward the exit. Then the wall behind her exploded.

CHAPTER 22

The impact threw Vesper and her hand-guards to the floor. Dust and screams filled the air, and Vesper felt the grips on her limbs loosen. She'd fallen hard on her hip, but she hoped she'd merely bruised it. Light streamed in through a hole in the bottom half of the wall, three times the size of the one she'd created with her compass. The top portion of the wall looked on the verge of collapse as well.

Vesper crawled, then got up and staggered toward the hole. As she reached it, a man's silhouette filled the gap and entered.

Jules barreled through, grabbing her by the hand. "Move!" he shouted over the sound of rumbling, and he pulled them through the hole, just before an entire section of the ceiling collapsed with a roar.

They ran, but only for a moment, as Jules yanked them to a stop and flicked his wrist—one, two, three times. An eyeball and two hands fell to the ground, and only when Jules bent to retrieve three tiny darts from them did she even realize what he'd thrown.

"We have to get away from here," he said. "Most of the available soldiers have been sent after the escaped prisoners, but they'll be back here soon enough after that explosion."

They both heard it then—the crack of a stick, an indrawn breath—and Jules' wrist snapped back again, ready for another flick. Then Vesper caught a glimpse of a pale, frightened face in the grass, wide, slightly protruding blue eyes.

Jules saw him too, checked his movement, and lowered his hand. "Nim," he acknowledged, and he pulled Vesper down so that the three hunkered down in the grass together.

"Am I ever glad to see you," Nim said.

"Shh," Vesper said, as a contingent of eyeballs flew above them, an ominous cloud of silent, jellied white sight.

Whoever had told Vesper what spot on the wall to open had chosen rightly. The palace gates did not surround that portion of the wall. Because of its thickness, its seeming impenetrability, the wall formed part of the border of the palace grounds themselves, and no guards had been posted here.

The three of them waited for what seemed an eternity, watching the last of the soldiers marching out after the escapees. Finally, no more feet tromped past, and the rustling of organized body parts no longer filled the air. Jules pulled Vesper to her feet, and Nim followed them into a milling crowd of observers from town, all still pointing in the direction of parts flying into the distance.

"Where are we going?" Vesper asked.

"Herland," Jules said. "It's the only place that's safe now, and we need to warn the people before Bugger finds some way of sending the disease there."

Vesper felt the blood leaving her face. "Zinfel said something about using a tincture I'd made in order to get through the force fields of his enemy."

Jules' mouth thinned to a line. "Then we have all the more reason to get there quickly. Herland's defense system is all about force fields."

Vesper's chest constricted, with anticipation or apprehension, she had no idea. She did know the source of her reaction, though: she was going to see Garth.

Even in the few short weeks Vesper had been isolated in the palace, much had changed in town. Trained body parts had taken over the roles of the soldiers and police in many places—armed parts staffed each checkpoint, and even in the streets, knife-wielding hands, watchful eyes, and noses imbedded with rock-sensors to smell out magic whizzed by, creating heights of surveillance never before dreamed of in Malland.

The parts hadn't yet been trained to recognize specific faces, so without magic Vesper, Nim, and Jules were safe enough so long as they avoided the few who might recognize them. They went to an inn where even in the privacy of the room Jules had rented for the day, they found a pinky finger and an ear hidden in the curtains. After imprisoning the eavesdroppers in multiple layers of cloth, to be discovered by whoever cleaned the room after the travelers left, Jules sent Nim down to request food, leaving him alone with Vesper.

Only a few weeks had passed since she'd spent those early morning hours in conflicted agony lying six feet away from him, but much felt changed. Jules looked different—he'd cut off all that silky hair. It revealed a nicely-shaped head with a brown shadow of fuzz on top, bringing out the stark angle of jaw and cheekbone, and eyes that regarded Vesper so intently that she felt her ability to pull breath into her lungs rapidly receding. He was looking at her like *that* again...that same soul-searching look that had bothered her so much when they'd first met. She thought that perhaps she might not mind so much, now.

Mind or not, though, one could only take so much of having one's soul scrutinized. "I...I'm sorry I didn't believe you," Vesper blurted, to break the tension. "About the king's motives. You were right...he's completely crazy...and he's behind the spread of the disease."

Jules took a step toward her. "Well, yes," he said. "I think I was wrong, too, to be so against your going to the palace. Granted, you were in danger...but now that you're safe, it's easy to appreciate what you did. You freed most of the people in the quarantine dungeon, with fewer casualties than my group projected if we'd gone through with our own plan. And what you did with those walls—what was that?"

She blushed. "It's what the mushroom does in concentrated form—it amplifies magic. I figured out the cure for the split-disease, too." She had no more of the tincture, but she took out the other vial.

"You did?" A smile broke out on his face, and only then did she see how many cares had worn their way onto his shoulders as she watched him relax them, just a little. "Then that will take care of my biggest worry—that the disease has already infected Herland. Vesper, you're wonderful."

She beamed under his approval. Then his smile faded, replaced by the weirdest expression she'd ever seen on Jules; he was giving her that soul-searching look, but combined with a sort of constipated torture. She wondered if he had a stomachache when he muttered something under his breath and strode the space between them, seizing her in one arm and pulling her close. "To Mae's twat with Garth," he said, before he bent to kiss her.

She felt her body go up in flames, dry tinder to his spark. She kissed him back, ravenously, pressing her body up against his, rubbing up against him in some primal erotic reaction she never could have choreographed in fantasy. Her fingers ran across the dark velvet buzz of his hair as she opened her mouth against his, feeling the tentative flick of his tongue, meeting it with her own.

He pulled back a little, eyes raking over her, half-smoldering, half-cautious. "Were you like this with him?" he asked, voice husky.

She blinked. *Him?* Who was *he*? He couldn't be referring to—"Is that all you can think about? *Garth?*" Pulling out of his embrace, she nearly fell over, unsure if the kiss had set her off-balance—or sheer anger at his pigheadedness.

Jules seemed to be fighting an internal battle, lips pressed together, forehead furrowed as he stared at the floor. "No, it's not the only thing. I'm also thinking about how I can't seem to be anything but utterly selfish around you. It's been a struggle to become someone who sticks to his vows, and I thought I'd achieved it—until now. Breaking them makes no sense to me, because we don't fit in each other's worlds."

Vesper thought no differently herself, but somehow, hearing that she wasn't worth his breaking his vows irritated her, and she wanted to argue. Nim's entrance at that moment cut off her retort. "Hey, Jules—this is heavy, please take it quick!"

Nim, oblivious to the tension in the room, staggered in under the weight of a tray laden with covered dishes. Jules took it and set it down while Vesper pressed her lips together and turned away, toward the window.

As Nim chattered on, full of gossip about wizards and witches being run down in the streets by pursuing parts, Jules and Vesper avoided eye contact until the implicit agreement to forget the kiss and the ensuing argument became clear.

They stayed at the inn until evening. Vesper changed into the clothing Jules had brought for her—pants, tunic, cloak, and boots that had probably belonged to an adolescent boy who'd outgrown them.

Nim got a spare set of Jules' clothes, similarly appropriate for travel. Vesper's trip to, and escape from, the dungeon had ruined her silk and lace confection beyond repair, but she folded it to drop off in the poor-box—the cloth itself was still worth the monthly income of the average citizen of Malland. She wished she could bring it home with her—but she would have to think of something else to do to pay off the debt to Ruben, because there was no way she could lug a ruined dress across the kingdom. The few jewels that had remained on the dress she'd given to Jules, who used them to purchase their clothes, horses, and travel provisions.

Under cover of darkness they began their journey. They went cross-country, avoiding roads, as checkpoints staffed by soldiers occupied every major fork. Although the checkpoints were intended to ferret out witches and wizards, the travelers could not predict anything of King Bugger's actions—they had no way of knowing if he'd had every checkpoint alerted to Vesper's escape.

The extended warm season and a recent period of rain gave them bearable nights and land rich in forage. Jules proved to be handy with setting up traps for animals and using a slingshot that brought down a rabbit and several squirrels on their first day out. To Vesper's surprise and his own, Nim, too, proved to be a fast learner with hunting and particularly good with the slingshot. Vesper found greens that she knew to be edible. They drank water from streams or holes dug next to their campsites. They avoided towns, but they stayed close enough to access the richer land and waterways along which civilization had reached. Vesper could ride—at least she'd had plenty of practice on Jack—but she hadn't been on any animal for weeks, and now her muscles ached. Despite the pain, she made no complaint, and although Nim did whine a bit at first, he soon stopped when no one paid any attention. So, for the most part they rode in silence, Jules only offering terse instructions regarding the terrain.

As much as the days stretched on, Vesper almost dreaded the nights more. When they could conceal it, they kept a low fire burning through the night, but more often than not they preferred not to call attention to their camp, and they went without. Those nights, they slept in close proximity—Vesper sandwiched between Nim and Jules.

She'd never slept with a man before. Before these past weeks, her visions of sex had been either of something ethereal and gooey, not at all connected to her body, or as something base, something animals did. Now, with an awakening forced on her in several forms, she couldn't help being hyper-aware of Jules, how good he smelled despite the lack of bathing. Lying next to him stimulated a subtle form of emotional, mental, and physical torture. The contrast of feeling slight repulsion offrom Nim on her other side made it all the more painful, and she found herself often imagining herself sandwiched by tall brick walls to try to avoid reacting to anyone at all.

On the morning of the eighth day, as she woke up to find Jules gone and Nim still fast asleep by her side, she tucked her hands behind her head and relaxed, relieved to have a moment alone. The fire had fresh wood piled on it—Jules must have left only recently, either to forage or to climb a bit to scout their path, as he'd done on the days before.

Herland wasn't far now—they had been ascending steadily for three days, and the peak of the smallish mountain forming the border between the countries had become a visible smudge in the distance. It wouldn't be much longer.

She sat up and stretched, scowling as she scratched at a cluster of insect bites on her leg. Then she felt the telltale prickle of awareness that someone was watching her.

She whirled. Trees surrounded her and Nim, and only the occasional chirp of a bird disturbed the silence.

It must be nothing, she told herself, although she remained on edge as she began to pack up their camp—folding and tying the blankets, then unwrapping some leftover greens from the day before and nibbling on a wilted frond, so preoccupied she didn't even grimace at the bitterness.

She couldn't stop the prickles that continued their cold march down her spine, the uncomfortable feeling of being observed. Time and time again she turned, seeing nothing.

Then she caught a glimpse of something small—about as big as an eyeball, and floating in the air amidst the branches of the nearest tree.

It *was* an eyeball. Dirty white, pale blue iris and dilated pupil, it stared at her. When it saw her staring back, it turned and fled, faster than if she'd thrown it.

She shook Nim, who jerked to a sitting position with a shriek. "Wake up. We're being watched." Then she started up the nearest hill. "Jules! Where are you?"

She smelled something funny—reminiscent of city back-alleys and chamber pots that hadn't been emptied for a day...in fact, it was just like—

"Aaaaa—" Her scream was cut short by the enormous, jiggling, hairy, pale buttocks barreling into her face.

She ducked, but a sharp pain stabbed through her ankle as it twisted and she rolled down the hill.

Then the buttocks came again, this time making contact with the side of her head. She managed to deflect it with her elbow.

"Get away!" she shrieked, slapping at it. It laughed, its voice deep and growling, as if coming directly from the small pink rosebud between those cheesy dented globes of horror. With the laughter came a rush of that foul odor again. She got up, resisting the urge to pass out, and she limped toward the fire, arm protecting her face as the buttocks rammed her again and again, so hard her teeth rattled at the impact. It was strong—powered by the *gluteus maximus*, one of the strongest muscles in the body, she recalled—and if she didn't manage to get rid of it, it could certainly bludgeon her to serious injury, or worse.

She had to take her arm away from her face to reach for a burning stick. At that instant, the buttocks slammed into her face, cheeks squeezing her cheeks, foul odor assaulting her nose and closing off all air. She choked, flailing wildly, but the buttocks had flown too close for her to hit it with much impact. Her vision went black, leaving her with the thought—*this isn't the way I thought I would go...*

Then she gasped in clean air as something ripped the weight off her face. As she coughed, the foul odor still clinging to her face, she saw Jules thrust his dagger into the buttocks, which gave a high-pitched squeal, twitched, and went still.

Vesper sat up and opened her mouth to thank Jules, but he dove for his pack, grabbing that lightning-stick he'd taken from the palace soldiers before, and he whirled to meet a new attack. A flesh-colored cloud swarmed toward them, composed of eyes, ears, noses, whole arms or legs and various bits and pieces of others. "Run," Jules said, but too late. All escape routes blocked off, the body parts encircled them and began to move in. The first feet came running in to kick them, the first fists flying in to punch, stray fingers going for their eyes, other eyes and ears hovering to observe.

The horses screamed. Nim yelled. Vesper could hardly see her companions through the sea of flesh. She scrabbled for the burning stick and began swinging it wildly about, but doing almost no damage, screaming when she felt something biting her calf, fingers pulling her hair, unidentifiable wet things smacking against the rest of her. She remembered Zinfel's games, in which the body parts had killed the wizard within moments—even when he'd fought them with magic.

They did have Jules' shock-stick—which turned out to be better than either magic or knives. After a few zaps, blood and smoke spewing out in rhythm with the sound of electric shocks and squelching flesh, the parts began to fly off, lifting away in a collective mass of airborne panic. They'd been tortured by such a stick, Vesper remembered—making it the ideal weapon to use against them. She also noticed, though, that the shocks seemed to be diminishing in strength. Did the stick have limited power? At the rate at which it seemed to be losing efficacy, it would certainly not be enough to scare off each of the remaining parts individually.

Jules seemed to recognize this, for he was using his arms and hands to deflect and attack just as much as the stick now, waving it in a way to scare rather than make contact. It was working—but would the parts realize what he was doing and regroup? They still had the numbers to defeat him.

Little by little, Jules and Vesper thinned the ranks of the parts through death or flight, and finally the last of them, flew off. Blood, hair, and the stink of copper and singed hair permeated the campsite. Nim and the horses had disappeared.

Vesper stumbled over to where Jules was standing, his tattered shirt covered with congealed blood. "Are you all right?" she asked.

He waved her off impatiently. "We need to find the horses and go," he said. "That was no random attack. If they come back—which

I have a feeling they will, with reinforcements—I don't think we can hold them off. This stick's out of juice." He tossed the lightning-stick to the ground.

They found Nim passed out nearby, with one of the horses grazing close to his head. After they'd determined that he had only fainted, Jules took the horse to search for the other two; he'd found one of the missing horses by the time Nim had woken up and he and Vesper cleaned and bound what wounds they could—fortunately, all of them were superficial, although she did worry a little about the bite on her calf becoming infected. The third horse was nowhere to be found—but some of the dead body parts at the campsite did look horse-like, and Vesper feared the worst.

Vesper rode double behind Jules, which slowed their pace, but they had almost reached their destination and were already beginning a slow ascent up the mountains. "We should reach the border by nightfall," Jules said, although the tension in his body did not slacken.

At dusk, several hours later, they were crossing the mountain's peak, and Vesper finally began to relax. Only then did she notice a strange cloud in the faded dark blue sky behind them. "What's that?" she asked.

Jules took one look and kicked the horse into a gallop with a growled "Hold on. Nim, follow me!" Vesper clutched at Jules' waist as the horse, exhausted already, surged into its second wind.

The cloud grew closer, and Vesper knew now that body parts, in much larger numbers than the last time, approached for another attack. This time, she could see some of the parts—any of them that could actually hold something—carried knives or bludgeons or sharp-edged rocks. Now Jules had no more lightning-stick.

The horses ran, both of them frothing and now spurred by their own fear. Metal and flesh sang in the air above them—premature night descended as the parts arrowed in, knives at the ready—

The air thickened, as if they moved through honey. Within that honey-mass, Vesper felt a sort of static running across her body, and then a pressure building up in her chest as if her heart would burst at any second. She could hardly breathe—and as the honey released them into fresh air again, something popped out of her and flew out the top of her dress.

She caught sight of a lumpy roundish object, bright red and slick with blood, tubes protruding from its top. Its sides moved in and out—she could hear a faint *lub-dub, lub-dub*. Her heart!

It whizzed beyond the reach of her outstretched hand, although as it grew smaller she thought she could still see its sides fluttering. Her breath caught, and she waited for death—how could she survive without her heart? OnlyBut when she reached down the neck of her dress and touched the unbroken skin of her chest, she realized that somehow, her body had adjusted to the absence of that major organ, f. For she remained alive and standing.

Jules grunted, and out of the bottom of his pant leg flew a soft purplish-brown ball. He managed to snatch it out of midair before it could escape.

"Mae's twat!" he said. "Herland's magical border defenses. They should have disarmed us, stopped us from entering if we had any evil intent—but it seems they're totally corrupted by the split-disease, and now this is all they're good for—'liberating' parts."

A horrible sound, half a sob and half a squeak, came from behind them. It was Nim. Oh, *no*, Vesper thought. She didn't want to turn around—she knew, she just knew what she would see. Unable to avoid it any longer, she turned.

She needn't have been afraid of meeting his eyes and witnessing his shame through that contact; he had no eyes left. Instead of those slightly protruding blue orbs, he stared at her with two sunken holes. *Oh, Nim...*

Jules turned the horse, scanning the space where they'd just emerged—all they could see was clear moonlit sky and empty hills rolling downwards. "No sign of those parts," Jules said. "I suppose they've got orders to stay in Malland." He scowled at the squirming testicle. "What am I going to do with this thing?"

"Let me go!" it squeaked.

Vesper ripped off a strip of her cloak. "Wrap it in this," she said. "Then I suppose you could carry it—well, in the same place as it's supposed to be."

He did as she suggested, muffling the testicle's pleas within the cloth, then his pants. "Nim," he said. "Can you still ride?"

"I—I don't know," Nim said, voice uneven, on the breaking point. Then he steeled himself. "I think so. My horse will follow yours."

"Good," said Jules. With no more than that, he urged the horse forward again, heading for a path that wound its way around the mountain and then down. Vesper watched Nim, worried. Thankfully his horse followed, and Nim kept his seat.

"Did you lose a part?" Jules asked as they descended.

He hadn't noticed! She swallowed. Now that she knew he didn't know yet, she didn't think she wanted to tell him. The part someone lost reflected something about that person—and admitting that she'd lost her heart would reveal too much about her. It would show all her weaknesses and her faults. Perhaps it would show that she'd lost it because she had no skill at loving—or at being loved.

"I don't think so," she said, keeping her voice convincingly expressionless.

CHAPTER 23

Once over the honey-mass border, the mountains of Malland, shaped like carnivorous teeth padded with thick strips of arid forest, shifted to Herland's round bunny-hills covered evenly with grasses that looked as if they were waving "Hi!" to the passing breezes. Jules and Vesper could see clearly by the light of the moon, and as they descended, they saw flowers carpeting the hills, and the riot of blossoms bled into a village. Many small cottages dotted the land in a ragged circular pattern around a lake and a central gathering area beside it, marked by a larger building made of earth, with an open timber roof.

"Something's wrong," Jules said as they headed down toward the village. "I see no lights or fires anywhere. It's early enough that people should be coming out to greet us. Herlanders are very friendly. No one's here."

"You've been here before?" Vesper asked.

Jules nodded. "I came here after I left the king's military service. I wasn't really welcome anywhere in Malland...My family was really upset with me. They sided with Garth. Here, where they particularly like pacifists, I was accepted."

"Why did you go back to Malland then?" The flowers overwhelmed the grasses in increasingly large splotches, and she could smell them—a wild, sweet scent that made her think about tumbling off the horse and burying her face in blossoms. How could anyone leave this place?

She felt his shoulders lift in a shrug behind her. "Well, for one thing, I'm not really a pacifist, if you haven't noticed. And too many things need to be changed in Malland. How long could you stand living in a paradise if you're existing next to a dictatorship?"

Soon it became evident that this was no paradise—not any longer, at least. If people had lived in the approaching village, they had deserted it. Buildings with no doors and shuttered or boarded-up windows exposed the lack of movement or life within, and the evenness of the dirt showed few recent footsteps. Only as they reached the central gathering area did they see a lone torch lit, and holding it, an old man, featureless save for his mouth, as he'd lost his nose, ears, and eyes. As he shuffled toward them, Vesper turned toward another movement in the corner of the open circle—a leg lurked in the shadows of the flickering torch, hopping about in an endless circle. To his side, it looked like a stomach was sucking on a potato.

Jules dismounted, and Vesper slid down after him, following him as he went to take Nim's horse by the reins. "Come down, my friend. We're going to rest the night before continuing." Nim did so, and Jules kept a hand on his shoulder as the old man approached them.

"Visitors," the old man said. "Welcome, welcome!" His hand shook as he placed the torch in a holder. He held out both his arms, teetering from side to side as he inched toward them, fingers outstretched and massaging the air.

"Where is everyone?" Jules asked, and the man headed for him with more confidence. Jules gamely held his ground as the arms pulled him into an embrace, then added Nim for a group hug. Finally, the old man broke into sobs, face in the crevice between Jules' and Nim's shoulders.

"Gone, gone, all gone. All save Ject and me. Nothing here to eat, you see. It was always so easy, the magic in the land just made the food for us, and we didn't have to lift a finger, could spend all our time on art and music, on harmony...but now the land's turned against us. The magic is all weird now. We've had to farm, but we keep losing a finger here, a foot there whenever we till or plant or harvest. Everybody's scared to work, but they have no choice."

Jules patted the man's thin shoulders as they shook.

"Why have you stayed behind, and how do you survive here, with nothing to eat?"

"Someone has to greet the visitors," the man said, straightening a little. "And every couple weeks someone comes by from the capital. They usually give us some of what they picked up there. The Goodpeople are trying to get everybody to work together so we don't starve. Ject!"

Out of the building, an even older man emerged, a pale prune of a fellow whose shirt fell loosely over a caved-in abdomen. He held three small bowls of rice, one piled atop another. "Here, Reg. Warming up the rice for our guests." Trembling hands held the bowls out.

He lacked some internal organs. Vesper felt, in a somewhat separated way, a vague disgust, or a memory that she would have found such a thing disgusting. "I'm not very hungry," she started to say, but Jules looked at her and held her gaze for a moment—*Take it*, his eyes said. *They have little else except their hospitality.*

"We thank you," he said, and accepted a bowl, taking another for Nim. After an instant, Vesper took one as well.

She frowned down at the unappetizing bits of purplish grain. Tasting one, she found it bland, but oddly satisfying; as she ate more, the rice settled nicely in her empty belly, easing a tightness from days of under-eating. As she scooped up the last few grains with her fingers, she felt oddly satisfied, and that she needed nothing more. She basked in that fragile moment of contentment.

"We need to go to the capital," Jules said, as soon as he'd finished his rice. "Are there a couple of horses we could borrow—or better yet, three horses, so we don't have to ride double?"

"No horses left," said Reg. "We had nothing to eat while the first crops were growing. We had to eat the animals."

Vesper's moment of contentment abruptly ended. Still, her reaction to Reg's words was less than what it should have been; instead of horror, she only managed a numb discomfort.

The old man scratched his head. "Should be a wagon passing by tomorrow morning, going to the capital," he said. "You could ride in the back."

"Thank you," said Jules. "We'll do that."

"Take you someplace to rest now, if you'd like," said Reg. He rolled his head from side to side as if orienting himself, then shuffled to face the building and in a lengthy, lurching walk, led them inside what was little more than a roof over a large open space. Wwith such a mild night, and plenty of blankets from Reg, they slept in unaccustomed comfort until dawn.

Within an hour of their waking, the wagon going to the capital rolled by, and the driver, friendly as all Herlanders—well, considering Allegra, most Herlanders—agreed to give them a ride. So they gave up their horses—Vesper hoped no one would eat the poor beasts, but she couldn't muster enough compassion to exhort Reg and Ject not to do so—and an hour later she lay curled up against a mound of blankets in the back of the wagon. Jules and Nim lay on the other side, both dozing again, catching up on many days of missed sleep.

Jules' mouth had softened in repose, and Vesper stared at him, trying to remember how she'd felt about him—she'd been so conflicted about something…but now it was all gone. Aside from the dried blood and unidentifiable gore that smeared his clothing and matted his hair, he wasn't bad looking--she noticed he'd gained weight since she'd first met him, and it looked good on him—but beyond aesthetic appreciation, her strongest sense was of his unsuitability for her and her ambitions. It was somewhat of a relief, actually; all the agonizing about choices between men had disappeared with her heart. She would see Garth soon, and now it seemed clear to her that for a number of reasons he was the logical partner for her. She could almost hear her mother's voice in her head listing the reasons for his suitability—Vesper would certainly never get a better offer, and marrying Garth would open every door she could ever want with regard to her career as a scientist and philosopher at court—whatever court looked like after the political dust settled. With wealth, status, and a man beautiful enough to make her the envy of every woman in Pecktown, Vesper would have a chance to live the life she'd always dreamed of. So what if Garth wasn't always completely honest? That quality was offset by his apparent dislike of collecting wives.

Something about the idea made her feel hollow inside—the habit of reacting to things emotionally had her repeatedly hitting a dull ache where her heart should be. *Never mind*, she thought. *Life is easier this way*.

She scooted toward the edge of the wagon so she could watch the land as they drove past. Even in her state of heartlessness, she could appreciate Herland's beauty as something out of a dream or a fairy tale. Flowers carpeted the fields, burst from the crannies between rocks and trees, from tiny blossoms that dotted the ground like stars, to enormous exotic blooms as large as dinner plates. She wondered if there were extra-large bees to match—but she saw only butterflies and rainbow-breasted hummingbirds, as flamboyantly colored as the flowers around which they hovered.

She would have found it peaceful and relaxing here, but in every town they traveled through, people radiated anxiety under uneasy masks of optimism. Their dependency on magic had made them nearly helpless now that everything magical was corrupted. As the wagon traveled past, Vesper saw people working the land. They raked and shoveled and weeded with oddly jerky movements, as if the land might jump up and bite them. Then she saw why they feared the land so when a man pulled a weed and his hand came off at the wrist, flying away still clutching the plant. She remembered what Ject had said—the land had been infused with magic that allowed it to farm itself and provide food to the Herlanders, but the split-disease had infected the land. People now faced the choice of starvation or slow dismemberment as they toiled for their food.

As they arrived at their destination, Vesper observed that Mallandina eclipsed Herland's tiny capital. Here, no palace dominated and commanded those inferior to it. Instead, in a larger and somewhat less rustic version of each of the villages, a great round structure in the physical center of the populated area acted as the base and meeting point for its people. From an earthen foundation rose crystalline walls carved into a great spiral rising up to a round, flat rooftop that overlooked the land. This structure, Jules told Vesper, had been built with magic by the Goodpeople—the council of wizards and witches who governed the country.

Jules jumped down first, held out his hand to help Nim, then helped Vesper down. He wrinkled his nose. "You don't smell good."

"You're one to talk." She snatched her hand away.

He chuckled then. The laughter softened the planes of his face, and Vesper found herself smiling in return.

A cloud passed across Jules' face, squelching the laughter, leaving it devoid of expression. Vesper turned, still smiling, to see what he was looking at, and then she saw him, too: Garth.

CHAPTER 24

Two Herlanders, a woman and a man, accompanied Garth. All three wore loose white clothing—tunic over trousers or skirt—plain of adornment save for a few necklaces and bracelets of wood or crystal beads. The outfit flattered Garth's broad shoulders, emphasizing skin tanned a shade darker, eyes exuding a soft clarity that spoke of being well-rested. The Herlanders were older, the woman's hair streaked with gray and the man's pure white, but for all that they stood straight and now moved forward with the ease of youth.

The woman opened her arms to Jules, and they embraced. Her face scrunched into a sunburst of wrinkles as she smiled. "Welcome back, Jules," she said. "We have missed you."

Garth's scowl indicated that the sentiment was not shared, but Jules paid his brother no heed. "Kalma, Pefar, these are my companions: Vesper and Nim," he said.

Something about the woman's gaze, when it met Vesper's, had an almost hypnotic effect; instantly Vesper felt at ease, and she returned the smile and inclined her head.

Kalma went to Nim and took his face in her hands. "Poor Nim," she said. "You've come a long way from home, haven't you? And you've suffered greatly for it. I can feel your pain, your loss. You will find a little healing here, I think."

"Th-thank you," Nim said, almost inaudibly. Vesper saw Garth's mouth curl in revulsion at the sight of Nim's eyeless face, lids squeezed shut and sunken into their empty sockets. She threw him an angry glance, and he caught it and smiled lazily at her. She pressed her lips together and looked away.

"He lost his eyes coming into Herland," Jules said. "That's one of several pieces of news I bring you. Do you know that Herland's defenses don't work now?"

The white-haired man, Pefar, nodded. "Yes. It is unfortunate my daughter brought Garth here, even though it is, of course, no fault of his. Garth explained to us how the disease is spread. We didn't even try to heal him with magic, but what we discovered too late is that because magic is even in the air here, constantly working its spells on the earth and all creatures in Herland, an infected person simply setting foot here has been enough to set off a contagion that has reached every corner of our land." Garth had the grace to look ashamed.

Vesper stared at the man—he must be Allegra's father, she realized, and now she saw the resemblance in their fine-boned frames and in his face, an older male version of hers, although an infinitely more pleasant version.

"What are you doing about it?" Jules asked.

"What we have always done," Kalma said. "We accept and we adjust to the environment we are provided. We meditate and seek the wisdom to deal with these shifts, and perhaps to heal them. We nurture the parts that are born and make them feel welcome in Herland, as we do all who come here."

"Are you going to make Bugger's army welcome when it comes here, too, then?" Jules asked. "Not just his men—an army the likes of which you've never seen. An army of body parts that have been tortured into mindlessly obedient killers."

Kalma's expression remained unchanged, but Pefar shook his head, suddenly looking ten years older.

"We feared this," he said. "We are ill equipped for defense. I will call the rest of the Goodpeople to confer how to adjust to this unwelcome situation in the most bloodless way possible."

"Uh-uh," Garth said, looking at the two Herlanders and shaking his head.

Vesper and Jules both turned to him, waiting for him to clarify his vehement denial. Instead, he punched the palm of his hand and pointed at Kalma and Pefar.

"I assume you're saying that Bugger will easily subjugate Herland, which I agree with," Jules said. "What's wrong, Garth? You've never had a problem being articulate before."

Garth glared at his brother in silence, lips pressed together.

Pefar patted Garth on the shoulder. "Like so many others, our friend has lost something," he said. "He cannot speak."

Vesper stared at him in consternation. She wanted to feel compassion for him, but instead all she could think about was how this affected her calculation that he would make a good marriage partner. She pinched her arm hard, admonishing herself for having such a cold thought.

"The news we bring isn't entirely bad," Jules said. " We have brought the cure for the split-disease."

At the mention of the cure, Garth's face grew eager, and he took a step forward, reaching out his hand, gesturing for it. Vesper took out the small vial of remedy and the mushroom she'd brought.

"It hasn't really been tested," she said. "I've seen it work, though, and quickly. I think...judging by how the disease spreads here...you could put it in wells, and other places which supply drinking water. You make the remedy through putting a small crumb of the mushroom in pure water, and diluting it to about ten percent and shaking it for a minute, and repeating the process—I'd say at least ten times."

"Yes, I know that process of making a remedy," Kalma said, and she reached for the vial and mushroom.

"This is wonderful," Pefar said. "If it works, I will get the cure into the major water supplies. Once some of us can use our magic again, we can seed it into the skies and use the rain to disseminate it."

Just then, an eyeball came whizzing over to hover in front of Pefar. Vesper looked about in alarm, sure the cloud of body parts that had pursued them was not far behind,. bBbut Pefar knew this particular eyeball.

"What is it?" he asked.

"An enormous host is leaving Mallandina, heading in this direction," said the eyeball in its tinny voice. "Men on foot and horseback, and many, many body parts. They are armed."

She could still feel fear, Vesper realized, and she shivered.

"I'm afraid it's our fault they're coming so soon," said Jules. "Those parts who followed us to the border could have flown back to Malland within hours, and now they're bringing the whole army with them."

"But you're also the reason why we have hope of defeating them," Kalma said.

"We must move," said Pefar. "There is much to be done."

Pefar entered the building, and Garth began to follow. Then he turned to Vesper, meeting her gaze for the first time since their reunion. Taking a step toward her, he seized her in his arms, his sudden movement making her gasp. He kissed her, so hard her lips were smashed against her teeth—and then just as quickly, he pulled away and strode into the building. Vesper wobbled on her feet, her sense of gravity upended and reset, too fast.

Vesper glanced at Jules, who was already following his brother. Even though she had no heart, she still could feel guilt.

"Wait—where are you going?" she asked, running to catch up to him.

"I will take care of you," Kalma said, looking at Vesper and taking Nim by the arm.

"Go with her," Jules said, not meeting her eyes. "Stay safe."

"Jules—" she stopped, unsure what she wanted to say. *It's only practical that we not be together*. Or, *you have your life, and I have mine, and they just don't work. Let's save ourselves the pain of entertaining it*. Or, *the best part of me wanted you, and now it's gone. So don't feel bad, because it's making me feel bad*. She felt herself breaking into a sweat, and she wondered that she could still feel such conflicted affinity for him, even without a heart.

Jules turned slowly, his expression so pained that he almost looked ill. "Maybe if I hadn't lost my testicle, I'd have the balls to fight for you. I guess my losing it shows that I never had it to begin with. So good luck with my brother. You'll always have my friendship, at least."

What could she say to that? It left the way clear for her and Garth. Still, she turned to avoid watching him disappear into the building. "What can I do now?" she asked Kalma, gathering the shreds of her pride about her.

"We will go to the Sanctum," said Kalma. "Rest and relax. The army could be here within a week, but we have some time to prepare."

"It took us a lot longer than a week," said Vesper.

"But you didn't go the direct route, did you?" Kalma asked. "Come to the Sanctum. Make yourself comfortable. You'll want to get used to it, for if there is an attack, you will be safest there."

"Okay," Vesper said, after a moment. "I'll go there for now." She would have preferred doing something a little more helpful, but it wouldn't hurt to have a little rest, and to see Nim situated somewhere at least. So she followed Kalma into the building.

Within the Goodpeople's central building, walls of opaque crystal spanned out in circles that contained circles, interconnecting passageways leading up or down as if outlining an enormous three-dimensional spiderweb. The Sanctum could be located by always going in and down; beyond that, Vesper had no idea how they were getting there. Perhaps the confusion in its layout was what made the building safe. Other than that, though, it seemed to have no defenses at all. Finally they arrived at a large crystalline room, cave-like in its rounded shape, its lower half indented and sparkling with a shifting rainbow of color in the crystal. An odd calmness descended over Vesper—the equivalent of the feeling of walking through water, except with her emotions. All the anxiety she'd been feeling, all her worries about the impending attack, the traumas of the past weeks—everything seemed to dissipate, becoming remote echoes that sounded far away. Nim, too, allowed his shoulders to sag, and even the tension he'd developed around his empty eye sockets eased.

"How can this place exist?" Vesper asked in wonder. "Isn't everything magic infected in Herland?"

Kalma shook her head. "Not everything. This building, more than anything else in Herland, is alive...within it is a spark of pure consciousness. It is whole, a mirror to Mae, who unites all. The magic of Herland is like planes refracted off that mirror, and thus it can be distorted and infected with split-disease. But this place is inviolate."

"It's so beautiful," Vesper said. "A part of me wishes I could stay here always."

"One thing to remember," said Kalma. "It is nearly impossible to feel anything negative in here. Because you're really connected, to everything, here...but it's only meant to be a temporary sanctuary, a place to remember yourself. In time you'll want your negative thoughts, your emotional baggage back, and you'll have hopefully bolstered yourself enough with the Sanctum's reminder of your Source that you can come out with fresh perspective. When you've had enough of it, you'll know, and then come and join us outside."

"I'll remember," Vesper said, but she wasn't listening. She was watching Nim, whose hand just touched the edge of the wall; she felt no pity for him here, only kinship—and relief, to not pity him.

"Are you all right?" she asked him. She still couldn't get used to his lack of eyes. For so long, she'd been judgmental about how his eyes bulged like a fish's; now, she missed his eyes, exactly as they'd been.

"I'm thinking of Begonia," he said. "She really admires me. I don't think anyone ever has before. I think...I don't know if she'd ever come here...but if I could bring her here, to this room, I think she still would admire me."

"Oh, Nim." Vesper felt a pang of sadness even through the soporific calm induced by the room. "If she's a good person, she would love you even out of this room. Everybody's lost parts."

Nim turned his head toward her. "What about you, Vesper?"

She thought about lying, but in this room, shame did not exist, and besides, she'd known Nim forever. What did she have to hide from him? "My heart."

"Ah," he said, nodding. "That would make things weird with Jules, I guess."

"Jules?" she asked. "I think you mean Garth." She found herself fidgeting, and the crystal buzz seemed to increase in proportion to the spike in emotion.

"I feel like I'm drugged in here, but I'm not delusional. Come on, Vesper. I had to sleep next to the two of you all this week."

Vesper's spark of irritation quickly died. Nim was right, she realized; the disappearance of her heart had changed things between her and Jules much more than with Garth. She recognized now that she had paid a price for the simplification of her choices—that something in her was deprived of the opportunity of finding peace, and that she could have possibly found that in this room.

The split-magic wouldn't work in here, Vesper thought. She could tell, looking around at several body parts that floated about in the room, that the beneficial effects did not extend so far as re-uniting the parts with their former bodies. PBut perhaps—if someone spent enough time in here—they would become integrated enough so the split-magic would no longer be effective on them outside the room as well.

She thought all of a sudden that she could bring Aren here, and perhaps her sister would realize that her unhappiness with being supplanted in Bugger's affections, and misunderstood by his wives, was caused by loving the wrong man. She wondered if Allegra had spent much time in here at all—it seemed unlikely, with the amount of pain she still carried about Garth. Vesper herself felt expansive and generous toward the redhead, and toward Garth himself despite his lies. He had his reasons, she thought; he was trying his best. And Jules...he would stop being upset with her in here, would understand how torn she'd been and how his own self-torture over choices made or prevented was unnecessary. He would forgive her.

If everybody would just come to the Sanctum, no one would have any problems at all! She would bring Jules here first. Overcome with her enthusiasm, she rushed to the open archway entry and passed through.

She thought she would have to ask for directions a dozen times in order to get back out through the maze of the building, but she could have sworn the way was much faster and more direct this time. Back in the entrance hall, she looked behind her suspiciously, as if she might see the paths arranging themselves before her very eyes. All remained still. Was it just her terrible sense of direction?

She went through the hallway, retracing Garth's steps, and tried to find Jules. After passing under two arches, she found herself looking through a sheet of crystal into a sun-infused greenhouse where, to her astonishment, she saw masses of yellow poisoned grass growing and bright red peeking through the blades—the mushroom-cure was growing there! HBut how could so much have grown so quickly, in just a few hours?

"Things grow at an amplified rate in this greenhouse," Jules said from her side, as if he'd heard her thought. "The cure has been given to the strongest wizards and witches, the rest put in the city's water supply, but no doubt we'll be needing much more, for a long time."

Vesper turned, unsurprised to find him there. She opened her mouth to ask him to come to the Sanctum with her, but then she looked closer at him. He wasn't angry with her now, she realized. There was something about this place...

"It's amazing," she said.

Jules shrugged. "They act as if so. But a positive attitude is so automatic for the Herlanders that sometimes I wonder if they're simply going to be very surprised one day when things go utterly wrong."

Vesper shivered. She felt the spell of the Sanctum loosen its hold on her and let her go. SAnd she remembered what Kalma had told her—when she was ready to face her negativity, she would know, and that would be the time for her to be out of the Sanctum—when she needed her fear and worry to push her into action to change things on the outside.

Jules glanced at her, his expression softening. "They do have some cause to be positive. Herland is very powerful, and not entirely as ridiculous as it may seem—they've kept Malland and all their other neighbors in check for many years. Let me show you."

This time, they took a passageway where stairs wound up in a translucent spiral. They emerged at the top of the building, much higher than Vesper expected. Breathtaking views extended out for miles around them. From here, the round earthen houses that dotted the landscape didn't look so primitive; rather, they reminded Vesper of the mushrooms themselves in how they grew organically from the land, complementing its geometry rather than overpowering it.

An enormous circular courtyard was etched on the rooftop where they stood. On the edges of the circle, many dozens of men and women stood chanting. Even without much sensitivity to magic, Vesper could tell that magic was responding to those voices. Palpable in almost-visible swirls and waves within the center of the circle, the energy rose and expanded as a sort of tingly heat.

Vesper and Jules watched the scene for some time: wizards and witches came when energized and left when fatigued. The magic continued to expand, to whirl, to dissipate again.

"What are they doing?" she whispered to Jules.

"Creating a collective vision," he said. "Most of the land's natural defenses have been contaminated by the split-magic, so they are building new protection from scratch. There is time yet; from what others have said, it seems Malland's army is moving, but they have a ways to go. Another few days, perhaps."

Of the people in the circle, Vesper only recognized Allegra. That flowerlike face and that mane of red silk stood out despite her small stature. She appeared to be unaffected by the disease, unlike many others who shared the circle, wizards and witches missing limbs or facial features. Here, people didn't hide the ravages of the disease with either decoration or replacement of parts.

Vesper noticed that Allegra avoided Garth during the times they worked the ritual together. Allegra stood in a place in the circle where she couldn't see him. Whenever they passed each other, it looked as if a numb patch might be forming in the atmosphere.

After some time, Jules made a motion with his head, and Vesper followed him back down the stairs to a hall where women were setting out food on a long table. The floor was strewn with fur mats and pillows for people to sit and eat. "We were in there a while," Jules said. "I thought you might be hungry."

Vesper nodded, just realizing that she was. The last thing she'd eaten had been Ject's bowl of dry rice, and she found the vegetable soup served here much more to her liking—thick, spicy, and warming.

"I'm going to see how preparations for defense are going around the city," Jules said once he finished. "If you don't want to go back to the Sanctum, you could offer to help in the kitchen, if you'd like."

Vesper felt she'd rather keep her wits about her than return to the hypnotic peace of the Sanctum. She wandered into the kitchen, and after a brief conversation with a stout fluffy-haired woman of indeterminate age, she started carrying food to the table.

She was just arranging plates on the table when Allegra came in. The redhead stopped short upon seeing Vesper, narrow face stiff with disdain.

"You shouldn't be here," she said.

"Why not?" Vesper asked after a moment of resisting the urge to run. The woman was obviously spoiling for a fight, and backing down would be like an admission that Allegra was right.

"You're not one of us. You're not a witch, and you're not a Herlander. So that means you're either a deserter, or a spy. I don't think you should be trusted to touch the food. I know I'm going to use my magic to test it for poison."

Vesper felt herself turning red with humiliation. Then she looked at Allegra—really *looked* at her. Maybe she'd had such a problem with people not seeing *her* because she wasn't seeing *them*. Did Allegra's mask of rage hide pain and doubt that anyone would ever truly love her? She thought that it just might. Vesper didn't quite feel compassion, but she no longer took Allegra's behavior personally. "I'm neither a deserter, nor a spy. I think you know that."

"Then why are you here?" Allegra huffed. Hair flashed fire-bright as she flipped it back. "You think you can have Garth, don't you?"

Vesper shrugged. "Think what you want. I doubt I can make you have a better opinion of me, no matter what I say."

"That's right," said Allegra. "But I'll have you know that Garth is mine. We've known each other since we were children, and we always knew we'd marry. He's distracted by you—thinks you're different. Well, he's been distracted by a dozen others before you. You're just one more in a line of women for him. In the end, he always comes back to me."

She might be right, Vesper thought. She wasn't sure it mattered. If they had true love, it would be mutual...she believed that. So Garth's past wouldn't matter at all. Still, her confusion remained about that true love business. Was she in love with him? How could she tell, without her heart? Still, these weren't concerns to be shared with an angry ex-lover. "Then you shouldn't be worried about him being with me. You can have him back when I'm done with him."

With that, she hurried back into the kitchen. She knew she hadn't been kind, but understanding Allegra's pain didn't mean she had to suffer, too.

The entire group of magicians, now numbering over one hundred, took a break that evening. "They've made force fields over all the towns," said Jules, sitting cross-legged in the dining area. "They are stretched kind of thin over some, but the bulk of them are here;, at least here we should be able to withstand any attack."

Vesper breathed a sigh of relief. "That's wonderful," she said. "Maybe the wizards can help restore order to Malland after this is all over. This is all so strange and surreal…I'm hoping that things can be fixed enough that I can see home again. I have…some unfinished business there." She imagined her father in prison, thinking she'd abandoned him, and the numb space in her chest gave a twinge.

Jules put his hand over hers. Her eyes flew up to meet his at such an odd, deliberate contact, whose motivations remained murky in the clear amber of his gaze.

"Uuugh!" a voice called, and both Vesper and Jules turned to see Garth striding over. He snatched the hand Jules held, pulling her up to her feet. "Uungh. Uuunngh? Unnh!" he said, pointing to himself, then moving his finger all around the room and then pointing at her.

"Oh—you were looking for me," Vesper translated, and Garth nodded.

She glanced back at Jules; his face bore no expression yet again. *I don't care*, his face said, but somehow she knew he did. She didn't need to look across the room to sense similar feelings emanating from another source—a certain angry redhead. *They shouldn't feel so upset*, she thought. *They should feel sorry for me. Who wants to have a conversation with someone who can only grunt and point?* It would be rude to say so, though, and so she let Garth pull her down a corridor and into a small room, with no more than a pallet on the floor and a few clothes tossed onto a built-in bench.

Garth closed the door and in two strides, swept her in his arms, and kissed her.

Her mouth softened under the consummately skilled pressure of his; strong fingers wound into her hair as he trailed his lips along her jaw to her ear, then down her throat. It felt so nice that she almost forgot about his lack of a tongue.

"Umm," he murmured against her, hand sweeping the clothes off the bench to sit and pull her toward him.

Vesper's lips met his again, and she felt as if she teetered on the brink of a cliff above a fast-moving river.

She found that without the troublesome concerns of her heart, it was easy to jump in. All her self-consciousness and feelings of inadequacy were gone as she felt this odd, unfettered lust blossoming inside her, and she kissed him back, her mouth ravenous, clinging to his, her tongue exploring the spaciousness behind his teeth. Her hands slipped inside his tunic, helped him lift it up over his head; she splayed her palms over the smooth, hard expanse of his chest, sliding down the fascinating ridges of his stomach.

"Ahhh, Vehhpuh," Garth said. Vesper winced, and she kissed him again so he would say nothing else. He certainly was handsome enough to make her forget his shortcomings—if he'd just remain quiet.

She felt as if part of her was coldly watching herself do this from a corner of the room, while the rest of her traveled on a wave of physiological stimulation. They paused a moment to pull Vesper's shirt off and her trousers down, and Garth's blue eyes blazed with invigorated passion as he ran his eyes and his hands over her body. He lifted her in his arms and carried her to the bed, and Vesper experienced a sense of déjà vu, remembering when he'd done this in his retreat in the mountains—except she'd been such a different person then—with a vulnerability in her idealism, her fractured sense of self-love. Neither of those were problems now, as she recognized that her desire was born of a base and uncomplicated physical attraction—nothing more. Still—was it worth it, she wondered, to risk pregnancy and forming a permanent tie to a man for whom she simply felt lust?

His fingers found her, dipping into the silky wetness between her legs, and Vesper fought back the wave of euphoria and grabbed his hand.

In that instant, several ideas emerged in crystal clarity in Vesper's mind.

The first was that Garth genuinely seemed to like her, to respect her, and to think that something about her was different from his usual taste in women. Without the distraction of her heart, she could see more clearly when he'd been lying to her, and when he'd told the truth.

The second was that she liked him too. Beyond her thinking that he was a great "catch" and would impress anyone, including her mother, she admired his intelligence and his charm.

The third was that he was the sort of man who tired easily of a woman, which was probably the reason why he preferred serial monogamy over collecting wives. One clingy woman was too much for him; a whole slew of them would make him run. Even if it was true that Vesper was different, and that she managed to keep his interest, his tendencies to run would probably always exist. She would have to be very secure in herself to enter a partnership with him. Did she have that security? Perhaps...but something in her said that maybe she shouldn't have to.

Her analysis said that this could work, because she had no heart, and because Garth no longer had his smooth tongue—not only could he no longer lie without it, but he wouldn't be charming other women.

She imagined how it would be. They'd marry. Afterward, the happily ever after would take place living in Malland court, perhaps under a saner version of Bugger...Garth would be court wizard again, with her by his side as an official court advisor on scientific and philosophical matters. Every day they would spend a few hours listening to petitions and helping solve problems of Malland citizens, then maybe meet with the king to advise him on wider matters of policy, and then they'd spend evenings eating delicacies, dancing, listening to music. After that they'd go to their luxurious joint quarters where they'd have great sex...

Except—something in her objected to this, and she couldn't put a name or a reason to it—it was just a feeling that this wasn't right for her. For everything about him fitting her fantasy image of what she wanted, she still didn't feel *seen* by him...and that made her all the more aware that maybe her fantasy wasn't what she wanted at all. It didn't matter, suddenly, if Garth had lied to her about anything...because she knew that if she continued to insist to herself that he was the perfect man for her, she'd be lying to herself.

She half-turned to tell him some diplomatic version of her realization, but then she saw something out of the corner of her eye. As she glanced back at the window, her gaze was arrested by the strangest object floating outside. Dark pink in color, with a couple of petals, it looked like an organ—like...she looked closer. A vagina definitely hovered in front of the window.

"Garth," Vesper said, her voice nearly faltering, "There's a vagina outside the window. It looks like it wants to come inside. Um…it's beating its labia against the glass."

Garth made a sound of annoyance. He got up and stood in front of the window. "Go away!" he enunciated slowly. He pulled the shade down over the window.

A sudden suspicion occurred to Vesper. "Whose vagina is that?"

Garth shrugged, not looking her in the eye.

"Now I know you're lying," Vesper said.

He met her eyes then, and smiled a little sheepishly. "Isss Aregra's," he said, struggling to form the words. "Oooeee fought. UDuhfemndemd myhhelf."

"A fight!" Vesper repeated. "How could you? So she lost that… and I suppose that's when you lost your tongue."

Garth nodded, sighing.

So that was the reason for the tension between him and Allegra. Suddenly Vesper felt sorry for her.

"Iiiih wohn' go away!" Garth said, shaking his finger at the window. "Wanh iiioou, noh her."

"I have to go," she said, and she headed for the door.

"No…pirll…peeess…," Garth said, and Vesper realized that he was trying to say "please," but couldn't manage. His voice grew cold then. "Iiiouu go, no coming backh!"

"That's exactly why I have to go," she said, and she left.

She had to find Jules. She didn't know why, or what she would say to him, but she knew she followed a compulsion she'd developed ever since first meeting him to reach out to him, to talk, to know what he was doing…to be near him. It didn't matter if she had no heart, or if it would never work out practically with him, or if he had vows preventing him from being intimate with anyone. If they were all to die tomorrow...none of that would matter anyway.

Outside, Jules was talking to a round-faced young man. Behind the man a wagon brimmed with arm-length sticks topped by crystals of various colors, bound with copper wire. Behind him, a large group of town citizens had started a spontaneous drum circle, and within it several women and a man swayed in an odd sort of dance.

"These won't do any good at all. I asked you to collect weapons,"

Jules was saying, his endless patience apparently ending as he argued with the man, who was picking up sticks and making enthusiastic stabbing and waving motions.

"But these special crystal wands will ensure we win," the man said, eyes big and puppy-like. "Each color corresponds to a different major center in your energy body, and it's amplified by the metal binding and the shape of the wand. It's impossible for you to hurt another human being if you're integrated, and these will do the trick. Here, try it." He handed Jules a stick topped by a giant amethyst.

"But you'll be fighting against a bunch of body parts, don't you understand?" Jules said, then gestured with the stick at the cavorting citizens. "And why are those people dancing? They should be evacuating to a safe place."

"Anyone who comes here will be swept up in our vibration of joy, and they'll want to join us rather than defeat us," the man said, smiling. "You just have to have faith."

Jules seemed to be developing a facial tic. "I have nothing against faith. But you have to have faith *and* back it up with action!"

The peaceful expression didn't budge. "If you back it up with action, it means you don't have true faith."

Before Jules could continue the argument, a buzzing sound filled the air, as if millions of invisible wasps had circled them and were having a pre-attack conference.

"Jules," Vesper said, reaching out to catch his sleeve.

He rounded on her. "Get back to the Sanctum! That sound—what is it?"

Something flickered in the air, like lightning, but lasting an instant too long. No thunder followed, but something in the distance appeared that resembled a black cloud, enormous and dissipating across the sky into thousands upon thousands of fragments flying steadily closer. As they came closer, Vesper saw that some of the larger fragments were actually body parts clumped around and transporting men, horses, and one enormous throne.

"The king is here," Jules said, and in the calmness of his voice, Vesper heard dread. "Somehow, he's moved much faster than we ever thought—and somehow, he's gotten through the force field."

CHAPTER 25

No one had time to distribute the crystal wands, so the Herlanders' theory of balancing the energy-body centers of the intruders had no opportunity to be tested. A problem with the theory was that the army was composed of thousands of body parts, and just a few hundred Malland soldiers who were more or less whole. It would have been fodder for a long philosophical discussion, whether separate body parts also had the same energy-body centers and if so, where they might be found, but no one was thinking about philosophy as parts flowed in from every direction. The invaders ignored the beckoning hands of the dancers that faltered only a little at seeing what they faced.

Possibly the most peaceful conquest of a country's capital in the history of the world was occurring, but possibly the most pathetic as well. Not much material for any bards or minstrels to turn into songs of epic heroism had been created, certainly. The Herlanders didn't run and scream when their city was hemmed in by the black cloud of body parts, but they did drop any makeshift weapons and clutch each other or hold hands, and a considerable number of them fainted. Jules pulled Vesper back toward the Hub, but in moments all exits had been blocked off—within the crowd of quietly panicking Herlanders, they were trapped.

The parts parted to allow the throne on which King Bugger sat to settle on the rooftop of the crystalline Hub of the Goodpeople. The circle of wizards and witches, who had remained to continue to try to resurrect the force field, broke and attempted to flee. Body parts descended, immobilizing many of them until more parts deposited more soldiers to accost and take them prisoner.

King Bugger's head lifted off his body and spun slowly about, taking in all the activity around him. He watched a few of those on the rooftop muster a magical attack, bringing down parts or creating miniature force fields around their own bodies—but whatever the Mallanders had used to take out the force fields around the cities easily dismantled these small ones. As more whole soldiers arrived, resistance became more half-hearted and then petered out completely.

The army of parts had beat all estimates of speed—arriving in hours rather than days—and the takeover took barely any time at all.

A wall of living, hovering body parts hemmed in people from all over the town, herding them to the center.

Perhaps it wouldn't be so bad—perhaps it was time for new leadership, the Herlanders whispered to each other. They tried to make the best of it as Malland soldiers, whole and parts, worked on containing the only real weapons the country had—the magic of the wizards and the witches. Drained of power from maintaining the defenses and fazed by the summary destruction of a force field they thought impenetrable, it took little persuasion for the remaining witches and wizards to descend from the heights of the central building. Soon the Malland soldiers had restrained all the magical defenders with the blue-metal cuffs.

King Bugger had conquered them so easily, Vesper still couldn't believe it. All their effort, that crazy flight to Herland had been for nothing. Now, for sure, nothing good lay in store for them.

Those in the amassing crowd didn't have to wait long for the details.

"Your lives will be spared," the newly styled Emperor Bugger said from his throne on the rooftop. The acoustics of the building ensured that his voice boomed out over the onlookers. Behind him, body parts deposited a number of members of court—all twenty-eight wives, it looked like, and several richly dressed men. Two of them were already jotting down the king's words even before their feet touched ground—his secretaries, who Vesper had learned wrote down everything Bugger said to be run to all the towns in Malland—and now, she supposed, in Herland.

"However, you cannot be allowed to retain any trace of magic," continued Bugger, "because that is where rebellion lies, and the seeds of pride—the foundation of thinking that you are above the law, that you can take from others what they've earned by a genetic coincidence. In my empire, all shall be fair. You shall remain citizens with all your rights, but you must willingly give up the rest of your magic. Most of it is probably drained anyway by the disease that has spread throughout this land; you can take it as a message from the gods that they think you have aspired to too many of their own powers and now you need to humble yourselves, and be just like everybody else." The people behind Bugger had organized themselves as best they could, trying to absorb the presence of all the wives in attendance. Behind Bugger and to one side stood Magnus, and on his other side, for his preferred companion of the moment, lounged a buxom blonde—Vesper barely recognized Daisy, the woman who'd serviced Bugger under the dining table, for the richness of her clothing and hair accessories. The favorite fiancée, apparently, and behind her stood the rows of Bugger's wives, and his second-favorite fiancée—Aren, pale and wilting in a dress of gold chiffon and gilt-edged lace. From down here, Vesper couldn't catch her sister's eye, although she willed Aren to look out at the crowd and see her. However, Aren's attention remained on the golden-shod toes that peeked out from underneath the hem of her gown.

Six soldiers emerged onto the rooftop and strode toward King Bugger, whose head swiveled to observe them. The soldiers led a chain of a dozen manacled Herlanders.

"Your Highness, these are the surviving wizards who put up resistance against us," the soldier in front said.

Bugger's floating head gnashed his teeth and glared, but on his body that still faced the crowd, his hands rubbed together in anticipation. "An example shall be made of them—soso you will not repeat their mistake. You—that one, he shall go first."

Bugger pointed to a stocky young male wizard with short yellow hair; he reminded Vesper a little of Nim.

"You don't need to take away our magic. Let us teach you about the magic within you—" the man began, his voice shaky but earnest.

"Silence!" Bugger shouted. "Bring the secret weapon," he commanded, and from the rooftop entrance, two men emerged bearing a large cloth-covered square object. Bugger's head swiveled about in a complete revolution around his neck, surveying the crowd about him with a gleeful gaze that didn't want to miss a single gasp of fear or tremor of dread.

Vesper noticed a third man emerging from behind the object, and she cringed, recognizing Zinfel.

"I think three will make for an apt demonstration," Zinfel said, and with a flourish he swept the cloth away, revealing a golden cage crawling with thick pink worms. Sliding open a small door, Zinfel stuck his hand inside; the worms shrunk from him, but he grabbed one, two, three and pulled them out. The worms squirmed in his hand.

No, not worms. Penises.

Zinfel took a small vial of red-orange liquid from one of his many pockets, and he poured it into a bowl that he set on top of the golden cage. Red-orange liquid—it could only be one thing. Zinfel was using Vesper's mushroom tincture for some other nefarious end.

"In the name of Malland, attack!" Zinfel cried, and he pointed at the offending young wizard.

At his words, the penises went from timid, pink, and floppy to engorged, erect members sitting atop tightly drawn testicles. Each one dunked its head into the bowl of liquid before straightening, turning, and arrowing toward their goal. The penises surrounded the hapless wizard, hovering midair while they grew even longer, and streams of liquid shot out of their mushroom-heads.

They were using Minimus' trick—and amplifying it with Vesper's tincture!

Even though she knew what came next, and that she might throw up, Vesper couldn't tear her eyes away as the man screamed, arms flying up to protect his face. Large chunks of his forearms, his fingers and elbows, detached and flew away, and he had no more arms. His scalp tore itself off his head, revealing the smooth gray of his cranium—the bowl broke off, and next came chunks of brain.

"Back to the cage, you dumb cocks!" Zinfel shouted, but even before the penises stopped shooting, he ordered three more to the attack. Fresh gobs of sperm reduced the wizard to a featureless hunk of bloody flesh, and he toppled to the ground.

If Bugger had wanted silence, he surely had it now. The quiet of the assembled Herlanders, and the host of parts and people ringing them in, poised amongst them like a breath held or a heart stopped—and Vesper could almost see the crowd shrinking down, making itself invisible, containing no one who could possibly stand out or be considered in rebellion. *They are only human*, Vesper thought, suppressing her disappointment that Bugger's bullying could so easily squelch their vibration of joy and love. TBut then again, she had not shown herself to be any different.

"You saw how easily we dismantled your force fields. And as you can see, along with that, our newest biochemical technology makes Malland invincible. Any more refusals to cooperate?" Bugger asked. The chained wizards, faces ranging from blank to aghast, made no sound.

Bugger held up something pinched between thumb and forefinger, so tiny Vesper could only see it as a sparkle of blue in the sunlight. "You people like pretty stones, I know. I'm going to give each of you one of these as a present, in honor of the joining of our two countries into one. You'll each wear it in the back of your neck so you won't lose it."

Jules bent his head close to Vesper's ear. "It's the magic-blocking metal," he whispered. "Doubtless with some other properties to control everyone who gets one of those."

"What can we do to avoid it?" she whispered back.

"Right now, nothing. Wait—we'll find a moment to slip away. There's no way there won't be an opening."

Unfortunately, the crowd hemmed them in so surely she saw no means of escape unless they developed the ability to fly—and even then, they'd have to out-fly hundreds of body parts, each as fast as Minimus. Already Malland soldiers were organizing Herlanders into rows, and several more began advancing down the lines, pressing an oblong device against the back of each neck. Judging from the cries and winces, it wasn't a painless process. Only those who had the metal chip inserted were permitted to leave the circle.

Vesper waited and watched, but the circle of parts guarding them remained as tight as ever. She could see no potential opening for escape.

Then her gaze traveled across a yawning Magnus, who just that moment looked across the crowd—and met Vesper's eyes. He straightened, suddenly wide awake.

Vesper tried to shrink into the crowd. However, Magnus had hopped to Bugger's side; he tapped his father on the shoulder and whispered excitedly in his ear. Bugger's face darkened. He gazed in Vesper's direction; not spotting her, his head came off, flying over until his fiendish eyes stared directly into hers, red mouth twisted into a smirk. The press of Herlanders around Vesper scrambled back, Jules melting into their front ranks, and she faced the king's triumphant head alone.

"I would very much like to punish you," he growled. "Or at least to get you to accept a favor when I'm generous enough to give you one. You aren't allowed to leave a party when you're the guest of honor! I would also kill you for rejecting my poor son—except he seems to still want you. So you're to go to him, and when he tires of you, then I'll kill you. Or maybe I'll just cut off your feet. Guards!"

Armed parts closed in on Vesper—hands bearing knives, mouths with artificially sharpened teeth, and even a couple of whole Malland soldiers, swords drawn at the ready. Jules, weaponless, thrust himself in front of her.

He glanced over his shoulder, and she caught his eye and shook her head. Their gazes locked for a moment—and she saw the anger, and the friendship he would always offer. Behind both she saw something else—something that made her almost think she still had a heart, the way something in her began to ache. She offered him the tiniest of smiles before the soldiers dragged her away.

CHAPTER 26

The Goodpeople's Hub had no facilities for imprisonment, nor did any other place in all of Herland. The few people who did present problems were rehabilitated in the Sanctum—for all infractions, Kalma explained to the guards, were just a cry for help to remember one's true self.

The lack of even doors, let alone locks, did not deter the Mallanders. They imprisoned Vesper in one of the crystalline rooms, manacling one of her ankles and attaching a long chain to it that was anchored to a crystal the size of her torso, so she could move about the room but couldn't easily flee. With the addition of a host of hands, ears, and eyes at the entrance, along with one whole soldier and bars hammered across the window, the king had her well and truly contained. To add to the indignity, before imprisoning her they'd stripped her of her trousers and shirt, forcibly washed her, and put her in a tight-bodiced red dress that they declared Magnus would like much better than her men's clothes.

Magnus stopped by soon after, finding Vesper secured and sitting on an oversized floor cushion. He was scowling down at his pants as he entered, but then he straightened and grinned. "Hey, Vesper!"

"Why am I shackled?" she asked, regarding him warily. He looked at her as if they were still friends—as if he hadn't tried to rape her back in the palace.

Magnus' grin never budged. He threw himself onto another floor cushion, leaning back on his hands with long legs crossed in front of him. "Aw, don't be so mad. It's so you don't have to be implanted with the chip yet. I got in another argument with Dad about it—he wants everybody with the chip, but it dulls the brain, and I need you to be able to think."

Put in that light, Vesper thought, maybe she did prefer the shackles after all. "Why?"

"Zinfel told us that you found the cure for the split-disease after all, Vesper," Magnus said, leaning forward. "It's not going to be used much, you know—butbut here's another chance for you. If you find this other cure for me that fixes the messes the disease made, you can come back to Mallandina. You'll have whatever position in my father's new court that you want. You'll be rich and famous, because this is a cure that everybody, absolutely everybody would pay tons for. I know you can do it."

"A cure for what?" Vesper asked, stalling. No one had realized that her initial discovery of the split-disease cure had very little to do with science. Now she had no magic book to help her.

"Reattach Minimus to me. So he works like a normal prick again."

Vesper shook her head. "I can't do that. I already tried—"

Magnus' face shifted, a gradual darkening that took over before Vesper even had the chance to feel fear. The flesh around his brow and mouth tightened the tiniest bit, nothing more; still, the look in his eyes—as if she were less than an object—could not be mistaken. He'd never directed at her that sliver of cruelty she'd seen in him when he'd hunted, and now she found it terrifying; even when he'd tried to rape her, he still seemed a lackey controlled by his father. This, now, was all Magnus, and Vesper saw herself a fool for ever trusting his easy charm. "You'll try again," he said.

Then that dangerous look was gone, replaced by a panicky frustration that almost bothered Vesper more. He began to pace. She stood as well, feeling a sudden urge to be out of kicking range of his feet.

"You turned him against me," he said. "Now he's against everything I do. He makes me piss in my pants in public, or get erections whenever some gross hag—or even my dad—comes in the room, and he won't shut up, even when I thrash him. I've tried everything. I personally got twenty magicians infected by having them work on it. And you—you who made Minimus hate me—you found a cure for the disease. Even the Egregian scientists couldn't do that! So now you'll find a cure for the infected objects. Find a way to get Minimus back to normal, and I'll release you. If you don't—you'll regret it. I'll—I'll cut off your fingers one by one! And I'll let my men rape you, even if I can't." Magnus stopped pacing and fixed his glare at Vesper again, fists clenched, face red, looking as if he were two years old instead of over twenty.

"But I found the cure by accident," said Vesper in a small voice. "I can't possibly find one for the infected objects. If the best scientists and magicians in the kingdom couldn't do anything, I certainly couldn't. What you're asking is completely unreasonable."

"My dad says I haven't been taking advantage of the benefits of being a prince. He says that being unreasonable is one of them," said Magnus, and he backhanded her, sending her flying against the wall. "And that is, too." He stomped to the entrance.

"What are you looking at, chump?"

The round brown eye hovering in the doorway fled with a shriek before Magnus' fist.

That afternoon, Vesper's guards moved her to a different room, and they shackled and chained her once again, this time to a ring welded to the floor. This larger, windowless room, with the exception of her two guards and a large mesh cage full of body parts clinging to the sides, gave Vesper a sense of déjà vu as she stood there—because everything looked the same as in the laboratory in the Mallandina palace. Bottles and beakers full of liquids of varying colors, jars of herbs, the cool box—everything was arranged as Vesper had last left it. Except that other laboratory was many miles away. As a group of a dozen hands flew into the room and placed yet another set of bottles onto a shelf, she realized that the hands had been the means for transporting everything here.

What to do? How to start? She could think of nothing. She could more easily shove a baby back into a mother's womb or force two people into one body. She stared at the caged parts. They flitted about in circles, moaning or muttering in low voices. They didn't seem very intelligent, but she knew by now that they were fully separated and independent, each with a functional body of its own. How to reverse a birth? It was impossible.

With the chain at its fullest extension, Vesper could just reach the wall, and she sat down and leaned against it to think. Hours passed, but no ideas, no inspiration stirred her. She found herself wishing for *The Book of Offhand Truths*. Jules had scorned Garth's use of the book. He would probably say that each person's consciousness could access those same truths by meditating on it, without the need for outside aid.

Well, she was looking, and she couldn't see a thing. *Maybe I should meditate*, she thought. She closed her eyes and breathed in, out. In, out. She forgot about her breathing for a moment as she slipped into a light doze...woke up, re-focused on her breath. Soon her lids grew far too heavy, and she slept.

She walked through the flowered fields of Herland. They were coming alive again. She could sense the magic like the hum of the crystal walls of the Sanctum; it flowed through the dirt beneath her bare feet and made them tingle. No longer chaotic, but organized, focused. Seeds beneath the earth birthed and bloomed forth with food. The land would take care of its people.

"But you haven't done anything to fix the damage that's been done to the people already," she said to the earth, the burgeoning flowers, the food. "The disease that infected you has split them into pieces. How can they be made whole again?"

The breeze blew its concern, and she could feel it brushing her cheek. The land would take care of its people, the wind whispered, and it pushed her gently forward.

She walked until the fields shifted from emerald green to yellow grass, speckled with red mushrooms. The poison grass, she realized, and only then did her feet start to burn and blister. She saw a small pond ahead—if only she could get there, she could save her body from falling apart—as each step she took, the grass ate more of her flesh; alive, it crawled up her legs to burn steadily up her calves, knees, thighs.

She reached the water and collapsed on its bank. Now the earth offered her a mug of crystal, and she scooped it full and drank down deeply. The burning ebbed, modulating its heat with a sensation of cooling wax dulling the pain and then replacing it with a rush of such heady euphoria that she felt her toes curling with pleasure in the grass. She looked down and saw that her legs were whole again, and the euphoria dissipated, leaving in its wake a sense of well-being, body and mind, along with a comfortable drowsiness. As she slipped back into slumber, she noticed a blade of yellow grass at the bottom of the glass.

A noise startled her awake. She wobbled to her feet to see a pinkish-beige organ, resembling a mass of congealing pasta, fly into the room and come to rest on top of a table. She identified it as a brain—she'd never seen one live, but it could be nothing else.

"I'm told I'm to assist you," it said. "I don't see how *you'll* be able to do anything about reuniting parts to their bodies, though. You're just a girl—not even a scientist, let alone one of the greatest minds Egregia has ever created. I can't believe I've been displaced in your favor. If *I* couldn't find a solution, no one can."

"That's what I tried to tell Magnus," Vesper said, now quite awake. "You're welcome to have the job back, if you'll just unlock these shackles."

"Humph! Stop mocking my lack of a body. You know I can't do that. It's my lot to do damage control on your incompetence. Oh, what has the world come to! My mother would cry an ocean if she could see what's become of her favorite, her brilliant one, her genius of a son."

Escape, she thought, trying to tune out the brain's continued complaints. She should focus on that. She could try to dissolve the metal of her shackles...and make a sleeping draught for the guards. She could probably make something out of the substances here acidic enough to wear away the metal, but she saw nothing that could cause sleep but not death.

Sleep, she thought. She'd dreamed of something that had made her sleep. A slip of a memory recalled the entire dream to her. *The land takes care of its people*, she remembered. It had led her to a field of poison grass, and a single blade of grass in a crystal mug. What would it do? How could it help people reunite with their parts? Perhaps she would be as insane as Bugger to try out a random solution offered by a dream. *Jules would*, she thought. Would she? Maybe, maybe not. At least she could get rid of the brain while she worked on her shackles.

"I need some of the mushroom that's growing in the greenhouse," she said to the brain. "The red one that grows under the yellow grass. Get someone to help you gather it, and make sure they don't touch any of it with their skin. Better yet, they should put on gloves and take the grass together with the mushrooms—a few handfuls should do."

"What do you think I am, a servant?" hollered the brain. "I am the greatest mind on the continent. I should have—"

"You said you were here to assist me," Vesper cut in. "So assist me. Please."

"Well, I never!" The brain rotated in mid-air and flew out the door.

Vesper got to work. She located several acids among the chemicals; she knew a rough recipe for an acid that would dissolve metal, and in the next hour she experimented, trying different proportions and testing it on a metal spoon. When she found an effective combination, she glanced out of the door; the two guards were playing cards, not paying any attention to the goings-on inside the room. She tipped several drops of the acid solution onto her chain, watching it bubble slightly. She would need a lot of time for this, but at least now she had a plan.

She had burned through a quarter of the thickness of a chain link by the time the brain returned. She put the items away, then turned to watch the brain shouting orders at two hands holding a basket filled with yellow grass and red mushrooms. The hands deposited the basket on the table. They left, but the brain hovered above the basket, peering at the mess of red and yellow. "What are you going to do with these? You know the split-disease cure doesn't do anything about the ejected parts. You're stupid if you think those mushrooms will do anything else! Where did you learn chemistry? Mixing your mother's rouge-pots? You don't know *anything*!"

"I need silence to work," Vesper said, pretending she believed what she said as she glared at the brain and pulled the basket out from under it. "Why don't you take a nap or something?"

"Well, I never!" huffed the brain, but it descended to a floor pillow and settled itself like a cat, circling until it made an indentation so deep that the cushion obscured half its wormy folds.

Vesper pulled on gloves. She cut off a single blade of yellow grass and dropped it into a glass of water, watching as it floated for a moment, then drifted slowly to the bottom.

It seemed far too simple. How could drinking this do anything at all? Perhaps it had hallucinogenic properties, and she'd have a vision of the answer—but then why the extra step? She could have dreamed the answer instead of dreaming of drinking this solution. It was likelier to kill her or to do nothing at all than to solve anything. Had her dream been a true vision, like a page from *The Book of Offhand Truths* after all, or had a collection of wishfully thought images overcome her during sleep?

The brain began snoring so loudly that its wormlike strands vibrated. The hour must be quite late—she couldn't see outdoors, but her eyes hurt and her body ached from exhaustion. She looked at the small decanter of liquid. Well, why not? If it made her sick, that too might get her out of here.

Stretching her chain to its limit, she could just reach the small cot in the corner; she sat down on it, and before she could change her mind she swigged down the contents of the glass.

She lay down and waited. She thought she would become sleepy, and that another answer would come to her in that state. Instead, an odd sort of tension began growing inside her, originating a little below her belly—and she found warmth washing through her genitals, and that she was growing wet and aroused. What was happening? Could the poison-grass, in its diluted state, actually be an aphrodisiac?

She crossed her legs on the cot, annoyed. This sort of distraction was the last thing she needed! She had to focus on figuring out a cure, not think about sex!

Groaning with frustration, she yanked up her skirts and slid her fingers up across the slippery groove between her thighs. Curious despite herself, she explored, feeling the texture of her inflamed labia between thumb and forefinger, tugging a little, then gasping as she sunk her middle finger in between them as deep as it would go. She found her hips lifting involuntarily as she moved her finger in and out. Then she pulled her finger up and touched her clitoris, circling, first with just a feather's weight of pressure, then deepening her contact so the pleasure washed through her and she moaned aloud and writhed so enthusiastically that she ended up hitting the wall with the side of her head and body.

She felt a shock run through her from where she contacted the wall, and she felt stuck to it as if it were made of ice—numbness spread through her whole body until she could no longer feel anything except for a soothing liquid crystal infusion flowing through her pleasure-opened veins. *The Sanctum*, she realized. With her heightened senses, she could touch its effects just through the walls.

Slowly, she began to feel her body again. It seemed, though, to stretch out beyond the limits of the city, the country, the entire world.

Was she dreaming? If so, she had never had a clearer or more lucid dream. Her awareness reached out in undulating waves, feeling all the small movements of her body. Some parts of her laughed, some wept, others were calm; she touched them all with her thoughts, a brush of affirmation. Then, she noticed some blank spots in her awareness—places where she couldn't quite touch parts of her body, even though she could see them as connected to her still. Those parts of her—they solidified into forms of people—behaved as if they were independent of her. Only her being encompassed them all. Those physical structures believed that their delineations of separate function, of temporary purpose, meant that they were actually separate beings from each other... although why they would want to be so alone, she had no idea...

That aloneness struck a familiar chord. As she looked at those beings, each a glimmering splotch of color, she saw that one of them had a special significance to her...she'd identified with it strongly for a while. It had a name. She thought. She felt. She wondered. Then, she remembered.

Vesper, she said. *I'm Vesper.*

She saw herself then—this arbitrary delineation of beingness called "Vesper"—as if from outside. She saw in Vesper a microcosm of the same dynamic she'd observed in looking at all the beings that made up the world. Within her, places existed that looked almost cracked, where pieces denied their being part of the whole, and thus had splintered off into a new, compartmentalized identity as a piece of not-Vesper, a piece of Other.

She identified the biggest splintering in the center of that arbitrary body—in the heart. She stared at it, and her gaze magnetized her closer, until she found herself descending straight into the splinter.

Waves of pain battered her. A man stood there, broad back facing her, waves of bronze hair brushing the nape of his neck. She couldn't see his face, but the yearning that awoke in her at the sight of him told her that this was someone she deeply desired. *Turn around*, she begged him, but he only shifted a little—enough for her to see him embracing another woman. Long dark hair, small features—*she looks like me*, Vesper thought. However, somehow that other Vesper was everything Vesper had ever tried to be but could never embody. He could love that Vesper, but not her. She felt the conflict, the desperate desire to become another—and a hatred of those parts of herself that didn't deserve his love.

An endless moment of agony shredded her, consumed her completely, until nothing remained of her. Then she sensed, beyond the pain and the husk of shattered identity, a space—not a place, but a way of being. She filled it with a sudden bubbling up of the love that the poison-grass had given her, or perhaps allowed her to feel; buoyed there, she felt no pain at all.

Euphoria lifted her above the place of confusion inside her. At the same time as it deposited her gently back into her heart, now clear and open, she saw herself from the outside—embracing the unloved and rejected parts, and then the parts that judged herself for rejecting and not loving herself, and then the parts that judged herself for being judgmental, and so on. Filling her heart with self-love, she saw her essence seeping into the splinters and the cracks, and healing them...

Then she was looking at another splinter, much deeper, much older, in her solar plexus. She heard her mother's voice—*Nobody will ever want to marry you...*

Other voices chimed in. *Is she stupid? Why can't she speak properly?...*

Weirdo...thinks she's better than us...

The girls in her village taunted her. The old biddies snubbed her at gatherings. Her sisters talked without listening. Then she saw Perrin forcing himself on her, Bugger's face as he ordered Magnus to rape her. The pain surged up again, and Vesper saw her own being in thousands of pieces, each rejected into some buried place labeled with a *That's not-mine*. She was fine, she said, but inside she was a network of shattering glass.

The pain beat a tattoo against her eyes and down her chest and into that place of the splinter, and she felt her old reaction building—

she would build a wall and never feel the pain again...she would study, and she would show them how little she cared, and how superior she was to them or to the part of her that believed them. She would pretend she wasn't listening until she actually could no longer hear what people said...she would say, *I'm not interested in marriage or love because I don't want to lose my identity. I only want to be a scientist or a philosopher, just someone who thinks and doesn't feel...*

The part of her that believed them...the part of her...the part...

A brain floated by in slow motion, shouting in exaggerated slow tones, "You could never be a sciiiiiiientist..."

She saw herself again as the body-of-all, the beingness of all connecting her with the Egregian brain, with her old tormenters, and with the parts of her that held all sorts of different beliefs. They were all the same.

The pitch of pain shifted a notch and became ecstasy—so clear and lovely that she...,

Came to, her body trembling in pleasure. She lay curled on her side on a small cot in a room of earth and crystal, her ankle shackled to a long chain. Still in the same place—but not...she inhaled, still basking in the aftereffects of that bliss-place. Touching her chest, her heart beat against her fingers, slow and steady. Tears of relief sprang to her eyes.

She swayed as she stood. Her chains clanked; she ought to work on dissolving the metal again...but her eyes strayed instead to the cage of body parts, a rhythm of cries in minor, their banging against the metal mesh keeping disharmonious time. Some flew in moth-like circles, but no light burned away their misery. The brain still slept; now it muttered in its sleep and yelled, "No! Don't! Don't!" in such terror that Vesper actually felt sorry for it.

She understood now. All the detached body parts were physical manifestations of those denied and rejected places of each person from whom they'd been ejected. She'd seen the same in herself—she'd been full of places that would have created an autonomous body part, if the split-magic had been directed at her. The solution was so simple—with the help of the Sanctum's energy permeating this building, and a dose of amplified love, these parts could reunite with their former owners, and in joy and cooperation, not enslavement.

That decided it. She put a blade of yellow grass into a wide bowl, and a fresh one into her emptied glass, and she topped them both up with water. She opened the cage; most of the parts flitted to the far end of it, out of immediate reach of her hand. She grabbed a nose who flew a little slower than the rest, and she removed it and closed the cage.

"I'm not going to hurt you," she said as it struggled in her hand. "I want to try something. What is your name?"

The nose quaked in terror, but finally it squeaked out, "Toobig. That's what she called me."

Vesper winced. "Who is 'she'?"

"Melly," the nose said, beginning to sniffle. "My girl."

Better to do it quick. She dunked the nose into the bowl. It struggled at first, and then its movements became languorous, nostrils flaring sensuously.

Then she took a sip from her water glass, gasping as she felt her body's immediate erotic response. She went back to her cot and leaned back against the wall, simultaneously pressing the nose against it. She entered the other-space this time with a little more awareness. She spent a shorter time basking in that initial state of expanded being-ness, before remembering that she'd come here with a purpose. *I'm Vesper*, she thought, and she found herself amidst the swirl of beings-within-being. Who was the other she sought? A nose named Toobig, and a girl named Melly who lacked a nose.

She found the nose first, in close proximity to her own body-being. It vibrated at a dark brown color, and within that color she saw its depression, its feeling that it took up too much space. It would prefer not to exist. *Where is Melly?* she asked it. Toobig flickered in response to the name, and Vesper followed its line of thought that stretched out in a literal line of gold to another being—a young woman, asleep here in this other dimension, pulsating a steady yellow ocher.

As Toobig floated near the sleeping Melly, Vesper could see the crack in her space that had separated them. As she looked at the crack, it showed a story of Melly hating her enormous nose, but because Herland valued a positive attitude above everything, she judged herself a bad person whose negative thoughts kept her nose growing ever larger.

The ultimate punishment had been when she'd asked a visiting wizard to change her nose, and instead it had come off...

Some of the pain released, and love filled the cleared space, uniting, magnetizing more self-love to it. Only something deeper held the rest apart, and Vesper went toward it.

Melly, when was the first time you thought your nose was too big? Vesper asked, and the crack exploded into a memory.

Three-year-old Melly was collecting eggs from the chicken coop, and she'd seen a teen-aged boy kissing a girl inside, and doing other strange things to her. Melly watched them and waited for them to finish. Then the boy opened the door and hit Melly with it—so hard she fell and hit her head on a rock. She bled, and she couldn't think straight. "It's your own fault for sticking your big nose into others' business," the boy said.

So much pain arose, Vesper found herself reeling, almost swept away by it. *Tree*, she thought, and one burst from the ground, an enormous oak rooted deep in the earth. She clung to it and felt her own roots steadying her. *He wasn't saying Melly had a big nose*, Vesper said. *It's just an expression!*

In the dream-state they were in, Melly awoke, eyes opening, brightening, clearing, love fountaining up from her core to her long-hated facial features. *I see that now,* she said. *I don't have a big nose!*

With a gasp and an orgasmic shudder, Vesper pulled herself away from the wall, coming back to herself. She looked down at her empty hand. The nose had disappeared!

Did it reunite with Melly? Or did it truly disappear into nothingness? Or was it just hiding somewhere? She looked around the laboratory, finding no traces. She couldn't very well ask the guards to go find a girl named Melly, somewhere in Herland. She felt it must have worked...but she didn't know for sure. She ought to test it more...

No, she would trust herself on this one. Did she have time to do all these other parts, though, or should she escape now and take care of the parts later? If she did escape—where could she go?

She went to the cage. Did it seem the parts feared her less, floated about with a little more purpose, a little more pep? Was she just imagining it? "I need some help," she said. "I can help you to reunite with the bodies you separated from. But I have to plan an escape route for myself. If any of you could go out there and tell me what you see... maybe draw me a map or something, showing where are any places where there are fewer guards, a path I might run to for cover...just a little scouting."

"Why would we want to reunite with our old bodies?" asked a liver in a truculent tone. "Are you saying there's something wrong with me, as I am now, that I would need your help? You could just let us out of this cage."

She could think of several reasons, but she doubted philosophy was the forte of the liver, or any of these body parts. "I could, but it seems King Bugger has a device that compels body parts to go where he wants them to, and once you go there, he's perfected ways of torturing you into submission. So there aren't too many opportunities to live a free life as a body part. If you rejoin your old body, at least you won't have to be a slave or a soldier."

She spoke truly enough, and the body parts responded to her conviction. An ear drifted forward. "I could scout for you," it said.

"I'll help if it'll get me out of this stinking cage," said a nose.

"All right, me too," added the liver, after a pause. "Better to do something than sit around here waiting for torture or death."

Vesper opened the cage and the three volunteers came out. One of the guards was awake while the other slept, but he didn't notice one ear, one nose, and a liver creeping past his feet and out the door.

Vesper spent the next few hours dunking body parts in the poison-grass-turned-aphrodisiac-water, which somehow helped them "tune in" to the resonance of the Sanctum that reached out through the crystalline walls. Then Vesper helped reconnect those parts through accessing the Sanctum's healing energy, guiding the parts to recognize old denials and self-rejections, and filling the cleared spaces with love. The parts, somehow aware that something was happening, cooperated now. Vesper even started remaining at her place leaning against the wall, staying in her blissful trance-state as part after part dunked itself in the bowl of water containing the blade of grass and met her in the other dimension, leading her to their respective persons and their memories. The pathways to healing became clearer and clearer to Vesper, and she barely needed to do anything to nudge each part to a new and different relationship with its owner.

After some time, Vesper felt she needed to sleep. The trance-space rested her, and the sexual energy energized her—but neither allowed her to go into true sleep, so as dawn approached her need for rest increased. She had just finished reuniting a tongue with its person—she had a suspicion, even as she observed from some distance the lies that had kept this tongue from being truly united with the rest of the person's body, that it might have been Garth's tongue. Its pain had been particularly difficult to release. Instead of breaking contact with the wall afterward, she slid down along it until she was supine on the cot, still basking in sensual languor, and she slept.

"What did you do with those parts?"

Vesper sat up with a gasp, ripping open crusty eyelids to see the brain right in front of her. "Tell me! Did you let them escape, you idiot girl?" The gray wormy mass trembled with rage midair.

"Of course not," Vesper said, rubbing her eyes. "I've just been doing my job. Reuniting them with their owners." She stood. It must be morning now—she shouldn't have slept. Who knew how much time she'd lost? She would have to send the brain off somewhere...get to work on the metal-dissolving again...

"Liar," hissed the brain. "You couldn't have figured it out. I don't believe you!"

"I could do it with you, too," Vesper said. "It even works with parts who don't believe it'll work."

"You think you can trick me into drinking your poison? I don't think so. And you know very well that I have no body to return to."

"I didn't know that," Vesper said. "I'm sorry to hear that."

"Yeah, sure, sure," sniffed the brain.

Vesper knew she would get nothing done in the brain's presence, nor would she be able to rest. "I need more mushrooms. Can you arrange for that? About twice as much as you got for me yesterday." That would buy her at least two hours, she calculated.

"Oh, I'll get you something all right," the brain huffed, and it turned and flew out the door.

The brain had become increasingly irritable as Vesper worked, as opposed to the body parts in the cage, which grew more lucid and calm. That made her curious about something. She asked the remaining parts in the cage whether they knew if the bodies from which they'd been separated were still alive; they all knew with a certainty, and they unanimously answered *yes*. She wondered if the brain felt a subconscious frustration because it had no body to reunite with. Would it take that frustration out on her? Unfortunately, she had no time to even entertain this concern. She began to assemble the ingredients for dissolving the shackles again and tried to focus.

"Hey! You can't be in here," she heard one of the guards say. The singing of a short sword slicing through the air and a scream followed.

"Get that ear!" Cursing, then another high-pitched shriek.

The nose whizzed into the room, followed by a bleeding ear. "Liver is down," the nose panted. "But we got this for you." It inhaled and then snorted an impressive gust of air; out of one nostril shot a small rolled-up cloth. Vesper caught it and tucked it into her bodice just as the guards came in.

"Give me that nose," growled one of them, face a cross between a bulldog and a porcupine. He held a bloody dagger with a piece of ear still stuck to the tip.

"These are my test subjects!" Vesper said, opening the cage of parts, gesturing for the nose and ear to enter. They rushed in, and Vesper slammed the cage closed and stood before it. "You can't kill them. I need them for my experiments!"

"No one allowed in and out without authorization from the prince. No exceptions. Let me have the nose and I won't hurt you."

Vesper grabbed the beaker full of her metal-dissolving acid. She wasn't sure she would actually be able to kill someone—doing so with this acid would be a particularly disturbing way to commit a murder. Still, she wouldn't sacrifice the nose, who'd risked himself on her behalf.

She lifted the beaker, and the bulldog-porcupine face bared its teeth.

"What's all this?"

Magnus strode in, followed by the brain.

If the brain could have pointed and hopped up and down, it certainly would have. "I told you she was up to no good! Trying to escape, no doubt."

Magnus pointed to the guard. "You—lower that knife and get back to your post. Actually, I'm relieving you of your post. She's shackled down—she can't leave, and I won't be spied on. You go, too," he said, nodding to the brain.

"But—"

"I want to be alone with Vesper," he said, turning to her, flashing the smile that had won a thousand hearts, as if he hadn't had a tantrum and hit her the day before.

The guard and the brain obeyed. They hadn't even cleared the doorway yet by the time Magnus took Vesper in his arms and kissed her, full on the lips. She still held the decanter out in a stiff and nerveless hand.

Magnus pulled back, still holding her. "You wonderful thing!" he crowed. "You found out how to do it! That stuffy old brain told me that parts were disappearing, and then I explored a little in town, and rumor has it that some miraculous recoveries are taking place all over. I knew you could do it!"

Vesper wouldn't look at him, and finally Magnus released her, a hint of the sulk returning. "You aren't still mad at me because of yesterday, are you? Because you know, if I hadn't put you here and made you do this, you wouldn't have found the cure. We're a team, Vesper! I've half a mind to put you on the throne beside me once I'm there. Wouldn't that make all the girls in your hometown jealous—if you become first wife to the heir to the kingdom? Dad won't be able to say anything about it, because I'll only get the throne when he's dead. I assume his ghost won't hang around to keep judging me." He laughed.

Vesper could think of some fates worse than being Magnus' queen, but she still did not welcome the thought. Magnus remained jubilant; Vesper found it amazing that he found it impossible to contemplate that there might be a woman who didn't want him.

Magnus arranged himself on several floor pillows, lying on his side with his head propped on one elbow. He looked up at Vesper and smiled lazily. "Now it's my turn, lovely lady. Get Minimus back to his proper place. Attached…and silent! And the reward—I'll not only take you to dinner, but I'll give you the best fuck of your life!" He grinned. "Half the girls in the kingdom would kill to be in my bed, you know. You act like it would be torture—but, you know, I'm going to call your bluff, because I think you're just pretending—playing hard to get. And you're damn good at it—because your looks are growing on me, and I think I do want you as my queen. Admit it, won't you? You want me, too."

Magnus hadn't lost his sunny personality, but it had mixed with that other, cruel side that Vesper had seen so little of, and the combination made it even worse—made him as unpredictable now as his father. She admonished herself to stay casual, and she tried to slow her breathing, the rapid beat of her heart.

"I don't know if it's possible for me to reattach Minimus," she said. "It takes a long time with each part—there had to be some trust between them and me—"

"I trust you," he said. "And I know Minimus trusts you. The damn prick won't stop defending you. Don't you trust me?"

She didn't want to make him angry, but she couldn't bring herself to lie, either. "Sometimes," she said. "When you're yourself. I don't think the mean version of you is really you. I think...I owe it to the Magnus I do trust and like, to try."

Her hands shook while she donned her gloves and removed another blade of grass. It occurred to her that she could leave it on the top, so it floated...if he drank it, he would die. She doubted she'd ever have a better chance to escape, with no guards at the door.

She just couldn't do it. Even with Magnus being so nasty to her right now, she didn't want to kill him—nor would she willingly endanger Minimus.

No, she would do it this way—heal him, then hold him to his promise of her choice of positions at court. She could make the best of a terrible situation. From within Bugger's new regime, perhaps she could temper the suffering he would surely cause.

"Come lean against the wall," she said. The last thing she wanted now was a horny Magnus on her hands. He obeyed with a smirk as if he knew her reasons, and he blew her a kiss as he accepted the glass she handed him and downed the contents in one draught. As the aphrodisiac took hold, so too did the crystal, and his eyes closed, his body going slack against the wall.

Vesper sat down beside him, sipped from her glass, and leaned back.

CHAPTER 27

Vesper sank easily into that other-place; it ebbed and swirled about her. *Magnus*, she said.

Her voice percolated into empty space about her. *Magnus*, she repeated.

Nothing.

Minimus.

She felt rather than saw a response, and that response, as a new point of focus, magnetized her close. She floated toward Minimus' presence, which pulsated pale red, and beside it a much smaller yellow light winked faintly. Magnus.

Hello, Minimus, she said. The red brightened, solidified further. *Show me where Magnus isn't whole—where he denied you were a part of him.*

She looked at Magnus. For some reason, she could see nothing—no cracks, no appearance of splintering. In fact, if anything, he looked simply blank.

I won't be a part of him any longer. I don't like him, Minimus said.

Vesper ignored the penis-blob, focusing on something that looked like a hairline crack in Magnus' aura. She honed in, and she felt as if she were falling, diving into an abyss…

Of utter, unendurable agony.

Vesper screamed. Minimus screamed. Magnus twitched. Waves of pain battered them.

I won't! I won't go back to being with this blockhead! Minimus shrieked.

Vesper jerked out of the trance, just in time to see a struggling bulge in Magnus' pants. With a mighty rip, a hole broke through the pants and Minimus tore free of Magnus, eliciting a yelp from the prince.

"Magnus—are you all right?" Vesper asked, even though through a hole in his pants, blood oozed out of newly opened scars where a penis should be. , Vesper hoped that, since the penis had already torn itself off twice, a third time couldn't be so bad; he must just be unconscious from the shock...

She got up and paced, unsure of what to do next. Something was very odd about what had just happened. Somehow, it was important, and she felt she needed to figure it out. Why had her attempt to reunite Magnus and Minimus turned out so differently from all the other reunifications?

The root of the problem must lay with the split between Magnus and Minimus. Magnus himself showed an inconsistent personality, usually kind, but sometimes cruel; Vesper theorized that a person who had one split within themselves had an infinite number more potential splits, and if she wanted to talk to that part of Magnus that she liked, she somehow had to talk to all of him—the cruel side, and the part of him he'd rejected and projected into his penis.

Or...could it be the other way around? Minimus had dominated that trance-conversation. He had also always shown himself to be cleverer, a better leader than Magnus. Could Minimus be the main 'brain' in the prince's body—the one who initiated the split, because he had rejected and projected Magnus into the larger prince-body?

Her heart beat a little faster. She had to test the theory. She had to get Minimus back in here to dip into this bowl, to reenter the Sanctum-energy...but knowing how little he wanted to reunify with Magnus, that might be close to impossible.

Unless the bowl-dipping was connected to something else Minimus liked more than anything.

Vesper searched through the contents of the laboratory. She found what she was looking for—a small rubber funnel. She sealed the end of it so it became a cup. If she just could insert this cup into the willing vagina of some woman, for certain she could get Minimus to oblige. And she would use her own, iIf she could find no other, she would use her own.

She spent a good five minutes trying to push the cup into herself.

She might have succeeded, but then Magnus moaned. If she didn't escape now, she might lose any chance to do so.

She remembered the rolled-up cloth her body-part spies had paid so dearly to bring her, and she reached into her bodice, tucking the rubber cup into it and exchanging it for the cloth. She unrolled it and peered at something written on it in charcoal. Parts of it were smudged beyond recognition, but she could just make out the words:

Sanctum, as soon as you can.

Who had sent it? Garth? Or Jules? Could it be a trap? No—none of the Mallanders would ask her to go to the Sanctum.

She poured the metal-dissolving liquid onto the chain attached to her shackle, watching the metal fizzle and bubble. The chain thinned, but didn't break until she hammered at it a few times with the dagger she took from Magnus' belt sheath; it broke, and she was free.

She had to do one more thing. She turned back to the cage and opened the door. "Go! Go and hide somewhere. I don't know if it's safe outside—if it isn't, stay in the building. I don't want to leave you in here where anyone could get you. We'll find each other later, and then I'll help you get back to the people you belong with."

She headed for the door without waiting for them to agree, but behind her she heard a rustling and a bang of the cage door as they emerged. A few of them whizzed past her as she ran toward the Sanctum.

Any minute, she feared, she would feel the rake of a fingernail or the zap of Zinfel's shock stick, or she would hear the sounds of discovery and pursuit. She needn't have worried; her footsteps echoed through empty hallways on a suspiciously short path to the Sanctum—as if the building conspired to bring her there.

Jules waited for her just outside of the room, and Vesper's heart leapt—and then again, as she remembered that she had one now! Jules' eyes searched her face. "What's happened to you?"

"It's a long story," she began.

"Wait," Jules said. "Better if you tell me later. We have plenty of time—we're going to stay in the Sanctum for a while." He took her hand. Instead of leading her into the Sanctum, they moved to one side of it, into another passageway Vesper hadn't noticed before—a narrow one with walls of dark, opaque crystal and steps that curved downward as far as she could see.

They descended in silence; the one time Vesper tried to say something, Jules lifted a finger to his lips, and his eyes said: *trust me on this*. After a few moments, the passageway broadened and then opened to the outdoors—idyllic Herland scenery, with not a Malland soldier or body part to be seen. Turning back, Vesper saw that they'd emerged from a hill of white rock, with the Goodpeople's building nowhere to be seen.

Jules still had Vesper's hand, and he led her in silence down the hill to where the land flattened into green fields and enormous slender trees that thickened in the distance. Then, at Jules' whistle, a black horse appeared from behind one of those trees.

"Where did—" Vesper began, but again, Jules put a finger to his lips. He turned, pointing to the back of his neck, and Vesper saw a raised lump of red flesh directly over his cervical spine, a drop of dried blood showing that this was a recent injury. He pointed to his ear, and back toward the city.

The injury showed the location of the chip—that much she could guess. He'd been freed after its insertion. He'd told her that the chip could do other things, but he hadn't specified what. Magnus had implied that it could dull thoughts. Was Jules trying to tell her now that the chip could be used to track him somehow, or overhear his conversations? She couldn't believe Malland had the technology to track every single person in two kingdoms, even if they all were chipped. Maybe... if someone wanted to find someone else, they could use the chip to hone in on them somehow—perhaps by using their voice.

Jules mounted the horse and pulled Vesper up to sit behind him, and they surged into motion.

They rode at a canter for as long as they could at that pace, then slowed to a trot that lasted until the trees thickened beyond easy passage. Vesper couldn't shake the sense of being in a dream at times as they traveled through a forest, so different from any of Malland's. Sunlight dappled ground where feather-soft brush nestled dots of bright flowers, and warm breezes touched them even in the shade. This place felt alive. The land had changed in some subtle way from what Vesper had seen of Herland upon entering—as if an energy like that of the Sanctum had percolated out to calm an element of hysteria, of chaos, that had taken over with the disease. *The cure's working*, she thought. She had helped, and she almost felt as if the land knew it.

They stopped at a small clearing, secluded by trees. A space amongst the clusters of leaves opened to sky up top where late afternoon sunlight streamed through and warmed the ground.

At the sound of a faint burbling noise, they searched beyond the trees and discovered a running brook.

Jules slid off the horse and helped Vesper down. The horse bent its head to drink.

They walked back to the clearing. Jules picked up a piece of wood and pointed to it, then out among the trees. Collect wood for a fire, he was telling her. As Vesper went to oblige, she could have sworn that the trees were shedding dead wood directly in her path; she nodded to them with a whispered "thank you" and went back.

Jules stood, hands on his hips, looking down at something. When Vesper neared, she saw that the grass there had grown into a soft raised platform—almost like a bed.

Their eyes met, and Jules shrugged as he smiled sheepishly. The glade, like the Goodpeople's Hub, conspired to help them—that bed hadn't been there when they first arrived. What would the glade serve them for a meal?

A quick walk through the immediate surroundings answered that question. Fruit trees hung heavy with pears and cherries, and a lush crop of edible flowers soon filled Vesper's skirt. They returned with their bounty back to the clearing.

Vesper felt a settling inside as she sat on the bed and watched Jules build a small fire in the growing dusk. She wondered how she could feel so worry-free when terrible things were likely still happening not a few hours' ride from here. Only right now something distracted her—she was admiring the fineness of Jules' hair, which lay across a particularly well-shaped skull in short silky waves, like a windblown field. Her eyes traced lower, to the plane of his cheeks, down to the line of his mouth that had softened in a way she'd never seen it.

She swallowed as he sat next to her on the bed. His eyes flashed clear gold for an instant, and she realized that the angle of the light was changing as he leaned in, no hesitation in him physically or otherwise as his mouth touched hers.

She felt the *rightness*—but a part of her struggled to second-guess it, and Jules started to pull away—and in that instant, she had enough space to make the choice, and she grabbed his face and held on.

His mouth smiled against hers. *If you're sure*, that smile said, and his hands wound into her hair as he relaxed back against the grass bed.

From all the nights they'd slept back to back, his body had become familiar, its contours and its smell. Now, she found so much that was new—his hands running over her, redefining her borders so she could feel each cell in her body awake and alive and moving in concert to make her own explorations—touching him, not only with her hands and mouth, but rubbing up against the front of his body until he sucked in a breath and rolled her onto her back.

He pulled her dress off her shoulders to bare her torso, then yanked it completely off. Her smallclothes went next, and she shivered as dappled shade touched her bare skin. He nudged her legs apart, and she couldn't help her thighs tightening in resistance.

She liked Jules, maybe even more than she'd thought she liked Garth,. bBut she didn't want to get pregnant by him either—not just yet. She placed her palm on Jules' chest, pushing; he backed off immediately, withdrawing with respect if not understanding. She smiled and held up a finger, bidding him wait.

Reaching for her discarded dress, she picked it up and shook it until the rubber cup that had been in her bodice fell on the ground. Under Jules' interested gaze, she began anew her attempts to push the cup up inside her vagina. Her natural lubrication this time made all the difference, and the cup slid in easily.

She reached for Jules then, pulling him back down over her. She couldn't help but brace herself slightly for the intrusion.

It didn't come. What she got instead was a shock of sensation as Jules' tongue licked across the groove of her labia and settled at her clitoris, where he lapped, sucked, and swirled while her fingers ripped up chunks of the grass bed and her thighs, no longer resisting, twisted and squeezed. She felt herself tensing up as something built up inside her—and then, she thrashed about in her first orgasm induced by another human, further decimating their bed.

Only when her shuddering subsided and she gasped and laughed, pushing at him, did he crawl up her body, divesting himself of his clothes—neither of them caring as a testicle freed itself from a cloth and flew off. He kissed his way up her belly and breasts and throat and ended at her mouth, tongue dipping just inside her lips as he mounted her and slid his cock into her still-spasming pussy.

She felt so open, and what was happening felt so good, that it couldn't possibly be an intrusion. She gave herself up to the rhythm and the pleasure, grass-stained hands reaching around to grip him by the buttocks as long slow thrusts became a shallower stutter that became a groan as she felt him pulsing inside her.

He held her afterward. She sighed in contentment, feeling nestled in an oasis in a sea of chaos. One small thing bothered her, though. If they couldn't talk because they would be overheard, were they going to have to stay silent forever?

Apparently, Jules had already thought of a solution for this, because he moved away from her, fiddling with his discarded trousers, and he drew out a folded piece of white cloth and a piece of charcoal. He unfolded the cloth, smoothed it out, and began to write.

You are beautiful.

Vesper stared at the lines, blushing. Then she took the cloth and wrote underneath it. *Your vows?*

He smiled a little.

Flexible, he wrote.

She would get no more answer for now, as he was already writing something else.

Tomorrow I go back to city to help. Get chip removed. You wait for me here.

He was suggesting they separate? That she hang out in the woods while he went back into danger? She shook her head violently. Snatching the cloth from him, she rubbed out what he'd written and took the charcoal.

I go with you.

Jules wrote in reply: *No. You're safe here, no chip. I can be tracked.*

Vesper shook her head, pointing to herself, then him.

Jules shook his head.

They sat there, both naked in the glow of firelight, staring daggers at each other, until Jules broke the deadlock by kissing her again; they had no more discussions that night, written or otherwise, but Vesper resolved to stay awake all night and make sure he didn't leave without her the next morning.

She hadn't realized, though, the extent of her exhaustion in the delicious aftermath of lovemaking. She fell into possibly the deepest sleep of her life, and when she woke the next morning, Jules was gone.

CHAPTER 28

Vesper scowled at the piece of cloth Jules had left under a rock placed by the grass bed. On it he'd scratched just two words in charcoal: *Back soon*.

Therefore, she couldn't even pretend that he'd been kidnapped or gone off to find food and gotten eaten by a wild animal—not that wild animals existed in Herland; the land probably tamed them all and kept them as happy, dancing pets.

"Sorry, Mae's tits," she muttered, kicking the ashes of the fire.

He'd taken the horse, too. She kicked again.

He probably thought he was protecting her. Despite herself, she felt a gooey warmth uncurl in her belly as she flashed back to the night before. No, she shouldn't be thinking of how great he was—she should be angry with him! With herself, too—she should have found some way to explain to him what she'd accomplished in the laboratory, how she'd learned the key to reuniting parts to people. Maybe she could have done some good...if she could get to the king, for instance, and reattach that head of his, perhaps that would take care of most of his insane behavior.

She had to go back.

Decision made, she readied herself quickly enough. Nothing needed to be done here. She collected a few of the uneaten fruits from the day before, went to the brook to drink and wash her face, and set off. She tried not to think about how long it might take her and what she would do when she ran out of food or needed to sleep. She'd already wandered around by herself in Malland for days on end, and here the land took a proprietary interest in its inhabitants. She would be all right.

As she walked, her anger dissipated. Herland was too beautiful a country to walk around in feeling upset. On foot, she could appreciate scenery she'd not even noticed in passing yesterday. She left the forest and now crossed green and flowered fields with willow trees whose leaves rustled in the breeze.

She had definitely not noticed that the grass grew shorter right where she was walking, almost as if it had been trimmed in a neat path stretching out in exactly the direction she was going. She frowned.

"Are you changing things just for me?" she asked the air, then felt silly. Then she stopped feeling silly as a breeze appeared out of nowhere and blew across her cheek, feeling almost like a caress.

"Very well," she said. "If you are going to insist on making things pleasant and easy for me, won't you get me some sort of transportation back to Herland's capital city?"

No response, of course. Who was she kidding? Still, as she continued to walk, she felt that she was being watched.

Someone tapped her on the shoulder.

She whirled. A detached hand waved at her. Behind it hovered several dozen body parts. She thought they looked somewhat familiar... had she released those parts from the cage? She got her answer when she saw an ear with a missing piece of lobe, the wound scabbed-over but fresh.

"You told us to come look for you," the hand said.

"I'm so glad you've come!" Vesper replied, smiling. "You'll be wanting to go back to the laboratory as well, so we can get you all reattached. Do you think I could get a ride?"

Vesper rode back to the capital city in much more comfort than she'd had on her other trip with a body part. Many more parts held her, and she expended no effort at all lying in the hammock of her own dress, with hands and legs and mouths and noses supporting her from every place underneath. These parts, friendly and aware that she was on their side, chattered to her the whole way of inconsequential subjects, keeping her excellent company.

She grew concerned as they neared their goal, however. She had imagined that they would come upon a heavy presence of Bugger's army in the middle of its continued occupation of the city—but as they approached, she heard the faint sounds of metal or stone clanking against other objects, and cries and screams that grew louder every moment.

"Please turn me over so I can look," she asked, and the parts rolled her over so her belly faced down, and she could observe without hindrance.

For a few moments, she could make no sense out of what she saw. From this distance, it looked as if Malland soldiers fought the air—swinging swords, stabbing, whirling in some sort of insane dance. As they got closer, though, she saw that they were fighting body parts—groups of organized parts that used weapons. Zinfel's body-part army had turned against Malland.

A reddish-pink arrow shot through the air toward them, then stopped, hovering in the air in front of Vesper and her retinue, forcing them to slow and stop as well.

"Minimus," she cried. "Why are the parts fighting people? Have they gone crazy?"

The penis shook his mushroom-cap. "No," he said, and Vesper noticed that something was different about him. She suddenly recalled that the last time she'd seen him, he'd ripped free of Magnus and screamed his way out of the building. Now...the sweet, slightly lewd character she'd known had transformed into something harder—almost hostile. "They've come to their senses. And the only thing they're fighting for is the right to be free. New parts—you are joining the battle late, but there is still much to be done. Put her down and contain the people so I can free more of our fellows!"

The parts holding Vesper went still. "Is he talking to us?" she heard from behind her buttock.

"Can't be."

"Why should we listen to him anyway?"

"He's the crown prince."

"No, he's the crown prince's penis."

"That's right—he's the crown prince of the crown prince."

Vesper didn't understand why Minimus was acting this way, but she saw her danger. She eyed the space below them—if they dropped her, she would at least break some bones, if not her neck. She tore her eyes from the ground and made herself look the penis in his eye. "Minimus, let's talk about this! I went about your healing all wrong—I wouldn't make you do something you didn't want! Parts—please head to the room we were in before so I can help you..."

"You would have made me a servant to that incompetent idiot of a prince," shouted Minimus, voice cracking. "I thought you were all right! I thought you supported my right to autonomy, as a free and conscious being. No, you want me back in the dark in those nasty smelly pants—back being a slave—that's what all you people want to do to us parts, even though we are breaking free because we can have a better life in independence. Fellow parts, come and fight with me. We'll end the tyranny of so-called 'whole' people once and for all! You've been nice to me, Vesper, so I'll spare you this time. You can go—but you only have this one chance. If you're not gone from here in fifteen more minutes, I won't be responsible for the consequences. Put her down, parts!"

Some of the parts holding Vesper detached themselves and flew to join Minimus. The remaining parts, trying to obey the penis' order, fell with Vesper, unable to support her weight in the air.

She crashed to the ground.

For an instant she thought she couldn't move. Had she broken something? No—bones had broken, but none of hers. Several parts had cushioned her fall and suffered the consequences; two she'd smashed so badly that they had to be dead. She picked up the hand who'd tapped her shoulder that morning, the friendly one who'd waved; its fingers splayed in unnatural directions, bent and broken beyond repair, and it did not move.

She'd already witnessed the killing of many parts, and she'd even stabbed one herself in self-defense, but this hand's death, she knew, would haunt her dreams.

"Noooooo!" Minimus cried. "I can't let you get away with that, Vesper—deal or no deal!" He came barreling down, growing so engorged Vesper could see a vein throbbing on the side of his shaft—and she had no time to duck when liquid came shooting out of the hole on his head, blasting Vesper on her bare face and head.

She gasped and cringed, waiting for her parts to start detaching and flying away. A vision of General Perrin's bloody mass of meat flashed in her mind.

But—nothing happened. She remained whole.

"Impossible!" shouted Minimus. He bulged, grew taller, shot more sperm. Still nothing. Enraged, he turned and began shooting randomly at the nearest group of soldiers, and screaming newborn body parts shot free wherever the sperm touched.

Vesper ran a sleeve across her face and shook off the slimy fluid. Filthy and disgusting she might be, but she felt jubilant, because she'd beaten the disease.

Getting to her feet, she made a run for the buildings, dodging parts who sailed by to attack Malland soldiers and the few Herlanders who happened to be about. The Herlanders, more resourceful than they'd led Vesper to expect when they'd been waving around those crystal wands, contained the parts in nets and under crates with stones piled atop. Against Minimus and his recruitment of new parts at every moment, though, the whole Herlanders and Mallanders fought a losing battle.

Vesper dashed into the Hub. The sound of running footsteps made her shrink back against the wall. Magnus burst through, followed by Jules. They sped up the stairs leading to the rooftop ritual area. An instant later, Garth ran by. King Bugger chased him; his head floated two inches above his body, flushed and shrieking laughter and incoherent insults.

She started after them, then stopped. She'd be more help elsewhere—better to stick to her initial plan. As she turned to go down the hallway that would lead to the makeshift laboratory in which she'd been imprisoned, she heard a sound that made the hairs on her neck stand on end—a series of simultaneous screams that were coming closer every second.

A stream of women burst forth into the corridor, and Vesper threw herself against the wall, flattening herself there out of an instinct for self-preservation. Watching the rush of flying hair and sparkly gowns in disarray, she realized that she'd seen these same women earlier today, standing behind King Bugger on his transported throne. They were his wives—and they appeared to be running for their lives.

Vesper's eyes quickly scanned the crowd for Aren, and after a few heartbeats she found her sister in the middle, dark hair disheveled, golden dress hiked up to her knees as she ran.

"Aren!" Vesper called, and Aren turned wide dark eyes toward her, and she slowed just long enough to grab Vesper by the hand and to pull her into a run.

Caught up in the wave of terror and adrenaline, Vesper knew well enough not to question Aren now. Still, she couldn't resist a glance behind her—and then she almost wished she hadn't looked.

Half a corridor behind them, Daisy pursued them, her teeth bared in a feral kind of smile. She held two golden leashes in one hand, and in the other a spray bottle filled with red-orange liquid. On the other ends of the leashes two penises flew above her. "I won't be Wife Number Twenty-Nine or Thirty or what-have-you. I'm going to be Wife Number One, and none of you can stop me!" Daisy cried. Then she laughed and squirted bursts of liquid at the penises. Vesper could see them growing harder and longer in mid-air, preparing to blast any unfortunate targets into parts. Daisy had already been busy; behind her Vesper could see dozens upon dozens of parts floating mid-air.

Vesper had an idea. "The Sanctum," she said, and she put on a fresh burst of speed. She overtook the crowd so she and Aren ran in the front, and then she simply put the intention out there that they would head for the Sanctum. Then, she ran, and she prayed.

As if pulled by an invisible string, she dashed up one fork of a passageway, then another. Through several twists and turns, she sensed herself going into the core of the building.

She came through the open archway at a dead run. The soporific calm of the room, an energy so familiar to her this past day, yet not any less of a shock for all that—hit her so hard she stumbled. Aren was no less affected; she grabbed at Vesper's hand for balance, then stood there, wavering on her feet, a look of surprised contentment wiping the panic and worry clean from her expression.

the

is The other women spilled in behind them, and they, too, slowed to a halt, filling the entranceway so that when Daisy arrived, she crashed into a knot of women clogging the front of the room.

The women paid no attention to Daisy except to make a little room for her to enter.

Daisy, too, no longer was paying attention to anyone. She stood, mouth slightly open, blinking at the crystalline walls. The leashes hung slack from her hand, the two penises now flaccid and floating about above her.

"Oh," she breathed. "How silly I've been."

"How silly we've all been," said another of the wives. "We shouldn't be fighting each other. Our problems don't lie in any of the relationships we have with each other."

"The problem is our entire social system," chimed in another.

"Bugger has turned us against any new wives who join us—and we should be working together instead of fighting them."

Aren bowed her head. "I'm so sorry I didn't believe it when you tried to warn me against him," she said.

The women forgave her, and each other. Would it last? Vesper didn't know, but she thought it just might.

Vesper caught Aren's arm. "I've got to go," she said. "Will you be all right?"

Aren smiled, an expression Vesper hadn't seen for weeks. The sight warmed her heart—and she lifted a hand to touch her own chest, again marveling at its presence. Her sister nodded. "I'm already all right," she said. "You go. I've got some things to talk about with these gals." SAnd she turned and joined the circle of women that was already forming, hands being held, heads bent forward to talk and scheme.

One more look, and Vesper left the Sanctum at a run. The building seemed to sense her urgency, creating a hallway that got her to the laboratory in under half a minute.

It was deserted. No guards stood by the open archway, and she entered, observing with satisfaction that everything remained as she'd left it. The mushrooms and the yellow grass lay in their basket next to a bowl filled with water. The door to the cage remained open, with no indication of what had been inside, save for a few drops of smeared blood.

on the window Vesper refilled the bowl with water, donning her gloves to add a fresh blade of grass. The fastest way to end most of the killing, she decided, was to disable Minimus. She could do that if she could just try to cure his split with Magnus once more—if she could get him to dip into the bowl.

She'd already thought of a way that could be achieved. Squatting down, she reached underneath her dress, grimacing as she slid her middle finger up into her vagina, hooked the rubber cup with her finger, and pulled it out.

If this becoames an invention that more women used to prevent pregnancy, Vesper thought, *probably best to not share them between women*—but in this case, she would make an exception. She cleaned the cup with alcohol and set it aside. Then she moved to the window and yanked open the curtain.

"You—Allegra's pussy," she said to the sad pink genitalia that still floated outside, crying. "You're up next for being reunited back with Allegra. But only if you help me first."

The vagina flapped her lips petulantly, as if tossing her hair. "I don't know," she said, sounding bored. "Why should I care about Allegra? She's always just used me to get things she wanted. I'm sick of being used. Minimus says we aren't meant to be servants. We're our own persons."

"If that's right, then you should keep on liberating more parts of yourself," Vesper said. "Each of your labia serve you, don't they? And your clitoris? And then they have parts too...it could keep on going forever until you're reduced to atoms, each with a right to its own personhood!"

The labia continued to flap in silence, as if thinking.

"You can't possibly be happy like this," Vesper continued. "Sitting next to the window, hoping for some man to want to have sex with you. Does that make you feel any less used than when you were a part of Allegra? I think you know deep down that the only way you're ever going to get the kind of love you want is if you're united with her again, as a whole."

Vesper thought she'd gone too far. The vagina remained unresponsive, and even began to float away a little. Her heart sank—it wasn't going to work.

"What can I do to help?" the vagina whispered then, so softly Vesper almost didn't catch it.

Vesper restrained an urge to whoop, as the vagina seemed skittish. "Come in here. I have a plan."

The vagina followed Vesper into the laboratory, flapping softly as she watched Vesper pick up the rubber cup, lubricate the outside with oil, and pour in a little of the water from the bowl she'd already prepared. She would have to hope that this was enough liquid to absorb into Minimus—and that the cup was enough to stop Minimus' sperm from blasting Allegra's pussy into further parts.

"Now I'm going to ask if I can insert this inside you," Vesper said.

"It looks uncomfortable," the vagina replied.

"You won't notice it after it's in," Vesper said. "Especially after you do the next thing I want you to do. What do you think of Minimus?" Vesper gently inserted the cup.

The vagina lifted up her labia in a shrug. "He's not bad," she said. "Nice-sized. Definitely the best of the penises I've seen flying around here."

"I'm glad you like him," Vesper said. "Do you think you might like him enough to have sex with him?"

The vagina wiggled. "I guess I wouldn't mind."

"Your job won't be so bad then. I want you to go out there—and seduce him. Your job then will be only to lead him over to the Hub—just touching the side of the building should be enough."

The vagina crossed her labia. "What if he doesn't want to?" Her voice throbbed with all the rejection she'd experienced hovering outside this window, waiting for Garth.

"Listen. The most important thing for being attractive is that you simply be yourself. Stop wanting people who don't want you—only *because* they don't want you! Just be yourself, and he won't be able to resist you."

Pink lips fluttered, considering. "I'll try..."

"Don't just try. Do it!"

Vesper grabbed her own glass of water. Then they left the laboratory and went outside, spotting Minimus easily. In full battle lust, he howled as he rocketed around the battleground the city center had become. As they approached, he started slapping a man across the face. The man screamed, reaching his arms up to try to protect himself.

"There he is," said Vesper.

The vagina clenched, steeling herself, then shot over to the fray. She landed smack on the man's face right before Minimus landed another slap, and his contact made a squelching sound, hitting her instead of the man's face. Minimus sprang back.

He turned his one eye on her and stared.

"Hi," the vagina said, sashaying her labia to show just a hint of enticing clitoris.

Minimus grew even bigger, if that were possible. "H-h-h-hi," he stuttered.

Allegra's vagina opened her lips invitingly. Minimus moved forward, hypnotized, as if hardly able to believe what was happening. His head just touched the labia, and then he seemed to come to, and he began to batter forward, pushing until he was only visible by his ball-sac, and the vagina's tunnel was fully extended to contain him within.

Minimus groaned as he pulled out. The vagina moaned as she pushed herself back on. It took a few thrusts to get the other's rhythm, without any bodily muscles behind the pump and pull. Then, both of them began to speed up.

Vesper held her breath, wondering if Allegra's vagina had forgotten the part about bringing Minimus to touch the side of the building. Then, she saw the copulating pair pulling slowly backward toward the Hub even as their thrusting became a blur, a kaleidoscope of red-pink bliss. Then, more groans and moans, and a foot shy of the building, two yells of continuous pleasure sounded as the two spasmed midair, and sperm gushed out of the edges of Allegra's vagina.

Not close enough, Vesper thought, her heart sinking. Still merged as one fleshly unit of erotic satisfaction, the two floated to the ground, like two falling leaves one tucked within the other.

Allegra's vagina shuddered then, and with a languid jerk of her labia-petals, she pulled them both to land softly against the wall where it met the earth.

Vesper nearly sobbed her relief—although the battle was not yet won. Steeling herself, she sipped her water, then leaned back from her position next to the building until she had full contact between the crystalline wall and the backside of her body.

This time, in that other dimension, she headed unerringly toward the bright pink blob she identified as Minimus. Magnus' blob pulsed, faint and yellow and small.

"Minimus," she said, and the pink blob glowed in response. She focused on it until she saw the fracture, a long rent that went from top to the end of the shaft. Then—she and pink blogb and yellow blob all went tumbling into the gap.

A dark ocean contained and protected them in an embrace of smooth, warm walls. They floated, content, until a ripple of pain shivered through the walls and into their body. It made their body want to move, to squirm and spiral somewhere...anywhere to escape this pain... and then they realized that the only direction was out, and that they were headed toward a cold, bright, and terrible place.

No, they cried. *Let me stay.*

They clung to the darkness, but the warm walls surged with pain and pushed at them.

They struggled. It went on until the rippling of pain began to subside...but numbness replaced the pain...

Cut her open.

Yes, Your Majesty.

The sudden light hurt eyes they hadn't realized existed. They felt cold, and gravity, and they discovered lungs and screamed.

It's a boy, Your Majesty. Your heir.

Who are the parts of "they"? Vesper asked Them.

I am Magnus—I am everything my father wanted me to be as a prince, said one.

I am Minimus—I am everything else that I wanted for myself, said the other. *I was not allowed to be. But I have still ruled this body, from the place I have occupied.*

The denial of their duality caused the pain. The healing came from simply acknowledging the other, and Vesper saw and felt the pain release.

Vesper exhaled at the surge of pleasure and opened her eyes. That fading radiance from her dream-space still warmed her, and for a moment the cold of the ground and of the wall behind her disoriented her. It helped her feel the borders of her body, and to awaken. Only then did she remember where she'd just been, and what she'd achieved.

Or had she? Adrenaline flushed through her body and she sprang to her feet, spun on her heel to swing into the Goodpeople's Hub, and headed up the stairs for the roof.

The clash of swords, the battle howls, the grunts, and some hyena-like laughter that sounded like King Bugger alerted Vesper to the ongoing battle before she burst onto the scene. Jules still struggled against Magnus, and Garth fought the king. She wondered why both brothers were struggling—she'd never seen them fight with swords, but she'd seen Jules in hand-to-hand combat and he'd easily defeated multiple armed men before. Why was he having such trouble against one lazy prince? Garth, against an insane old king? Neither of them had any visible injury, but why then did Jules keep shaking his head between parries and thrusts, as if some invisible insect dogged him?

Then she saw Zinfel standing off to one side, wearing an odd contraption of multiple strips of black metal that joined in a band around his scalp. It looked like a giant spider sat on his head. He stared at the fighting men, eyes narrowed in deep concentration.

The chip, Vesper thought. Magnus said the chip dulled thoughts. Jules had been chipped—probably Garth as well—and now Zinfel was doing something to sabotage their ability to attack and defend themselves.

Vesper didn't think she could attack him, but maybe a distraction would do. She ran at him, shrieking and waving her arms.

Zinfel turned, rat-face baring teeth. However, Vesper's shriek also had the unfortunate effect of distracting someone else...Jules turned toward her, and Magnus' lunge pierced him through his belly. Jules sagged, and Magnus pulled his weapon free and raised it again, the blade wet with blood.

"No!" Vesper screamed.

Magnus' eyes sliced toward Vesper.

He blinked. "Say," he said. "I...I..." He looked down at himself in wonder. "I got the body!" A smile broke out on his face. Something was different about him...something indefinable...but then Vesper knew—or at least hoped—

"Minimus?" Vesper breathed.

"You can still call me Magnus," he said. "But the two of us are both here...as one."

Bugger and Garth struggled on the edge of the parapet. Garth thrust his sword into the king's neck—but the head flew off, and Garth, overbalanced, teetered on the edge of the roof. The king's head swung around and rammed into Garth's back to help him over, and Garth fell with a scream that abruptly cut off.

Bugger staggered toward Jules, who had fallen to his knees and was struggling to stand again. Zinfel, still in action, muttered something under his breath, and Jules froze.

Bugger lifted his sword. Vesper started forward—she could do nothing, wouldn't be fast enough. No one could be that fast.

No person could be, but at that moment a flurry of body parts zoomed out of the entryway in a cloud of pink and mauve and peach flesh. This mass of pieces of breasts, vaginas, ovaries, and uteruses split into two clouds. The majority of them headed straight for Bugger, imposing themselves between him and Jules. The rest—mainly female breasts—attacked Zinfel, clinging to his face like barnacles. He beat at them with his hands, but he could not dislodge them. He made choking sounds as he fell to the ground and beat a tattoo on the ground with hands and feet for one horrible moment before going still.

The parts took their time with Bugger, still hovering around him in silent condemnation even as Zinfel was dying. "No! I don't want you! Get away!" shrieked Bugger. "I like feet...and mouths...the occasional asshole...not all these ugly women-parts! Who are you all? What do you want?"

"We're rejects from your army," they said. "The pieces of them at least. All two thousand eight hundred and eighty-three of us. And we think you are a terrible role model for men."

He screamed, once, twice. His second scream cut off as the parts moved in against his face and began to stuff themselves into all his orifices—through his ears, eyes, nostrils, going so deep they must be boring into his brain. His scream went on and on, echoing across the rooftop—and then it died out to a whimper, and silence.

His body fell heavily. His head remained in the air. Abruptly, the parts that had disappeared into his orifices shot out, and they let his head go; it bounced to the ground and rolled to the edge of the precipice, eyes open and staring, quite dead.

Vesper saw Jules slump again—whether from relief or something else, she didn't know. She ran to him, taking in his paleness, the blood-soaked gash in his shirt. She bent to examine the wound; one trembling hand reached to the rent in the shirt—and brushed against something hard and round. She pulled at it to get it out of the way—and out came one of the crystal-topped sticks. Beneath it, Vesper could see that the slice in Jules' skin was long but superficial. The crystal had borne the brunt of the sword thrust and saved his life. "I'm all right," he said, and Vesper embraced him as gently as she could given her desperate relief.

He held her close. Then, "Garth," he murmured, and Vesper lifted her head, aghast. How could she have forgotten? She turned and ran for the stairs.

Magnus stood at the edge of the parapet, staring down at the battle that still raged. "It is time for this fighting against ourselves to end," he said.

He raised his voice, which boomed out, an edge of command new to its baritone. "Combatants! Mallanders and Herlanders, all," he said. "Stop fighting, and put down your weapons! King Bugger is dead. I am your new king. And as for all you body parts—" He opened his pants and exposed himself—the proud, silent penis dangling long and limp and in perfect harmony with his larger counterpart. "Minimus and I have reunited, and we work together now. As all of us shall."

Everyone was listening to him now. Body parts hovered; Mallanders' sword arms stayed still by their sides; Herlanders had dropped their nets and crates and shovels.

Magnus looked all around him, sadly. "We've all been fighting shadow parts of ourselves," he said. "Herlanders and Mallanders, you are reflections of each other, just as these body parts are microcosms of our own souls. We have nearly self-destructed by allowing our views to become increasingly narrow. But now, Herlanders, we shall stop forcing you to be peaceful and annoyingly positive. And Mallanders, we shall stop being so power-hungry and chauvinistic. We will try to be authentic people, and think about coming together as community rather than this continual emphasis that there is an Other to be beaten.

"Bury the dead. That is our first task at hand. Then, we will rebuild what we can."

Magnus' integration with Minimus brought him to heights of regality, grace, and charity never before seen in either kingdom. When he descended and went outside, he caught something fluttering in the air. He walked a few paces to where a man lay after having fallen from the roof—Vesper blinked, remembering that vision from *The Book of Offhand Truths*. She recognized this moment—with the difference that in this image, a young woman with long red hair wept over Garth's fallen body.

Magnus bent down over Allegra. "Beautiful young lady," he said. "I believe this is yours." He held out her vagina, which lay curled against his palm, deep rose petals fluttering in a slow, contented rhythm.

Allegra averted her face. "I'm so embarrassed," she muttered.

Magnus took her hand and helped her stand. "Do not be," he said. "For this, your pearl of womanhood, is the symbol of the bliss of union that will represent our united countries. It was what turned me from my chaotic bloodshed. It stopped the fighting and gave me the purest, most amazing pleasure I've ever experienced. The only thing that would make me happier is if I could make love to it integrated with its owner."

Allegra blushed, and Magnus kissed her hand.

She looked down at Garth. "It's been so many years that I loved him and thought he was the right one for me," she said. "But the past couple of years, he kept showing me that he wasn't. And now that he's dead, I don't know...I keep thinking about all the time we both wasted."

"It's never too late," Magnus said.

Garth groaned.

"He's alive!" Allegra said, turning toward him. Still, she clasped Magnus' hand.

"Alive," Vesper said. She knelt and touched his face lightly.

His eyes opened and met hers.

"Vesper," he croaked. "I'm so sorry..."

"Nonsense," she said. "You're going to recover."

A ghost of a smile touched his lips, but it was a self-mocking kind of smile. "My body...it's got a chance, I suppose...it's always been a hardy thing. Glad I got my tongue back, too. I heard a rumor that you're responsible for that. Still, since you've rejected me, I'm not so sure my heart is going to recover."

Vesper smiled at him. "I think you believe you're telling the truth. Still, I suspect it's your pride injured, not your heart. You didn't really see us married in the *Book of Offhand Truths*, did you?"

Garth's attempted smile turned into a grimace. "I stopped seeing anything in it after I got infected with the disease. I still wish we could give it a try."

"Well—you're a lot more attractive now that you can talk properly. And by talking properly, I mean telling the truth," Vesper said. "But being with you doesn't feel right to me, and I'll go with that. Do you really think you wouldn't get sick of me?"

Garth drew in a quick breath—then exhaled and shrugged, the motion causing him to grimace. "I don't know," he said. He began to cough then, and Vesper stood and watched as a couple of burly Malland soldiers and a Herland healer took Garth in hand.

Vesper surveyed the battlefield, parts with no purpose floating around as people tried to organize the injured and the dead. There was much work to be done. She sighed and headed for the laboratory.

CHAPTER 29

Bugger's widows, who had considered entirely overthrowing the present system of monarchy and taking charge through installing themselves as a governing council, ended up agreeing that Magnus had proven his leadership abilities in the aftermath of the Battle of the Parts, as it was now called. Magnus agreed that ruling a kingdom was too much work for one person, so he was fully amenable to sharing the power with a council formed of the widows and a few select others.

To bridge the gulf between Malland and Herland, Magnus proposed a two-year marriage to Allegra on the rooftop of the Goodpeople's Hub. She'd been reunited with her vagina the day of the battle and had already had numerous additional encounters with the newly integrated Magnus, so she agreed with a contented sigh. Together, they began to undo the damage King Bugger had wreaked upon the two countries.

With the spread of the infection neutralized, most of the work lay in removing the metal magic-blocking chips from everyone's necks with a time-consuming but simple surgery, and then the more complicated reuniting of people with their separated parts. Nim, whose time in the Sanctum had gone far to integrate him with his eyes already, became one of the first newly whole people. Once Vesper shared her discovery, parts and people came together with ease, and rehabilitation of the tortured parts forming the army also began in earnest. The Herlanders, already interested in issues of body-being integration, were natural therapists and soon took over the work.

Many of the parts had died during battle, but even now scientists were working on new technologies to replace or regrow organs, and for the most part it became a worthy battle scar when someone could claim that a part of them had died on the field.

On a personal level, Vesper got all the recognition she'd ever desired—she returned to Mallandina as an official scientific-social advisor, complete with her own medallion, and she sat long hours with Magnus and his new council, arguing about policies and directions for the new united kingdom. She sent home all the money due Ruben, plus interest, along with a copy of her certificate of self-guardianship—not that she would need it for much longer, as the council of Bugger's widows was swiftly changing laws in Malland, particularly for its women.

She'd imagined that attaining her goals would feel a bit more satisfying than this. She was contributing, helping people...but maybe she'd gotten too used to all the excitement of traveling around, running from parts, and being thrown into dungeons and cells all the time, because she felt bored. No—it was silly to miss those things.

She had to admit that what she missed was Jules.

They'd argued when she told him she was going back to Mallandina to become an advisor.

"You were right before—the system couldn't be changed from within, not when Bugger was king," Vesper told him. "But now it's different. Everything's in flux. Don't you want to be part of the change?"

"No," said Jules. "It's not enough, you know. It's still basically a dictatorship, even though the dictator is a better one—probably—than the last. It's not an organic expression of the will of the people for what they want to lead them. So I don't want to give it my approval by participating in the so-called change."

"But if you don't participate, you can't edge it over more toward your ideal government." Vesper felt as if they were having the same discussion as they'd already had before, but she couldn't help it. He was so stubborn!

"I'll be participating…but not by ego-stroking and having boring meetings and losing touch with the real world. I'll be living my life according to my principles."

"Like how you kept your vows?" She bit her tongue, but couldn't take it back.

He looked at her, and his eyes had gentled into acceptance—of a life on his own terms, which didn't include her. "I do keep them. Organic and flexible."

Vesper snorted, and he'd ruffled her hair a little and turned, leaving her. Vesper had seen no more of him. She didn't know how to convince him to stay with her; all the reasons she rehearsed to herself sounded pathetic to her own ears. Then, when she thought she would just tell him that she loved him, and would he please reconsider for no reason she could think of—he had gone. She cried at that, but then thought that it shouldn't matter, if their lifestyles didn't suit.

It was too bad she didn't want Garth at all, because *his* lifestyle was compatible with hers. He'd come back to Mallandina after his injuries healed, and he took up his old position as official court wizard, charming lords and ladies alike—with the added benefit of a new reputation for being truthful. He was excellent at his job, and Magnus used his assistance for much less trivial matters than had Bugger, which made Garth happy.

Magnus was also much more liberal on the issue of relationships than his father had ever been. He declared that not only men, but women could have multiple spouses, and he even suggested to Vesper that she might consider marrying both Garth and Jules. "I could order

Jules to come back here and marry you," he told Vesper. "I could see how much you liked him. And Garth still wants you. He sometimes accidentally calls Allegra by your name when he joins us in bed. You should see how mad she gets!"

Vesper restrained herself from clapping her hands over her ears. "I can imagine," she said. "Thank you, but no. I'm not interested in marrying both—or either, not right now."

"I'm sure that it would keep both of those men crazy about you if they're always fighting each other for your attention. Don't you like that idea?"

"No," Vesper said firmly. "No more fighting."

Aren accosted her one evening after dinner. "I'm going home," she said. "Nim just found out his father died and he's going to go help his mother. He's bringing Begonia. And even though Magnus and Allegra have been really sweet, I don't belong here. I wasn't even a wife. Thank goodness, though—it would feel nasty being even the widow of that asshole Bugger. Anyway, I miss Mother and Father. They've been asking to see you, too, if you want to come."

Did she? She hadn't thought about them much since she'd sent the money two moons ago, but she'd been aware of a nagging feeling that she was avoiding dealing with them. She'd come to accept that they would never apologize for the business with Porter, but it bothered her that resentment tinged that acceptance. Owning her heart fully again, as well as all her parts, it felt wrong to begrudge anything now. Maybe true forgiveness would come if she saw them again. "I'll come," she said. Being in a backward place like Pecktown, she'd probably appreciate court life all the more when she returned.

So it was that Nim, Aren, and Vesper set out again in a coach, but with Begonia as the fourth passenger, adding a different dynamic to the group than their initial journey had had. Shy and quiet at first, once she opened up a little, the four chatted like old friends all the way home. The ride was uneventful; they stopped every night at inns, ate well, and rode in relative contentment.

Once at home, Nim and Begonia took over Oggen's shoe-making business and soon decided to stay. "Making shoes for normal people is so much better than endlessly churning out dancing shoes for court," he said. "And Begonia and Mother like each other."

Nothing had changed in Vesper's old house, with the exception that Medalla had had her baby, and her husband and his second wife had moved in. Her mother's temper and her father's passivity still created the same dynamics in how they communicated and behaved, and even though changes were already obvious in women's roles in their town, Sharrua had always been in charge in their household. Still, it was because they had not changed that Vesper found it so easy to forgive them once she saw them—because it made her realize how different she had become, that what had happened in the past no longer controlled her.

Bobbin was happy to have his middle daughter home, and Vesper slipped easily into her old role of going around to farms to purchase animals for slaughter with him. She found that she'd let go of her self-consciousness enough to find a pleasure in these simple visits and their quiet interactions with customers; it helped as well that the idea of an intellectual women had suddenly gained respect for the first time, and people regarded her with a sort of awe.

Her less easily impressed mother had not been pleased with her returning without a man or wealth to show for her time away. "You're not getting any younger," her mother told her. "In fact, you look tired! Old! The spark gone from you! Who's going to want an old maid who's been labeled 'scientist' by the king? You might as well write 'Bluestocking' in red on your forehead! And I don't want to hear any more about reading becoming fashionable. It's scandalous, absolutely scandalous!"

Vesper smiled at her mother. "I wouldn't say reading is becoming fashionable, but that fashion is becoming less important," she said. "I think you were right that I did read too much, though, Mother. Because I was reading just as much to escape living as to learn about life."

Sharrua stared at her daughter, the momentum stolen from her argument. "Well…yes. That's what I said." She started speaking again, stopped, started again. "Will you be going back to live at court, then?"

"I don't know," Vesper said slowly. "I had thought I would…but now that I'm here, it doesn't seem so important. I'm thinking I'd like to try something different…to learn something new for its own sake, not as the means to get somewhere else."

She had no idea what that something was, though, and in the following weeks, she felt as if she were drifting, unable to take action; nothing felt quite right, although she wasn't unhappy—more just lethargic. Was this a fallow period, the end of a cycle, or was it just how she would feel from now on?

She felt some relief of her lethargy in visits to Neela. Her old friend and mentor's business had taken off as more and more people took an interest in whole-body healing methods that didn't involve magicians excising away pain and unwanted body symptoms. Since Neela had assistants now to run her shop, she took Vesper out several times on herb-collecting excursions, which did much to calm Vesper's restlessness, although it would always return.

Then, one late morning several weeks after Vesper had come home, someone knocked at her bedroom door. "Vesper, are you in there?"

Vesper recognized Aren's voice. She'd been lying in bed and contemplating getting up, although so far she hadn't come up with a convincing reason why. Now she roused herself and answered the door. "What?"

"You'd better go downstairs," her sister said. "Mother and Father are throwing a fit. Well, Mother is at least, and she's making Father stay, which is making him tense."

"She's always throwing a fit," said Vesper, but she didn't mind dealing with them now, and she was already on her way.

She froze—for seated there in the receiving room, being glared at by her mother and offered a sausage on a fork by her father, was Jules.

"Vesper!" her mother snapped. "This young man here says he's here to pick you up. He won't go away. I'm just about to send someone to fetch the constable, but I thought I would first have your explanation. He is awfully fresh and demanding."

Vesper stared at him, eyes already starting to water slightly, unable to move, but something in her that she hadn't known was asleep began to wake.

Jules looked different—his face somewhat drawn through his tan, and body almost as thin as it had been when she'd first met him. Only the way he looked at her, as if he could see into her soul—she'd dreamed of that gaze every day since she'd last seen him—had not changed one bit.

"Vesper," he said, standing, and his voice held a question.

"Yes," she said, sure of her answer, even if she didn't quite know what the question was. What had woken up inside her was interest—stimulation—an expansion of her universe. Jules would always bring that with him.

Bobbin, sausage rejected by the guest, munched. Sharrua shifted slitted eyes from Jules to Vesper and back. For once, she seemed unsure. "You know him then?" she asked.

"Yes," Vesper said again, still gazing at Jules.

"I'm going to Egregia," he said. "The Children of Mae have gotten pretty disorganized under the new regime...more than half of our members left. They wanted me to help recreate their mission, but I figured that since I already broke my vows, I might as well take a complete break and expand my horizons a little. You know they have the best scientists in the world in Egregia. Will you come with me?" He took two steps toward her, and she two steps toward him; it might have gone on like that for a while longer, except Vesper stumbled, and Jules dipped down to catch her. Then, as Sharrua uttered a high-pitched shriek, they embraced, and their lips met in a long kiss.

Bobbin made his escape then, and Sharrua eventually relented after admitting grudgingly that Jules was not a bad-looking fellow, and Vesper could do worse, and she was sick of having all these people running around her house anyway. So Jules ended up staying for dinner and overnight, which was good, for the two of them had weeks' worth of pent-up passion to spend on each other.

"Not marrying!" Sharrua shrieked at them the next morning. They were in the stables, saddling up their horses to leave. "How could you not! You spent the night together...under my very roof! It's utterly scandalous!"

Vesper smiled at her mother. "Jules and I haven't been together very long, Mother. I don't know if we want to marry yet. But I have a good feeling about him." She reached out and took his hand, and she felt the same syrupy expression as he wore stealing onto her own features, which made her giggle. She couldn't help either, the giggle nor the expression.

"I'll take good care of her," Jules said. He took hold of both horses' reins, and he and Vesper walked them outside, Sharrua trailing them.

Bobbin was waiting for them. He clapped Jules on the back and presented him with a package wrapped in brown paper. "Just something for the road. Don't wait too long to eat it or it'll spoil."

Vesper threw her arms around her father. "Thank you," she said.

"It's just a little barbecue," he said, patting her, eyes blinking rapidly. "You're all right, daughter. Made me proud with all that stuff you did. Don't think I don't know anything about it. Official scientist and all that."

This was one of the longest speeches anyone in Vesper's family had ever heard coming from Bobbin, and it had them all momentarily stunned. Sharrua shook her head, but her anger had gone.

"Not things a girl should be doing," she said. "Scandalous. But I suppose you...know what you're doing." She looked as if she might vomit as she said the last few words, but she accepted Vesper's kiss with a pinched nod.

As Vesper and Jules nudged their horses into a walk past the neighboring house, Nim watched them from behind the fence, one arm around a beaming Begonia by his side. From horseback and at this distance, his eyes actually didn't appear to bulge today.

"Good choice, Vesper," he called. "I always liked him!"

The couple waved, and they rode away, saddlebags full of specimen containers clinking in merry concert with their movement.